MY TEN-YEAR CRUSH

FROM FRIENDS TO LOVERS...

OLIVIA SPRING

HARTLEY PUBLISHING

To my brilliant bestie, Cams

CHAPTER ONE

Present Day: July 2010

We all have those moments.

The moments when we agree to do something and regret it.

Like when you go for a run to support a friend who's started a new fitness regime, then it ends up raining.

When you say 'Of course I'll come out tonight,' when really, you wish you could just stay at home and chill on the sofa.

Or when a well-meaning neighbour sets you up on a date and you get the feeling it's going to be as successful as a trip on the *Titanic*.

Yep.

We've all been there.

In fact, I was there right now: sitting in a bar with Edwin, my neighbour's brother.

I'd met him briefly once before, and during our limited exchange, he'd seemed nice, polite and handsome.

My neighbour, Gina, was convinced we'd be great together and kept asking if I'd meet him. I said I'd let her know, but then last Sunday she'd knocked at my door, offering me a plate of freshly baked chocolate chip cookies. The sweet cocoa scent was intoxicating, so of course I'd accepted. But seconds later, she'd said, 'So, about that date with Edwin… is this Thursday okay?'

I couldn't exactly say no. She'd caught me when I was hungry. At the time, a quick drink with a guy who came highly recommended seemed like a fair exchange for satisfying my sugar fix.

There was no denying that just like when we'd first met, Edwin was good-looking. He had brown eyes and well-cut short dark hair and was dressed in a three-piece suit with a bow tie. Very different to the relaxed orange maxi dress and gold sandals I was wearing. But whilst he had the looks, so far, the jury was out on his personality.

He'd already asked me why I was single, which was one of my least favourite questions. I knew it was something most people wondered when they met someone new, but Edwin had asked it in a kind of 'what's wrong with you, woman?' way, which wasn't cool.

The red flag was well and truly raised when he asked if I'd had many boyfriends. I told him that question was too personal, so didn't answer.

And it wasn't just his personality. There was no chemistry either. I didn't feel that connection.

The thought of making up an excuse to get out of here had crossed my mind approximately fifty times in the last sixty seconds. But then the logical part of my brain reminded me that even though I hated dating, I had to keep an open mind. Plus, I couldn't just get up and leave. I'd only been here twenty minutes, so that would be rude.

Although I was certain that he couldn't be further from being *the one* if he lived on Mars, I'd promised Gina I'd give him a chance, because he'd been out of the game for a while, so I should at least try and stay for an hour out of politeness. It'd be fine…

'Yummy, yum, *yum*!' Edwin sipped the red wine he'd recommended we order, because apparently it was 'full-bodied' and had a 'silky texture', with 'an aroma of cherry wood, juicy berries…' and some other stuff I couldn't remember. Personally, I preferred to drink Chardonnay, but said I'd give it a go. 'This is absolutely *sublime*. Just like I knew it would be. The explosion of berries is like an orgasm on your tongue.'

Did he just…

'I'm sorry?' I frowned. 'What did you just say?'

'The wine.' He licked his lips. 'It's like an orgasm on your tongue. Not a small whimper of a climax. *No, no, no.* I'm talking about when you've had an unusually long dry spell and after months of waiting for a woman to accept your invitation to spend the evening together, you finally seal the deal, get to release and the explosion is cata-clysmic. It's just boom! POW! *Whoosh!* Like a rocket! *That's* what drinking this wine feels like: the sweetest, juiciest orgasm on your tongue.'

'Right…' I took a sip and it tasted surprisingly like… red wine. Nothing spectacular and definitely not compa-rable to an *orgasm*. Admittedly, it had been a while since I'd had one, but I was pretty sure it was better than this.

'So!' Edwin sat up straighter in his seat. 'Are you ready?'

'Ready for what?' I frowned.

'For the date to begin.' Edwin rolled his eyes like it should be obvious.

'I thought it already had?'

'No, silly!' he scoffed. Edwin snapped open his black briefcase, then pulled out a stack of cards. Reminded me of the ones I used to help me revise for exams. He gave them a quick shuffle and cleared his throat. 'Where do you see yourself in five years' time?'

No way. I thought I was here for a date, not a job interview. I took a deep breath, wondering how my love life had come to this.

'Doing a career that I love and settled down, hopefully.'

'I see.' Edwin put the cards on the table, pulled out his phone and started typing. 'Ready-to-get-married-and-have-children. Exclamation mark. Good-sign. Exclamation mark.'

I quickly covered by mouth to stifle my surprise at the fact that he was actually taking notes and reading them out loud. And if that wasn't bad enough, somehow he didn't seem to realise that he was doing it.

'So you intend to work after you've had children?' He frowned.

'Yes. I'd like to. Even if it's part-time.'

'I see…,' he said with a disapproving tone before typing out, 'Career woman. Dot-dot-dot. Potential-question-mark.'

I sat there for half an hour as Edwin quizzed me on everything from where I'd gone to school to what A levels I'd studied, what my parents did for a living and my favourite hobbies. It was exhausting.

'And you?' I asked, attempting to make this date a two-way conversation. 'What do you like doing in your spare time?'

'No, no, no.' He wagged his finger. 'I haven't finished *my* questions. Actually, let's switch to the quick-fire round.'

Oh dear God. So now we'd gone from an interview to a game show? I was losing the will to live.

How could Edwin and Gina be so different? If she wasn't such a good neighbour, I would've attempted to make my excuses and left. I deserved a lifetime supply of home-made cookies after this ordeal.

'Ah, yes!' He selected the next card. 'This is always a fun one: Which way should the toilet paper go on the holder?'

What the…?

I scanned the room. I refused to believe this was happening. I must be part of a secret camera show. Ashton Kutcher was going to jump out at any second and tell me I'd been punk'd. It was the only explanation.

'Time is ticking!' Edwin tapped his fingers impatiently on the table.

'Over,' I answered. 'It should go over rather than under.'

Edwin gasped. 'That is incorrect.'

'Incorrect?' I huffed. 'Seriously, though: does it really matter?'

'Of course it does. Let's try another. Skiing in the Alps or relaxing on the beach?'

'Well, I've never been skiing, so I'd have to say beach…'

'This isn't going well…' Edwin tutted and waved his

finger again. 'Next question: What is your favourite television series?'

'That's easy. *Friends*. I used to watch it all the time with… with my old best friend.'

'Of all the television series you could have picked, you chose *Friends*? Dear oh dear oh dear.' He shook his head.

I'd just about managed to put up with being interviewed, but now he'd insulted *Friends*, he'd taken things too far. If I hadn't been before, now I was certain that Edwin was *not* the man for me. I'd felt it in my gut when the date had started, not to mention when he'd started comparing wine to bloody orgasms.

Forget the cookies. There weren't enough biscuits in the world to compensate for putting up with any more of his rubbish. Once I explained to Gina, she'd understand why this absolutely couldn't go any further.

'Bella, I'm sorry to break this to you, but I'm going to call this a night. I'm afraid you're just not a suitable candidate for me. You're just a bit too, you know…? Never mind.'

A bit too what? Actually, I'd rather not know.

Arsehole.

I should've left earlier, when I'd first realised this wasn't going to work.

Story of my life. Even when men waved more red flags than an overzealous football referee, I ignored the signs because I wanted to be kind and give them the benefit of the doubt. And then they dumped me without giving my feelings a second thought.

'Here.' He tipped a pile of coins onto the table. 'This is for my wine. I would've paid for yours too if I thought this could go somewhere. Should be enough. If there's any extra, you can keep the change. My treat!' He winked. 'Bye.'

And just like that, Edwin left.

I was rooted to the spot for a good thirty seconds. My cheeks burned with frustration. I wish I could have told him *exactly* what I thought of him and his stupid questions.

I needed to leave. Right now.

After handing my cash and Edwin's money (including the extra ten pence he'd so generously left) to the waiter, I rushed out of the bar.

I couldn't wait to get home and put this nightmare behind me. Although I wanted the date to end, I still felt like I'd been punched in the stomach. This was exactly why I hated dating.

I couldn't believe Gina had said he was a catch. If Edwin was the only fish left in the sea, I'd rather starve.

I'd told her my ideal man would have a good personality, not be an annoying snob. I was hoping to meet someone normal that I could have a decent conversation with. You know, chat about everyday stuff, like what was happening in the soaps, but also be able to talk about heavier topics too. Someone down to earth, who could make me laugh. Someone like M—

No.

Stop it.

What was wrong with me? I had to get a grip and stop comparing everyone to him. It had been a decade for goodness' sake. I'd cut myself off. Moved on. I was over him.

Thankfully, it didn't take long to get home. I opened the door, kicked off my shoes, hung up my jacket, tied my dark curly hair into a bun, then flopped down on the sofa.

My phone rang. Gina, who lived in the flat below

mine, had probably heard me come in and was calling to find out how the date went. Saying I thought her brother was a patronising dickhead wasn't going to be fun.

'Hi, B!' *Phew*. It wasn't her after all.

'Hey, Melody!' I breathed a sigh of relief. 'How are you?'

'I'm good. Thanks for the cool bracelet. You're such a luv, thinking of me like that. It really made my day!'

'Glad you liked it.' It was nothing extravagant. Melody always wore a million bracelets, so you could usually hear her jangling before you saw her. When I'd spotted the colourful beads on a stall in Camden Market last weekend, I couldn't resist getting it. She'd had a tough time lately, so I'd thought it might cheer her up.

'Anyway, what you up to?' she said.

'Just back from a terrible date.'

'Sorry to hear that, my lovely. Dating is pants.' *Exactly what I'd just been saying*. 'Let me guess: you deliberately picked someone crap who you knew wouldn't go the distance, so either butt ugly or a boring old fart.'

'What?' I gasped. 'I don't do that!' Yes, Edwin was boring, but I hadn't known that when I'd agreed to the date. I'd thought he had potential, and he was handsome.

Melody made my dating patterns sound so prescriptive and it really wasn't like that. I'd gone out with all kinds of guys over the years. I was an equal opportunities dater: I pretty much said yes to anyone who asked me. Tall, short, slim, big, good-looking, less aesthetically blessed.

Don't get me wrong: I was no supermodel, so it wasn't like I was inundated with offers. But whilst my friends shied away from the guys who were under six foot, even though I was five foot eleven, I didn't. Finding someone seemed impossible enough, so I couldn't afford to rule anyone out.

It made no difference, though. Sooner or later, they always found a reason to dump me.

I'd come to the conclusion that the perfect man for me just didn't exist. I was never going to meet anyone who ticked all three of my important boxes: great personality, chemistry and good looks.

It was like that saying. When it comes to choosing a service, there are three options: fast, cheap or good quality, but you can only pick two. So if something is fast and cheap, it'll be poor quality. If it's fast and good quality, it won't be cheap.

The way I saw it, the same principle applied to men. It wasn't possible to find one with the complete package. They'd either be hot with sizzling chemistry, but have zero personality. Or have a great personality, but there'd be no chemistry. If I could find a guy who had a great personality and good chemistry, I wouldn't be so bothered about his looks, but nope.

I'd only ever met one man with the complete package, but that hadn't ended well either. Because I'd discovered that even if by some major miracle a guy *did* have all three qualities, he still rejected me.

Which proved my original point: my perfect man didn't exist.

But I still wanted a partner, so rather than expecting to be swept off my feet and find the love of my life, I now considered dating a numbers game. It was a case of just persevering until I found someone to settle with who could tick a couple of boxes and was ready for something long-term. Realistically, that was all I could hope for.

'Say whatever you want, but I know you better than you think, B. Anyway, I was calling to check you were coming the Friday after next?'

I racked my brain trying to think what she was talking about. I'd known Melody for ages. We'd gone to university together, and although we texted and spoke often, we only saw each other a few times a year. Whilst I lived in South London, she was based miles away in Coventry, raising her daughter on her own, so it wasn't easy. I definitely didn't remember arranging to meet up.

'What's happening in two weeks?'

'The reunion!! Can you believe it's been ten years since we left uni! Crazy! So, anyway, Heather and a few of the others thought it would be cool to organise something. They said they'd sent you an invite?'

Oh. *That*.

'Erm, I'm behind on opening my post, so I must have missed it…' I crossed my fingers and prayed I wouldn't be sent to hell for telling a little white lie. I remembered seeing the invitation a few weeks ago, then putting it where it belonged: in the dustbin.

'No worries! It's pretty relaxed. You can still come. I'll just let them know. It'd be great to see you! They've hired a venue and everything. Tickets are really reasonable. Even includes a couple of drinks, a buffet and a DJ. It's going to be amazeballs! I've had my childcare booked for weeks. Can't wait!'

'I've actually got plans for that Friday…' My second lie of the evening. *Heaven help me*. Although, technically, staying at home could still be considered as having *plans*. If not, I'd find something to do. Plucking individual hairs from my bikini line, walking across hot coals barefoot… *anything* except going to the reunion.

'Oh really? What you up to?'

'Um, I've been invited to… I'm just busy… sorry. I'm sure you'll all have a great time, though! Maybe we can meet in a couple of weeks or something so you can tell me all about it.'

'Hold on! I'm coming!' Melody shouted. 'Sorry, I've got to go. Andrea needs me. Think about it, though, yeah? See if you can change these *plans* of yours.' Something told me she didn't believe me. Melody had always had some sort of sixth sense. I was glad the conversation was ending. I was rubbish at lying, so if she hadn't already guessed, it wouldn't be long before she realised I was telling porkies.

'Thanks for calling. And say hi to Andrea from me.'

'Laters!' Melody hung up.

As nice as it would be to see Melody, I definitely would not be changing my mind about going. It wasn't a good idea.

Not because of *him*. That had happened ages ago, so I was definitely over it. He'd probably forgotten all about that night too. Like me, I doubted he'd given it a second thought.

All the same, in the interest of avoiding any potential awkwardness, I'd leave that memory under lock and key.

Yep. Some things were best left in the past. Which was exactly where all thoughts of him belonged.

CHAPTER TWO

Give me strength.

I was stood at the front of the classroom, trying to have a serious discussion about *The Fault in Our Stars*, the book we were reading together. And rather than focusing on the important issues raised in the novel, such as serious illness, the misfortune of fate, and the story of falling in love in the midst of tragic circumstances, what were a few of my troublesome pupils focusing on? The brief sex scene, which wasn't even detailed. God help them when they were old enough to read *Fifty Shades of Grey*.

Loud chatter and giggles vibrated throughout the room.

Holding the attention of thirteen-year-olds was tricky at the best of times, but especially during the last lesson on a Friday afternoon, when I knew they'd already checked out mentally and were counting down the seconds until the weekend. *Same here.*

'Settle down, please.' I raised my voice.

Kieran, who I suspected was the ringleader of the

commotion, was teasing Mandy, one of the quieter, more studious pupils.

'Do you have something you'd like to share with the class, Kieran?' I folded my arms. 'What are your thoughts on the healing power of love explored in the novel?'

'What, miss?' Kieran turned to face me and frowned. I knew he wasn't listening. Gradually the class quietened down.

'I said, tell me what you think about the story of Hazel and Augustus and how love helps with their pain and suffering.'

'What I think, miss, is that Augustus felt *much* better when he finally did it with Hazel!' He smirked and the whole class erupted into laughter.

'Is that your answer?' I raised my eyebrow.

'Do you have a man, miss?'

Here we go.

The *asking personal questions stalling tactic routine.* The more they got me to talk about myself, the less work they'd have to do.

I almost wanted to laugh at the lunacy of the question. Me having a boyfriend! *Chance would be a fine thing.*

Highlights, or I should say *lowlights*, of my last ten years of dating flashed into my head. It wasn't a pretty sight.

For the first four years after uni, I'd gone for the handsome, fun guys, so Greg, Leroy and Heath. But none of those relationships had lasted for longer than a year. They'd all dumped me because they thought I was too sensible. A word I took to mean *boring*. That was when I'd decided to change my dating strategy. It was clear that if I continued choosing guys who loved partying and doing wild things, then of course sooner or later they'd realise they couldn't stay with someone like me, who enjoyed quiet nights in, watching a good TV series or reading a book.

So then I'd decided to date less adventurous men like Howard. He was sweet and okay-looking, but boring as hell. We'd spent our Sundays trainspotting and only had sex twice a month (always on a Thursday evening, don't ask me why) and always in the missionary position.

I remembered one Saturday lunchtime after two years of bedroom boredom, I'd suggested we try the sofa. He'd looked at me like I'd just asked if he wanted to go to a swingers club and have a threesome.

I couldn't bring myself to dump him—after all, you can't expect one man to satisfy all your needs (and at least having a rigid sex regime meant I knew what day to wear my best underwear), and I didn't want to hurt his feelings. So imagine my surprise when *he* broke up with *me*, because *he* wanted more from life. Pff!

I'd then had two failed relationships with Shawn and Ade that I'd stayed in way past their expiry date, just in case. Even though we hadn't had great chemistry, or I hadn't found them massively interesting and I'd known I should call it a day, I'd lived in hope that something might change.

They weren't perfect, but neither was I. Everyone had their flaws. *Better the devil you know*, I'd reasoned. I knew things could always be worse, so I'd stuck it out. But sooner or later, they'd both ended up rejecting me.

Just like my last boyfriend, Lee, had done over a year ago, when our relationship had ended after just five months. Since then it had been one disastrous date after another. And as the Edwin encounter last week showed, the idea of me finding love anytime soon was about as likely as the entire class volunteering to come in for extra grammar lessons on a Saturday night.

'Do you really want to know if I have a boyfriend, Kieran?'

'Yeah!' His eyes widened.

Kieran and the whole class were captivated. The room was so silent you could hear a pin drop. It was as if I'd cast a spell over them.

I walked towards him slowly.

'Come on, miss! Tell us his name!' He strummed his fingers on the desk.

'Okay!' I smiled. 'His name is MYOB.'

'MYOB?' He frowned. 'That's a strange name, miss. Is it short for something?'

'Yes, Kieran. It's short for mind-your-own-business. Now, let's get back to the book…'

I was about to move on to the next discussion point when there was a knock on the door.

'Come in,' I called out.

'Hello, class.' His deep voice vibrated around the room. Everyone immediately sat up straighter as the head teacher entered.

'Hello, Mr Walker,' they said in unison.

I hadn't noticed when I'd seen him earlier that he'd had a haircut. His silver strands were much shorter at the sides than usual. The smart navy suit he was wearing fitted his tall frame perfectly, and those black shoes were so polished and immaculate, you could probably do your make-up in them.

'Hello, sir,' I said. He nodded in acknowledgement.

'Good to see the commotion has settled down. When I walked past a moment ago, there was an awful lot of noise... anyhow, just confirming our meeting at 3.30 in my office.'

'Yes, that's fine.' I smiled through gritted teeth. Trust him to walk by when the class was playing up.

'Very well.' He opened the door and left. The class let out a collective sigh of relief and I dug my nails into my palm, wishing that I was clutching a stress ball.

I glanced at the clock on the wall. It was already after three, which meant in less than half an hour I'd know whether I was being promoted to second in department.

Even though the interview had only taken place earlier today, so it didn't seem like a long time to find out the verdict, it felt like I'd waited ages for this opportunity. My heart thudded. I thought it had gone well and I'd worked my arse off all year, so I was confident, but it could go either way.

Before I knew it the bell rang. The class wasted no time in rushing out the door, and I admit, I did a happy dance inside my head too. Once this meeting was out of the way, I'd have two whole days away from this place. Then after that, there were only five more working days until we broke up for the summer holidays. Not that I was counting or anything...

Don't get me wrong: I still enjoyed teaching. It was rewarding to help my pupils realise their potential. To take a teenager who thought they had no interest in reading at the start of term and see them transform into a bookworm by the end of the year, or help someone who struggled with grammar finally get to grips with it. I loved all of that. It was just that I'd been here for nine years, and aside from a few curriculum changes and a new intake of students each year, the classes were pretty much the same.

I knew I needed some kind of career advancement, but I didn't really want a big change, because that would be too scary. If I got this promotion, I could keep my current job but just add some new responsibilities. That way I wouldn't have to worry about looking for a position at a different school that might be worse than where I was now.

Yes, with the promotion, hopefully next term everything would be better.

I filed away my notes, tidied my desk and packed my bag so that as soon as I left the meeting, I could go home.

I looked up and saw Mandy hovering by the door.

'Um, miss, can I chat to you for a minute, please?'

'Of course.' I glanced at the clock. I only had four minutes until my meeting and I didn't want to be late, but it sounded important, so I couldn't just turn her away. Maybe she was upset about something Kieran had said. It was so frustrating when pupils who didn't want to learn made it difficult for those who did. 'How can I help?'

She walked over cautiously, placed her rucksack on the desk in front of mine, pulled out a chair and sat down.

'What do I do if I want to go to college when I leave school so I can get my A levels and then go to uni, but my parents want me to go out and get a job? They said it's a waste of time and money and only stuck-up rich people go to university, but that's not true, is it, miss?'

'People from all backgrounds go to university these days,' I said diplomatically. 'What would you like to do?'

'I really want to continue studying English. I'd love to become a journalist, miss, and travel the world. Maybe become a foreign correspondent for the BBC or something like that. But when I tell them that, they just laugh.' She hung her head. It really annoyed me when I heard stories like this. Mandy was a bright student. Smart, hardworking and naturally talented at writing. She was always the first to hand in her homework and always hungry to learn. I could totally see her becoming everything that she dreamed of. Hearing that her parents wanted to trample over her dreams made my heart sink. 'What should I do, miss?'

'I can see how this is a difficult decision for you. What I'd suggest is that you—'

'I've been waiting for you in my office!' The head teacher burst into the room.

'My apologies…'

'Um, I better go.' Mandy's face reddened. She grabbed her rucksack and scuttled away.

I dug my nails into my palm again. At that point I wanted to forget about the meeting and run after her, but I knew he didn't like being kept waiting. Thankfully Mandy wouldn't have to start applying for colleges until her final year, so she still had time, but I'd make it a priority to speak to her on Monday. Would have been nice to reassure her today, though.

'I'll just get my things and I'll be right there,' I said as he stormed off.

After picking up my bag, I walked quickly down the corridor. I took a deep breath, then knocked on the door.

'Come in,' he called. I sat down on the seat opposite him. I looked up at the clock. It was 3.39 p.m.

'Apologies for being late, Dad,' I said quickly to break the ice. 'But Mandy needed my help.'

'I see,' he said softly. That was a good sign. Seemed

like he'd calmed down. Although he didn't always have the best way of showing it, he cared about the pupils' well-being just as much as I did.

'Anyway, Isabella, I'll cut to the chase.' He leaned forward. *Uh-oh.* He'd used my full name. He only ever did that if I'd done something wrong or he was being extra formal. This didn't look good. 'I'm afraid you won't be getting the promotion.'

Just like that, I felt like I'd been struck around the face with a hammer. I wanted to say I was shocked, but that wouldn't be true. It wasn't as if this was the first time this had happened.

'Is this because I was late?'

'Of course not! The decision was made earlier today after completing the interview process.'

That would have been done by late morning. I wondered if he'd known when I'd seen him in the corridor earlier this afternoon or in the staffroom at lunchtime, when he'd offered me some chocolate digestives because he knew they were my favourites.

This was one of the many reasons I hated teaching at the same school as my dad. The blurred lines between our professional and personal lives.

'Why, then?'

'It's a big responsibility and you're not ready.'

I wanted to scream. *Not ready?* I'd been here for almost a decade. I was good at my job. My pupils got solid grades, year after year. I was dedicated, committed, hard-working. What more did he want?

'I don't understand. That's what you said before. But then last year, when I got offered that job, you said if I stayed, there would be opportunities for me here. You said something would come up soon. And now that it has, you've rejected me again.'

'You're far too sensitive Bella,' he sighed. 'You get too emotionally involved. This is a professional decision.'

'But I'm a good teacher,' I insisted.

'I agree. You have the ability, when it comes to teaching, but you're not strong enough to handle the pressure. A role like this would require a lot of additional responsibility. And you would come up against many challenges and additional scrutiny, particularly because you're my daughter. I have to give the job to the strongest candidate. I'm sure you understand.'

Dad was still talking and I heard every word that flew from his mouth, but all I could think about was what an idiot I'd been passing up the role I was offered last year. I should have jumped ship whilst I'd had the chance.

'You're growing into a very fine English teacher, Bella. You've got a good, stable job, with a decent salary. That's the best role for you right now. We all have our lanes and sometimes we need to just stick to them. Perhaps things will change again in a few years.'

My cheeks burned and beads of sweat trickled down my forehead. The thought of enduring goodness knows how many years of waiting and hoping that one day he'd believe in me enough to give me a chance to try something more challenging made me feel sick.

I wondered who'd got the job. Probably Julie. Even though I'd been here longer than her, the governor and head of department, who had also been in the interview, always sang her praises. I wanted to ask, but hearing who I'd been passed up for right now was too painful. I was sure I'd find out soon enough.

'Right, okay, um, so that's it, then?' I stuttered. I needed to get to the toilet. Better still, get to my car and drive away from here.

'Yes. I've said all I have to say on the matter. Will you be coming for lunch on Sunday?'

How was he able to switch so seamlessly from telling me I wasn't good enough to be promoted to inviting me around to play happy families with him? Unbelievable.

Once again I wanted to scream at him, but there was no point. That was just Dad. He blew hot and cold like the British weather.

'No, I have plans. I have to go.' I grabbed my bag and walked out.

As I drove home, my dad's words swirled around my head.

You're too sensitive…

You're not strong enough to handle the pressure…

I have to give the job to the strongest candidate…

We all have our lanes and sometimes we need to just stick to them…

A tear ran down my cheek. *Oh God.* Dad was right. I *was* too emotional. At least I hadn't started crying in front of him.

I parked up, opened the building door, climbed the stairs to my flat, kicked off my shoes and collapsed on the sofa. I was so glad I'd be meeting my best friend, Sophia, for dinner in central London in a couple of hours. After the afternoon I'd had, I needed to let my hair down.

At least I didn't have to worry about what to wear. I planned my outfits for the week ahead every Sunday afternoon before I did the ironing.

It wasn't like I had day-of-the-week underwear or

anything. I just found it was easier to wear certain clothes on particular days. For example, Mondays were all about being formal to get my head back in the professional zone after the weekend, so I'd wear my black trousers with one of two smart dark blazers (navy or charcoal), whereas Fridays were more relaxed, so wearing either my light blue or peach maxi dress with a cream blazer was more appropriate. I'd been in this outfit all day, though, so I'd picked out something different for tonight.

I walked in the bedroom and saw the long green dress laid out on the bed along with my gold sandals. *All set.*

I was about to start getting ready when the phone rang.

'Hello?' I frowned, looking down at the number to see if I recognised it.

'Is that Isabella Walker?'

'Speaking.'

'This is Zainab from the JCH London Language School. We had your name on the waiting list for the PEFLITC course, which starts a week on Monday. One of our students has had to pull out due to illness, so a space has just become available and I wondered if you'd like to take it?'

My eyes widened and my knees wobbled. Of all the people I had been expecting to call me, they were the last on my mind. I remembered Sophia convincing me to apply last year when I'd turned thirty. Around about the same time, an old colleague of mine had put me forward for a role at a school she'd just moved to. I was going through a *what am I doing with my life?* crisis, and both of them were trying to help me out of it.

One of the ideas I'd explored was studying for a PEFLITC qualification, which was a professional English foreign language international teaching certificate, so that I'd be qualified to teach English abroad. Something I'd always been interested in trying.

I'd spent months researching the course and it all sounded really exciting, but Dad hadn't thought it was a good idea. Plus, the more I thought about it, the more overwhelming the idea felt.

I'd plucked up the courage to look into it again a few months ago when I'd turned thirty-one. After more encouragement from Sophia, I'd applied and even gone along for an interview.

That was when the enormity of it all had dawned on me and I'd got cold feet again, so I'd been relieved when they'd emailed back to say although I'd been accepted, the one-month intensive course for this summer was full. When they'd said they'd put me on the waiting list, I'd thought they were just being polite. I hadn't known they were actually serious.

Even though I was sure the course was something I wanted to do at some point, I didn't know if I was ready to do it so quickly.

'Thanks for calling me. That sounds very exciting, but it's all very sudden. Can I think about it and let you know?'

'Sure. I can't guarantee that the place will still be there, though, because we do have other people on our waiting list.'

It was a difficult decision.

Dad's comments flashed back into my head. He thought I couldn't manage extra responsibility or pressure, and this course would be intense, so maybe now wasn't the right time.

On the other hand, I'd said earlier that I wanted to develop my career, and this would definitely help me do that. Once I passed, I'd have the certificate for life. So if a promotion didn't come up again at work in the next few years, I could look at teaching overseas then. I'd have options.

But what if I failed? Then there was the money to think about. It was a big investment, and…

'Isabella? Are you still there? If you're not ready, then perhaps you can sign up for the evening courses we offer or look at applying again next year.'

That seemed like a much more logical option. Big changes had to be planned with precision, not just done on a whim. If I did it next summer, that would give me time to think it through properly and do some more research. After all, maybe something had changed since I'd last looked into it.

Yes, I was still angry about being passed over for promotion, but that didn't mean I should just make rash decisions.

Did I like having Dad as my boss? Not really, but no job was perfect, right? Things could be much worse. I knew colleagues who'd left to work at other schools and complained that the head was even worse than him or had feral pupils, so the grass wasn't always greener.

'Thanks very much for thinking of me, but I think doing the course next year sounds like it would be better.'

'No problem. Have a good weekend.'

'You too.'

I breathed a sigh of relief. Panic over. I'd carefully consider my options over the summer holidays and work out my next move.

Both my career and my romantic prospects might not look rosy right now, but I was sure things would improve at some point. If I kept working hard, I'd get promoted eventually.

As for my love life?

Something told me *that* would be a lot more challenging to sort out…

CHAPTER THREE

I stepped out of London Bridge train station, crossed the road and headed towards the restaurant Sophia had booked, which was only a few minutes away.

After I gave my name to the hostess, she showed me to our table. *Right by the window. Perfect.*

The restaurant had wall-to-wall views of the River Thames and Tower Bridge. I watched a boat gliding across the water, then looked over at a couple posing for photos outside with the iconic bridge as a backdrop. Didn't blame them. I'd lived in London all my life and still never got tired of looking at it.

It was probably a good idea to order some drinks now so that they'd be here before Sophia arrived.

We didn't get to meet often, so I wanted to make the most of the time we had together. Sophia had her own business, running a beauty PR agency, so rather than relaxing at home or being out with friends, her evenings and weekends were usually spent burning the midnight oil.

Once the drinks came, I scanned the menu. It shouldn't

take long to decide what I wanted. I always went for the chicken dish. Just like I always drank Chardonnay. Life was so much easier when I stuck to the same thing. No worrying about whether or not I'd like something. Change and variety were overrated.

'So sorry I'm late!' Sophia put her bag and jacket on the chair, then opened her arms to give me a big hug.

'No worries, hon,' I squeezed her tight.

'Literally a minute before I was about to leave, a client called to discuss a project and I got stuck on the phone.'

'Don't worry! I know you're building a PR empire. I haven't been here long.'

Sophia exhaled, smoothed down the back of her fitted blue dress, then sat down. She was looking glamorous as always. Her shoulder-length dark hair looked freshly blow-dried, and despite it being seven-thirty in the evening, her make-up was still immaculate. And how she walked in those three-inch heels was still beyond me.

'Thanks for understanding and for getting the drinks in —I definitely need something strong after the day I've had.'

'You and me both.' I took a large glug whilst Sophia quickly checked her glass. She had a bit of OCD. I'd already given it the once-over to make sure it was clean when the waitress had brought it to the table, but I let Sophia do her thing anyway. It was important she felt relaxed.

'Oh no, what happened?' Her face creased with concern. 'Is it about the promotion? You didn't reply to my text about it earlier.'

'Yep. I didn't get it. He said I wasn't ready. *Again*.' I filled Sophia in on what had happened. The more I talked about it, the more it felt like someone was twisting a sharp knife inside my stomach.

'I know you won't like me saying this, and I know he's your dad and everything and he loves you, but he's also stifling you. You need to get out of there.'

I'd tried leaving. Even though I hated the pressure of applying for jobs and the whole interview process, I'd forced myself to go for a second in department role an ex-colleague had put me forward for last year. Surprisingly, they'd offered it to me. Probably because she'd put in a good word. But when I'd told Dad, he'd said he needed me to stay.

I remembered how awful I'd felt when he'd told me that if I left, it would damage the school's reputation. "How would it look?" he'd said. "My daughter—my own flesh and blood abandoning me to work at a rival school? We're *family*, Bella. We have to stick together. I know you want to progress, and don't worry. We don't have any roles available at the moment, but just be patient. Something will come up."

And so I'd listened to him. The last thing I wanted to do was let my dad down or cause him any unnecessary stress. I owed him a lot. Teaching was definitely my calling and I probably wouldn't have got into it if it wasn't for him. He'd given me a job when I'd completed my teacher training after I'd been rejected by some other schools. Of course I'd applied and been interviewed for the role fair and square like everyone else.

As harsh as he could be, I knew that deep down, Dad wanted the best for me. So I'd decided to stay. After all, he'd said there would be opportunities for promotion, so why upset him by leaving if something would be coming up soon? Staying meant I could keep my dad happy and still have a chance to rise up the ranks once a position became available. At the time it had made perfect sense.

'It's difficult,' I sighed. 'On the one hand I want to progress, but on the other I'm not sure about going somewhere new or making drastic changes. That reminds me, can you believe that I had a call this afternoon about the PEFLITC course? Someone dropped out, so they had a space to start a week on Monday.' Just saying it out loud sent a shiver down my spine.

'That's amazing! So you're finally going to do it, right?'

'Um, no. Not exactly…'

It was Sophia who'd inspired me to look into the course. She'd studied French at uni, which involved a year teaching English in France. I didn't travel much, but when I'd taken the Eurostar to go over and visit her, I was amazed by the experiences she was having. The different people she met, living in a new country, experiencing a new culture and getting paid to teach at the same time. It sounded so exciting. But by then I had already applied for my teacher training course. My career path was already mapped out, so I'd pushed the idea out of my head.

'Why not? I thought you wanted to do it. You've been talking about it for years.'

'I did… I do… it's just—it sounded intense. Plus, it was too short notice. I just don't think I'm ready.'

'Now you're starting to sound like your dad,' Sophia sighed. 'You're *more* than capable and you know it too. What else are you going to do this summer? Go to Cornwall again with your parents? Try something new, Bella.

Give yourself a new challenge. Call the language school back and say you've changed your mind.'

I hadn't, though. Sophia was always trying to encourage me to *grow* as she'd call it. She consistently excelled in her career and was much braver than I was at making big decisions. Running a company meant she had to be. But for someone like me, signing up for this course was a big step.

'Maybe… it's too late now. I've already told them no and they had a waiting list, so someone else is bound to have snapped up that place.'

'Hmmm…' She rested her finger on her chin. 'Not necessarily.'

'Anyway, enough about my work stuff,' I quickly changed the subject. 'What's new with you?'

'Oh, no, you don't! We're not done talking about you yet. So…!' Sophia leant forward. 'Tell me more about that date you had last week!'

From one failure in my life to another…

Because she'd been so busy, I'd only texted her to say that it was a disaster and that I'd let her know more when we met up. As I filled her in on the excruciating details, Sophia couldn't stop wincing.

'Jesus… hats off to you for lasting that long. What a nightmare.'

'Tell me about it. Count yourself lucky that you're coupled up and don't have to deal with the dating world.'

'Yeah.' Sophia's face fell a little and she took a large gulp of her G&T.

'How are things with you and Rich?'

'Fine. Good! He's *so* supportive of the business and the

long hours I have to work. I'm very lucky!' Her voice went up several octaves.

'You are. Finding a decent man is like trying to run in quicksand. I just don't—' My phone started vibrating on the table. I glanced at the screen.

'Aren't you going to answer?' Sophia frowned.

'No, we're out at dinner. It's Melody. I'll call her tomorrow.'

'Melody—your uni friend?'

'Yeah.'

'I *love* her! Don't worry about me. Especially since *I* kept *you* waiting because of a phone call earlier. You don't speak often, so if she's ringing, it must be important. Answer it. It'll give me time to look at the menu.'

I definitely did *not* want to answer. I was pretty sure I knew *exactly* why she was calling and it wasn't important.

'Honestly, it's fine. She's probably just ringing about the stupid reunion next weekend.'

'Oh yeah! I remember you mentioning that when you received the invite. That came around quickly. Have you decided what to wear yet? Please tell me you've changed your mind and that you're going?'

Sophia took one look at my blank face and immediately knew the answer. Before I could stop her, she swiped my phone off the table.

'Melody! Hi! It's Sophia! Long time no speak. How are you?'

What the hell?

I was just going to leave it to go to voicemail. Now Sophia had answered, I knew they'd form an indestructible tag team and start concocting ways to persuade me to go.

I could hear Melody talking at a million miles an hour and Soph was nodding and smiling.

'No way?' Soph's eyes widened. 'Really? Oooh! I definitely agree.'

I could only imagine what Melody was saying to her…

'Erm, Soph? Give me my phone, please.' I narrowed my eyes.

'Yeah, you're absolutely right. Well, you can tell her yourself now. She's just come back to the table, so I can hand you over. Great talking to you! Have fun next Friday, and take care. Yeah, you too. Here's Bella.'

Sophia handed me the phone. At least she'd covered for me by making out I'd gone to the loo. I took a deep breath, preparing myself for the incoming lecture.

'Mel, hi! How are you?' I mustered up all the enthusiasm I could.

'I am sooo excited! This time next week, I'll be partying at the reunion. I cannot wait! Anyhow, I spoke to Heather and she said she still hadn't received your RSVP. What's going on, B?'

'Glad you're excited! I'm not coming, though. Remember I said when we spoke last week? I've got plans.'

'Liar!' Sophia said loudly. My eyes popped out of my sockets. What was she doing, throwing me under the bus like that?

'Whatever you've got going on, you need to cancel. Like, now. It's not confirmed, but word is that none other than Mike Jones might be there, so you *have* to come.'

My phone slid out of my hand and hit the table. Luckily, I managed to catch it before it bounced onto the floor.

Shit.

I took a deep breath to try and stop my heart from racing, then put the phone to my ear.

'That's nice. Say hi from me. I'm sure you'll all have an amazing time, but I really can't make it. Our main courses have just arrived and I'm starving, so I'd better go, but I'll call you soon, okay? So we can get a date in the diary to meet up. Bye!'

I hoped I wouldn't get sent to hell for cutting her off so abruptly, but I knew her. Melody was persistent. If I didn't end the call quickly, she'd persuade me to do something I didn't want to. I had no choice.

Melody had only dropped that bombshell literally a minute ago and already my mind was all over the place.

I could feel sweat pooling on my forehead. Maybe they'd just turned on the heating. My heart was pounding and suddenly my throat felt drier than the Sahara Desert. I reached for the carafe of water, filled up my glass and downed it in one gulp like a sambuca shot.

She'd said his name.

It had been ages since someone else had mentioned it out loud.

'You okay?' Sophia frowned.

'Yeah. Yeah, I'm fine.'

'You are so *not* fine. You look like you've just seen a ghost.' She rested her finger on her chin. 'Did she tell you? About the fact that you-know-who might be going next Saturday? Is that why you don't want to go? Because of that night?'

'No! Of course not!' My voice sounded like I'd just sucked on helium. 'Ancient history. We were just kids back then.' I waved my hands dismissively.

Sophia knew the basics of what had happened, but not

the full story. It was way too embarrassing. That was the kind of thing you kept to yourself and took to your grave.

It was easy to hide the fact that after it happened, I'd locked myself away at home, bingeing on *Friends* and eating enough Häagen-Dazs to fill an Olympic-sized swimming pool. Sophia had gone to France and Melody had gone travelling, so neither had been around to see how devastated I was.

Eventually, though, I'd seen the light and realised that I had to forget about him. Sever all contact. Put him out of my mind. Focus on my teacher training. Start preparing for my career. Move on with my life.

So that was what I'd done. I was over him. I was doing well. I had taken on more shifts at the department store I worked at to keep myself busy during the summer. And when term time came around, I threw myself into my course.

As far as Sophia was concerned, since I'd graduated, I hadn't given him a second thought. I was strong and sensible Bella. A woman who knew that it was absolutely ridiculous to pine for a man who wasn't interested in her. Whenever Sophia asked, I brushed it off and told her I'd been too busy to even think about him and that we'd lost touch.

It was absolutely the right thing to do. It was much better to find someone who *did* want to be with me.

I knew that unrequited love was painful and toxic. It would eat away at you slowly and there was no way I'd succumb to something like that. Yeah, it was fine to have feelings after a few months. That was understandable. But I certainly wasn't dumb enough to still like someone a decade later. *Pff.* Having a ten-year crush would be crazy.

I mean, okay, occasionally I thought about him, usually whenever I was on a date. Particularly a rubbish one, so probably more often than I would've liked. Or worse, when I was in a relationship and I knew things weren't going well. Somehow, thoughts of him would pop up, but I always made sure I pushed those feelings out of my head, quickly.

Like now: I absolutely *wasn't* thinking about tall, dark, sexy Mike. The guy that had been my best friend for three years at uni. The man that I'd spent all day with during lectures and then studied with at our student digs late into the night.

The one who'd always made me laugh.

The friend I'd fallen in love with.

Who hadn't loved me back.

Anyway, like I said, it was water under the bridge. At the time, I was barely an adult, so what did I know about love or men?

'Oh, *come on*! You're not even a tiny bit curious to go and see if he's still as hot as he was all those years ago? I know things didn't go how you wanted them to back then, but that was ages ago and you guys always got on so well. What if he's single now too? And what if you two hit it off again? This could be your second chance!'

Ha.

I bet he was nothing like as good-looking now as he was before, and his personality had probably gone down the toilet too.

In any case, unlike Sophia, I knew the full story of what had really happened that night, and he'd made it very clear that he didn't see me that way. Like I always said, *if someone tells you something, believe them.* The past should stay in the past.

'Nope,' I said firmly. 'We were great friends back then, and yes, I briefly had feelings for him, but not anymore. It doesn't bother me that he'll be there. I just don't see the need to go, that's all…' I shrugged my shoulders, hoping I'd said enough to convince her to drop the subject. 'Anyway, enough about him and the reunion. I really am starving. Let's order.'

I'd told Melody our main courses had arrived, but we hadn't even called the waitress yet. *See?* This reunion was bad news. It was making me snappy, and I'd told more lies speaking to Melody this past week than I had in months.

Still, in just over seven days, the whole thing would be over and I wouldn't have to think about the reunion or him ever again.

Next Saturday morning couldn't come quickly enough.

CHAPTER FOUR

Pizza. Oh how I love thee.

P I sank my teeth into a large slice topped with pepperoni and extra cheese and it tasted like heaven.

Tonight I'd decided to treat myself to a takeaway and a bottle of wine to celebrate the end of term. I'd been good throughout the week, cooking healthy dinners from scratch and bringing the leftovers to work for lunch, and I'd even had a chicken salad last night when I'd gone out for dinner with a few colleagues, so I deserved this.

An evening at home with a good feed and a couple of DVDs would also help take my mind off the 'R' word, which had started an hour ago.

Melody had been messaging all week about the reunion. Pleading with me to come, but I'd stuck to my guns. The more I'd thought about it, the more anxious it made me.

It wasn't just the stuff about seeing Mike, which might be awkward. The idea of seeing everyone also made me shudder, because it meant I'd have to face up to the reality that I wasn't happy with my life.

I'd thought that by now, I'd have everything together. I'd have a great job and be married with a child. Or at least be thinking about having one soon. But I wasn't even close. I was failing in every aspect. So the last thing I needed was to go to some stupid reunion and be reminded about how much I'd fallen short of my expectations, hopes and dreams.

I bet loads of my old friends had done lots of cool things. They were probably racing up the career ladder, travelling to exciting places, raising an adorable family or doing fun stuff. And then there'd be little old me. Boring Bella who was still stuck in the same job, with zero relationship prospects or romance on the horizon.

No, thanks. I felt bad about myself already. I didn't need to go to the reunion to feel even worse.

My phone pinged. It was another text from Melody.

Melody

Music is ace! About to have a boogie on the dance floor. Wish you were here! xoxo

That was the fourth text she'd sent this evening. The first one had said:

Melody

I've arrived! Place looks fab! Lots of decorations and pics from the good old days. Spotted a few of you! The spread seems pretty good, so I'm going to get stuck in. Will keep you updated! xoxo

.   .   .

That had been swiftly followed half an hour later by:

Melody

Great turnout! Loads of people already here. Miss you! xoxo

The third text had come twenty minutes later:

Melody

Just seen little Hayley! Can you believe she's got five kids now? FIVE?!! I'm struggling with one. She was always so prim. I thought she'd end up joining a convent and now I discover she's had sex at least five times! Just shows how much things can change in a decade. I've heard Duncan's here. Gonna find out if he ever became a playwright like he always boasted he would. I'll keep you posted!! xoxo

It was as if Melody had been appointed the unofficial roving reunion reporter. I hadn't asked for these updates, but she insisted on sending them. Okay, I admit, I was kind of interested to know what was happening. And I was just as shocked as she was to hear about Hayley. She'd always said sex was the root of all evil. Pretty sure she'd also said there was no need for procreation, seeing as the world was already overpopulated. Hmmm…

Still, at least she had her own family, so she was way ahead of me.

My phone pinged again. If Melody kept up this level of texting, I wouldn't need the film to entertain me.

Melody

OMG. OMG. OMG. Haven't found Duncan yet, but I

can confirm that Mike Jones is in the building. I repeat: MIKE JONES IS IN THE BUILDING.

Melody

Holy mother of God, he is H-O-T. Not just Nando's chicken hot. I'm talking extra spicy with chilli sauce and a side order of one thousand jalapenos HOTTTTTTT!

My heart stopped for a second as I tried to take it all in.

He was there.

He was *really* there.

If I wanted to, I could see him again.

For the first time in ten years.

No.

It's a bad idea.

If I went, it would be awkward. He'd ask why I hadn't kept in contact and then I'd have to explain that it was because I'd liked him so much back then that it was the only way I could move on with my life. Even though of course I didn't feel that way anymore, just saying that out loud would sound so cringey.

So Melody reckons he's still hot…

As I pictured his face, my heart restarted with a vengeance and pounded through my chest.

I supposed it made sense that he'd aged well. Mike had always taken care of himself. Playing basketball or working out in some form or another. Most students cured their hangovers with a full English breakfast or a Bloody Mary. Not Mike. He'd get up and go running.

I remembered one evening when I was feeling down about my ex breaking up with me, Mike had invited me to the gym because he'd said exercise would take my mind off things. But after being there for all of half an hour, I'd said I needed to leave.

He'd thought it was because I was chickening out, but in truth it was because I'd hated the illicit thoughts going through my head. Watching the sweat trickle down his biceps and chest as he lifted weights. Seeing the firmness of his thighs and his tight bum as he ran on the treadmill.

It was wrong. He was my best friend. And he had a girlfriend. One that didn't deserve him, but that wasn't the point. I had morals and that was a line I wasn't going to cross. So I'd never gone to the gym with him again and always tried to avoid looking at his body. Pretty hard, especially during the summer months, when he wore those sexy tight vests and had his arms on show.

Oh, I remember those arms and that chest…

I wondered whether he was still built like a god.

I felt another tingle race through me.

Stop it…

Anyway, knowing Melody, she'd had a few drinks and was drunk on nostalgia too, so was probably exaggerating about how good he looked just to persuade me to come. But it wouldn't work.

Even if he *was* still hot, looks weren't everything. I doubted he was single anyway.

My mind wandered, thinking about what Mike was doing now. We'd both always wanted to teach. He was ambitious, so I bet he was already on track to become the head teacher of a top school. I may have been tempted once or twice to Google him over the years to find out…

I had one moment of weakness when I actually did and was shocked to find a bald, overweight guy at the top of my search. Then when I'd clicked on the picture, I'd realised that it wasn't him. Mike was a popular name (at uni there were three Mikes in our year—that's why we'd often called him Mike *Jones*) and I guessed his surname was pretty common too. After that, I'd vowed never to look again.

I knew I could find out the answers to *all* of my questions and more, if I just went along tonight. But the sensible voice shouting loudly in my head told me there was no point and to keep my bum firmly on the sofa and stay at home.

Melody

Did some detective work and Heather told me he is single!!!

Melody

I repeat: MIKE IS SINGLE!!! Once word gets out, he won't be for long. Get your arse down here pronto, Isabella! xoxo

My stomach flipped. He was single? That was a surprise.

Every time he broke up with Rebecca (I lost count of how many times they were on and off—could easily be in the hundreds), there was always a queue of women longer than the January sales, eager to take her place.

My mind whizzed again, thinking about what might have happened. Maybe he'd just got divorced. Then again, Mike never had really done the whole commitment thing, so I couldn't see him being dragged down the aisle. Marriage and long-term relationships had never been his thing. Shame, because he was smart, kind, funny and gorgeous.

Looking back, it seemed like he had the total package:

looks, personality and chemistry. But I knew he couldn't have been as perfect as I made him out to be.

My memory had clearly become distorted over the years. That was the thing with time: it romanticised things. Everything always seemed like it was glossier in the *good old days* when we were young and naïve, but in reality it wasn't true. He'd rejected me. Case in point. It was just a silly little crush.

Sophia had said she had something important to tell me this evening and would be calling me any minute. Otherwise, I would've just switched off my phone.

I'd just text Melody and tell her I couldn't come. *Again.*

Me

Thanks for all the updates. Not going to be able to read any more of your texts now, though, so don't worry about sending them. Just go and enjoy yourself! Say hi to everyone. xxx

Melody

What the hell is wrong with you, woman?!!! I've just told you your Mr Right is here, in this room, and is SINGLE and you're still spouting BS about being busy?!

Melody

The other day you were complaining about how hard it was to date and find someone decent and I've just told you your perfect man is RIGHT HERE. TONIGHT!!

Melody

You tried to play it cool, but I know you liked him a lot more than you let on. I never understood why you guys didn't go out when you both became single. You would've been so good together!!

Melody

The timing might have been off back then, but this could be your chance to secure a lifetime of happiness!

Melody

Just in case my previous messages weren't clear, let me repeat: MIKE JONES is HERE and UNATTACHED! Come NOW! xoxo

Her constant use of CAPS was so aggressive. I was beginning to wish I'd never confessed to her about my crush on Mike a few years after we'd graduated. I knew it would come back to bite me in the bum.

Me

NO! I know you're trying to look out for me Mel, but I CAN'T. Sorry.

Hopefully, now I'd replied in CAPS and given her a hard no, she'd *finally* get the message.

I pressed play on the remote control and took a sip of Chardonnay, wondering what that Edwin guy would have to say about it. Was this wine just as orgasmic as the one we'd had at that bar? I shook my head and chuckled. As soul-destroying as it had felt at the time, I had to admit I wouldn't forget that date in a hurry. And if I didn't laugh about it, I'd have to cry about the sorry state of my love life.

I knew Melody thought going tonight was going to magically resolve it and that I'd end the evening riding off with my Prince Charming, but she was wrong. As rubbish as things were on the romance front, I'd still be better off staying in.

Just as I thought I was finally off the hook about tonight, my phone rang. No prizes for guessing who it was. She was like a dog with a bone. Clearly I hadn't been firm enough. No more pussyfooting around. I had to be more direct.

'For the last time, I am *not* going to the stupid reunion! I don't care if Mike is there. Hell, I don't care if Brad Pitt and George Clooney are cavorting on the tables right now doing a striptease. I. Am. Not. Coming!'

There. I'd done it. I rarely raised my voice, so she'd definitely know I was serious. If she didn't get the message from that, I didn't know what it would take.

'I reckon, Brad and George will be *very* disappointed to hear that. I would be too…'

OMG.

Ground swallow me up now.

I held the phone in front of me and studied the name on the screen. Yep. It was definitely Melody that had called me, but it wasn't her that had spoken. I'd recognise *that* voice anywhere.

It was *him.*

Mike Jones.

My heart raced and my stomach plummeted.

'Bells? Are you there? It's me. Mike.'

Shit.

My body tingled at the sound of him saying my nickname. He was still the only one who called me that.

My brain scrambled. I knew I needed to say something, but it was like someone had pressed the erase button. I couldn't find the words. And I'd apparently lost the power of speech too. My mouth opened and closed repeatedly like a hungry goldfish, but nothing came out.

'Mike! Hi… erm… long time no speak! Sorry about that. Just… before… I didn't mean… it's just… *of course* I'd want to see Brad and George. I mean, who wouldn't want to have a look at their meat and two veg? I definitely would! And I'd like to see you too. Not just your willy, obviously—I'm interested in seeing all of you… I mean…'

Oh God.

Seriously?

Please don't tell me I'd just told Mike I wanted to see his dick. Yes, I'd dreamt about it many times, but I was never supposed to say that out loud.

Bloody hell.

'Sorry, I… I've been drinking. I'm not thinking clearly. You remember what a lightweight I was. I always speak gibberish when I have alcohol.' I laughed awkwardly, praying he'd see the funny side.

'Well, if George and Brad are looking for someone to join their Chippendale act, I reckon I could make myself available for special bookings,' he chuckled. *Phew.* Glad he still had a sense of humour. 'Still a lightweight, eh? You were always so cute when you were tipsy.'

My heart fluttered.

Mike just called me cute.

No. No. No. Get a grip.

'Yeah, so anyway, nice speaking to you. Er, h-have a good time this evening. Better go…'

'Wait!' Mike shouted. 'Are you really not coming tonight? At *all*? I know you've got plans and stuff, but I'd really love to see you. Even if it's for half an hour. It's been *ages*.'

'I—I don't know, by the time I get there it'd be late and—'

'There's *loads* of time! Apparently they've got this place until one, maybe even later, and it's only just gone ten. Please come, Bella. *Please. For me?* I've *really* missed you.'

As those words tumbled from his mouth, it was like my brain started playing a montage of rainbows, sunsets and every romantic scene in a romcom.

The world's population of butterflies simultaneously took up residence in my stomach and began fluttering like crazy.

Game over.

'Okay, I'll come.' The words flew out of my mouth before I had a chance to stop them. I'd always found it hard to say no to him.

'Amazing! See you soon!'

'Yeah… see you soon.' I dropped the phone on the sofa and tried to take everything in.

I'd just spoken to Mike.

Agreed to go to the reunion.

I was going to see my old crush.

The guy who'd crushed my heart.

What the hell was I thinking?

CHAPTER FIVE

Sometimes I wished I could be bad. That even if I'd agreed to do something, I could cancel without feeling guilty. It just wasn't me, though.

That was why I had to go tonight. Now that I'd told Mike I was coming, I couldn't back out. I'd made my bed, so I just had to lie in it.

Plus, Melody had followed up Mike's surprise call with a text, threatening to bring Mike to my flat if I didn't turn up. So as much as I didn't want to go, I'd rather see him in a crowded room where I could just say hello, then slip away a couple of minutes later if it became too awkward, than be left alone together in my flat.

No way.

I jumped off the sofa and went into the bathroom.

After showering, I ran some product through my curls to give them some definition, swiped on some eyeliner, mascara and clear lip gloss, then went into the bedroom and opened my underwear drawer. For a fleeting second, I considered whether I should put on my frilly bra and knickers, just in case. Then I came to my senses and reminded myself to get real. Comfortable black cotton underwear would be just fine.

Time to get dressed. I opened my wardrobe and started rifling through the hangers. I had no idea what to wear. When I'd planned my outfits for the week last Sunday, obviously I hadn't included anything for tonight because I wasn't supposed to be going. Dammit. I hated doing things off the cuff.

I couldn't think about it for too long, though, if I was going to get there in time. I decided on a long pink cardigan and my favourite yellow skirt, which came just below my knees. It was bright and colourful and made me feel more confident.

Now for the shoes. I pulled out some brown leather sandals. Nice and practical. *Hmm.* Maybe practical wasn't the best idea for a reunion. I was going to see a lot of people for the first time in a decade, so maybe I should put in a bit more effort. Make an impression.

I pulled out a box from the bottom of the wardrobe.

So pretty.

It was a pair of pink-and-yellow heels that Sophia had given me as a gift. She'd said she'd bought them for herself and they didn't fit, but I knew that wasn't true because they were in my size. I rarely wore heels, but what the hell. If I didn't wear them tonight, when would I?

I slid my feet into the soft leather shoes, fastened the straps around my ankles, then looked myself up and down in the mirror. A cardigan and skirt with heels might not be most people's idea of glamour, but I felt pretty good. At least it was an improvement on how I'd looked at uni.

Just as I was checking the train times, Sophia's name flashed on my phone.

'Hey,' I answered.

'So, are you ready yet?'

'Ready for what exactly?' I said suspiciously. Somehow it sounded like she already knew I was on my way out.

'The reunion, of course!'

'How did you know I was going?'

'*Come on.* You're one of the smartest women I know. So sooner or later you *had* to realise that grabbing the opportunity to see Mike after all these years was a much better use of your time than sitting on the sofa eating pizza.' How did she know I was eating pizza? I considered telling her she was wrong about Mike, but then thought better of it. 'And if you hadn't, then I'd just come and drag you there myself.'

'Yeah, right! You may *think* you know me, but I know you too, and I'm guessing that right now, you're in the office, working at your desk, where you'll be until at least midnight.'

'Just because you're right doesn't mean I couldn't have taken a break to take you there… and anyway, I'm almost finished. I've got a big pitch on Monday morning. If we get this account, it could really propel us into the super league of beauty PR.'

I believed her. Sophia was on fire. If I'd achieved as much as she had, there was no way I'd be nervous about going to a reunion. She ran her own business and was in a serious relationship with a decent guy. Sophia was such an inspiration. The rate her agency was growing, she could literally take over the world. I loved that she was doing so well. At the same time, though, sometimes I worried that she worked too hard. She'd been the same ever since we'd first met at college when we were sixteen.

'That's brilliant, Soph. I know you'll smash it. You always do.'

'Thanks, hon.'

'Was that your exciting news?'

'Um, no… I'll tell you about that tomorrow. Anyway, why haven't you left yet?'

'I'm about to. I was just checking the train times when you called.'

'Train? There's a time and a place for public transport and now isn't one of them. This is your Cinderella moment. Do you think Cinders would have got the bus and tube to go to the ball and meet her Prince Charming?'

'Firstly, I'm not going to the reunion to meet my Prince Charming. He doesn't exist.' I rolled my eyes. 'And secondly, I'm not a high-flying PR star like you. A cab to the city will cost a small fortune.'

I'd thought about driving—that way I could give Melody a lift to wherever she was staying if she got legless, which she often did on a night out—but I'd already had a couple of glasses of wine myself and I wasn't sure how easy it would be to find parking near the venue. Getting public transport was definitely the best option.

'Don't worry about the money. I'll pay. You need to arrive calm and composed, not be fretting about train times and cancellations. What's the point of me working all these long hours if I can't treat my best friend to a bloody taxi?'

'But—'

'No buts! I'm calling them now. I've already got the address from Melody. I'm booking it now. Have fun!'

Sophia hung up. Melody? I knew those two would be scheming. I wanted to be annoyed but couldn't. They were good friends who were only doing what they thought was best for me. If they knew how hurt I was and the full extent of my feelings at the time, they probably wouldn't be so eager for me to see Mike again.

It'd be fine. I wasn't going to waste time fretting.

Minutes later, I received a text to say the cab was outside.

I was really going…

I opened the taxi door. As I slid onto the back seat, my mind wandered to the first time Mike and I had met. It was at a freshers' event during the first week of uni. He'd accidentally stepped on my foot when we were queuing at the busy student union bar and turned around to apologise.

The attraction was instant. Well, from my side anyway. I didn't think I had ever seen such a perfect specimen. *Ever*. Not in real life anyway. The man that was stood in front of me looked like he'd belonged in an edition of *Cosmopolitan*'s Sexiest Men or stepped out of a Hollywood romcom.

Six foot four, broad shoulders, muscular arms and chest, dark hair, chiselled jaw and a smile that made your stomach do backflips. He was *everything*.

I often struggled to find men that were taller than I was. But Mike was the perfect height. Like he was made just for me. And after we'd spoken for a while, I realised that he didn't just come in pretty packaging. He was funny and smart too. Not only that, he was also studying English. What were the chances? How had I not seen him in my class? Yep. Mike was perfection personified. There was just one problem: we were both in relationships.

My boyfriend, Lance, had gone to study in Newcastle, so we'd decided to try the long-distance thing. In hindsight, I should've just called it quits before we'd started uni. I'd fallen out of love with him long before that, but we'd been together for almost two years and I knew ending it would break his heart. The last thing I wanted to do was hurt him, and cheating was definitely *not* an option.

In any case, as far as I was concerned, the chances of hooking up with Mike were about as likely as me winning a trillion pounds. In short, zero. I was a geek with frizzy hair, thick-rimmed glasses and a dress sense that was more *shabby* than *chic*. Plus Mike was dating Rebecca, aka the most beautiful girl in uni. I had no chance. So I accepted my fate. I pushed my feelings back where they belonged, deep below the surface, and we became best friends.

It wasn't easy keeping those desires locked away. Especially when I eventually broke up with Lance, and Mike also became single. Ever since we'd first met, I'd told myself that guys like him didn't go for women like me. If only I'd remembered that on that fateful night of our graduation three years later, when I'd tried to break from the friend zone, I could have saved myself a lot of heartache…

Anyway, that was then, this was now. It would be okay. It'd take at least another half an hour to get to the venue, by which point the reunion would be almost over.

I'd say my hellos to everyone, Melody would be happy I'd come, and once I'd engaged in some small talk with Mike and we'd said our goodbyes, I could finally show her and Sophia that he wasn't some magical version of my Mr Right. They'd realise I was over him.

'We're here!' the taxi driver indicated, then pulled up on the kerb.

'Already?'

'I took a shortcut. The lady who booked the cab said it was urgent and getting here quickly was a matter of life or death.'

Typical Sophia. She could be so dramatic sometimes.

My heart thudded as the reality hit me. I was about to come face to face with Mike for the first time in a decade.

I had no idea what I'd say. How I'd act towards him. How he'd act towards me. Whether it would be awkward or if it'd be like no time had passed.

Now that I'd finally arrived, there was only one way to find out.

CHAPTER SIX

M elody was right. They'd done a great job of decorating the venue. As soon as I stepped inside there was a huge red-and-gold banner hanging across the entrance—*Queen's University, Hertfordshire, Class of 2000: Ten-Year Reunion*, it said—along with matching balloons.

Large collages lined the walls with photos of the many events and parties we'd enjoyed during those three years. Okay, full disclosure: I'd been a total nerd at uni (truth be told, throughout my entire education), so I couldn't pretend that I was at most of them. Only when Mike used to drag me from my room, literally kicking and screaming, to whatever function was going on at the student union.

Mike was one of those annoyingly talented people who barely had to study and still got straight A's. I, on the other hand, had to put the effort in if I wanted a decent grade. It didn't help either that I did my best work at night, which was of course when everyone wanted to go out.

Bloody hell.

I spotted a very unflattering photo of me holding up an alcopop. How had I not realised at the time that the glasses I wore were so hideous? I knew most people looked back at old photos and questioned their fashion choices, but they really weren't pretty.

As I walked down the corridor, my heart beat faster. The music was getting louder, which meant I was getting closer to the main part of the venue, where everyone was. And of course it was the thought of seeing *everyone* that was making my stomach extra jumpy and definitely *not* the idea of coming face to face with one person in particular…

'Hey, Isabella!' said a brunette with a big smile.

'Hi…!' I scanned my brain, trying to remember her name. I recognised the smile, but I couldn't quite place her.

'It's Frances,' she said, reading my mind.

No way.

'You look amazing!'

'You mean *fat*.' She winced.

'No.' I frowned. 'I mean exactly what I said: you look *amazing*!' Frances was always dieting, and if I was honest, I often worried that sometimes she took it a bit too far with skipping meals and manically exercising. She'd never looked well. Yeah, she'd gained weight, but to me, she looked much healthier.

'Thanks!' Her shoulders relaxed. 'You look fantastic too. I love your hair, and what happened to your glasses?'

'Thank you—I discovered contact lenses and the wonders of anti-frizz hair serum!' I laughed.

'Good for you! Everyone's in there. Nice seeing you.'

'Okay!' My stomach churned. 'You too.'

I entered the large main room. There was a bar and a buffet table towards the back, a dance floor in the middle, and a DJ in the corner at the front. It had mellow lighting, bright enough to see people's faces clearly, but dim enough to create an atmosphere at the same time.

As I looked around, it felt really surreal. In some ways, it was like I'd stepped back in time and was at uni all over again. Whilst some people looked more or less the same, just with different clothes, others showed that a lot could change in ten years. They'd undergone complete transformations. So much so that it took several glances to place them.

There was Winnie, who used to wear ripped fishnet tights, leather skirts and a biker jacket and had purple hair, with one side shaved, the other long, now sporting a very sensible-looking brown bob and wearing a floaty floral dress. It was only when I heard her infectious raspy laugh that the penny dropped and I recognised her.

Bryan, who'd always had shaggy shoulder-length hair and walked around with his head low like he had the weight of the world on his shoulders, was now bald (or had decided to shave it all off) and seemed a lot more smiley and confident.

I continued walking around, smiling and waving to people I knew whilst scanning the room. I told myself I was looking for Melody, but really I knew I wasn't. I was just about to get a drink when I spotted him.

Oh…

My…

God…

As soon as I laid eyes on Mike, my heart announced it was competing in the Olympic gymnastics.

It flipped. Jumped. Did backflips. Somersaulted. Twirled…

The acrobatics became so intense, I was sure my heart was going to fly from my chest at any second.

Melody wasn't exaggerating after all. Mike looked HOT. And this time, the use of CAPS was entirely necessary.

He'd been gorgeous before, so how was it possible that he was even more attractive now?

It wasn't just my heart that was in danger of escaping my chest. My eyes were in danger of shooting from their sockets too.

Even though he was unsurprisingly surrounded by a group of women who were dribbling like starving babies, I could still see him clearly. And as much as I tried to resist, I couldn't help drinking him in.

He towered over everyone like a god. His hair was shorter than it was at uni. Dark and slightly mussed up, but in a good way. And that face. He was still clean-shaven, with skin that looked like it was smoother than the finest silk. I had to fight the urge to race over and run my hands over his beautifully chiselled jawline.

Mike was wearing a crisp white shirt with a couple of buttons undone at the top, giving a glimpse of his rock-solid chest. I could tell by the way his pecs strained against the fabric that he still worked out.

Because of the bees surrounding him like a pot of sweet honey, I couldn't see what trousers he was wearing, but whatever they were, I already knew they'd look magnificent.

Just as I was reminiscing about how good he used to look in his Levi's, our eyes locked.

He'd seen me.

His dark eyes widened and his face broke into a smile. Mike excused himself from his conversation, much to the disappointment of a girl I think was called Angie, then made his way through the crowd.

He was now just metres away, striding towards me in his dark blue jeans. My heart clearly approved and was thudding like crazy.

There was no doubt about it. As much as I hated to use a wine analogy after that cringey date, this time it was warranted. Mike was like a fine wine. He just got better with age. And unlike that underwhelming glass of red, I was sure that *he* could definitely give me the sweetest orgasm…

I quickly pushed that illicit thought out of my head and attempted to compose myself.

'Bells!' Mike threw his arms open, picked me up and spun me around.

Talk about knowing how to make a woman feel welcome.

I wrapped my arms around his broad back, squeezing tight.

Mike's scent was divine. He'd graduated from the supermarket body sprays and upgraded to a delicious woody aftershave. I didn't know what it was called, but All Man would be an accurate description.

The sensation of having his big, warm muscular arms wrapped around me was just insane. Mike had always given the best hugs. I hadn't realised how much I'd missed them until now. I felt like I'd come home.

No, no, no, no, no.

I mustn't allow myself to get carried away. Yes, Mike

looked phenomenal, but looks weren't everything. And just because I was enjoying this hug, that didn't automatically mean that we were romantically compatible or some nonsense.

He gently put me down on the ground, took a step back and looked me up and down from head to toe. If I didn't know better, I'd think… *No*. Of course not. Mike was probably just wondering if I'd become even taller, that was all.

'Fuck! You look absolutely *incredible*! Come here!' He pulled me in for another hug. My mind raced. Mike seemed genuinely happy to see me. He'd complimented me multiple times. Had all these years apart changed things and made him see me differently?

'Thank you,' I said graciously. I almost told him that he looked pretty amazing too but stopped myself just in time.

He released me and stared with disbelief again.

'Wow…' He shook his head. 'My old bestie is all grown up!'

'Less of the "old", thank you!' I poked him in the ribs. Yep. Those abs were still as rock-solid as ever. 'We're the same age.'

'You wouldn't think it, though. You haven't aged a bit. And look at your hair.' He stroked it gently. 'I love it!'

Suddenly we were surrounded by a group of women. *I knew they wouldn't leave him alone for long.*

'Hey, Mike!' A woman I recognised as Ursula twirled her long hair around her fingers seductively.

'Ursula!' He threw his arms open and gave her a hug. A twinge of jealousy shot through me before I quickly suppressed it. That was just Mike. He'd always been a big hugger. 'You remember my friend Bella, don't you? She was my best mate all through uni—one of the sweetest girls I know.'

Friend. Mate. Bestie.

Earlier he'd called me *cute*, and now I was the *sweetest girl* he knew. All really *nice* compliments, but also words used to describe a puppy or your little sister. The answer to my question was clear: the way Mike saw me *hadn't* changed. He might have thought I looked all grown up, but I was still well and truly in the friend zone.

'Yeah.' She fake-smiled.

I remembered Ursula all right. She was always trying to get her claws into Mike. I understood why, but unlike me, she hadn't cared whether he was single or not. She would openly try it on with him. At a New Year's party, she'd actually walked up to Mike, clutching a handful of mistletoe, and asked him for a kiss when his girlfriend, Rebecca, was standing right beside him. No shame.

'Hi,' I said.

'Hold on… you don't have a drink!' Mike glanced down at my empty hand. 'Let me get you one. I'm guessing you've moved on from Hooch and Bacardi Breezers. What you drinking these days?'

'Chardonnay… definitely *not* tequila.'

'Got it,' he replied, his face falling a little. *He remembered.* It was tequila that had got us into a sticky situation before, and I hadn't touched the stuff since. The last thing I wanted was a repeat of that disastrous night.

After asking some of the others who'd come over if they wanted anything, Mike disappeared towards the bar and Ursula stood in front of me.

'So… *Bella*. Are you and Mike going to be, like, a *thing*?'

'Sorry, what?'

'Are you two going to get together? I know you always liked him at uni and it's obvious you still do, so with him being single and all, I wasn't sure if you'd be trying to hook up tonight.'

Ha. Never going to happen.

And how did she know I'd liked him? I'd always thought I did a pretty good job of hiding it.

'N-no… we're just friends.' Something he'd stated several times already tonight. Just in case I was in any doubt.

'So you don't mind if *I* make a move, then?'

Ursula hadn't changed. But who could blame her? She saw what she wanted and went for it. Her asking 'permission' was new, though, not that it was mine to give. If Mike was looking for a hook-up, judging by the women swarming around him tonight, he'd have rich pickings. 'Course not!' I squeaked. 'Go for it!'

Even if I did mind, it was irrelevant. Mike had never been interested in me in that way, so it didn't really matter.

I wasn't about to make a fool of myself again like I had that night. When I'd done something stupid that had led to us not speaking for over a decade.

That night had been unforgettable for all the wrong reasons.

Yes.

That night was the worst…

CHAPTER SEVEN

Graduation Night: July 2000

I t'd been the best day. Mike and I had graduated!

Three years of blood, sweat and tears had finally paid off. Going onstage dressed in our gowns, shaking the dean's hand and posing for official photos before doing the obligatory hat toss in the air, was so cool.

Even several hours later, it still hadn't quite sunk in. I was a *graduate*. Someone who was supposedly ready to go out into the world and start my career. It was exciting and scary all at once.

I had mixed emotions. Happiness and pride for what I'd achieved: a 2:1 with honours in English (of course, Mike had got a first-class degree, like I'd known he would). But I also felt a little bit sad. I'd no longer be spending my days with him. Studying, laughing, joking and hanging out. My stomach plummeted at the thought of it.

We'd already moved out of the house we shared with

Melody and Jim, and in a few months, I'd start my teacher training and he'd be—well, *who knows*? Mike didn't like thinking too far ahead, so he still hadn't decided whether to travel or go through with doing his master's.

But the good news was, we still had a whole summer to enjoy together. I'd been doing lots of extra shifts and saved up a fair bit. I'd also had a brainwave. What if Mike and I took a trip to Bali—together? He'd always wanted to go. I had too. I knew Dad wouldn't be happy with me flying so far, but what the hell. A trip there with Mike would be worth it.

With its lush landscape of hills and mountains, sandy beaches and idyllic clear waters, it looked like paradise. Mike had a whole mood board with pictures he'd cut out from travel brochures and magazines of all the places he wanted to visit and things he dreamed of doing. It was in the top ten of his bucket list, which I knew Mike was eager to tackle ASAP, and what better time to tick it off than our last summer of freedom before we were thrust into the world of proper adulthood?

I remembered thinking that the only thing that would make the day perfect was if I was brave enough to finally tell Mike how I really felt.

I'd been wanting to do it for weeks. Ever since he had broken up with Rebecca. But I'd decided to wait. I mean, they were always on, then off again, and then back on. Swooping in straight away would be heartless. Even though he said he was fine, it was only natural he'd need some time to get over her. I was definitely over Lance. It'd been three months since he'd dumped me out of the blue, saying that the whole long-distance thing just wasn't working, so I was single and ready for another relationship.

Mike and I had become even closer those past couple of weeks and I was convinced we'd had a few *moments* together. I felt it. Right in my gut. We were meant to be. We made each other laugh. We knew each other inside out. We got on like a house on fire and I fancied him like crazy.

Actually, 'fancying him' was an understatement. I *loved* him. Utterly and completely. He was the first thing I thought about when I woke up, then he was on my mind what felt like every second of the day, and I dreamt about him at night. I had it *bad*.

Was it one-sided? I'd wanted to think it wasn't. I was sure he had feelings for me too, but Mike was a gentleman. He was probably too worried about overstepping the boundaries by making a move. So I'd promised myself that if it felt like we were having a moment again, I'd act on it. Tell him how I felt.

Easier said than done, though. I'd known that declaring my feelings was a big risk. *Huge*. Mike was my best friend and his friendship meant everything to me, so the last thing I wanted to do was to mess things up. But at the same time, I recognised that I couldn't go on like I was. It'd become harder and harder to hide my emotions. I'd wanted to tell him how I felt so many times but just didn't know how. How did you tell your best friend you were in love with him?

Go for subtle with something like:

Mike. I fancy you. What do you say about being more than friends?

Or full-on declaration:

Mike, I'm madly in love with you. I have been since the first day we met. We belong together.

Hmm. I'd decided that the second option was a definite

no-no, but knowing the right words and getting the timing right seemed impossible.

I'd considered doing it before we graduated but thought it best not to, just in case it made things awkward that day. But now, I reasoned, uni was officially over. We were no longer living in the same house or going to the same lessons. It was the ideal time to try. If only I had the guts to—

'We should toast our success!' Mike said as he walked into my parents' living room.

One of Dad's friends had booked tickets to see a show in central London, followed by a night in a hotel, as an anniversary gift for his wife, but then she'd fallen ill, so he'd asked Dad if he wanted the tickets and accommodation so he could treat Mum instead. Dad was never one to pass up a freebie and quickly accepted. Mum said she felt bad about leaving me on the night of my graduation, but I told her that I was going out with friends anyway and would be fine.

After Mike and I had left Melody, Jim and the others at the bar, I'd just planned to come back on my own, but because it was late, Mike had offered to get the bus home with me. By the time we got here, he was bursting for the loo, so he'd come in and then just kind of ended up staying.

'I agree!' I smiled. 'You can never toast graduating enough!'

'Exactly. We have to live our lives to the full, Bells. Not everyone gets the chance to. We're very lucky…' His voice trailed off, then he spotted the drinks cabinet and perked up. 'Oooh! Is that where your parents keep the good stuff? I'm sure the booze in that bar was watered down, so it'd be great to get a decent drink.'

Mike and my dad didn't get on, so Mike had only been here a handful of times. Usually when my dad was out, or in the summer, when he and Mum went on holiday.

'That's their dinner party stash, so I'm sure it's good,' I said.

Mike opened up the cabinet and pulled out a bottle.

'Tequila! Yes! This is perfect,' Mike said, whilst I wondered whether Dad had marked or measured the contents of every bottle so he'd know if anyone drank it. I wouldn't put it past him. But Mike was right. It was our graduation night. We deserved to enjoy ourselves a little.

'Confession: I have never had tequila before.'

'What? You've *got* to be joking. We are going to fix that immediately.' Mike strode into the kitchen and opened the fridge.

'What are you looking for?'

'Found one!' He'd plucked out a lemon, took a knife from the block and cut it into wedges. After putting it on a saucer, he grabbed the salt that was on the counter, took my hand and led me back into the living room. 'Ready to pop your tequila cherry?'

'Put so elegantly…' I said.

'This is a *big* moment. You never forget your first taste of tequila. Mine was on my last holiday with my best friends from college when I was seventeen, just a few months before… the… anyway… lick your hand,' he commanded.

'What? That's gross.'

'You've led such a sheltered life, Bells. Come on.' He licked his own hand, and the sight of his tongue made my body tingle. At that moment, all I was thinking about was how good it would feel to have it roam all over me. But I told myself to focus. It wasn't the time. I was sure I'd know it when it was.

That was when I decided that maybe the tequila wasn't a bad idea after all. It would help me relax more and maybe even give me some Dutch courage…

I tried to make adding saliva to my hand look seductive like Mike had, but failed miserably. I was rubbish at flirting.

He took my damp hand, sending shockwaves through me, sprinkled salt over it, then poured tequila into two shot glasses and put them on the coffee table.

'So when you're ready, you need to lick the salt off your hand, drink the tequila quickly, then bite and suck the lemon straight away. Got it?'

'Okay,' I replied. 'But you go first.'

I watched as Mike made light work of downing the shot. If I was with anyone else, I probably wouldn't have admitted that I'd reached the age of twenty-one without trying tequila. Most of my peers had experimented with every type of alcohol available and a lot more, so they'd probably laugh. But I could be myself around Mike. He never judged me.

I was always nervous about being too adventurous with alcohol. Before I'd gone to uni, I'd never really drunk that much. Maybe a glass of wine for special occasions with my parents or a Bacardi Breezer if I was out with my friends, but never more than one bottle. I usually just opted for a Diet Coke.

There was no denying it. I was a lightweight. A few sips of anything remotely alcoholic and my mind went all wobbly. Plus I didn't really like feeling out of control. It just always seemed safer to stay sober so I could remember what I'd said or done the night before, rather than hiding my head in my hands as someone recounted cringeworthy stories of me dancing on tables or doing something embarrassing.

Tonight, though, I told myself that I'd try living a little. Yep, that about summed me up. Drinking a tequila shot was my idea of living life on the edge. *Jesus*. No wonder some of my friends called me Grandma…

I winced once as I licked the salt off my hands, then again when I downed the shot, and grimaced repeatedly as I sucked on the lemon.

'Why?!' I stuck my tongue out in disgust. 'Why would anyone do this to themselves *voluntarily*? It tastes awful!'

'I thought it tasted pretty good, actually. This is quality tequila. You should taste the one at the student union bar. That could strip paint off the walls.'

'Sounds like I had a lucky escape.'

'I think you'll like the second shot better.'

'Second?'

'Yeah. You didn't think you were just having one, did you?'

'Well, yeah…'

'Don't worry, Bells. Just because I'm having more shots doesn't mean you have to. If you don't fancy drinking, just have a Coke or water—it's up to you.'

That was Mike all over. Always wanting to make me feel comfortable.

'Screw it!' I said, deciding to loosen up. The tequila had already started to hit my bloodstream. 'We're celebrating. I *will* have another!'

How bad could it really be? I didn't have to worry about passing out drunk in a bar or how I was getting home. I was with Mike. Despite what my dad thought of him, I knew I was completely safe.

As the night went on and more shots were consumed, more of my inhibitions evaporated.

'So are you and Rebecca definitely over now?' The words flew out of my mouth before I could stop them. I didn't know what I was thinking. Correction. I knew *exactly* what I was thinking. I was checking whether the coast was clear. Whether I should test the waters and see if Mike was interested. I probably wouldn't have the guts to go through with anything, but I reasoned doing a little research wouldn't hurt…

'We are done. *Over*. I am single and ready to mingle!' he shouted emphatically. Which I thought probably meant he was lining up a new woman for every night of the week. That was what normally happened when he broke up with Rebecca. He'd mope for several days, then go on a booty-call binge-fest. Then again, this time round, he hadn't brought anyone home. 'What about you? Think you'll patch things up with Lance?'

'No way.' I shook my head.

'His loss. I'm surprised you haven't been snapped up already.'

'Ha!' I laughed. 'Most guys just think I'm boring and too sensible,' I blurted out. I was so annoyed at myself. I was supposed to be convincing Mike that I was a catch, not reminding him why all my relationships ended with me getting dumped.

'You're not boring!' Mike frowned. 'You're smart and funny and beautiful…' He shuffled up closer to me on the sofa and brushed a stray curl off my face. Feeling the heat from his fingers was like being struck by lightning.

Mike called me beautiful. And smart. And funny. My mind went crazy and my body fizzed with excitement.

I looked into his dark eyes and thought he was the most perfect man I'd ever laid eyes on.

'Thanks.' I blushed. 'But it's not true.'

'It *is*. Any guy would be lucky to be with you.'

'I don't just want *any guy*, though. There's only one man I'm interested in.'

I'd put my foot in my mouth again. At first I wasn't sure that I should have said that, but I then told myself it was okay. After all, it didn't have to mean anyone specific…

'Oh really…?' Mike edged closer. 'And do I know this guy?'

'You do…'

Mike held eye contact with me. His face was just inches away from mine. All it would take was for one of us to lean forward and our lips would be touching. I felt the sparks of electricity firing between us. *This is it*, I thought. *I should tell him.* This was the moment I'd been dreaming about for three years. The timing was perfect.

He'd just complimented me. We were both unattached. He'd confirmed that things were definitely over with Rebecca and there was no one else on the scene. We didn't have to worry about exams or dissertations or deadlines. We were free. To be together. After years of fantasising and dreaming about him, it was finally going to happen.

'Who is he?' Mike smirked, moving forward another inch.

That was the closest we'd ever been. I could smell his

favourite body spray, mixed with the sweet scent of the lemon he'd just sucked on.

Mmm. Those lips. All I'd have to do is move a few millimetres and they could be all over me.

It was now or never.

I lurched forward and planted my lips on his.

Our mouths collided and before I knew it he'd gently slid his tongue inside.

Oh. My. God.

It was finally happening.

I was kissing Mike Jones! The man I'd been in love with what felt like forever. And it was even more sublime than I could have imagined.

Mike tasted all citrusy and fresh. As we continued kissing passionately, I ran my fingers through his hair and then down his big muscular arms. This was bliss. I felt like I was floating. With every flick of his tongue, the feelings of ecstasy grew. I wanted him. I had never wanted a man so much before in my life.

The tequila had given me some kind of newfound sexual confidence, and before I knew it, I'd pushed Mike back down on the sofa, climbed on top, then reached for his belt buckle.

Normally I wouldn't sleep with a guy so quickly, but this was different. This wasn't just *anyone*. This was Mike. I couldn't wait for us to be together. Properly. To have all of him. To *feel* all of him.

Just as I went for his zip, he grabbed my hand. 'Wait…' He bolted up from the sofa. 'This is a mistake. I-I should go.'

I was rooted to the spot.

What was happening?

Less than sixty seconds ago we were kissing. Enjoying the most magical, blissful kiss I'd ever had, and now he was leaving?

'What? Why? I thought you…'

A mistake? Never had anything felt so right in my life. He wasn't making any sense. I'd felt it. Every fibre in my being told me that kiss was real. That we were meant to be together.

I climbed off him sheepishly, feeling like a fool. Wondering if I'd come on too strong and that was why he wanted to leave.

'I'm sorry. I've got to go,' he said, avoiding my gaze. He grabbed his jacket and walked out of the room, then I heard the front door slam.

Just like that, Mike was gone.

And little did I know that, apart from one other awkward exchange, we wouldn't see each other again for another ten years…

CHAPTER EIGHT

Present Day: July 2010

'A Chardonnay for the beautiful lady.' Mike passed the glass to me. I took it from him in a trance. The sensation of the cold liquid inside instantly helped to cool my clammy palms.

Thinking about what happened that night had brought a load of feelings flooding back and my body was reacting to all the emotions. My head spun at a hundred miles an hour as I tried to process everything.

For a few seconds I felt wounded as I remembered how hurt I'd been, but then I reminded myself that it was ten years ago. It wasn't important anymore. I pushed the flashbacks out of my mind.

'Thank you.' I realised he'd just called me beautiful, and before I could stop it, I caught myself blushing. So annoying that I still found him charming.

'You're welcome. So… we've got a lot to catch up on! I don't even know where to start.' He sipped his beer.

'Going to be pretty hard to summarise ten years in ten minutes,' I said.

'Why ten minutes?' Mike frowned. That was roughly how long I reckoned we had until we were surrounded again by the Mike Jones fan club. 'The night is still relatively young, so we've got time. Actually, let's make it more fun. Let me see if I can guess what you've done and then you can tell me if I'm right.'

My stomach sank. This was why I'd been nervous about coming to the reunion. Doing a *my life since uni* summary would only highlight how little I'd achieved.

'So I reckon you became a kick-ass teacher, travelled around the world and had some romantic adventures along the way. Am I right?'

Describing my love life as a series of *romantic adventures* was a bit of a stretch. More like *dating disasters*. Although I'd dreamed about going to far-flung destinations like Asia and Australia, I'd hardly travelled anywhere abroad. Just to short-haul destinations like France and Spain a few times. He *was* correct about me becoming a teacher, though. Kick-ass might be overstating things, but it was sweet of him to say that.

'Actually, I enrolled to do my training, then I decided that teaching wasn't for me, so I dropped out and got a job as an exotic dancer in a nightclub where I met my first husband. We then travelled around the world on his private jet for several years until we got divorced and I married my current husband, who's a seventy-year-old billionaire, so now I'm just a lady who lunches.' I smirked.

'*As if!*' he laughed. 'We may not have seen each other for a while, but I know you, Bells. And there's no way you'd give up your dream of being a teacher to become the wife of a sugar daddy. You're too good for that.'

'Well, you know what they say about good girls…,' I teased.

'I do, but you don't have a bad bone in your body. Come on, truthfully: what have you been up to? And whatever happened to staying in touch and being friends forever? I tried to message you so many times.'

This was what I'd been dreading. I knew Mike would bring this up. He was right. He might have rejected me that night, but the reason we hadn't spoken since was primarily down to me.

I'd wanted to keep in touch and wished I could have spoken to him every day, but I just couldn't bring myself to. I was embarrassed. I'd stupidly mistaken our friendship for something more. I didn't want to know why I wasn't girlfriend material. Or hear all about who he was dating. It was already too painful.

Cutting all contact was the only way I could make the pain go away. Every time I saw Mike's name flash up on my phone, it was a reminder of the rejection and also how much I missed him. And I didn't want to spend the rest of my life pining over Mike, so I had to try and forget about everything that had happened. I couldn't tell him that, though.

'You were right the first time,' I added quickly to avoid answering the question on why I hadn't kept in touch. 'I became a teacher. How about you?'

'Same. You and I were always going to go into education somehow. It was in our blood. I couldn't imagine doing anything else. Where are you teaching now?'

'A school in Clapham,' I said, being deliberately

evasive. Maybe I'd mention my PEFLITC plans for next year. That would sound much more exciting. 'But I'm thinking about—'

'There you are!' Ursula grabbed hold of Mike's bicep, causing him to almost spill his drink. I was wrong about the ten minutes. I think I'd had Mike's attention for less than five. 'I've been looking for you *everywhere*.' She gazed up into his eyes, fluttered her lashes and ran her fingers seductively down his arm. I wanted to be sick. 'Bella, Melody was looking for you. Think she said it was urgent.'

'Really?' I wasn't sure whether or not to believe her. It was true that I hadn't seen her all night, though, so I should really go and find her and say hi. After all, it was Melody who'd been so insistent that I come. 'Where did you see her?'

'By the toilets. If you hurry, she might still be there.'

'Right… well, I'd better go.' I smiled at Mike.

'See you later, and I hope everything's okay with Mel.'

'Thanks.'

It took me almost half an hour to track Melody down. Partly because I kept bumping into so many different people. Seeing everyone again was bittersweet. On the one hand, it was nice to catch up and hear about what they'd been doing. But on the other, as I'd suspected, hearing about their amazing jobs only highlighted how unhappy I was with my own.

Whilst of course it wasn't true for everyone, some people had gone on to do fantastic things. They'd travelled the world, tried different careers, and had adventures. But what had I done? Just stuck to the same old thing. Ten years on, I was still boring, safe, predictable Bella.

I could have done more with my life, but the truth was, I was afraid.

Take tonight: I almost hadn't come because I was worried about seeing everyone again. But although talking about what I'd done over the past decade was uncomfortable at times, it hadn't been as torturous as I'd feared.

How was I supposed to get promoted to second in department and handle all the extra responsibility if I shied away from anything that seemed too frightening? How could I inspire pupils like Mandy to achieve their goals when I wasn't actively pursuing mine?

When that woman from the language school had called me last week about the PEFLITC course, instead of finding a load of reasons to say no, I should've had the courage to say yes. Maybe Dad was right. I *was* too sensitive. I had to get stronger. Something had to change.

'Bella-boo!' Melody had so many nicknames for me it was impossible to predict which one she'd use. There was also La, B, Aunty B. I couldn't keep track.

'Hey!' I said as she practically jumped me, throwing her arms around my neck. My hair got caught in one of the many colourful bangles on her wrists. Melody was wearing a low-cut sparkly gold dress, with bright red Dorothy shoes. She also had a matching big red flower in her brown hair, which she'd styled into a beehive.

'The party finishes in half an hour. Where have you been, darling?' she slurred before knocking back the rest of her drink. Smelt like vodka and Coke. 'Please tell me you've been in the toilets shagging big Mike!' she giggled.

'Sssh!' My eyes bulged. Even though the music was pretty loud and most people were chatting, dancing or drunk, I didn't want anyone overhearing. As far as I knew, she was the only one at uni who officially knew about my stupid crush (I reckoned Ursula was just bluffing). I didn't want anyone thinking I was some saddo who still carried a torch for him.

'It's okayyyy! It's our secret!! Do you wanna know another one?'

'Okay.' I linked my arm in hers to help steady her on her feet.

'I just snogged Danny!'

'Computer Science Danny?'

'Uh-huh! Danny the nerd. Except he's not a nerd anymore. He's fit! And it's been pretty hard to find any eye candy here tonight. So many of the guys have let themselves go. Already! We're barely thirty-one and some of them are receding with beer guts. Not just the blokes either. I mean, I'm no oil painting, but crikey, some of them look a right state! Good news for me, though: more chance of getting lucky, if you catch my drift.' Melody winked and threw her head back, laughing.

'I do…'

'I told Danny to take me home with him, but he said I was too drunk. *Bloody cheek*. I'm as sober as a judge.'

'Course you are, Mel.' I rubbed her back gently. I didn't want to burst her bubble by telling her she was about as sober as a bride-to-be on her hen night. 'Where are you staying?'

'Crashing at Fatima's.'

'Good. I know you're having fun, but you still need to be careful, okay?'

'Don't worry, Aunty B. I'll be a good girl. Not too good, though. Do you know how long it's been since I had a decent snog? Or any snog come to think of it. Since before the dinosaurs walked the earth! It felt amazing. I got the fanny flutters and everything. I've only got another twelve hours before I have to go back to being a mum. Cooking and cleaning… blah, blah, blah. I wanna enjoy my freedom whilst it lasts.'

'I get that. Just be safe, that's all.'

'Okay, *Grandma*.' Melody rolled her eyes. I knew I was being a bit serious, but Melody had got herself into trouble on more than one occasion when she'd drunk too much. There was the time she'd fallen down some steps and broken her ankle—oh, and when she'd ended up punching a guy who'd pinched her bum. Although he was out of order and deserved to be put in his place for his sleazy behaviour, it was her that got in trouble. I was just trying to help her avoid spending another night in a police station, or worse, at the hospital. 'I'll promise to be a good girl if you promise to be bad for a change. Deal?'

'I don't know about that…'

'Come on, B! Take that stick out your arse and let your hair down. You shouldn't be here chatting with me, you should be over there with Mike.'

'I was, but then Ursula said you needed me. That it was urgent.'

'Lying cow! All I said was how nice it was to see you and Mike together again. Nothing about needing you urgently. She's playing you. She did that so she could get him all to herself.'

Classic Ursula.

I scanned the room and spotted Mike on the dance floor, swinging his hips to a '90s dance song that sounded vaguely familiar. Ursula was shaking her bum like she was auditioning for one of those music videos where the women dance around the pool in skimpy bikinis. A few other women had gathered too. God. It was as if he was some sort of teenage heartthrob surrounded by a bunch of groupies.

'Uh-oh…' Melody's face dropped.

I looked over again and saw Rebecca striding towards him. She still had long hair, which she swooshed over her shoulders. Rebecca was in her signature miniskirt, which she always wore all year round. Even when it was winter. Surprised she didn't catch hypothermia.

Rebecca had her arm draped over Mike's shoulder. I felt like I'd been punched in the stomach. Ursula didn't look too pleased either. Especially since she'd only just managed to corner Mike again.

He'd stopped talking to her about half an hour ago, gone to get a drink or go to the toilets, then had started chatting to Tunde (not that I was watching Mike or anything), and Ursula had tracked him down for what must have been at least the third time tonight. She wasn't giving up easily.

'Oooh, this should be interesting.' Melody rubbed her hands together. 'Rebecca and Ursula fighting over Mike.'

He'd choose Rebecca. He always did. No matter how many times they broke up, or what women he went with whilst they were apart, he always went back to her. I'd had first-hand experience of that…

'Well, he certainly looks happy to see Rebecca,' I said. 'It's almost the end of the party, so I'm surprised it took her so long to track him down.'

'Oh no: this isn't the first time they've seen each other. They were chatting for ages earlier. Heather told me that they hadn't spoken for years…' Melody came closer.

'Don't tell anyone, but word is that Rebecca got divorced a few months ago and is on the prowl for her next victim. She reckons Mike's the one that got away, so is trying to rekindle stuff with him.'

'Doesn't surprise me.' I shrugged my shoulders.

'You should get your butt over there! Both those ladies know that there's now only fifteen minutes until the party finishes'—she squinted at the clock on the wall—'so they're giving their get-Mike-into-bed campaigns one final push. You need to throw your hat—or should I say *knickers*—into the ring and claim what's yours.'

Hardly.

'You must be joking.' I rolled my eyes. 'There's no way I'm going over there.'

'Come on! You're here now. What have you got to lose?'

'My self-respect for starters…'

Before I knew it, Melody had dragged me across the room and we were just inches away from Mike, who had Ursula on one side and Rebecca on the other. So awkward.

'Hey, Mel, hi, Bells!' Mike smiled. 'Good to see you on the dance floor!' His hips were now gyrating to an R&B track. I tried and failed not to imagine what it would be like to be beneath them. He'd always been such a good dancer. If he could move his body like that here, God knows how amazing he'd be in bed.

Oh God. It really was time for me to go home.

'Bella…' Rebecca looked me up and down. I pulled my mind out of the gutter and forced a smile.

'Hello, Rebecca.'

'I see you've got rid of those glasses at long last,' she sniped.

'I see you've become *very* observant,' I snapped back. She was just as salty as she'd always been. We'd never got on. I'd really never understood what Mike had seen in her. She had a horrible personality. Then again, I'm sure he wasn't dating her for that.

'*Always*.' She gave me a fake grin. 'So anyway, Mike, you'll definitely come round on Monday night?'

'Sure,' he replied. The song ended and Mike stopped dancing.

'And you're coming for drinks now, Mike?' said Ursula quickly.

Wow. He'd made arrangements with both of them already.

What was I even doing here? Standing in front of him like a desperado, fighting for his attention?

This was pathetic. I wasn't some lovesick twenty-one-year-old anymore. I wasn't going to get sucked in by Mike's charms again.

I was worth more than that.

I turned around to tell Melody I was leaving, but she had already gone. I scanned the room and saw her stumble onto the floor. She really wasn't in a good state. She could call me Grandma all she wanted, but I couldn't leave her like that. I had to find Fatima and make sure she got to her place safely.

'I better go and help Mel…'

'But you'll be back, yeah?' Mike said.

'Hmm-mmm.' I walked off.

I absolutely would not.

After I'd sorted things with Melody, I was leaving.

I'd done what Melody and Sophia had encouraged me to do. I'd come to the reunion, seen some old friends and held a civil conversation with Mike, so mission accomplished.

Surprisingly, coming here had given me some clarity about my life too.

As much as I hated change, seeing Mike and everyone tonight combined with being passed over for the promotion showed me that it was time to do something different. Starting with my job.

I wanted to do a career that I loved. So instead of spending another second watching Ursula and Rebecca cooing over Mike, I would go home, get a good night's sleep, wake up early and start working out how to do something more constructive. It was time to be brave and start facing my fears.

The romantic side of things would need to take a back seat for now, but if I'd had any doubts before, tonight had definitely confirmed that I was over Mike. One hundred percent.

I was glad that we'd exchanged pleasantries and cleared the air, but that was it. Like I'd said to Melody and Sophia a thousand times, Mike wasn't the one for me. Never was, never would be. *End of.*

CHAPTER NINE

W*ow*. 11.27 a.m.

I hadn't slept that late in ages. I'd got home from the reunion just before two in the morning, but hadn't fallen asleep until about three.

I couldn't stop tossing and turning. I was fighting a battle with my thoughts. On the one hand I had the image of Mike and how hot he looked swirling around my brain, doing all sorts of crazy things to my body. When I closed my eyes, I could still smell his woody, intoxicating scent. Feel his warm, sweet breath tickling my skin and the desire pulsing through me. Wishing he was there on the bed, ravishing me…

But then I remembered the farce of the reunion. All the women cooing over him. *Ugh*. What I'd felt last night was just physical attraction. Nothing more.

Hot or not, even if things had changed and he'd magically decided he liked me, there was no way I could be with a guy who had women throwing themselves at him all day and night. He was only human, and sooner or later he would succumb to temptation. Adventurous, popular guys like him weren't designed to be with women like me. That was just the way the world worked.

Anyway, enough about him. I needed to check on Melody. I'd put her and Fatima in a cab before I left. Thankfully Fatima was relatively sober and replied to the text I'd sent to check whether they'd got home safely.

I was glad Melody had a good time—it wasn't often she got to get out and enjoy herself. I bet she was feeling like she'd been hit by a high-speed train this morning, though.

Me

How's the head? Hope you're okay? Remember to drink lots of water to rehydrate and have a decent breakfast. Perfect excuse for a good fry-up! xxx

I had a feeling that it was going to take a lot more than a full English breakfast to help Melody feel better today, though. Hangovers at thirty-one needed a longer recovery time than they did at twenty. Plus she had to get back up to Coventry. That would probably feel like the longest journey ever.

I made myself some toast and cereal, then flopped down on the sofa. I took a sip of tea from my favourite purple mug and thought about the day ahead.

On Saturday mornings I did the weekly food shop. Shouldn't take long. To keep things simple, I had a food menu for the week, so for example, Saturday lunchtime was normally a chicken burger and home-made potato wedges. Monday lunch was chicken salad, Tuesday dinner was roast salmon, and I always had cod on Thursdays and a supermarket pizza on Fridays (unless it was a special occasion, in which case I'd order one from Domino's). Planning in advance just made things easier. I always knew what to buy and never had to worry about what to eat. It was good to have a routine.

This afternoon, all I wanted to do was chill and start thinking about how I could make some improvements with my life. Then tomorrow I'd go to lunch at my parents', which, with the exception of last week, when I was too annoyed to face my dad, I did every Sunday.

My phone pinged. Melody must have surfaced.

I picked up my phone. But it wasn't a text from her. It was a number I didn't recognise. I read the message.

Hey, Bells!

Great to see you last night! Sorry we didn't get more time to talk. You left without saying bye… Melody gave me your number. Fancy meeting up?

Mike x

My stomach flipped. I wasn't expecting *him* to text me.

Oh God.

I really wished Melody hadn't given him my number. I'd said last night that chapter was closed, and now look.

I read his message again, zeroing in on his question:

Fancy meeting up?

No way.

One of the reasons I'd gone last night was to avoid

Melody bringing him round to see me and ending up alone with him. Imagine being sat in front of him at a bar. Just the two of us. Gazing into those dark brown eyes…

I wasn't going to risk getting sucked into the Mike Jones cyclone. I knew how charming he could be, and I didn't want to end up getting my friendship wires crossed again.

My phone started ringing. It was Sophia. Perfect timing.

'Hi,' I answered quickly. I needed the distraction from my thoughts. 'What you up to? Please don't tell me you're at the office, working?'

'Working, yes,' she said, 'but not at the office. I'm on the sofa with my laptop.'

'You work too much,' I sighed. 'Your body needs to rest sometimes.'

'I know, I know. I'm almost finished. Just need to go over these slides again, rehearse the presentation and then I should be good for tomorrow. Anyway, enough about that. How'd it go last night? With Mike?'

So much for distracting me. It was understandable that she wanted an update, though. I'd be the same. I filled her in on everything.

'Seriously, Soph, it was so cringey. The way all the women were swarming and fawning over him. He agreed to have a drink with Ursula last night, then see Rebecca on Monday night. And now he's just texted me to ask if I wanted to meet up. Probably because he didn't have anyone scheduled for the weekend.'

'He texted?'

'Yeah. Literally right before you called.'

'Amazing! The fact that he wants to see you is a good sign. I reckon he likes you. If you ask me, he always did.'

'He doesn't. He must have called me his *friend*, *mate* and *ex-bestie* about a hundred times. It was embarrassing. Like, *okay. I got the message ten years ago. You don't see me like that. You're not interested. No need to rub it in.*'

'Have you ever thought he was doing that to remind himself *not* to cross the line?'

'Why? We crossed the line ten years ago with that silly drunken kiss and it didn't work out.'

I didn't elaborate about the fact that he couldn't get away from me quick enough. Despite what Sophia said, I knew that yesterday, Mike was just emphasising the whole friends thing to stop me from embarrassing myself again. The way I'd thrown myself at him that night.

'I'm sure that the fact that he kissed you back, even if it was briefly, meant that the feelings were mutual.'

Yeah, right. That's why he left and ended up in bed with her…

I winced as more memories came flooding back. Soph didn't know the full story, so I didn't blame her for thinking that way.

After Mike had left that night, I'd felt awful. Embarrassed, hurt, confused. That kiss had felt like it meant something. But if it had, why had he run? Why had he left so abruptly?

Before that night had happened, we'd planned to spend the day in Brighton. So I'd told myself that even though it might be a bit awkward at first, after we'd talked it out, blamed it on the alcohol, somehow we'd find a way to get things back to normal. At that point, I'd wanted us to stay best friends.

We were due to set off at nine that morning. But Mike didn't arrive until after nine-thirty, which was unlike him. He was always on time. That was when I really started to think that the very thing I'd been trying to avoid—ruining our friendship—was really happening. If only I hadn't kissed him.

When he arrived wearing the same clothes as he was in last night, I knew something was wrong. I went to hug him and it was limp. Weak. Mike was the king of hugs. Big heartfelt hugs with feelings. But this one was stilted. Cautious. That kiss really *had* messed things up. Ever the optimist, I ignored the signs.

'Ready to go? I've packed some cheese balls for us to eat on the train,' I'd said, trying to keep things light.

'The thing is, Bella, I'm really sorry, but I'm not coming…' He'd hung his head. And he'd called me Bella. Not Bells like he always did.

'Look, if it's about last night…'

'No… it's just that, when I got home, Rebecca was in her car waiting for me. She was really upset and said she needed to talk, so because I didn't want to wake Dad and Lyra up, we kind of went to her place…'

I remembered wanting to collapse on the floor and curl up into a ball when I heard he'd spent the night with Rebecca. I bet they'd done a lot more than just *talking*.

That was blow number one. Hours after rejecting me, Mike had jumped into bed with her.

Mike told me Rebecca said she missed him and wanted to try again. Give their relationship a proper go. And to prove it, she'd bought him a ticket to Bali. His dream destination. The one on his bucket list and the very place that I wanted to go with him. *We'd* always talked about going there. Together.

That was blow number two.

'I was so shocked,' he'd said. 'Rebecca has never done anything like this for me before. I didn't even realise she'd been listening when I said I'd always wanted to go. The thing is, the tickets are already booked and paid for, so I couldn't say no...'

'When do you leave?' I'd asked.

'This afternoon...'

I can still remember how hard those two words hit me. It was like a wrecking ball ploughed into my stomach. He was going. *Today*. And they'd be there for a month. *A whole month*. That must have cost a fortune. Her parents were loaded, so she'd probably asked them to pay. At most I could have only afforded to go for ten days. I wasn't surprised that he'd said yes. It was a once-in-a-lifetime opportunity.

'Oh wow...' was the best that I managed.

'I'm just going home now to get my passport and pack. You don't mind, do you? I feel bad about bailing on you today.'

Mind? I was gutted. Heartbroken. Crushed. But what could I say? *Please don't go because I'm in love with you?* He'd already made it clear that he didn't feel the same way. Maybe some distance between us would be good, I reasoned. Now that we'd finished uni, this was how it was always going to be anyway. The sooner I got used to it, the better.

'No, course not... you'll have a great time.'

'Thanks for being so understanding. And, um, and

about last night…' He'd paused for what felt like hours. 'I'm sorry, I…'

'Forget about it.' I was already embarrassed. Before I knew he was getting back with Rebecca, I'd wanted to talk about it. But now that had changed. Hearing the reasons why he'd rejected me would only add to the hurt and make everything worse. The last thing I needed was him launching into some speech about him being drunk, not seeing me like that, me being like a sister to him and telling me how he and Rebecca were made for each other.

I'd started to wonder if he'd told her about what had happened. I imagined her doubling over in fits of laughter. Of course someone like Mike wouldn't be interested in someone plain like me.

Those thoughts took me even further back to the last year of secondary school. It was already challenging there. We'd moved because Dad got a promotion and I still hadn't gotten used to the horrible big change that happened when I was thirteen, where I had to leave a school that I'd loved and where I'd had lots of friends and move to a new school where they called me Daddy Long Legs. Anyway, there was a big summer dance, and it seemed like every girl had a date except me.

At the time, my dad was also the head of year, which I was sure didn't help. Desperate not to go to the dance alone, I'd asked a boy called Timmy and he'd turned me down. When word got out, everyone at the school laughed at me. Worse still, Dad heard about it and told me I was too young to be thinking about boys. It was so humiliating. Rejection was the worst. And being rejected by your best friend stung even more. I just wanted to forget it had ever happened.

'Like you said, it was a mistake, so…'

'I didn't mean… I…,' Mike had said. 'Maybe we should talk about it…' Then his phone started ringing. 'I've got to take this—it's Rebecca…'

Hearing her speaking to him on the phone made the reality of everything that had happened hit even harder. We'd kissed and Mike had said it was a mistake. Clearly I wasn't exciting enough. I didn't measure up to the other women Mike had been with, so he'd run. Run straight back into the arms of his ex. Not only were they back together, he was also going away with her for a month to the place I was hoping we would go together this summer.

It was at that moment that I truly understood heart-break. All the lyrics in those sad love songs took on a whole new meaning.

I loved Mike, but now he'd just confirmed it once and for all: he didn't love me. It felt like my heart had been ripped out of my chest and shredded into a million pieces.

I could feel my eyes beginning to water, and I knew it wouldn't be long until I turned into a blubbering mess.

'Well, you'd better go.' I passed him and opened the front door. 'You don't want to be late. I'm bursting for the loo, so… have a great trip.'

'Oh… right. Okay.' Mike hung his head and slowly stepped outside. 'Erm—thanks. Sorry again. I'll… I'll send you a postcard and we'll catch up once I'm back, okay?'

'Yeah. Okay. Bye.' We'd looked at each other awkwardly. I could tell he was trying to decide how best to say goodbye. Normally we'd hug, but somehow it just felt weird. So we didn't. He walked down the path and turned back to wave again, and that was the last time we'd seen each other.

True to his word, he'd sent postcards and even emailed some photos. But seeing him bare-chested in his tight trunks only made things worse. All I could think about was him lying on the beach with Rebecca all day and the two of them curled up together at night. It was too much to bear.

After his trip with her, Mike caught the travel bug and went straight off to Australia with his cousin. When he came back, I was visiting Sophia in France, where she'd returned for the summer after spending the year teaching English as part of her French degree. Then Mike decided to take a gap year to continue travelling, and I saw the light and decided I had to cut all contact.

I'd started teacher training by then, so whenever Mike did get in touch, I told him it was super intense and I was busy. Eventually he'd stopped asking and we'd lost contact altogether…

I pushed the painful memories out of my head and brought myself back to the present and my conversation with Sophia.

'Just because things didn't work out before doesn't mean the same will happen this time. Why don't you give it a try?' Sophia said. 'Reply to his message. Meet up with him.'

'I went to the reunion like you and Melody encouraged me to, so that's that. Right now I need a clear head. I need to forget about men, dating, speaking to ex–best friends, and silly old crushes and just focus on working out how to sort out my career. You of all people must understand that.'

'True. Not the men stuff, obviously, but I know how

important a new career direction is for you. Speaking of which, that was the other reason I was calling…' Sophia paused. 'Remember I said I had some exciting news to tell you?'

'Yeah…'

'Well, I hope you won't be mad at me, but I sort of booked you onto the PEFLITC course that starts on Monday…'

'What?' I swallowed hard, then flopped back onto the sofa. 'When did you do that? How?'

'I called them last week. The last space was still available and I just… I couldn't stand to see you spend another year unhappy in your job. I really think this will be good for you.'

I froze. I tried to process what Sophia said. When that Zainab lady had originally called me, there was over a week until the course started and I'd thought *that* was short notice. But if it was starting on Monday, *this* Monday, that meant that there was now less than forty-eight hours.

'Bella? Are you there?'

'Um, yeah. I'm just shocked.' I paused. 'That was so thoughtful of you, Soph, it really was, but there's no way I'll be ready by then.'

'I know you, Bella. You're freaking out. Making changes, even small ones, scares the shit out of you. I mean, how many times has your car broken down in the past few years? And yet you still refuse to buy a new one.'

'I will at some point. It's just complicated. I'd have to think about what one to get, research the different models, get a load of insurance quotes…' Bertie, my old VW Golf, had served me well over the years. Yes, it had a few blips from time to time, but I'd had it since after I'd graduated, so it was to be expected. And it was working fine now.

'And what about your dressing gown? I bet you still have that battered pink one that looks like it's been through a war zone.'

'It's comfortable!'

'This is exactly what I'm saying. You don't like changing *anything*. You like to stay in your comfort zone. You *think* about doing things. You make extensive plans about taking action, but how often do you actually follow through? I say this with love, but you just keep making excuses and pushing things back. Sometimes we all need a gentle push, don't you think?'

She was right. I knew she was. I'd thought the same thing last night.

'Maybe…'

'Don't worry about the prep. I've ordered the books they recommend, which I'll courier over to your flat this afternoon, and I've got a list of the other things they suggest you do before it starts. You're already a grammar whizz, you've got loads of experience teaching English— you're going to nail it.'

'And what about the payment and stuff?'

'All taken care of. Just pay me back when you can. Zainab is at the school until two today, so she said you can call if you have any questions and there's just a couple of forms you need to send back.'

Sophia really had thought of everything. I stood up and started pacing through the living room. My heart was thudding. It was a mixture of fear and excitement. Could I really do this?

I'd said last night that I wanted to make changes with my life, face my fears and do something that I enjoyed. I'd also said I'd wished I'd been brave enough to accept the place on the course when Zainab had first called me. And now, thanks to Sophia, I had another chance. All I had to do was say yes.

I was pretty sure that the course was non-refundable too, so there was no way I could let Sophia's money go to waste like that. And I couldn't let her down after she'd gone to so much trouble. She believed in me, and it was high time I believed in myself too.

I *was* a good teacher. I knew the course would be intense, but surely with my experience, that would give me an advantage.

Now that I thought about it, the timing *was* good. I had zero plans for the summer holidays, other than probably going to visit my parents in Cornwall at some point. But I did that every year.

Just think: if I did this course and if I passed, that would give me a huge sense of achievement. It would also show Dad that I was capable of more.

Having that qualification could also open doors. It might help me secure the next promotion at my current school. I'd be killing two birds with one stone: doing something that I'd always wanted to do and proving myself by showing Dad I *was* strong and *could* handle pressure.

And if I *did* decide to leave at some point, it didn't have to be to do something as scary as teaching abroad. That was still something I'd consider doing in a year or two when I had more time to plan. There were bound to be plenty of people wanting to learn English as a second language right here in London, so I didn't even have to travel to make use of it.

Time to stop being afraid. Time to bite the bullet.

'Yes,' I said quickly before I changed my mind. 'I'll do it.'

'You will?'

'Yes.' My heart was now pounding so much I was sure it might fly from my chest. 'But I need you to send me your bank details straight away so that I can pay you the money back.'

'You don't have to do it now. Honestly, there's no rush.'

'I want to. Please. You've been generous enough by arranging all of this.'

'Okay, hon. I'm really proud of you. I know this is a huge step, but I wouldn't have booked it if I didn't believe in you.'

'I know. And thank you. Focusing on this course could be good for me. I'm scared, but I think if I work hard, I might be okay. Which means I need to do it without any distractions…' And if I wasn't careful, drawing myself back to the past by seeing Mike alone had the potential to become one.

Right there and then, I decided that my life would be a man-free zone. At least until the end of summer.

That meant no meeting up with Mike and no dating.

I didn't want to be rude, so I would text Mike back, but not yet. Not today.

I'd spent too long stuck in a rut. Now wasn't the time to revisit the past. It was time to start focusing on my new future.

CHAPTER TEN

Faking it was hard.

Let me rephrase. Faking things for longer than a few minutes was difficult. I'd faked many things: smiles when I had to speak to someone I didn't like, even orgasms. But right now, sitting here playing happy families with my parents—mainly with my dad—was proving difficult.

'Wine?'

'Yes, thanks.'

Dad put the glass in front of me on the cherry wood dining table. Like most of the furniture in the house, it was antique. The decor had stayed the same since I was a child. Burgundy wallpaper in the hallway, dining and living rooms, with matching carpets and what felt like a thousand childhood photos of me lining the walls, which were always a source of embarrassment whenever my friends came over.

Seeing the glass on the table reminded me how long it had taken for Dad to accept I was an adult and wanted to be offered alcohol instead of just water or a soft drink. Think I was around twenty. I remembered he'd also insisted I use a 'Daddy's little girl' tumbler until I was thirteen.

'They'd sold out of the one you always drink from Sainsbury's, so I drove to M&S and got this one instead. It's won awards, apparently, so should be good.'

'Thank you.' That was kind. The nearest M&S was a few miles away, so I appreciated him going out of his way.

As sweet as it was, I was still frustrated about the promotion. I'd been right about Julie getting the job. Wasn't looking forward to being reminded of that next term. But at least now there was hope. I had the course to look forward to.

After I'd transferred the money into Sophia's account, I'd spoken to Zainab and sent off my forms, and I was all set. Once I'd got back from shopping, there was a box outside my door with a selection of books Sophia had ordered, bless her. So I'd spent the whole day going through those and looking over the course syllabus.

Truth be told, I just wanted to stay at home today and study some more to prepare myself as much as possible for tomorrow. But I knew how much Mum looked forward to our Sunday lunches, so here I was, pretending everything was fine.

'Looking forward to your holiday next week, Mum?' I asked.

'Yes, sweetie!' she said brightly. Even though she'd moved to London when she was twelve, you could still detect her St Lucian accent. Mum's smile was infectious. The laughter lines at the side of her dark eyes were the only creases in her skin. She was in her late fifties, with short, curly salt-and-pepper hair, but could easily pass for a decade younger. 'It'll be nice to spend some time by the sea.'

My parents were off on holiday to Cornwall. They'd gone every year as far back as I could remember, apart from one year where Mum had insisted that she take me to St Lucia to meet her family. I think I was only about seven or eight at the time, so I didn't remember a lot about the trip.

Mum had returned regularly to the Caribbean until she'd met Dad in her early twenties. He wasn't keen on flying and had always insisted that we holiday in England. His grandparents lived by the coast and he'd grown up spending his summers with them. So when I was born, I supposed he wanted to continue the tradition.

'I hope you'll be joining us?' Dad said, cutting his roast beef. We always had a roast on Sunday with potatoes and veg. It was Dad's favourite. 'You used to love our holidays there.'

I'd enjoyed them much more when I was a kid. Cornwall was a beautiful place, and when my younger cousin Cassie came with us, it was a lot more fun. But that was decades ago. It would've been nice to have more of a balance, alternating between Cornwall and St Lucia so I could've got to know Mum's side of the family better too. But that was how it was.

These days, I joined my parents on holiday more out of habit than desire. Every summer they invited me, and if I was free, I tried to go and stay, even if it was just for a few days. Things would be different this year, though.

'Yes!' Mum perked up. 'Come with us, Bella!'

'I'm sure it will be lovely, but I can't, I'm afraid.'

'I can drive back to London to pick you up whenever you're ready to go and we can travel together if you like?' said Dad. 'To make sure you get there safely.'

He offered to do that every year, but I knew it took at least five hours in the car each way, so it didn't seem fair for him to trek down to collect me when I could just make my own way there.

'Thanks, Dad, but I can't this year. I've got plans…'

Sounded so weird to say that. This time I genuinely couldn't. I really did have plans.

'Plans?' Dad's face crumpled. 'What plans?'

'I'm starting… going on… away…,' I stuttered.

I'd decided not to tell Dad about the course. When I'd first mentioned that I was thinking about doing it last year in the evenings and at weekends, he said I'd be taking on too much and it would distract me from my real job. The course did seem pretty intense, and it was true that it would be hard to juggle everything during term time. That was why doing it during the holidays was the perfect solution.

Even though his objection had been addressed, I still got the feeling that if I mentioned it, Dad would find another reason why it wasn't a good idea, and I wanted to start the course tomorrow with a clear head, without any negativity or doubts swimming around my mind.

Yep. It was better to wait until I'd finished it. Then I could show him what I'd achieved.

'You didn't mention any holiday plans for the summer.' He folded his arms. 'Who are you going away with?'

'Sophia,' I said without thinking.

'Sophia?' Mum frowned. 'She's actually taking a holiday? I thought she was a workaholic.'

It was confirmed. I was rubbish at lying.

'Yes… she is… it's kind of a spur-of-the-moment thing. I'm not even sure if it'll happen. But it *might*, so I'm on standby. I need to keep myself free. Just in case.'

'Hmmm…,' Dad muttered, clearly unconvinced. 'Nowhere far, I hope?'

'It'll definitely be in Europe. Most likely in the UK…' That was true, at least. Dad always worried about anyone close to him travelling far. Especially if it involved getting on a plane. He had a fear because of some sort of traumatic event that had happened when he was younger, apparently, that he never liked to discuss. I'd tried a few times, but Dad always left the room when I mentioned it, and Mum always said it was best not to raise it. Even to this day, I still didn't know exactly why. All I knew was that as far as he was concerned, air travel should be avoided at all costs.

'Well, if it doesn't go ahead, you can always come and join us. We'll be there for at least two weeks.'

'Thanks,' I said, being careful not to commit to anything.

'Speaking of friends'—Mum sipped her wine—'how did that reunion go on Friday night? I was so excited when I saw your text about it yesterday. I didn't even know it was happening. Must have been fun to see your old friends. Was that bubbly girl you used to live with there? What was her name again? Mirabelle? Melanie?'

'Melody.'

'That's the one! How is she? Is she the one who just had a baby?'

'Yes, well, her daughter Andrea isn't a baby anymore. She's three now. Melody's okay. Doing the best she can, but it's not easy being up there on her own with no family or support network.' Truth was, she was struggling.

'Poor thing.' Mum sighed. 'Such a shame she isn't in London. And what about Michael? Was he there? Such a lovely boy.'

'Ugh!' scoffed Dad. 'On the contrary, I thought that Mike boy was *awful*. Rude and disrespectful. I'm glad you stopped fraternising with him.'

The first time Dad met Mike, when he'd come to our student halls unannounced, we were in my room drinking a bottle of cheap wine and I was tipsy. Even though I was eighteen, as far as Dad was concerned, I didn't drink alcohol and Mike was about to take advantage of me.

The second time, a year later, Dad had dropped by and I wasn't there, but apparently Mike hadn't shut the front door when he'd brought a woman back to the house we were sharing. So Dad walked in and saw Mike with his hand up the girl's skirt when they were getting hot and heavy on the sofa.

The next time, I think, was when I was planning on going away with Mike, Melody and a few others on a cheap trip to Tenerife and Dad said he didn't want me to go because planes were 'too dangerous'.

Dad had always been overprotective. He never wanted me to wear headphones, because he said they'd damage my ears. I wasn't allowed to iron my own clothes in case I burnt myself. I had to really fight to go away to a uni just outside London because he wanted me to stay nearby.

Anyway, after listening to Dad lecturing me about how dangerous it would be for me to go on holiday with my friends, Mike had lost it.

'Jesus!' he'd shouted. 'Stop being such a controlling

prick! You treat Bella like she's a child. I don't know if you've realised, but she's twenty: a grown woman. That means she's old enough to drink, have sex, get married and do whatever she wants. If she wants to go on holiday, she can. Leave her alone!'

I was actually glad that he'd stood up for me. I'd never been brave enough to do it myself. It showed he cared.

His outburst had *not* gone down well with Dad. He wasn't used to people standing up to him. After calling Mike a 'foul-mouthed cretin', Dad had stormed out, then called later that evening, demanding I stop living with him.

He'd said this wouldn't have happened if I'd gone to a university in London and continued living at home, which was what he wanted. They'd rejected me anyway, so I'd gone to a uni in Hertfordshire that I liked. I told him I'd already paid rent until the end of the year, so had to stay.

I think that was the last time Dad ever dropped by uninvited. But he'd never forgotten their argument.

'He was always very polite whenever I saw him,' insisted Mum. 'I even thought you and him might get together…'

'Over my dead body!' Dad shouted. 'I know his type. Only interested in one thing. There is no way I would have ever allowed a boy like that to be with my daughter.'

'*Allowed?*' I narrowed my eyes.

'You know what I mean,' Dad said.

Some things never changed. Even now he treated me like I was thirteen, not a woman in my thirties. It was so infuriating.

'Anyway…' I dug my nails into my palms and tried to ignore the burning sensation in my cheeks. It felt like they were on fire. 'The reunion was fine. Like you said, it was nice to see everyone.'

I'd almost managed to stop thinking about Mike until Mum had mentioned him again. *Almost.* It was possible it had been a whole twenty minutes since he'd last popped into my head. Okay, maybe ten.

Dad didn't have to worry about me and Mike ever becoming an item. I'd only spoken to him for a few minutes, and he was already taking up far too much brain space.

The reunion might have brought him back towards the front of my mind, but it was still under control. In a day or two, I would've pushed Mike out of my head again completely and returned to normal.

Yes. I still hadn't decided what to do about his text, but I knew that as long as I didn't agree to meet him, I would be absolutely fine.

CHAPTER ELEVEN

Today was the day.

I woke up with butterflies. I hadn't been this excited about doing something work-related since... I couldn't even remember when.

After leaping out of bed, showering and getting dressed, I made some toast, then flew out the door.

I arrived at Charing Cross station and strolled towards Covent Garden, which was where the JCH London Language School was based. I was half an hour early, so I decided to kill time by grabbing a coffee. I checked my phone. Sophia had replied to the text I'd sent her on the train wishing her luck with her big pitch and also wished me well for today. Which reminded me: I must send her a thank-you card and some flowers later to show how grateful I was for her signing me up.

Cassie had texted me too. Although Mum was a child-minder and growing up I'd always been surrounded by children during the week, as an only child, sometimes I still felt lonely, so I enjoyed visiting my cousins. Cassie had three other siblings, but we were the closest. When we were kids, I always begged my mum to take me there at weekends. Mum didn't mind as it gave her a chance to catch up with her sister.

Cassie

Good luck with the course! Still up for meeting on Sunday? Then you can tell me all about it.

We'd been warned that the course was intense, so not to make too many social plans, but I was sure I could handle one afternoon off. Plus, with Mum and Dad on holiday, I wouldn't need to visit for Sunday lunch, so it'd be perfect.

Me

Thanks! Definitely. Have a good day at work. xxx

I stood outside the light-coloured brick building. It spanned several floors and had two large plants on either side of the grand glass doors.

I took a deep breath. *Time to go in.* Twenty minutes early was acceptable. Keen but not too desperate.

It was modern, light and airy inside. Even though the school had been around for years, everything looked so clean and new.

As I queued up at the long wooden reception desk, I glanced at the back of the ground floor, where there was a café. It was buzzing with students waiting in line at the oak-panelled counter and sitting around the cute blue tables and chairs. I liked the vibe of this place. Despite my nerves at the time, I remembered having the same warm feeling when I'd first come for my interview.

After greeting the receptionist and signing in, I walked across the shiny light grey tiles, through the barriers, then up to the second floor, following the signs to the classroom.

The door was open. As I came inside, I saw I wasn't the only early bird. Five other people, three women and two men, were already seated at the shiny white desks with their books in front of them.

'Is this the PEFLITC class?' I asked a lady with shoulder-length blonde hair and green eyes.

'Yes! There's a seat over here if you want it.' She smiled and took her bag off the charcoal-grey chair.

Like the rest of the building, this classroom was also modern. Light grey checked carpet and fresh white walls, with a lime feature wall at the back and a large whiteboard at the front of the class.

'Thanks. I'm Bella.'

'Hi, Bella. I'm Faye.'

'Nice to meet you.' I unpacked the brand new notepad Sophia had included in the box of books. It was bright yellow and had *Follow Your Dreams* written across the front. I loved it. I pulled out a pen and some textbooks.

'Have you done any language teaching before?' she asked.

'I'm an English teacher at a secondary school,' I said, turning to face her, 'but I've never taught English as a second language before. You?'

'I helped a couple of kids with their English when I was travelling years ago and did a stint as an au pair, but I haven't had any proper training or been in a classroom for donkey's years—not since I was at school, so I'm really nervous. Oooh. Looks like our teacher's arrived!' Faye sat up straighter.

'Great.' I spun around and…

What the…

'Morning, everyone. Welcome to the PEFLITC course. Let me start by introducing myself…'

Oh God.

He really didn't need to.

At least not to me.

I knew *exactly* who he was.

'My name is Mike and I'll be your tutor.'

What were the chances?

Just when I thought I'd be able to push him out of my mind, up he popped. Like a jack-in-the-box.

Yesterday I'd said I'd be fine as long as I didn't see Mike again. And now he was going to be our tutor: for a whole month. Four weeks of intensive lessons. Twenty solid days. Together. In the same room.

It would be impossible to avoid or forget about him now.

This course might be good for my career prospects, but not for my emotions.

With Mike back in my life, if I wasn't careful, my heart could become mincemeat.

I was completely and utterly screwed.

CHAPTER TWELVE

O f all the courses. Of all the teachers that could have been standing at the front of the class right now, it had to be *him*.

I'd heard of coincidences, but this was *crazy*.

If I'd taken more time to talk to Zainab about the course when she'd first called instead of rushing her off the phone and done more research, then I might have found out that he was one of the tutors. *Dammit.*

Just as I tried to process how spooky it all was, Mike clocked me and his eyes widened. His face broke into a smile and then he continued introducing himself.

'I've been teaching English as a foreign language to young learners and adults for eight years, and for three of those, I've also trained teachers to help them become PEFLITC qualified. I've worked all over the world: across Asia, so Japan, China, Vietnam and Thailand; South America, including Brazil and Argentina; and also throughout Europe, in France, Italy and Spain.'

Wow. I knew Mike would have travelled a lot, but I

hadn't realised he'd been to so many places. I supposed he always had loved travelling.

'So I'm sure you researched PEFLITC thoroughly before you signed up and everything was explained in your interview, but in a nutshell, this course is going to help you learn the principles and practical skills you need to teach English as a foreign language. We'll focus on communication and learning through tasks. There'll be a lot of group work, discussion and coming up with cool ideas and activities you can use for your learners…'

God. He'd only just started speaking and I could already tell he was great. Of course he was. He was Mike Jones for goodness' sake. He was always great at everything.

There I went romanticising things again. He wasn't great at *everything*. He had his flaws, just like everyone else. I couldn't quite remember them all now, but I know he did. Yes! For example, he wasn't great at commitment or holding down a long-term relationship. There were probably plenty of other things I'd forgotten about too.

Mike took us through the different topics we'd be covering, which included focusing on language skills, so reading, writing, listening and speaking, planning classes and preparing resources, that kind of thing.

Another tutor, Graham, a short, stocky man with receding blonde hair, came into the room, introduced himself briefly and said that he would also be teaching various elements of the course to us. He seemed sweet and very knowledgeable. *Two tutors for the price of one.* If only Graham could teach me full-time instead of sharing the role with Mike, something told me I'd have a better chance of focusing. Graham sat at the side of the room whilst Mike turned his back to the class and started writing on the board.

'Ding-dong!' said a woman behind me. 'No wonder this course was popular. I thought his face was beautiful, but look at those buns! I'd pay money just to sit and stare at him. He is *lush*.'

A pang of jealousy shot through me. Just like when Ursula had expressed her intentions, I wanted to spin around and say 'back off, lady', but I had no claim on him. Especially considering he'd texted me two days ago and I hadn't replied. *Awkward…*

Seconds later, Mike turned back to face us. That woman wasn't wrong. He really was a vision. Especially dressed in that crisp white shirt, colourful tie and smart trousers. As he spoke, I watched his lips moving. I'd always loved his lips. They were full and so evenly proportioned. Even though it was a decade ago that I'd felt his mouth on mine, I still remembered how soft they were. He was such a good kisser too…

'There's no final exam. You'll just be assessed throughout the course. To receive your PEFLITC qualification, you'll need to meet the assessment criteria for all of the written and practical assignments…'

Faye coughed, which jolted me out of my thoughts. *Damn.* This was only the first lesson and I was already getting distracted. If I wanted to stand a chance of passing, I'd need to concentrate. How, though? Mike was so confident. So commanding. So annoyingly sexy…

'I'm not going to lie to you. This course is intense. It will be like cramming a uni semester into one month, so you're going to have to kiss goodbye to a lot of your free time in the evenings and at weekends. I'm going to work you hard…'

Someone pass me the cold water.

'But it will be worth it. Both Graham and I will be here to help you every step of the way, and once you have your PEFLITC, it will open doors for you all around the world. Anyway, that's enough from me. One of the things you'll learn about is the importance of minimising teacher talk, so let's get straight down to it.'

I only digested about fifty percent of what Mike had said. Something about *kissing*, *working me hard* and *getting straight down to it*. That was the gist of it, right?

Oh God.

This was ridiculous. I shouldn't even be having these thoughts. Before I'd arrived I was worried about the work-load and the intensity of the lessons. But as I looked at Mike in front of me, I knew it wasn't just the assignments and teaching sessions I needed to worry about. It was how I was going to curb my attraction enough to focus on basic instructions.

Damn.

I knew this course would be tough, but with Mike as my tutor, it was going to be a lot harder than I thought…

During the coffee break, I'd messaged Sophia and Melody to tell them the news. I wasn't expecting a reply from Sophia until this evening. After her big pitch earlier, she'd be exhausted. Plus, once she'd started work, she usually wasn't contactable for the rest of the day. She was always rushed off her feet.

Melody, on the other hand, had sent me a string of messages. Andrea was having a nap and she'd taken the day off sick from her part-time office job because she was still recovering from Friday night. That must have been one hell of a hangover.

Melody
OMG!!
This is fate!
You were meant to be together. Told you!
Me
It's not fate! It's just a nightmare coincidence…
Melody
Bull! You're the one that used to harp on about the universe and stuff. If this isn't a sign, then I don't know what is.

It was true. I used to believe in all that universe stuff, but I'd abandoned hope ages ago. I'd been asking it to send me a decent man for an eternity. I'd placed my order in the relationship catalogue, and yet years later there was no word on a delivery date. That was when I decided to face the truth: there wasn't a Mr Right out there for me.

Anyway, signs from the universe didn't always have to be good. I had no idea why Mike had to be one of my tutors, but it didn't have anything to do with us forming some sort of romance like Mel kept thinking.

Melody
You've GOT to ask him out for lunch. DO IT!
Me
I've got to go.
Melody

DO IT!!

I went back into the class, my stomach churning. I couldn't…

There were a couple of women chatting to him as I walked in, so I took my seat. The room quickly filled up and he started the lesson again.

A couple of hours later, it was time for lunch. Surprisingly, everyone filed out of the classroom quickly and we were left alone. I supposed it wouldn't hurt to try and diffuse some potential embarrassment.

'So…' I approached his desk. 'This was a bit of a shock. I was *not* expecting to see you here today.'

'That makes two of us! I should have checked the register before the lesson.'

'Looks like we really *do* have a lot to catch up on…' I paused. I needed to get the awkward bit—well, one of the many awkward bits—out of the way. 'Sorry I didn't get to reply to your message… I only got a space on this course at the last minute, so you know me, always the nerd, I spent the weekend swotting up and preparing for today's lesson and time kind of slipped away from me. I was going to respond. Honest.'

'Yeah, yeah.' He smiled. God, that smile… 'I believe you.'

'Let me make it up to you. Let me buy you lunch. Well, don't get too excited. This week, I'm a student, so I'm not talking a slap-up meal or anything. Just a sandwich from Pret or something?'

I hadn't wanted to meet him for a drink before when he'd texted, but asking him to lunch now was completely different. Now I knew he was going to be teaching me for a month, I needed to resolve any awkwardness to get the most out of the lessons. If spending an hour over lunch with Mike would help me with the course, it would be worth the sacrifice.

'Oh… I…'

'Are you ready, Mike?' I turned to see a woman, who I assumed was another teacher, standing at the door.

'Sorry… I've already arranged to…'

'No worries!' I plastered on a smile. 'Just a thought. No big deal. Maybe we could just grab a drink later, then, instead?'

The question flew out of my mouth before I even realised it. *Shit.* Mike winced a little.

'I'm, um, I'm going to Rebecca's tonight…'

Doh.

Of course he was. I'd heard her gloating about it at the reunion. God. It was at times like these that I wished I could freeze time. If I could I'd also get myself a shovel, dig a giant hole to bury myself in, permanently. This was so embarrassing.

The woman came into the classroom, tilted her head and made a face that seemed to say *'awww… diddums. Poor little woman has a crush on the teacher. How sad.'*

I felt pathetic.

'Rain check?' said Mike.

'Yeah, sure.' I backed out of the room, hitting a filing cabinet on the way out. *Ouch.* As if I wasn't mortified enough.

I literally sprinted along the corridor and down the stairs, then raced through the barriers and out the front door into the fresh air.

My phone chimed.

Melody

So… did you ask him to lunch?

I quickly typed out a reply. Seeing it written down in black and white made me wince even more.

Me

Yes. But he already had a lunch date with another woman. So I stupidly asked him for a drink later instead and he reminded me he was seeing Rebecca…

Melody

Oh, love. I'm sorry.

Me

No big deal. I was just trying to avoid any awkwardness and apologise for not replying to his text. That was all. Probably best to keep things strictly professional anyway.

Right now, I wanted to run to the station, jump on a train and never come back. But it was too late. I couldn't walk away now. I'd already paid for the course—I couldn't afford to lose that kind of money. And if I wanted to give myself the best chance of developing my career, I needed to get this qualification.

Yep. There was no way around it. As much as I wanted to climb under a rock and never come out again, I had to continue. I was stuck on this course with Mike for four weeks, and if it was anything like how it had gone so far today, I had no idea how I was going to get through them.

CHAPTER THIRTEEN

Sometimes clouds really did have silver linings. On the way home yesterday, I'd still felt embarrassed. But after I had my shower, grabbed a bar of chocolate and started going through my notes from the course and the schedule, I realised I'd dodged a bullet.

Mike wasn't joking about the amount of work we needed to do in our spare time. So him not being able to come out last night was actually a godsend. It meant I was able to spend the whole evening getting a head start on the planning and research I needed to do for the first assignment, which was due by the end of the week. Apart from taking a break to make a salad for dinner, I didn't stop. Before I knew it, it was past midnight.

Throwing myself into the course was for the best. Otherwise I would have spent the whole night replaying what had happened. Today I felt much better. I'd woken up early and given myself a pep talk. I'd committed to the course and Mike was one of the tutors. There was nothing I could do about that now. I had to get over whatever minor attraction I was feeling and focus on what was important, and that was passing this course. My emotions would have to take a back seat.

As I walked into the classroom, I saw Mike was already there, chatting with Faye and two of the other students. A guy who I think I remembered was called Craig and Petra—the woman who'd commented on Mike's bottom yesterday. Whilst Craig seemed nice, I wasn't keen on Petra. Not because she was perving over Mike. There was just something about her that my gut didn't like.

'Good morning.' I pulled out my chair and sat down.

'Morning, Bella.' Mike smiled.

Every. Single. Time.

My insides melted like an ice cream under forty-degree sunshine. Saying I was going to focus and not be distracted by Mike was fine in theory, but now I was here, watching him at the front of the classroom, flashing that smile, it was hard to know how I could.

It was still weird seeing Mike in a shirt and tie, but he totally owned it. He didn't look corporate and stiff like that Edwin guy. He had his sleeves rolled up to his elbows and was wearing a colourful red, yellow and orange tie, which reflected his sunny personality.

I wondered how things had gone with Rebecca last night. If that gossip Melody had heard was true, Rebecca planned to win Mike back. Had it worked?

Stop. Thinking. About. Him.

I turned away from Mike. After saying hi to the others and chatting to Faye about her evening, which mainly involved fretting about the assignments, the lesson began.

The day was flying by. We'd learnt a lot about different strategies and approaches for developing learners' language awareness. As part of our preparation for the assessed teaching practice, Mike had given us some lesson objectives which he wanted us to take home and use to work on our own lesson plans. We'd then discuss them with him and the other trainees tomorrow.

I'd done much better in terms of focusing today. Partly because Graham did a lot of the teaching in the afternoon, but Mike was still in the room.

And I hadn't even entertained the idea of suggesting that Mike and I meet or chat or do anything at lunchtime. So, whilst Mike was chatting to Petra, I'd slipped out of the classroom, grabbed a sandwich, then gone straight to the library to get a head start on my lesson planning.

I'd thought I'd be able to get a lot of it done during lunch—after all, I'd been planning lessons for years—but I was wrong. It was a lot more challenging than I'd thought, so I'd need to dedicate time to it tonight.

It felt like I'd barely got back from lunch when Mike announced it was the end of the lesson. It'd caught me by surprise again. I was really enjoying the challenge of learning new things, and even though it was only the second day, despite having Mike as a tutor, I was glad Sophia had signed me up.

Everyone had left the room before I'd managed to pack up my stuff. Graham rushed off to take an evening class, so Mike and I were alone. My heart beat faster.

'Great lesson today.' I quickly headed towards the door. Best if I left before I did or said something to embarrass myself again. 'See you tomorrow.'

'Wait!' Mike called out. I turned around and looked over at my desk to see if I'd forgotten something that he'd spotted, but there was nothing there.

'What's up?'

'Have you got plans for this evening? If you're free, I thought we could go for a quick drink.'

Whoa. I wasn't expecting that. I tried to hide the surprise in my eyes. I knew he'd said to take a rain check yesterday, but I didn't think he'd actually meant it.

My first instinct was to accept because despite trying my best not to be, I was still really attracted to him.

But whilst my heart was throbbing with excitement at the prospect of gazing into his beautiful eyes, the principled, logical side of me was screaming:

Walk away. Right now. Nothing good can come of this. Spending more time with Mike is only going to make you like him again. Just go home and study. Focus on the course.

And what about Rebecca? You don't know what happened last night. For all you know, she could have got her wish and rekindled things with him. Should you really be going out for drinks with someone else's boyfriend?

All valid points. Especially the studying part. Just seconds ago I was telling myself I needed to go home and plan the lesson. I had other stuff to do too. This course involved at least thirty hours of home study a week, which worked out at five extra hours every day if I worked six days a week (I thought it was important to give myself at least one day off to rest). That was a lot. I couldn't afford to go out socialising. Especially on a weekday.

Mike had even said himself that we needed to curb our social activities, and now here he was, tempting me...

Then again, he did say a *quick* drink. So I'd only be out for half an hour. Thirty minutes wouldn't make much difference. I'd spent more than that in the library, so it would balance out.

And I'd said yesterday that I'd wanted to resolve any awkwardness to get the most out of the course. That was still true, so this would be a chance to do that.

Actually, our drink could be like an extension of the lesson. I was going home to study, so would it really matter if I did it in a pub instead? Okay, maybe that was stretching it a bit. I couldn't exactly get my notes out and start writing, but I could discuss what I had in mind or something and get his thoughts. That way, technically I'd be getting a bonus lesson for free, right?

If we spoke about the course, which hopefully wouldn't be breaking any rules, then our drink would be legit. All above board. Totally, completely fine. Nothing wrong with that whatsoever.

'On one condition…'

'What's that, then?' Mike raised his eyebrow.

'That if I have more than one glass of wine, you remind me that I have to go home and plan a lesson, and for that I'll need a clear head.'

'Deal. In fact I'll insist on it. I saw you in the library earlier, so knowing you, you've already started working on the plan, and with all of your experience, I reckon you'll be able to finish it quickly tonight. Otherwise I wouldn't have suggested it. Don't want to lead you astray. It'll just be a quick one. I've just got to get some stuff from the staff room, so I'll meet you outside in ten, okay?'

'Okay.' I smiled. 'See you in a bit.'

'So, teaching in Asia, South America and Europe. Sounds like you've done a lot in the last ten years.' We were in a pub in Covent Garden, not too far away from the school, and had just sat down with our drinks. It was more modern than a traditional pub, with cream walls and light pine furniture. I shifted my chair to the left a little to make sure I wasn't too close to Mike. I had to say focused.

'I've done okay.' Mike shrugged his shoulders. Still as modest as ever. He was so relaxed about everything. Top of the class? No big deal. First-class degree? Standard stuff. Even though he was the most intelligent guy I'd met by a clear hundred miles, he had never been boastful about it. That was one of the things I'd always loved—I mean, *liked*—about him.

'*Okay*? Sounds like you're doing more than okay.'

'I was just lucky. I tried coming back to London so many times, but I always ended up getting itchy feet after a week, so I just went travelling again. Obviously I needed to survive, though, so after spending a few months in Australia, I came back, got my PEFLITC, then started applying for jobs.'

'So you didn't do your master's in the end?'

'Nah. I just wanted to get stuck in with working, you know? And I had the bug. I needed to be somewhere different. I landed my first gig in Bangkok. It was amazing— waking up every morning and seeing banana trees from my window, the tuk-tuks, the delicious street food and all the colours. I loved experiencing a new culture. The school was great too. I think the guy that was there before me was pretty terrible, so they thought I was some sort of English Jedi and kept asking me to stay. Whilst I was there, I made friends with a bunch of other teachers who ended up in different countries, and whenever a position came up, they'd recommend me. That's how I got to go to so many different places.'

'You always were good at networking.'

'I just like meeting different people.' He shrugged his shoulders again. 'This year, though, something pulled me back to London. I saw that there was a temporary position available to teach this course, so I thought I'd give it a go and, well, here I am. Anyway, what about you? You said before you'd been teaching at a comprehensive?'

'Yeah…' My voice trailed off. 'Started when I qualified and been there for nine years.'

My life seemed so dull compared to Mike's. Once again I didn't elaborate and tell him I was teaching at the same school I went to as a teenager and that my dad was the head teacher. It sounded too lame. Plus, to say he was not a fan of my father was putting it politely…

'Wow. That's a long time. Longest job I ever had was two years. And that was a stretch.'

'You were never one for commitment…' I laughed, wondering if he knew I meant not just professionally, but in his personal life too.

'Bull! I went to school for a whole eleven years, college for two and uni for another three. If that isn't commitment, I don't know what is!' He laughed. I'd missed that laugh. Deep, loud and totally infectious.

I was actually enjoying talking to Mike. Whilst I'd waited outside for him earlier, I'd wondered whether this evening would be awkward, but it wasn't at all. The conversation just flowed easily. Like it always did. It was like no time had passed. Speaking of time, I'd been here way longer than half an hour, but even though I knew I'd regret it later, I couldn't bring myself to leave.

'How's your mum?' He leaned in. 'She still child-minding? Oh, and does she still cook the fried plantain, or —oooh… those delicious fried bake things. What were they called again? The round things that are like dough-nuts, but without the hole in the middle?'

'You can call them fried bakes.'

'I used to *love* those. They were always so light and fluffy and had the perfect balance of sweet and salty. I liked when she used to stuff them with the salt fish too.'

One day Mike had come round when Dad was out and Mum had just finished making some St Lucian dishes and asked if he wanted to try them. He did and he'd loved it all. So whenever I went home to visit, she always gave me Tupperware containers filled with food to take back to uni and share with him.

'She's well—on holiday with Dad at the moment…' Mike's face fell. Just like I'd thought it would. They hated each other. 'She does still make those dishes, and she's retired from child-minding now,' I said quickly. His shoulders relaxed again. 'Not sure if you remember that little girl that used to be there whenever you came round—the one who used to speak at a million miles an hour? Judy? Anyway, she's all grown up now and is getting married next month. Madly in love, apparently.'

Oh, wow! I remember her. She was full of beans. Always smiling.'

'Yep, that's her. Speaking of love, how did it go with Rebecca last night?' That transition was about as smooth as an old car driving over speed bumps, but it was the best I could think of. I was digging and he probably knew it.

'It was fine. We hadn't really spoken since we broke up... not long after we came back from Bali.'

I remembered that they'd separated, but they were always so on and off that I just thought maybe they'd got back together a few more times before she got married or something.

Actually, now I thought about it, it made sense that Mike would have wanted to be free and single to enjoy himself whilst he was travelling.

His answer hadn't really told me whether some sort of *reunion* between them was on the cards, but I couldn't ask him outright.

'Good that you're still on speaking terms,' I said diplomatically.

'Yeah, even though things didn't work between us, it was nice to catch up. It was her grandma's ninetieth birthday last night, so she invited me round to see her. I always adored her gran and she's not very well, so I thought it would be nice.'

Oh...

So he'd only gone to Rebecca's to see her grandma? Not to rekindle things like Melody said Heather had told her? *Interesting*... Clearly a case of Chinese whispers.

'She must have been happy to see you.'

'Yeah. I bought her some flowers and she cried. Said a man hadn't given her flowers for twenty years, which was when her husband passed.'

'Awww.' My heart melted.

'You know how I hate seeing women crying, so I gave her a hug. Then she wouldn't let me go. Think she kept me there for a good ten minutes,' he chuckled.

Lucky lady. It didn't surprise me. Whenever Mike

wrapped his arms around me, I remembered feeling that I just wanted to stay there forever.

'You always were the king of hugs.'

'Thanks! Afterwards, she did seem much brighter. When I arrived, I think she was still holding out hope of some sort of reconciliation with Rebecca, but I told her that was never going to happen.' I caught myself doing a mental fist pump, then reminded myself that whether he was with her or not made no difference. We were just here as friends. 'And after her hug, she said that seeing as I wasn't interested in Rebecca, maybe I'd consider courting her instead.'

'She didn't?!' I burst out laughing.

'Yep. Even squeezed my bum when I was leaving. I felt so objectified!' He chuckled.

'Ordinarily I would be against any form of sexual harassment, but hopefully in this case you made an exception.'

'I promised her I wouldn't press charges. This time anyway.' Mike smiled.

'That was very understanding of you. I reckon you made an old woman very happy. You were always good at doing that.' I felt a tingle race through my body.

'What, titillating pensioners?'

'You know what I mean, *Casanova*. The rumours that were always going around about you at uni.'

There were so many stories of Mike's prowess in bed. The women who claimed to have slept with him all gave stellar reviews. Said he was the best they'd ever had.

'I don't know what you mean…' He smirked. 'Anyway, my super shagging days are over. I've grown up.'

'*Yeah, right.*' I rolled my eyes. 'I was there on Friday, you know. I saw all the women pawing you.'

'They weren't *pawing me*, they were just being friendly.'

'Ursula told me point-blank what she wanted to do with you, and it wasn't something that friends did…'

Saying that out loud stung a little. Given our history, it was too close to home… maybe I needed to get off this subject. I didn't want him to think I was jealous.

'Just because a woman offers you a jar of something sweet doesn't mean you have to take it,' he said. *Ouch.* That stung too—knowing that I'd offered myself like dessert on a plate and he'd turned me down. 'I'm not saying she didn't try, but I politely declined and went home. *Alone.* My days of one-night stands were over a long time ago.'

Oh really?

So Mike was no longer into bedding different women? *Hmmm.* I never thought I'd see the day that he would turn down the opportunity to get his leg over when he was single. I wondered if it was really true.

Whether it was or whether it wasn't, it didn't change the situation, though. In fact, if anything, it just confirmed what I'd thought. If he wasn't interested in adventurous women like Ursula and Rebecca who had probably done a lot more exciting things in one year than I'd done in the last decade, he definitely wouldn't be interested in me.

Nope. We were just old friends, and for the next month he was my tutor too. Which was even more reason to avoid adding any extra complications.

CHAPTER FOURTEEN

I quickly lifted my notepad to cover my mouth. That was probably my tenth yawn in two minutes. I was shattered. I'd worked until after one in the morning to finish my homework.

I hadn't got home from the pub until nine last night, so I'd stayed a lot longer than half an hour. But I'd really enjoyed myself. It was just like old times. The ease of everything. After so many terrible dates, it was a breath of fresh air to spend the evening with someone smart and funny. Not that I was saying it was a date or anything, because of course, it definitely wasn't…

We'd chatted about everything from travelling to TV and mindless things. Just like we used to. Admittedly, we spent all of about ten minutes talking about the course, so I didn't get to 'study' like I'd told myself I would, but as well as burning the midnight oil, I'd also spent my lunch break studying too, so it balanced out. Sort of.

As happy as I was that we'd got on like a house on fire, I knew I was treading on dangerous ground.

Throughout the lesson, when I should have been focusing on our teaching practice preparation, some techniques Mike recommended we used and preparing for our first assignment, I couldn't stop myself from thinking: what if…? Each time, I'd pushed the thoughts out of my mind. I couldn't go there. Exploring them further would only lead to embarrassment.

'Fancy a sweet?' Faye reached in her bag. We were supposed to be working on an exercise together, but I was miles away, lost in my thoughts, and she'd clearly noticed. 'Might help your energy levels.'

'Yes, please.' I yawned again, almost on cue. There was only half an hour left until the lesson ended, but I was still flagging.

'What would you like? I've got Percy Pigs, Haribo Star Mix, Haribo Sours, Celebrations, Drumsticks… take your pick.' She put a stack of packs on her desk. We'd only known each other a few days, but Faye was like a walking tuck shop. She always seemed to have an endless supply of treats stashed in her bag. It was one of the reasons I liked her.

'I'll have some Percy Pigs, thanks.'

'Good choice. These kept me company last night.' She tipped several into my palm. 'I was up until all hours doing this lesson planning thing. I was so nervous about getting it wrong. I have no idea how I'm going to get through this course. I thought working in a call centre was stressful, but this is a whole different level. Maybe I'm out of my depth.'

'You're doing great, Faye.' I tossed a second sweet into my mouth. 'Remember, it's only the third day. You're still finding your feet. We all are.'

'It must be easy for you because you're an actual teacher, but I'm freaking out! The idea of doing this teaching practice session tomorrow has got me tied up in knots.' She winced like she was about to be physically sick. 'If I just had to stand and do a lesson, maybe I'd be okay. But it's all the formal stuff. Y'know, the writing down all the aims, sub-aims, procedures and stuff you're doing and why. It's mind-blowing!'

'I know it can be at first. It's just practice, though. We can sit outside at lunchtime tomorrow or something if you like and do it together?'

'Oh, would you?' She sat up straighter. 'You're such a star, thank you!'

Faye and I carried on working, shamelessly devouring several more treats, and before we knew it, the lesson was over. The days always seemed to go so fast. Probably because I enjoyed the classes so much. As she went to ask Mike a question, I found myself taking much longer than was needed to pack up my stuff.

What was I playing at?

In future, I should try and leave whenever Graham did. That way I'd keep myself out of trouble.

The devil inside of me wanted to speak to Mike. Find out what he was doing this evening, but that was stupid. I was tired. I'd been yawning all day. I needed to go home, study and get an early night. I'd just about managed to keep on top of things by staying up late and working during my breaks, but this wasn't sustainable. Or sensible. If I wasn't careful, I'd fall behind.

'Bye,' I said to Faye and Mike as I headed towards the door. 'See you tomorrow.'

'Bella,' Mike called out. 'Would you mind waiting a sec? There's something I'd like to discuss.'

Sounded very formal.

'Course. I'll be back in a minute. Just going to the loo.'

'I'll be right here.' He smiled and my knees turned to jelly.

After I'd been to the ladies', I found myself looking in the mirror, then scrunching my curls with my fingers to try and give them a bit of va-va-voom. The next thing I knew, I'd applied a fresh coat of lip gloss and popped a couple of mints in my mouth. I swear there was someone else controlling my actions.

I'd never been one to fuss over my appearance. The only make-up I generally wore was gloss, mascara, maybe a little eyeliner and that was it. And yet, this morning, I'd spent much longer than usual on my hair. I'd even worn my favourite hoop earrings. And now here I was checking I looked okay in the mirror at the end of the day, when I was supposed to just go straight home to study.

I'd love to pretend I didn't know why I was making an effort and that I was just doing it for myself, but I'd be lying. I wanted to look my best. Despite knowing that nothing could happen between us, I still *wanted* Mike to fancy me. It felt lame admitting it, but it was true.

Mike was still talking to Faye when I returned to the classroom, but it sounded like they were wrapping up their conversation.

'I know it seems overwhelming, especially when you look at the plan, but remember, you don't have to think of everything you have to do at once. If you tackle one thing at a time, it'll seem less overwhelming. I'll go through some organisation tips with everyone tomorrow, but don't stress, okay? I've got you, Faye. We've all got you. You're going to be fine.'

'Thanks so much!' Faye's shoulders instantly loosened. My heart felt so warm. I didn't know how he did it, but Mike just had a way of putting people at ease. Faye looked over and saw me hovering by the door. 'Um, anyway, I best be off. See you both tomorrow.'

Faye winked at me as she left the room. Did she sense something? She had no reason to. I think all of us had stayed behind over the last few days to speak to Mike at the end of the lesson. And I'm sure we all did it purely for educational reasons…

'You wanted to talk?' I perched on the desk in front of him.

'Yeah. What you up to now?'

'I was going to head home and study. I'm doing this course and the teacher is a real ball-buster,' I smirked. 'Got to make sure I'm up to speed before tomorrow's lesson.'

'He sounds like a right arsehole. Expecting you to do homework on a beautiful evening like this. We all know how shocking the British weather can be, so when we get balmy evenings, it's important to make the most of them. Want my advice?'

'Go on…'

'I say take a break and come for a walk along the South Bank with me.'

'Hmmmm… tempting,' I said, thinking it really was and that I absolutely should *not* go. 'But what will I tell my tutor tomorrow?'

'Tell him your dog ate your homework or something. If you flash that beautiful smile of yours, I'm sure he'll be putty in your hands.'

I blushed at the sound of him calling my smile beautiful. I'd known Mike for years, and yet still I had developed zero immunity to his charms.

'Actually, Bells, you're right.' He cleared his desk. 'You should go home. Even though you did a great job in class today, I already kept you out for too long last night. This course is super intense and I don't want you to fall behind.'

My heart dropped. I knew he was being considerate and I agreed that I really should study. It was what I'd been telling myself every time my mind had wandered, and I wished Mike and I could hang out again tonight. But the devil was dancing on my shoulder again…

It was only a walk. It wasn't as social as going to the pub. There'd be no alcohol involved, so I'd be less likely to lose my inhibitions and let the hours slip by.

As long as I was home by eightish, I'd be able to catch up. I could just stay up a bit later again. I tended to work better late at night anyway.

'Don't worry, it's fine. I can go for a short walk. As long as I get back at a decent time, I should still be able to work on my assignments. I got a lot done at lunchtime too.'

'Great! Meet outside at the Piazza in ten?'

'Yep. See you in a bit.'

CHAPTER FIFTEEN

I stood in Covent Garden Piazza, which wasn't far from the language school. Mike was right. It was a gorgeous evening. The sun was shining, the sky was blue. A large crowd had gathered on the cobbles to watch a mime artist dressed as Charlie Chaplin.

I loved coming here. It was always buzzing with tourists who'd flocked to see the street performers, visit the market or the museums, or just come to eat and drink at the many restaurants and bars lining the streets.

'Sorry about that.' Mike rushed up to me. 'One of the teachers cornered me.'

'Wanted to invite you to have a drink?' Oops... the question just slipped out.

'Something like that...'

'Must be exhausting for you, having to fend off female attention every day.'

'*Please!*' He rolled his eyes. 'It's not like I'm Robert Pattinson or some sexy rock god like Lenny Kravitz. It's only stars like them that get a lot of attention.'

I didn't know how he couldn't see the way women melted around him.

'You're either blind or stupid if you can't see the effect you have. And I *know* you're not stupid.' Now it was my turn to roll my eyes.

'Yeah—women talk to me, and I'm lucky that if I approach one I like, she's usually receptive. But it doesn't mean *every* female likes me. And it doesn't mean I like every woman that approaches me either. I'm not just a piece of meat, you know. I have feelings too!' He clutched his heart, then burst out laughing.

'*Awww.* Poor thing.' I rubbed his shoulder. 'Always being objectified.' I was definitely guilty of that. Could you blame me? Even his shoulders were sexy. So muscular… I pulled my hand away quickly. I needed to behave myself. 'Anyway, what's the rule on socialising with students outside of lessons? Are we even allowed to be seen together, or is that why we meet away from the building?'

'As a general rule, I'm guessing it's not encouraged, but we've been friends for years, so it's different. To me anyway. I think as long as they don't walk in on us going at it on the desk, we should be good…' He winked.

Oh my God.

I blushed as a mental image of Mike pushing me down on the desk and ravishing me flashed through my mind. My entire body started sparking and I wondered if he was just talking generally—you know, giving an example—or if there was the remotest possibility that he'd ever thought of doing that, to me.

As if.

Even if by some major miracle he *was* interested in me

(which of course he wasn't), despite what he'd said about not doing the one-night stand thing anymore, I knew he'd still only want something short-term, and I wasn't into flings. I wanted to find someone who was ready to commit and settle down. And that definitely wasn't Mike.

'Well, as long as you can control yourself, then we should be all good.' I smiled, thinking I was the one who needed to rein it in. Mike held my gaze and his eyes darkened…

Hold on…

I could have sworn that I felt something. Really subtle. It was the way he looked at me. There was a kind of twinkle in his eye. *No.* I must be seeing things. It was probably hay fever. My eyes always went funny at this time of year if I didn't take my allergy tablets.

'You hungry?' Mike broke the spell.

'Always.'

'There's a food truck along the South Bank that does the most amazing burger and fries. We could walk there and then sit on a bench and eat?'

It was Wednesday, so I already had tonight's dinner all planned. Maybe I could freeze it and cook it next Wednesday instead? Yes. That could work.

'Okay!' I grinned. 'You know how much I love a good burger.'

When we were at uni, pizza had been our go-to meal on Friday nights or whenever we were cramming for exams or trying to finish a dissertation. But burgers were what we ate for a treat. They were our special thing.

We experimented with different types. Everything from big fat juicy beef patties to chicken burgers and spicy bean burgers. We tried different fillings and attempted to make our own versions before deciding it was easier to just buy them. We even had our own poll of the top ten. Everyone thought we were sad, but it was just another thing we bonded over.

Maybe for me it was like a form of rebellion or freedom. My parents never let me eat fast food when I was a kid and so it wasn't something I was used to having. But then one day Mike brought back a burger from somewhere in town and it smelt so delicious, I asked if I could have a bite. Mike happily cut off a big helping (he always shared his food with me) and after one mouthful I was hooked.

'Well, I don't know. You're all grown up and sophisticated now, so you could be a vegetarian or exist solely on a diet of spinach or something.'

'I do eat pretty clean most of the time,' I said, 'but I haven't had a big dirty burger in ages, and you worked us hard in the lesson today, so I deserve it.'

'You haven't seen anything yet, Bells. Wait until you see what I've got lined up for tomorrow…'

We weaved through Covent Garden, then over to Embankment, where we walked across the Golden Jubilee Bridge to the South Bank. I saw multiple iconic monuments in all their glory from across the Thames. To my left was St Paul's Cathedral in the distance, and to my right I spotted Big Ben, the Houses of Parliament and the London Eye.

We went down the steps and strolled beside the river. Just as I watched a boat cruising down the Thames, Mike took my hand and led me to the truck that was now just metres away. Feeling the heat from his palms sent shockwaves through me. The sensation of my fingers woven between his felt so natural. It was like my hands were made to fit perfectly in his.

It wasn't unusual for Mike to hold my hand like this. He was very tactile. Where others might greet each other with a simple hello or kiss on the cheek, Mike went all in with big bear hugs. I remembered whenever he was excited to show me something, he used to always take my hand to drag me to see it.

'What do you fancy?' He released my hand and pointed to the board with all the options. *Shame. I was enjoying that.*

I resisted the temptation to say '*you*: you're exactly what I fancy' and focused on the menu written in white chalk on the blackboard instead.

'I'd recommend getting Down & Dirty…'

'What?'

My eyes popped out of their sockets. Ever since I'd seen him at the reunion, and especially since we'd spent more time together last night, I'd been trying to push naughty thoughts of him out of my mind. Telling myself that we were just friends and could never be more. But my willpower was wavering.

I was already unravelling. All those years of hard work, trying to suppress my feelings, and just a few days of seeing Mike had sent them rushing to the surface. In fact, they were already bubbling over.

The truth was getting *down and dirty* with him was more than appealing, but I knew that wasn't what he was referring to.

'It's got the works. Cheese, tomato, lettuce, burger sauce, mustard and, of course, gherkins. They're still your favourite, right?'

'You remembered!'

'Of course!' I loved pickles in a burger. Mike used to take them out of his burger and put them in mine because he knew how much I adored them.

'And you? Still extra cheese with a part-time aversion to onions?' I raised my eyebrow. 'I'm totally on board with cheese. I love it almost as much as you do. But having a burger without onions should be illegal. You've *got* to have onions. Remind me why you didn't have them again?'

'It wasn't all of the time,' Mike said. 'Just sometimes I went without them out of courtesy.'

'Courtesy?' I frowned.

'You know, if I was going out and I had plans to get close to someone at the end of the night…'

'Ohhh…' Message received loud and clear.

'Can I help you?' said the server.

'Erm, two Down and Dirtys, please, with fries. Can we have one burger with extra gherkins, lots of mustard and ketchup for the lady and I'll have mine with extra cheese and no onions…' He faced me and smiled.

No onions…

Mike had that look in his eye again. Did this mean…? For a split second I considered if he was thinking of kissing me later, then quickly pushed the ridiculous thought out of my mind before my imagination started working overtime. *Again.*

It was just Mike being Mike. Being flirtatious. This was probably one of the reasons I'd fallen for him in the first place. He just didn't know how to turn off the charm. He flirted a bit with every woman he met, didn't mean he was interested. Just a habit of his, that was all.

Mike ordered two Diet Cokes and we laughed at how we used to always have it whenever we had junk food as if we were hoping it would magically cancel the thousands of calories we were about to consume. We found a bench, sat down and got stuck into our food.

'So what's the plan after you finish the course?' Mike took another chunk of his burger and then closed his eyes like it was the most delicious thing he'd ever tasted.

'Um…' I paused. I wasn't sure how much I wanted to tell him. 'The more I study this course, the more I love it and feel like this kind of career could be ideal for me, so naturally, teaching English as a second language to adults would be the dream—one day, but I'm not doing the course to get that kind of job straight away. First, I need to prove that I can handle the pressure and pass, so I can line myself up for a promotion. And if that doesn't work, then next summer I'll start researching opportunities to maybe teach abroad the following year or just look for opportunities in London. We'll see. The course is part of a long-term plan.'

'Prove yourself?' Mike's face crumpled. 'To who?'

'My… boss…'

'Where do you teach again?'

Last time he'd asked, I'd managed to avoid answering the question fully, but I wasn't sure I could get away with it again.

'St Andrew's…' I crossed my fingers tightly, hoping he wouldn't remember.

'Isn't that where you went to school? Where your dad's a teacher?'

'Yeah…'

'Wait…' Mike's forehead was now more wrinkled than a linen suit. 'So your *dad* is the head teacher?'

'Yes…' I hung my head. I felt bad for being ashamed. Dad was good at his job. He'd worked hard to get and retain that position for so long. Did everyone love him? Absolutely not, but most people respected him.

My embarrassment was more a reflection of myself. It always sounded so lame telling people we were related. I knew they'd assume I'd got the job because he'd handed it to me. That was why I always had to work extra hard to prove that I was worthy and had earned it fair and square. Which was why passing this course was so important. It had nothing to do with Dad. He didn't even know I was doing it, and he'd have no say in whether or not I passed. My achievements would be entirely down to my own merits.

'Oh, Bells! You shouldn't have to keep proving yourself to him. I know he's your dad, but if he's anything like he was when we were at uni, it must be a nightmare working under him.'

'It has its challenges,' I said diplomatically. 'Even after all this time, he doesn't think I'm ready for the promotion…' Once I started talking I couldn't stop. Everything just poured out of me. Being passed up for the promotion, feeling like I was stagnating, going round and round on a hamster wheel, not wanting to let my dad down…

'I hate to break it to you, but whether you wait one more year, two or three, he'll still say the same thing. He doesn't want you to change, grow or achieve big things because if you do, you'll realise there's a big world out there and will want to leave and he won't be able to control you.'

'Controlling? No. Overprotective? Definitely. It's true that if Dad had his way, I would always be his little girl and stay at the school forever, but I know deep down he wants the best for me.'

Dad knew how upset I got whenever I failed and didn't want me to get hurt. That was why he always encouraged me to accept my capabilities and 'stay in my lane'. It was like a vicious cycle, though. Whenever I tried something and messed up, I'd feel like he was right all along: that I shouldn't push myself too hard and should just accept that I wasn't able to change. That was why this course was important. To prove to him and myself that I was capable of more.

'If I was you, I'd leave ASAP. You'd be brilliant at teaching English to speakers of other languages. You could travel all over the world. Any school would be lucky to have you. Don't wait. Life isn't promised. Get the ball rolling. *Now.*'

'Now?' My eyes widened. I knew I wanted to make some adjustments to my life, but *baby steps...* 'I can't just swan off to another country. I've got responsibilities. I've got to think about my pupils—I can't up and leave. It would take a lot of time to plan such a big move. Huge changes need to be thought through carefully. I'd need at least a year. I'd have to update my CV, look for jobs, go to interviews, and even if I found a position, I'd have to give a whole term's notice. I couldn't just go anywhere on a whim either. I'd need to research the areas I'd like to teach in, go over there to visit in person...'

My head was spinning just thinking about it. If I did go abroad, I was thinking of heading to China. When I'd researched it last year, there had seemed to be a lot of opportunities for English teachers there. Plus, I'd always liked the idea of visiting Asia one day and it'd be much easier to travel to other cool places like Australia, Bali and the Maldives too.

'And then there's my flat. Renting it out would take time. I need to research estate agents, do viewings, vet the potential tenants…'

'Breathe!' Mike quickly wiped his hands on a serviette, then rested them on my shoulders. 'You're overthinking. All these things are easy to resolve. Like I said to Faye earlier, when you look at everything at once, it can feel overwhelming. But if you break it down, it's less scary. Take our burgers. We didn't just shove the whole thing in our mouths. If we did, we'd probably choke and die. Instead, we ate it bit by bit. It's the same for your career. You can't change it all at once. Think of it as stages—bite-sized burger chunks. Doing this course is a big piece, and obviously that needs to be your focus, but I'd also recommend updating your CV ASAP.'

'I will. Once the course is over.'

'I wouldn't wait until then to start. Teaching English as a foreign language is an amazing career, and the more people that get their PEFLITC qualification, the more competitive it'll become. Every time the course finishes, there's a fresh batch of candidates all looking for work. Thanks to your experience, you're already ahead, but why not give yourself an even better chance by preparing it now, so you're ready to seize any opportunities that come up? Isn't that what you're all about, Bells? Planning in advance?'

Hmmm. When he put it like that…

'What you're saying makes sense, but preparing a

strong CV takes time. I've already got my hands full, and after being in the same job for almost a decade, I don't have a lot of experience with doing them.'

I hadn't looked at my CV since applying for that job last year, and it was pretty basic. I'd wanted to improve it several times since then but always thought I was being disloyal to Dad because I'd agreed to wait and see what opportunities came up at the school.

'I can help if you want? As you know, I'm a bit of a professional tart. I never stay in one job for too long, so I've had to update my CV a lot. I'd be happy to give you some pointers.'

'Really?' My eyes widened. 'This is a whole new world for me, so any advice you can give would be brilliant. Thanks.'

'No worries.'

'Not right now, though. Maybe sometime next week, once I've got into more of a routine with the assignments and planning.'

'Okay. It'll be easier if we block out some time to work on it together. Just tell me when's good and I can come to yours and we can just bang it out.'

Bang it out…

Damn. I knew it wasn't intentional on Mike's part, but these double entendres were driving me crazy.

'Banging it out next week would be great…' I resisted the temptation to smirk. At least I hoped I did. I stuffed a few chips in my mouth as a diversion, just in case.

'Cool. It's a date.'

There he went again. I wondered if he really meant date as in… *No. Seriously. Get. A. Grip.*

'Great.'

'I see you still do that thing with your fries.'

'What thing?'

'Eating all of your fries before you eat your burger,' Mike said.

I remembered he used to tease me about this. I supposed it was a habit, and half the time I didn't even realise I was doing it.

'It's the logical thing to do,' I said. 'Fries get cold faster than burgers. And who wants to eat cold fries? Plus, when you let the burger sit for a few minutes, it gives more time for the cheese and everything to melt together. What?' Mike's mouth twitched. I narrowed my eyes. 'Stop looking at me like I'm crazy!'

'You said it, not me!' Mike laughed. 'I like to alternate. Eat a bit of burger first—after all, that's the main part of the meal—and then some fries. Then maybe some more fries at the same time as the burger. I don't really have any rules.'

When I thought about it, that was me all over. Always one to follow rules, rituals and routines, even with food. Eating cod on Thursdays and salmon on Tuesdays. Why was I so rigid? Having to finish all of the fries before I allowed myself to take a bite of the burger. If mixing up the way I ate a burger and fries was my idea of living on the edge, I clearly needed to let go a bit more. No—a *lot* more.

I took a big bite of my burger. It was delicious. And I loved the taste of the mustard and ketchup together.

'You've got…' Mike traced his finger just below my lip, wiping away some mustard, then licking his finger, slowly.

Damn.

My heart started fluttering and my blood raced through my veins. Who knew that dribbling a bit of mustard down my chin could turn into something so hot? I quickly took a sip of my drink to cool me down.

After we'd finished eating, we strolled down past the Southbank Undercroft—a skateboard park.

'Do you mind if we stop here for a sec?' Mike asked.

'No—go for it.'

We stood behind the barrier and watched different skateboarders skating past the graffiti-covered pillars and over the concrete ledges, banks and stairs.

'Brings back memories of when I used to come here as a kid.'

'I didn't know you skated?'

'Yeah—I used to love it. I started off at home. Y'know, just on the pavements, and then one of my mates brought me here. I was so terrified at first. Everyone else was so good, so I spent ages just standing behind this barrier, too scared to climb over and try. But once I did, I was hooked. I used to come here every Saturday afternoon. I even taught my sister here too.'

'Lyra skated?'

'Yeah. She loved it. Loads of people said it was for boys, but I didn't see why she shouldn't be able to enjoy skating just because she was a girl.'

Stood beside us was a woman, cheering on her son. He didn't look more than about seven and was skating up and down near the barriers. I liked how everyone, whether they were experienced or novices, respected each other's space.

'That's my boy!' she said proudly.

'He's very good,' said Mike.

'Thanks! He loves coming here.'

'I was just saying that I used to love coming here too. Back in the dark ages when I was young.'

The woman giggled and started twirling her hair around her fingers. Was there any woman who *didn't* fancy him?

Suddenly there was a scream. We looked over to see her son on the floor crying, rubbing his knee, which had been grazed and was now bleeding.

'Peter!' she shouted. 'Oh, my poor baby.'

Mike jumped over the barrier, rushed over to the boy, scooped him and his skateboard out of the way and carried him over to his mum.

'Owww! It hurts, Mummy!' he cried out as she assessed the damage.

'I told you to wear your knee pads!' He cried louder. 'Sorry to shout, darling. I just…'

'It doesn't look too bad.' Mike lifted Peter over the barrier and then climbed back over. 'If you come with me, I can carry him to the Southbank Centre to see if they have a first aid kit to get this cleaned up?'

'Would you? That would be amazing, thank you!'

He readjusted Peter in his arms and carried him effortlessly, like he was holding onto a bag of sugar.

Luckily, they had a first aid kit and Mike quickly cleaned the wound and wrapped it up.

'How's that?' he asked Peter.

'Much better.'

'I can't thank you enough,' his mum said. 'Your boyfriend is the sweetest. You're a very lucky woman.' She smiled.

'He's not my…,' I stuttered. 'We're just friends…'

'Hold on to that one,' she added as they both waved goodbye.

'Well, that was impressive,' I said.

'What, rubbing an antiseptic wipe over a graze?' Mike shrugged his shoulders. 'Not really. I just did what anyone would have done. If my son or daughter had fallen off their skateboard and hurt themselves, I'd hope someone would help them too.'

'You'd like kids?'

'Definitely.'

What? Who was this guy and what had he done with the Mike I knew?

'I thought you always said that you were going to live the bachelor life forever?' I remembered him saying that during our first year of uni.

'I know you've got this image of me being flighty, and yeah, to a degree I am with some things. I like variety. I like to try new things and be challenged, but that doesn't mean I don't want to settle down. I'd love to have a family. With the right woman…'

So Mike wasn't anti-long-term commitment anymore? Seriously?

This man was *killing* me.

Spending time with him over the past few days had reminded me of exactly why I'd fallen for him all those years ago and why my crush had been so hard to overcome.

Up until tonight, I'd thought the idea of him seeing me as more than a friend was ludicrous. A hundred percent never going to happen.

But after the few exchanges we'd shared this evening, the subtle looks, the way he seductively wiped the mustard from my lips… I was starting to believe that maybe that figure might be edging closer, perhaps to ninety-five percent.

Maybe, just maybe, there was a tiny chance that the feelings growing inside of me weren't just one-sided after all…

CHAPTER SIXTEEN

I flopped onto the bed. I hadn't even bothered to switch on the light. My eyes stung and my head felt like it had been hit with a brick. I was done with studying for the night. I'd been working non-stop for a week, and although I was still enjoying the challenge, it was taking its toll.

After my walk with Mike last Wednesday, I'd practically skipped all the way home. I was on a high. Thinking of the moments we'd shared and excited about what might be brewing between us. I still wasn't completely sure that he wasn't just friendly flirting rather than romantic flirting, but I sensed a vibe.

What if...? had quickly been replaced with *maybe* as my brain considered the possibility that Mike *might* be interested and churned out different ways we could make things work. *Maybe* him being my teacher wouldn't make things complicated. After all, there were only a few weeks left of the course.

I'd got so caught up in my fantasies that I hadn't started work until after ten-thirty, which meant I was still up after 2 a.m. trying to get everything done. Of course I was like a zombie on the way to class. At that point, I reckoned the majority of the liquid in my body was probably coffee.

I decided I couldn't have any more nights out for a while. As much as I loved being with Mike, there could be no more walks or drinks. Not forever, of course. I just needed to knuckle down properly for at least a week. Find my bearings. Then once I was in a good place and got myself organised, I could be a bit more social again.

So that was what I did. Last Thursday and every weekday evening since, I'd come straight home after the lessons. I worked solidly at the weekend too, even postponing my catch-up with Cassie. As intense as it was, I was still loving the course, but now, seven days later, I was shattered. I'd gone too far the other way.

I'd always said to Sophia that she worked too much and needed to take breaks, so it was time I took my own advice. I'd message Cassie later to see if she was free this Sunday and rather than spend tomorrow evening doing stuff for the course, I'd take the night off and see if Mike was free to help me tackle my CV.

I'd like to say that not hanging out with him in the evenings had helped me to control my feelings, but it hadn't. I still thought of him as soon as I woke up. I still got the tingles when I watched him at the front of the class and when he walked by my desk and I could smell his gorgeous woody scent. And I still dreamt about him at night.

But it could be a lot worse. If I'd continued meeting him every evening, by now I'd be a complete wreck. Keeping some distance was the better option. As long as I didn't see him too often outside of class, it should be manageable.

I closed my eyes to rest them for a few minutes, then remembered I'd wanted to check on Melody. I switched on the bedside lamp, reached for my phone and dialled her number.

'Hi, Bella,' she answered. Her voice was low and lifeless.

'How are things?'

'Pretty shit to be honest,' she sighed. 'I think I'm gonna lose my job. They need me to work longer hours, but what they pay me isn't enough to cover Andrea going to nursery full-time and it's another year before she goes to school. I can't seem to find another part-time job anywhere. I've tried the supermarkets, even the corner shop down the road, but there's nothing. I don't know what to do.'

Melody had been having a tough time for a while now. She was stuck in a run-down house in Coventry with her daughter Andrea, working part-time in an office trying to make ends meet.

'And Rodney is still no help?'

'Pff. That wanker is about as helpful as a chocolate teapot. His mum used to help out now and then, but after I was a bit late picking Andrea up that Saturday afternoon after the reunion, she's gone cold and stopped answering my calls.'

Rodney was her loser ex and Andrea's so-called dad. Melody never used that word, though. She usually referred to him as the sperm donor, dickhead or a myriad of other derogatory terms. Each one was well deserved.

After spending a few wild weekends with him, Melody

had fallen pregnant, and although he was initially shocked, Rodney had said she could move to Coventry, which was where he was from. They'd had their ups and downs living together during the pregnancy, but a few months after Andrea was born it had gone downhill, fast.

One afternoon Melody had come home to find all of Rodney's stuff was gone. All he'd left was a note saying: 'Sorry. Can't do this.'

Melody had obviously been distraught and tried calling him repeatedly, but he'd ignored her for days. In the end she'd had to resort to going to his workplace to get answers.

He'd taken her to one side. 'The baby cries a lot,' he'd said. *Duh*. That was what babies did. He'd told Melody it was too much. He wasn't ready for the responsibility and had never wanted a baby in the first place. Being with her was just supposed to be 'a bit of fun'. What a loser.

'Every time I ask for help, he says he's a bit short. He's got money for fags and booze, but none to keep his child clothed and fed. Well, not Andrea anyway. I'm sure he takes much better care of his son. Arsehole.'

To add insult to injury, just a few months after he'd left her, Melody had found out that Rodney had got another woman pregnant. When his son was born he'd moved in with them. He was still there, playing happy families whilst Melody had to move to a horrible place and do a job she hated just to pay the bills.

'Oh, hon, I'm so sorry. I wish I could do something to help. I wish you were in London—then I could babysit or help you look for work or something.'

'I wish I could move back, but it would be even worse there. Everything's even more expensive down south. I'd never be able to afford the rent or childcare. Don't worry, B. I'll sort something out.'

Knowing your friend was struggling and not being able to do anything was the worst. Melody didn't have any family or any form of support network in Coventry and she'd fallen out with her family long ago. All she had was me and a few other friends from our uni days.

'Well, just tell me if you need anything? Help with the rent or supermarket vouchers. Anything. Don't ever feel like you can't ask. Okay?' I wasn't flush with cash, especially after shelling out for the course, but I had some savings I'd put aside for a rainy day that I could dip into.

'Okay,' she said. I could tell she was crying but didn't want me to know, and it broke my heart. 'How did it come to this, B? How did I go from being at uni, getting my degree and having the whole world at my feet to being a single parent, living in a shithole dump of a house in Coventry, and doing a job a teenager could do, with no life and no money? I wish I'd never met bloody Rodney.'

'But then you wouldn't have Andrea.'

'That's true. I don't know what I'd do without my little munchkin. She drives me up the wall sometimes, but I love her more than melted butter on warm toast.'

'Wow. That's big. I know how much you love your toast.'

'That I do, luv. Bread is the *best*. I don't know how people go without it. That's why I was never good at dieting. I can't live without a tasty loaf. Especially with a nice bit of jam—ooh, or some melted cheese. Now my stomach's rumbling!'

'I'll let you go and eat, then.'

'Oh, no, you don't! Not until you fill me in on how it's

going with our mate Mike, or should I say your sexy teacher! Have you shagged him yet? Has he had you up against the filing cabinets or spread you over the desk? Come on, Bella-boo. You asked if there was anything you could do for me, and now you can. I've had a crappy day, so I need cheering up. Tell me some sexy stories…'

I wished I could have answered yes to Mike having his wicked way with me, but the only place that was happening was in my dreams, which were becoming more and more explicit every night.

If only there was a way to make those dreams become a reality.

CHAPTER SEVENTEEN

T he doorbell rang. I quickly checked myself in the
mirror, then pressed the buzzer.

'Hi, it's me.'

'Hi!' I replied, my heart pounding. 'Come up to the
first floor.'

Mike was here and in a few seconds he'd be in my flat.
I'd texted him last night to see if he'd be free to help me
with my CV this evening after our lesson. He said he had
to work late but could come to my place straight after.

On the one hand, of course I wanted to see him. It had
been a week and a half since we'd spent time alone
together during our walk, and even though I saw him in
class every day, it felt like forever. But on the other, I'd
hoped that because of the short notice he'd be too busy to
come.

Part of me was still holding back. For so long my
memories of Mike had been tainted with the rejection and
embarrassment of that night. But since the course had

started, thinking of him had made me happy. I was enjoying having him back in my life and I was scared that if we spent more time together, something might happen to ruin that.

'Welcome!' I said as he stepped through the door. As always, he looked so good. He'd taken off his tie and the top buttons of his shirt were undone, giving a glorious glimpse of his magnificent chest. His sleeves were also rolled up to his elbows, revealing his toned forearms. Concentrating in class was hard, but something told me that focusing tonight would be even more of a challenge.

'Wow, this is nice.' He slid off his shoes and walked down the hallway, peeking in the rooms. 'And so tidy. You haven't changed. I think your room was always the neatest.'

'That wasn't difficult, if you think about who we lived with,' I laughed.

During the first year of university, we'd stayed in student halls, and then Mike and I had shared a house with Melody and Jim. Mike's room was hit and miss. Sometimes decent, sometimes a bomb site. But the others always looked like they'd been ransacked by burglars.

'True. So do I get the grand tour?'

'Of course! Follow me.' I was glad I'd got up extra early to give the place the once-over. 'So this is the living room, which is also my dining room and study.' The design was pretty simple. Cream walls, purple sofa, wooden flooring and a plain white dining table. I had a tiny desk in the corner with a computer, printer, bookcase and blue chair. That was my little office.

'Nice. Good size too.'

'Thanks. And here is the kitchen.' It had light grey

cupboard doors and a yellow feature wall. The bathroom is here…'

'And the bedroom?' Mike asked. What was it about him saying the word *bedroom* that sent shivers down my spine and tingles between my legs?

'Um, that's down the hall on the left.' I walked towards it and opened the door. The king-sized bed, which was covered with a white floral duvet and several cushions, was in the centre, with white bedside tables on either side. The walls were painted a pretty peach, which made it look nice and bright.

Mike stepped inside, smiled, sat on the edge of the bed and bounced up and down.

Oh God.

Didn't he realise what that did to me? Thoughts of him climbing on top of me and how great it would be for us to be bouncing on it for real flashed through my mind.

'Cool bed. Firm, but with some movement and not squeaky.'

'Unlike your old one, you mean?'

Remembering that immediately poured cold water all over my fantasies. Now all I could think about was the days that Rebecca or his girlfriend of the moment stayed over and I'd have to listen to that bed squeaking all night. And when I said all night, I really meant *all night*. It was like he was powered by everlasting batteries. Then there were the endless moans of pleasure: "Oh, Mike, don't stop. You are a sex god!" That sent my jealousy off the scale.

When we'd moved into the house, I'd thought being in the bedroom next to Mike was a good idea because it would make it easier for us to study together. Big mistake.

'I remember that bed. It was pretty noisy.'

'Tell me about it… so, Goldilocks, now you've tested my mattress, shall I get three bowls of porridge for you to try too?'

'*Very funny*. I just appreciate a good bed, that's all…' Mike's eyes darkened, just like they had on our walk, and a frisson ran through me.

'So… ready to take a look at my CV?' I swiftly left the room before I misinterpreted his intense staring as some sort of attraction and ended up doing something stupid like trying to kiss him again.

'Okay.' He followed me down the hallway. I went to my desk in the living room and picked up a copy of the CV I'd printed off, handing it to Mike, who'd already made himself comfortable on my sofa.

'Here you go. Drink?'

'Please.'

I went to the kitchen, took a beer out of the fridge, poured myself a glass of wine and pulled an empty bowl out of the cupboard. After putting everything down on the coffee table, I reached into my bag and grabbed the snacks I'd bought especially.

'I thought you might like these…' I held the packet up and smiled.

'No way!' Mike grinned. 'Cheese balls! I haven't had those in *years*!'

Whenever we were pulling an all-nighter, Mike and I had always binged on these crisps. They were the perfect snack, crunchy and full of cheesy flavour. We could easily go through a couple of packets in one sitting.

'Me neither.' I tipped them into a bowl, then sat down beside him. 'Did we ever eat anything healthy whilst we were at uni? When I think back to my diet, all

I can remember is having pizza, burgers, crisps and Haribos.'

'And Pot Noodles.'

'Yes! Pot Noodles.'

'Well, you were the healthiest one. You always had salads or home-made sandwiches for lunch and used to tell us all to make sure we had vegetables with our dinner.'

'Oh God.' I winced. 'Really? I'd forgotten about that. It is true, though…' No wonder they called me Grandma. I guessed that growing up with all the little kids Mum used to look after caused me to fuss over people more than most. Having a helicopter dad probably played a part too.

'Yeah. I'm sorry, Bells, but I'm not going to be able to look over your CV…'

'What?'

'Not whilst there are cheese balls right in front of me. Unless you don't mind me getting orange dust fingerprints all over these pages?'

'Don't worry about that! That's just a rough draft I printed for you. I'm sure there's going to be loads of amends, so feel free to get stuck in and put your fingers all over it.'

Mike smirked. 'Well, if you're giving me permission to do that, I'm not going to say no…'

My face flushed. He was still talking about the CV, but I couldn't help thinking about other places I'd like his fingers to go…

This was getting ridiculous. All of these naughty thoughts. I hadn't had sex for ages and it was really beginning to show. It seemed to be the only thing I could think about lately.

'Permission is most *definitely* granted…' I smiled and

held his gaze whilst reaching for the bowl. Mike went for it at the same time and our hands brushed against each other. Feeling the heat from him was like being struck by lightning. He held his hand there for a few more seconds, then broke eye contact.

'Where are my manners? The lady should always go first.'

Mmmm…

He said go *first, Bella, not* come *first*, my brain shouted at me.

Stop it. Stop it. Stop!

When overheating around Mike, which used to happen frequently, I always found it best to remove myself from the situation to either splash cold water over my face or count to a hundred to calm down. Seemed like something I should do right now.

'Thanks. I think I'll take my handful into the kitchen and think about what we can have for dinner. It's a bit weird me sitting here watching you read through my CV in front of me. I'll get nervous.' Which was exactly how I was feeling right now.

'Okay. I'll give you a shout once I'm done.'

After shovelling the crisps into my mouth and washing my hands, I went to get my phone. I'd heard it vibrating earlier.

Melody

How's it going, luv? Have you two done the naked dance yet?

I rolled my eyes. She must be feeling a bit better today. That kind of comment was so *Melody*.

Me

There will be no 'naked dancing'! He's here to help with my CV. That's it.

Melody

If you say so…

When I'd filled her in on the evenings Mike and I had spent together during the first week of the course, she'd got so excited.

I'd texted her last night after Mike had replied to let her know that he'd be coming round, because I thought it might cheer her up. Should've known it would result in her sending multiple texts to egg me on. But if it made her happy, it was worth it.

Melody

I keep meaning to ask. Have you been to the opticians lately?

Me

No. Why?

Melody

Because you clearly need to get your eyes tested if you can't see that MIKE LIKES YOU!

I paused. I couldn't deny that even though he'd only been here a few minutes, I had already picked up a vibe again. When you combined that with the long stares I sometimes caught him giving me and the innuendoes, then maybe there *was* something. But that was what I'd thought before, the night we'd kissed all those years ago, and look how that had turned out.

Me

Anyway, how you feeling today?

I deliberately ignored her comment.

Melody

Bit better. Went for a walk in town with Andrea earlier.

Melody

Found a gorgeous bracelet in the market for only a pound! Bargain!! It's so bright and sparkly. Cheered me right up.

Me

That's good! You are single-handedly keeping the bracelet industry alive. You must have so many!

Melody

I am the queen of bracelets! I know a good'un when I see one.

Me

No doubt. Maybe you could start making your own?

'I've finished!' Mike called out.

Me

Gotta go.

Melody

Okay, luv. Happy humping!!!

Honestly.

'That was quick.'

'I was powered by cheese balls. You know I always do my best work when I have snacks.'

'So hit me with it.' I held my breath. 'What do you think?'

'It's a good start. But you need to change the angle. Link everything to your extensive communication skills. I'd talk up the teaching methods you use a lot more. Give examples of how engaging your lessons are. Once we have more practice sessions in the course, you'll get some feedback from the learners, so maybe ask if you can use a couple of short quotes as testimonials.'

'That's a good idea.'

'You mentioned the other day that you liked the sound of teaching business English, right?'

'Yes!' I said enthusiastically. When Mike was telling me about the opportunities there were to teach adults who needed to improve their language skills, particularly for use in a work setting, it seemed super interesting.

I liked the fact that they'd be really motivated to learn, which wasn't always the case with my pupils at school. Plus, they'd have specific, career-orientated goals that I could help them achieve, like how to speak with clients, phone etiquette, writing emails, building relationships with colleagues or giving presentations. Sounded really exciting.

'Well, if you're keen on teaching that at some point, it would also help if you could get some experience to put on here. Even if it's voluntary stuff. I know it'll be hard to do that right now because you've got a lot on, but maybe you could look into lining something up for when it's over. There are websites that list companies who are looking for volunteers. I can find some for you. Also, do you know anyone who runs a business who might deal with people who need to learn English for work?'

I started to think about it. *Oh yeah…*

'Actually, yes. Remember Sophia?'

'Your friend that used to study French at UCL?'

'That's her. Well, she's running her own PR agency now and I think some of the companies she works with might be French or Italian. So I could ask her.'

'Great! What would also help your CV stand out is if you can demonstrate some understanding of the business world. So if you've ever helped Sophia out with any elements of her company, adding that would be ideal.'

I thought I'd done my research, but I hadn't even considered half of the things Mike had just mentioned. He really was a fount of knowledge.

'Wow. Sounds like I've got a lot of work to do. Looks like I'll definitely need to wait until I've got some more experience.'

'Sometimes there's no perfect time. But if we hammer this out over the weekend and get the main parts done, it'll be much easier to slot in any additional things later on. You're already halfway through the course, and having PEFLITC on your CV and all your teaching experience will already give you an edge. The rest will come. Don't worry, Bells. You've got this. You're going to be starting your new career in no time.'

For the first time in ages, I really felt positive about my professional prospects. I was so used to hearing why I wasn't ready, but I was beginning to feel more confident about pursuing this path in the future.

I exhaled. I'd always hoped this career would be my calling, but I'd never really had the chance to speak to someone with Mike's level of experience in that field about it. So hearing him say those words and knowing that he believed in me meant a lot.

Not only was he helping me today, he'd also said that we could work on it this weekend too, implying he would be around to help me for more than just a few hours.

My stomach flipped.

I'd had my doubts before, but now I was excited. I'd be spending another afternoon or evening with Mike. We'd be alone. Together, side-by-side, working, eating, laughing and joking. And if Melody's instincts and the feeling growing in my gut were anything to go by, maybe there was a small chance it could lead to more…

CHAPTER EIGHTEEN

'I think we're there. You've nailed it, Bells.'

My shoulders loosened. That was a relief. We'd worked on the CV until eleven last night, when Mike had had to leave to catch the train and tube back to the flat in North London that he was renting. Then after spending the morning studying, I'd gone over it again—rewriting, rejigging and tweaking.

After Mike arrived around 2 p.m., he made some more suggestions, and now, a few hours later, it was looking so much better.

'Thanks! Seriously, I really, really appreciate your help. Especially on a day like this. Sorry for cooping you up in my flat when you could be out enjoying the sunshine.'

'Don't worry about it.'

I did feel bad. It would've taken him at least an hour and a half to travel home yesterday and he'd trekked here again today. Would have been so much easier if he'd stayed over. I'd thought about asking when I went to see him out and he gave me a big hug which lingered for longer than what might be considered normal, but I'd chickened out.

'It's still sunny, though, so if we're quick, we can take advantage. Fancy coming for a walk? I need to stretch my legs and get some fresh air.'

'Love to!'

'Great! I'll just go and change.'

Mike was already dressed for the weather, wearing a pair of khaki shorts and a vest top. I'd almost fainted when I'd seen him at my front door. He was casually holding a shirt over his shoulder, which only accentuated the shape and tone of his bulging biceps, and it was very distracting. He was gorgeous.

I put on a yellow maxi dress and slipped into some strappy sandals before we set off.

I knew exactly where I wanted to take him.

We walked along the busy high street all the way down until we reached Streatham Common, passing sunbathers, picnickers and a group of people playing football on the grass. As we turned the corner, there it was: the Rookery. It was a pretty landscaped area within the Common that had an ornamental pond, beautiful flowerbeds and a rock garden with streams.

'This is pretty cool.' Mike's eyes widened. 'It's like a little secret garden.'

'Yeah. It's been here for I think close to a hundred years, but can you believe I only discovered it recently? It's so pretty.'

'It is. That's the thing I love about London. We have so many beautiful parks. It's unlike so many other cities.'

'Definitely. What did you miss most when you were travelling?'

'Hmmm…' Mike paused. 'To be honest, apart from a handful of people, not much. Occasionally I'd get food cravings, you know, for things like baked beans or custard creams, silly things like that, but the pros of travelling outweighed that by miles. I enjoy trying new things and prefer to focus on making sure I live life as much as possible. I'm just lucky to be here…' Mike hung his head.

'Do you mean in general, or something specific?' I frowned. Mike had often made references like that, but never elaborated. His eyes looked glassy and I wondered if somehow I'd struck a nerve.

'Shall we sit?' He pointed to the wooden bench. 'There's something I think I should tell you.'

We went and sat down, and I turned to face him. Mike took a deep breath. My heart thudded, wondering what it was he had to say. It seemed serious.

'Do you remember I mentioned I was ill when I was seventeen?'

'Yeah, you had to take a few months off when you were at college and worked really hard to catch up?'

'That's right. Well…' He exhaled deeply. 'I've never really told anyone outside of my family this before, but it wasn't just an illness. I was involved in a serious car accident.'

'I didn't realise that. What happened?'

'I went out with a group of friends. Kev had just got his first car, so invited me and three other guys for a trip to Manchester. We'd planned to go there for the night and try and get into a few clubs. But Kev got a bit too excited, started speeding and…' Mike's voice cracked. 'He—well, the car crashed and everyone except me died.'

'Oh my God!' I gasped. Mike was trying to stay strong, but I could see his eyes watering. I threw my arms around him and squeezed tight. 'I am so sorry. I can't even begin to imagine how horrendous that must have been.'

Mike wrapped his arms around my back and rested his head on my shoulder. After a few minutes, he gently pulled away. His eyes were red and his face was pale. I squeezed his hands. It was so hard to know what to say.

'Yeah.' He broke the silence and wiped his eyes. 'It was pretty rough.' I reached in my bag, pulled out a tissue and handed it to him.

'A tragedy like that happening would be hard to deal with at any age, but at seventeen? I have no idea how you managed to pull yourself through.'

'I struggled for a long time. I still do. The grief was indescribable. I was just a kid. Up until then, no one close to me had died. Then, bang, all of my best friends were gone. Wiped out. Just like that. One minute we're driving down the motorway, music blaring, excited about being on our way to a new city, and the next I'm waking up in hospital with tubes coming out of me, my parents in tears, wondering if I'd survive.'

'Jesus. Grieving for one friend would be bad enough, but losing four?' I rubbed Mike's shoulder, then wrapped my arm around him again. Listening to this made my heart crumble.

'It wasn't just the grief, Bells.' He dabbed the tissue over his damp cheeks. 'I was just completely overcome with the guilt. I kept questioning why I'd survived and not them. It was so hard looking their parents in the eyes.

Knowing that they must be thinking the same. I mean, all of us had bright futures ahead of us, so why me? Kev was going to become a professional football player. He was so talented. Dwayne wanted to be a doctor. And he would have done it too. He was always so kind and thoughtful. Some days I wished I could just swap places with them.'

'That's terrible. I know it's hard, but you can't blame yourself. I really believe that you survived for a reason.'

'I believe that too… now. Took a while, though. For the first few months I couldn't even get out of bed. As you said, I was in my last year of college, but I couldn't even think about studying for A levels. It just felt so insignificant in comparison to what I'd been through. But then my dad had a word with me. Asked me if I thought this was what they'd want. Said that the best way to honour my mates would be to live my life. That I owed it to them and myself to make the most of this gift of surviving that I'd been given. So the next day, I dragged my arse out of bed, went to college, spoke to all my teachers and asked them to help me catch up.'

'That was so brave of you.'

'I didn't see it as brave. I just didn't want to let my friends down. To be honest, I didn't think I'd be able to cram almost a whole year's worth of work into just a few months, but my tutors and the college were really understanding and supportive. They'd lost four of their brightest students too, so they wanted to help. They put me in touch with a counsellor, who I started seeing, which helped a lot, and thanks to everyone's support, somehow I did it.'

'You more than *did it*. You *aced* it. Three A levels—all A's, wasn't it?'

'Yeah.' He shrugged his shoulders. 'Before the accident, I didn't believe in all that afterlife stuff, but getting those grades under the circumstances seemed like a miracle. It kind of felt like they were all there with me during the exams and coursework. Like angels sitting on my shoulder. Helping me.'

'That's a really lovely way to look at it, Mike.'

'Actually, I feel like they're always there. Guiding me. And I know that's why I've always done the things I have. It's why I wanted to travel the world. Why I never stayed in one place for too long. I suppose knowing how short life is, I've been afraid to stand still.'

Aha. So much started to make sense.

'That's understandable. I think you should be really proud of what you've achieved and all the things that you've done. I know your friends definitely would be.'

'Thanks. It hasn't been easy. I still think about them every single day, and ask myself whether I'm doing enough.'

'I get why you'd do that, but try not to be too hard on yourself. Remember, you're still human. You can't expect to do amazing things all the time. After what you've been through, sometimes getting out of bed and putting one foot in front of the other should be seen as a win. Making them proud isn't just about putting yourself on a treadmill, racing from one achievement to the next. Sometimes it's just enough to do whatever makes you happy. That could be as simple as taking a walk, like today.'

'You're right. And this has been nice. Thanks for listening. It's not easy to talk about something like this. And I'm sorry I didn't tell you before. It was just, at college, because everyone knew, they either tiptoed around me or ignored me because they didn't know what to say.

Uni was a fresh start. No one knew my past and I wanted to keep it that way. I didn't want other people's pity or to be reminded of the worst memory in my life. Does that make sense?'

'It does.'

'Even now I don't like talking about it with my family. Because it happened almost fifteen years ago, I feel like they'll just think I should be over it by now.'

'I wish I could tell you that you'll wake up one day and all the pain will be gone, but I don't think that's true. Sometimes it helps to just get your feelings off your chest. So if ever you need to talk about it, I'm here.'

'Thanks.' Mike strained a smile. 'Talking about it, telling you felt right today. I'm already feeling a bit better. You always were a good listener, Bells.'

'It was all part of your premium best friend package.'

'Well, I'm so glad I signed up for it!' His face brightened. 'I've really missed this. I've missed us…' Mike reached out and stroked my cheek. My pulse quickened and my knees felt weak. Any form of physical contact with him had always driven me crazy.

'Me too. More than you know.'

I really had. Everything was always so easy between us. We could talk about everything without judgement. Of course, there was just one thing that we'd never really spoken about properly, but now definitely wasn't the time.

'Hold on…' Mike pulled his hand away and looked down on it. He scanned his thighs then glanced up at the sky. 'Did I feel… is that rain?'

I touched my bare shoulders and looked down on the ground.

'Yep, looks like it.'

'That's one thing I haven't missed about being back in London: the weather. How is it that it was just beautifully sunny and hot less than half an hour ago and now the sky looks like it's about to erupt?'

'Now that's a question that every Brit asks what feels like almost every day.'

As the rain began pelting down, I cursed myself, wondering how I could have made the mistake of leaving home without either an umbrella or a coat. I never did that. I was clearly distracted.

'Here.' Mike untied his shirt from around his waist and put it over my shoulders. 'Take this.'

'Are you sure?'

'Of course. I'm not sure how much it's going to help you, but it's worth a try. Come on. We'd better get out of here.'

We ran out of the Rookery, over the Common and onto Streatham High Road. The rain had now become a full-blown storm. I could feel the water swooshing inside my sandals and I was completely soaked through.

We crossed the road and headed to a bus stop, but it was already crammed with people all huddled underneath the shelter. There was no room for us and not a single bus in sight. The mini-cab office was halfway up the road, and no doubt there would be a queue of people waiting.

'I can't believe this!' I pulled Mike's shirt over my head. My curls were already drenched, but I had to try and do something.

'We've got two options. Find somewhere to shelter and wait until it stops, or make a run for it back to your place. What do you reckon?'

'Neither option is that appealing, to be honest, but

maybe we can attempt to make a run for it? Who knows how long the rain will last.'

'Agreed.'

'Although, saying that, I'm not sure how far or fast I'll be able to run in these sandals. Feels like I'm trying to run through a river right now.'

'Fear not, m'lady.' Mike put on a posh accent. 'I shall carry you.'

'What?'

'Consider it part of *your* premium best friend package.' He winked. 'Hop on.' He scooped me up in his arms and put me over his shoulder. 'The Mike Express is ready to depart.'

Even though the rain was coming down hard and I felt like a cold, drowned rat, with every step Mike took, my heart soared. It was like I was a character in some sort of romantic film, where the hero sweeps up the damsel in distress. As a strong, independent woman, I knew I should tell myself that I didn't need to be rescued, but I had to admit, I was absolutely loving this. Having Mike's arms wrapped around me, my feet being protected from the giant puddles on the pavements, the closeness between us, feeling the heat from his body and the sensation of his heart beating so fast, all felt like the sweetest thing in the world.

Just when we were minutes away from my road, a bus sped past, causing a big dirty puddle to rise like an enormous wave and soak us in the process.

'Crap!' I screamed as the water hit my skin. 'As if we weren't wet enough already!' Mike just laughed. 'How can you be so cool about it? You're carrying me in the rain and now we're covered in muddy puddle water.'

'It's only water.' He shrugged. 'We'll be fine.'

He was right. After the devastating news he'd just shared with me, I understood why Mike didn't sweat the small stuff. Getting soaked was so insignificant in comparison.

Mike turned the corner, and seconds later we were walking down the pathway to my building.

'Got your keys?' Mike lifted me from his shoulder, moving me across his body so he was now cradling me. That made it much easier for me to reach into my bag.

I unzipped the pocket compartment and fished them out.

'Yep. Got them. You can put me down now if you want.'

'Nope. Only once I've delivered you safely inside.'

I wasn't going to argue. I was enjoying every second.

Once my flat door had been opened, Mike put me carefully down onto the floor, then stretched his arms back and forth.

'Thanks again. That's your workout for the rest of the year done now.'

'Not really. You were pretty easy to carry.'

'Suppose it helps having such big muscles.' I reached out and squeezed them.

Ooops.

That was the kind of thing I was supposed to imagine doing in my head rather than do in real life. Totally inappropriate.

'Sorry… I didn't mean to…'

'No need. I like you touching me…' Mike's eyes darkened. I looked at him and shivered. Partly from the cold water running down me, but mainly from the way his words sent sparks through my body.

There he was. Standing in my hallway, soaking wet. His muscles glistening with the droplets of water sliding down them slowly. Completely drenched, his wet vest clung to his chest and I could see every groove of his six-pack through the damp fabric too. Mike said he liked me touching him and that was exactly what I wanted to do. Rip off his clothes right now and run my hands over every inch of him.

Mike sneezed loudly and it brought me back to my senses. I shouldn't be thinking about things like that after what he'd just shared with me.

'Are you okay?' I asked.

'I'm fine. Honestly. Don't worry. I just had a moment, that's all.'

I accepted his response and promised myself to leave it at that. He'd kept it a secret before because he didn't want people tiptoeing or pitying him, so I had to make sure I didn't do that. If Mike wanted to talk more about it, he would.

'You need to get out of those clothes before you catch pneumonia. If you go in the bathroom and call me once you're in the shower and behind the curtain, I'll get your clothes and put them in the machine. I don't have a dryer, but if I turn the heating on, it shouldn't take too long to dry.'

'Sure you don't want to go first?'

'No, no. I'll get your clothes sorted whilst you're in the shower and try and find something for you to put on whilst they're drying. I'll bring you a fresh towel too.'

'Thanks, Bells.'

Just minutes later, Mike called out. I knocked on the bathroom door to double-check the coast was clear, then entered. I could see the outline of Mike's body behind the white shower curtain and my knees turned to jelly. Behind that flimsy sheet of material, he was fully naked, in all of his glory. What I wouldn't give to see that…

I whipped his vest, shorts, socks and boxer shorts from the floor and quickly left the room. It was getting harder and harder to push these kinds of thoughts out of my mind. And after his comment about him not minding me touching him, I was definitely starting to believe that he was having them too.

Although it seemed like it could be mutual, there was still that tiny percentage of doubt niggling away at me. If I was wrong, the rejection would be too painful and embarrassing. And with two weeks of the course still left, I couldn't risk it. Imagine how awkward the lessons would be.

No.

Even though I really, really wanted to make a move or at least say something, I couldn't. This time I had to keep my feelings to myself.

CHAPTER NINETEEN

I couldn't find anything. Unsurprisingly, there wasn't a single thing in my wardrobe that would fit Mike. Not even my baggiest T-shirt or jumper would squeeze over those big shoulders and biceps. Even if I *could* find something to cover his top half, there was definitely nothing to slide comfortably up those solid thighs. And judging by what I'd heard (not to mention what I remembered feeling when he was beneath me all those years ago), a pair of my pyjama shorts wouldn't be able to accommodate his package…

'So… what you got for me?'

Oh. Dear. Lord.

I looked up and saw Mike leaning against my bedroom doorway with a towel wrapped around his waist and I thought I was going to pass out.

I'd seen him topless during our uni days. We'd all shared a bathroom, so it was inevitable that I'd see him coming out of it at some point. He'd looked good then, but good Lord, he looked even better now.

His chest looked like it had been carved from the smoothest marble by the most talented stonemason.

'Um, er… I…,' I stuttered. *Pull yourself together, Bella*, my brain commanded. 'Nothing. There's nothing in here that will fit you.'

'Let me take a look.' He squeezed in front, rubbing his bum against me, which sparked a tingle between my legs. Mike reached inside the wardrobe, then paused. 'Do you mind?'

'Go for it. Don't rate your chances, though.'

He scrolled through the hangers.

'How about this?' He pulled out a purple cardigan.

'There's no way that's going to fit you.'

'Wanna bet?'

Thankfully the sleeves were wide and floppy, so he managed to get his arms through them, but it barely covered twenty percent of his chest.

'You look ridiculous!' I giggled as the cardigan strained against his pecs. 'Take it off before you rip it.'

'So you want me to strip?' he teased. 'Okay…' He removed the cardigan and every part of me wished his towel would come off with it. Sadly it was still firmly in place.

'What about this?' He plucked a floral kaftan from the wardrobe and held it up against his glistening chest.

'You have *got* to be joking?'

'Why on earth would you say that? Don't you think it'd suit me?' He burst out laughing.

'In a word: *no*.'

'I'm hurt.' He clutched his heart. 'I'm just messing around. I got way too serious earlier, so just trying to lighten the mood again. Oh, wow!' Mike plucked a hanger from the rail. 'You've still got this orange top.'

'What? You remember it?'

'Of course I do. You used to wear it with your light blue jeans and your favourite brown boots. I used to love when you wore this. Really brought out your eyes…' He smiled.

'Why, *thank you*.' My heart fluttered. There went the tingles for about the hundredth time today.

I knew I was very out of practice with men, but I was pretty sure Mike was flirting with me—like, *properly*—and I really wanted to do something about it. It was risky, though…

Just as I was weighing up my options and attempting to draw from my non-existent flirting bank, there was a loud thud followed by a heavy vibrating noise. Talk about ruining the moment.

'What was that?' Mike frowned.

'Probably my annoying washing machine. It goes a bit crazy on the spin cycle and bangs against the integrated door. I better go and check.' I really needed to get around to sorting that out. Sometimes it made so much noise it sounded like it was going to fall through the floor.

'Oh, okay.' He seemed disappointed. He wasn't the only one.

'Feel free to help yourself to anything you like in my wardrobe,' I smirked. 'After I've sorted out the clothes, I'm going to have a shower.'

Once the machine had finished spinning, I quickly draped Mike's clothes over the living room radiator, which was the biggest and hottest in my flat, and darted into the shower.

Just knowing Mike had been in here naked minutes before sent shivers all over my body. I imagined the stream of hot water trickling down every inch of him, rubbing the shower gel over his gorgeous skin…

I really needed to calm down.

When I came out of the bathroom, I peeked into the living room and saw Mike sitting on the sofa, still with just the towel around his waist.

Seriously. How was I supposed to control myself when he looked like *that*?

I darted into my bedroom, slipped a lacy black bra and knickers over my freshly creamed skin, then wrapped my silky dressing gown around me. Yes, I could have worn a T-shirt and a long skirt, but as Mike was half-naked, I'd be half-dressed too. It was purely a selfless action to make him feel more comfortable. Nothing to do with trying to look sexy at all. *Nope*.

I was tempted to check the progress of his clothes on the radiator, but I didn't want to. I was enjoying the view. He looked so good exactly how he was.

'I knew it'd be hot in here, so thought I should wear this, so I don't overheat.' I slid onto the sofa. It was true. That radiator made the room like a furnace when it was turned on full blast, and even though it had been raining earlier, it was still a pretty warm day.

'No complaints from me. I did spot a blanket that I was going to cover up in, but then I was getting pretty hot myself, so I thought I'd be better off staying like this. Hope you don't mind.'

'Definitely no complaints from me either…' The shoulder of my dressing gown slipped down, revealing my bra strap. Mike's eyes burned. And this time it was clear:

they were definitely, one hundred percent filled with desire.

'You're so beautiful, Bells.' He moved up closer to me on the sofa and brushed his thumb over my cheek. His touch sent shockwaves through my body. 'You always looked great. Even when we'd been up all night finishing assignments and had no sleep. You never needed to wear loads of make-up either—you were just naturally pretty.' He continued stroking my face. 'Being around you was always so fun and easy.'

I swallowed hard and tried to process what was happening. Mike had called me beautiful and fun to be around. He'd said something similar on our graduation night, but somehow over the years, I'd told myself he didn't mean it. Mike liked to travel and party. I was a geeky nerd who stayed in my room and studied or read books. I wasn't glam and outgoing like Rebecca, so I couldn't understand how someone like him could be interested in me.

But now, ten years later, I was starting to wonder if somehow I'd misjudged things. Maybe I'd been wrong to doubt him and have such a low opinion of myself.

Although I still didn't know what was going through his mind that night, as I looked into his eyes, right now, I knew Mike was being genuine. It really felt like he meant every single word.

I wanted to do or say something, to respond somehow, but I was scared. Truth was, I had been ever since I'd heard that he was going to be at the reunion. I was afraid to see him again and discover that the feelings I had for him back then *were* real.

I'd tried suppressing them for so long. Tried to deny

that I really wanted him. Made excuses and created reasons for why we could never be more than friends. But now it was obvious something was finally brewing, I owed it to myself to be brave and take a chance. Nothing crazy. Just flirt back.

Come on, Bella. You can do it.

'As I remember, you looked pretty good yourself back then too. But if I'm honest, you're looking even better now...'

'Oh *really*...?' His hand trailed down to the side of my neck and my stomach flipped.

'Yeah...' I reached out and ran my fingers down his chest. My heart thudded. My fear had suddenly been overcome with pure lust and desire and I couldn't seem to stop myself. 'With these insane abs'—Mike closed his eyes and let out a groan of pleasure—'and these big, muscular arms'—I squeezed them gently, imagining how good they would feel wrapped around me.

Our eyes locked and we both fell silent.

Mike began to stroke my bare shoulder. Oh. So. Slowly. My dressing gown fell around my waist and I could feel a pulsing sensation between my legs.

As I ran my hands across Mike's chest again, I felt his heart beating fast too. His eyes were now like flames. He wanted me and I *definitely* wanted him. After over a decade of waiting, it was finally happening.

Our faces started moving together, getting closer and closer. Mike leant forward and I tilted my head. Our lips were now inches apart and I could feel the heat of his warm sweet breath on my skin.

Just as he leaned in to close the gap, loud ringing vibrated through the living room, causing us both to jump.

Mike pulled back quickly, like the effects of a spell that had been cast on him had suddenly worn off.

'My phone,' I said. It was like I'd been in a deep dream and just regained consciousness. I jumped up, quickly wrapping the dressing gown back around me, and headed over to the house phone on the other side of the living room. I knew exactly who it was. 'It's my parents. I better get it—might be urgent.' They were the only ones to call my landline. Well, them and salespeople who always phoned right in the middle of *Eastenders* or at the most inconvenient time. If this was a sales call, I'd scream.

'No worries.' Mike's eyes darted to the floor. 'I'll just check on… see if my clothes are almost dry.' He looked guilty, like he'd just realised what we were about to do and felt bad about it.

'Hi,' I answered the phone quickly, wishing they could have called just a few minutes later. Even thirty seconds later would have been better. Then I would have got to feel Mike's lips on mine. I would've been able to see if they were just as soft and delicious as I remembered.

Ten minutes later and who knows? I might have got to feel his hard body pressed against mine. And with just his towel and my underwear between us, I was sure that it wouldn't have been much longer until I could have finally felt him. *All of him.*

Dammit.

After causing me to miss out on all of that, something I'd wanted for so long, my parents had better be calling to tell me their lottery numbers had just come up.

'There you are!' my mum shrieked. 'What's the point of always telling me to call your mobile telephone if you don't answer it?'

'Sorry.' I immediately looked over at the coffee table, which was where I normally kept it if I was in the living room. Then I remembered it must still be in my handbag. 'I left it in the hallway, so I didn't hear it ring. Is everything okay?'

'No. We thought we'd drive to Plymouth, but the car's broken down. Your father has got his head stuck under the bonnet, convinced he can fix it himself. I've said it's better to call the breakdown service people, but I don't have the number.'

'Where are you? On the motorway?'

'No, pulled over on a normal road. We didn't get that far.'

'That's good…' I saw Mike take his clothes off the radiator and head out into the hallway and got distracted. I wanted to call after him.

'How is that good?'

'Much better than Dad tinkering under the bonnet on the hard shoulder of a busy motorway.'

'Do you have their number, Bella?'

'Not to hand, but don't worry, I can get it for you. How come you didn't have it in your phone or stored somewhere safe?'

'Your dad has it, but he's being stubborn,' she huffed. 'So I'm going to call them myself.'

'Mum, if you give me a minute, I'll look the number up for you. Hold on…' My mother's phone resembled a brick and was so basic it didn't even have internet.

I went and got my phone from my bag in the hallway. Mike must be in the bathroom as the door was closed. I tried turning on the phone, but the battery was dead. I'd just get the number from my computer instead.

'Are you still there, Bella?'

'Yes, Mum. Just waiting for the computer.' Why did it have to take so long? I needed to get back to Mike. When it eventually did load, the spinning ball of doom popped up on the screen. It had crashed. I really needed to get a new computer. I went to charge my phone, but after hunting in the bedroom and living room, for some reason I couldn't find the charger, so I returned to my computer. By the time my internet browser successfully launched, almost twenty minutes had passed. So annoying.

Mike entered the room fully dressed. Dammit. He started mouthing something to me. I held my finger up to say *one second*.

'Everything okay?' Mike whispered.

'Yeah—my mum's car won't start. I'm just going to get the number for the AA.'

'Okay. Actually, Bells, I'm gonna go.'

'Oh no! You don't have to… I mean, are your clothes even dry yet?'

'I better get back. I've got a load of lesson planning to do, so… my clothes are fine. The sun's out again, so they'll be dry by the time I walk to the station.'

I hoped Mike was okay. For a moment I wondered if he was having second thoughts like last time and was trying to run off again, but I quickly pushed those ideas out of my head. Mike had spent most of last night and all afternoon helping me. He had a life of his own, and it would take him ages to get back. Mum's badly timed inter-ruption had just reminded him he needed to take care of his responsibilities, that was all. *Sigh*.

'Hello!' I heard my mum shout down the phone. 'Are

you there? Is that a man's voice I heard? Who is it? Where are you and why are his clothes wet?'

'Um, yes, I'm still here, Mum. I'm at home. With Mike —he was just helping me with my… he just popped round.'

I realised Mum didn't know about the course or that Mike was my tutor. And I couldn't exactly tell her he was helping me with my CV because I wanted to leave school. She'd tell Dad and all hell would break loose.

'Lovely Michael! I'm so glad you've met up with him again. You two were inseparable and I remember you fancied the pants off him. I always thought you two would get married.'

'Mum!' I winced. Thank goodness I didn't have her on speakerphone. I wondered if Dad could hear her. Hope-fully not. She said his head was under the bonnet and she planned to call the AA against his wishes, so Mum must be in the car or out of earshot.

'Let me talk to him!'

'Er, Mike has to catch his train, but he says hello.' There was no way I could let her speak to him. She'd give him the Spanish Inquisition, and once she found out that he was single and had been alone with me in my flat, she'd start saying a load of embarrassing things, and this situa-tion had already turned awkward.

'Hello, Mrs Walker,' Mike shouted.

I started walking towards the hallway, clutching the cordless phone to my chest. 'I'm just going to see Mike out.'

Mike followed me and put on his shoes. 'So, I guess I'll see you on Monday, Bells…'

'Yeah.' My heart sank. If only my mum had put the car

breakdown number in her phone or if Dad wasn't so stub-born, this wouldn't be happening.

No, no. I shouldn't be thinking about an almost-kiss when my mum needed me. 'See you then. Thanks again for your help.'

'No worries.' Mike gave me a half smile, turned and walked down the communal stairs, then out of the main door.

So close.

We were so close.

Damn.

CHAPTER TWENTY

Every time I thought about what happened yesterday with Mike, I cringed.

I'd had a hot half-naked man on my sofa, just seconds away from kissing me, and I'd passed up the opportunity just to answer the phone.

If it was just any man, that would be bad enough, but this was *Mike Jones*. The man I'd been craving for over a decade. My ten-year crush. The man that no matter how hard I tried, I just couldn't get out of my head.

For years I'd been secretly wishing for a do-over. A second chance to kiss him. I'd told myself that it was never going to happen. That he didn't see me like that. To him I was just a friend. And when the opportunity had come to break free from the friend zone finally happened, what had I done? Let it sail straight past me.

After I'd called the car breakdown service for my mum and they'd got back on the road, I spent the rest of the evening chastising myself for not ignoring the phone. Even though, realistically, knowing it was my parents calling me, that was probably never going to happen.

I told myself over and over that I should have just asked Mike to stay whilst I got the number, then attempted to pick up from where we'd left off. Turned up the flirting dial. Even though I wasn't good at the whole acting sexy thing, I could have tried. Mind you, if he had marking to do, that would have been selfish.

In any case, once he'd said he was leaving, I definitely shouldn't have hurried him out the door. Especially seeing as he'd helped me so much with my CV and literally offered himself on a silver platter. *Oh God.* I groaned as I pictured his beautiful body on my sofa.

Then again, if I thought about it logically, I knew what my mum was like. If Mike had stayed a minute longer, she would have forgotten all about her car and kept insisting on talking to him. And Mike, being the nice guy he was, would have chatted to her for ages.

She would have wasted no time telling him about my failed relationships over the years, my non-existent love life now, how she just wanted me to settle down with a nice man and have kids. Oh, and I'm sure she would have asked him if he fancied marrying me because we were made for each other. The word 'embarrassing' didn't even begin to cover how I'd feel if they'd spoken to each other.

Plus, at some point Dad would have come back inside the car and asked Mum who she was talking to. When he'd discovered it was Mike, he would've demanded to speak to me and I'd have had to listen to him banging on about how unsuitable Mike was. It would be like living back at home all over again.

Yeah… now that I thought about it sensibly, I'd dodged

a bullet. If Mike had stayed, there would have been no sexy time—not last night, not ever. My parents would have scared him off for good.

I couldn't change what had happened. I needed to focus on finding a solution. I'd decided that inviting Mike round for dinner this week was a good option. As a thank-you for his help with my CV. And if I was lucky, we'd have a *moment* again.

In the meantime, to take my mind off things, I'd go to the supermarket. What with working on my CV and Mike coming round, I hadn't had the chance to go yesterday like I normally would. Plus, in an hour Cassie would be coming over and we were going to cook lunch together and have a catch-up.

I nipped out to Sainsbury's and got the ingredients for the vegetable lasagne recipe Cassie had found on Jamie Oliver's website. Not long after I'd returned home, the doorbell rang.

'Hey! Come up.' I buzzed her in.

'Hey, you!' Cassie gave me a hug, then handed me a big bunch of flowers.

'Wow! These are gorgeous, thank you. What's the occasion?' I took a sniff of the pretty pink lilies.

'I'm just happy that you're finally doing this course! Call them an early *congratulations for passing* gift.'

'Thanks for the advance vote of confidence!' I went into the kitchen and took a vase out of the cupboard. 'So, how are things?'

'So-so. My flatmate's driving me up the wall. She hasn't done her dishes in three days and left the shower full of pubes. Still, at least I should be grateful she washed. I swear sometimes she goes a whole week without a drop of water touching her body. The whole flat stinks of her B.O.'

'Oh, hon.' I winced. 'I thought it had got better. Can't you just find somewhere else?'

'It *did* get better—because she went on holiday, but now she's back it's the same as before. I've still got a couple of months on my contract. And it was the only place that I could afford.'

Cassie used to live in a lovely little flat with a super clean flatmate. But then the lady said her boyfriend was moving in, so Cassie had to find somewhere else to live. Not easy in London when the rents were sky-high.

'Maybe try talking to her?'

'Pff. I've tried. She just says it's her place, so she can do what she wants. I just want to be somewhere clean. I mean, look at how lovely your kitchen is. Always so spotless.'

'Thanks.' I smiled.

'I even contemplated moving back home, but that would be a different type of bad, what with all the rules I'd have to follow. "Turn the lights off, Cassie. Don't bring any men home, Cassie." Then again, after my date last night, looks like that won't be happening anytime soon.' Cassie started unpacking a couple of bottles of wine and some snacks she'd bought for us, then washed her hands.

'Oh no! Who was this one with?'

'Just some guy I'd met at the coffee shop near work. How is it possible for a man to look so good on the outside, but have zero personality?'

'All style and no substance dates are especially disap- pointing.' I thought of that date with Edwin. When I'd told Gina what had happened, thankfully she'd sided with me and apologised. 'It's like seeing the most beautiful-looking cake through a bakery window, buying it, then sinking your teeth into it only to find it tastes like burnt toast.'

'Exactly. He had no chat. I had to make all the conversation. Whenever I asked him a question, he'd just answer with monosyllabic answers. It was like getting blood from a stone.'

'I feel your pain.' I rubbed her shoulder. 'It really isn't easy out there.'

'Sorry. I'm on a bit of a downer. It must be the Sunday Scaries. Or should I say the *Single* Sunday Scaries. Maybe it's just me, but sometimes Sundays feel like the worst day of the week when you're looking for love.' She pulled a printout of the recipe from her bag and placed it on the kitchen counter.

'Why do you say that?'

'When you're happy in a relationship, Sundays are the *best*. You can have morning sex and long lie-ins, then go for a nice walk or have lunch together and then spend the rest of the day snuggling up on the sofa watching TV shows. I really miss that.'

'You can have a long lie-in, nice walks, lunch and watch TV when you're single too. I know I do.'

'You know what I mean. I know there are loads of women who are happily single, but I'd really like to find a partner. It's nice to have someone to do things with. But when you're single, sometimes Sundays just feel like a double whammy of sadness. You're down because Monday morning is looming and you know you've got to go back to work and you're wondering when you'll meet someone decent. And morning masturbation isn't quite the same as real sex. I miss that.'

'Me too.' I nodded. 'It's been so long.'

'From what I hear, you have a man ready and waiting to service you in the bedroom…' Cassie smirked.

'Excuse me?' My cheeks burned.

'I knew it!' She grinned.

'Knew what?'

'That's why I didn't mention anything on my text last night. I wanted to see how you'd react in person.'

'React to what?'

'Look at you, playing all innocent.' Cassie raised her eyebrow. 'I know Mike was round here yesterday with his clothes off…'

'How did you know?' There was absolutely no point in me trying to deny it. As she'd just proved, Cassie could read me like a book. She'd know I was lying.

'Your mum called my mum and then she told me.'

See? This was exactly why I didn't want my mum to find out.

'Oh, no. What exactly did she say?'

I loved her dearly, but my mother was a hopeless romantic. It wouldn't surprise me if she'd told Aunt Janet that Mike and I were about to get engaged. She was so keen for me to settle down that she'd let her enthusiasm run away with her. I knew at least she hadn't told Dad. Otherwise I would have heard from him by now.

'Only that Mike had been in your flat getting naked…'

'What!? She… I didn't tell her that!'

'So it *is* true, then?' Cassie beamed. 'I need details. *Now!*'

As we chopped the vegetables, I filled Cassie in. On everything. Saying it out loud was even more cringey than it felt relaying it in my head.

'Er, so let me get this straight: after spending years *pretending* you were over Mike and finding every excuse under the sun not to get in touch with him because as far as you were concerned, the fact that you two were tipsy when you kissed or whatever *really* happened that night meant he definitely didn't fancy you, Lady Luck puts Mike in front of you, pretty much naked, and arranges for his lips to be millimetres from yours and you, what, decide to blow him off to speak to your mum instead and then kick him out?'

Cassie knew I still liked him all this time? That meant Sophia and Melody must have guessed too. Damn. I really thought I'd done a good job at hiding my feelings.

'What, so I was just supposed to put the phone down on my mum and tell her to wait until I'd finished snogging him? I couldn't do that.'

'Sometimes you're too kind for your own good. You could have just let the phone ring or go to answerphone. Anything! That was a once-in-a-decade opportunity.'

'You're right.' I hung my head, contemplating whether I should start banging it on the worktop in frustration. 'But it's done now. I'm going to invite him round for dinner this week. Hopefully I won't have to wait ten more years for another chance.'

'Actually…' She put down the knife. 'What am I even doing here today? You've waited ten years. *Ten years* to see Mike again, so why are you going to wait to invite him to dinner? Surely you should be seizing the opportunity for hot sex with your crush immediately. Call him. Right now!'

'What?' That was just the kind of thing that Melody would say. 'I can't. I'm with you. We're cooking together.

We've had today planned for ages and I already cancelled on you last week. I'm not going to blow you off for a man.'

'You're not! I'm insisting. I know how long you've liked him. And at least one of us should have a bit of fun.'

'But we haven't had a chance to catch up properly.'

'I've told you about my date. It was a disaster, just like my love life. I'm living with the world's worst flatmate. Nothing new to report at work. You're enjoying your course, you've updated your CV and you almost kissed Mike yesterday. Anything else to add?'

'No, but…'

'Call Mike now, and I'll help you prepare the meal so that everything's ready.'

'You really wouldn't mind?'

'I wouldn't suggest it if I did. Here.' She picked my phone off the worktop and handed it to me. 'Call him!'

I went to select his number, then put my mobile back on the counter.

I wanted to call him. I really did. But I was scared of misreading the signals and that it would make things weird between us.

'I can hear you thinking…' Cassie frowned. 'What's wrong?'

I paused. Maybe it was time to lay my cards on the table. Properly. Seeing as Cassie had realised I'd held a torch for Mike for so long, I might as well be honest. I'd bottled everything up for years and I needed to tell someone.

'Do you want to know the truth?'

'Of course!'

'It was Mike who stopped the kiss that night. It wasn't

because we both agreed to just stay friends like I'd said. He said it was a mistake and I was crushed. So now I'm just worried about being rejected again. It took ages to get over the pain last time. And like you guessed, I don't know if I ever did. I know there's a mutual spark there this time and I feel like things really could go all the way, which would be amazing. But I'm also worried what will happen afterwards if they do.'

'I'm sure Mike had his reasons back then and didn't mean to hurt you. Maybe the timing wasn't right. Maybe he was scared. I'm guessing you never got to talk it through properly back then, so it might be worth doing that now. People and circumstances change. Clearly you have a connection and he fancies the pants off you, so I'm pretty sure he won't be stopping it like last time.'

'But this is it for me, Cass. If we cross the line today, I don't think I'd be able to handle him leaving again, whether it's tomorrow morning, in a month or in a year. I'd be devastated.'

'If I was in your situation, what do you think my wise, logical cousin Bella would be saying to me?' She folded her arms.

'Probably that there are no guarantees in life and nothing ventured, nothing gained…' I sighed, wondering why it was so much harder to take my own advice and practice what I preached.

'Exactly! And if it didn't work out, which I'm sure won't happen, it's not as if you're still best friends, so you'd be throwing away years of friendship. You've survived without Mike before. You can survive without him again.'

Yes, I had survived. But when we'd stopped talking,

it was like being struck by a bullet. It had left a hole in my heart. It wasn't like I'd spent the past decade lying in bed, unable to function. I'd carried on. I'd pursued my career, had good friends, family, a decent flat, lived comfortably, but I'd always felt like a part of me was missing.

Now he was back in my life, it felt like Mike could be the missing piece of the puzzle. I didn't want to lose that.

I knew what I needed to do. I dialled Mike's number. With every ring, my heart beat faster. My brain swirled, wondering whether the conversation would be awkward. Things were kind of weird when he'd left last night. Plus, it was super short notice. He probably already had plans. Oh well. Like Cassie had just said, nothing ventured, nothing gained.

'Hey, Bells,' Mike answered brightly. He sounded happy to hear from me.

'Hey, um, sorry again for last night…,' I stuttered. 'Mum calling threw me, I…'

'Don't worry about it.' Relief washed over me. It was at times like these that I was so grateful that Mike was so easy-going. My shoulders relaxed and I felt more confident about asking him round. 'I'm sorry I had to rush off too.'

'So I was wondering, I know it's short notice, but if you're not busy today, I thought you might like to come round for lunch or dinner… just as a thank-you for all your help and to apologise for the interruption?' I held my breath, waiting for his response.

'No thanks or apology necessary, but yeah, I'd love that. I've just finished a basketball match in Crystal Palace, so I'm going to have a shower, then a drink with the guys, so I could be there in a couple of hours. That cool with you?'

'Great!' I said quickly.

'Want me to bring anything? A drink?'

'Can do, but no worries if not. Just bring yourself.'

'Okay! See you soon, Bells.'

'See you.'

Cassie was jumping up and down on the spot.

'*Bella and Mike sitting in a tree*, K-I-S-S-I-N-G!!' Cassie started singing and dancing around the kitchen. 'Tonight's the *night* that Bella gets it on with *Mike*!' Now she was thrusting her hips back and forth.

'Are you five years younger than me or five years old, because right now I can't tell!' I laughed.

I'd done it. Mike was coming round and Cassie was correct. All being well, we'd be getting it on…

Crap.

The realisation hit me fully.

Sex!

Sex with Mike was really on the cards. It could really happen. Tonight.

A shot of excitement raced through me. Followed by more fear. I was completely unprepared.

'You're freaking out, aren't you? Cassie rested her hand on my shoulder.

'Just a bit…' I took a deep breath. 'He's going to be here in a couple of hours and we haven't even put the food in the oven, I have no idea what to wear, I—'

'Calm down. We've already done all the prep. Once we put it in the oven, it's pretty much done. And this is Mike. Remember? You don't have to dress up for him. Just be yourself. He said yesterday how beautiful he thinks you are, so don't change a thing.'

'At least I have condoms.' I always kept a box in my drawer, just in case. Even if the likelihood of needing them was slim, I always liked to be prepared. 'I better check they're still in date, though…'

'Go!' Cassie shooed me out the kitchen door. 'Do whatever you need to do. I'll take care of this.'

I checked the box of condoms, then slipped into a purple lingerie set. I contemplated putting on the silky dressing gown again but dismissed it. If things were going to happen tonight, maybe it was better that they happened naturally. I opted for a vest top and pair of jeans instead.

It didn't matter that I hadn't planned my outfit in advance. I hadn't yesterday either and it was fine. I didn't always have to be so rigid. Like Cassie said, I was just going to be me.

I came back in the kitchen. Everything was in the oven and Cassie had poured me some wine and put some crisps in a bowl.

'Here, drink this.' She passed me the glass. 'It'll help with your nerves. And eat these too. We all know what a lightweight you are, so you need something to line your stomach.'

'When did *you* become the mothering one? As the older cousin, I thought that was my job.'

'It was. But then Mike came back in your life and turned it upside down, so I'm taking over Bella's motherly duties until you two do the deed, you both realise you're made for each other and then end up living happily ever after.'

I gave her a hug. I was so glad she was here, supporting me. I wasn't used to feeling so out of control.

'Thanks for everything.' I squeezed Cassie again.

'You're welcome. And don't worry. It's going to be amazing. Right, I better get going. Text me later to let me know how it all went.'

'Will do.' I walked her to the door. Once she'd gone, I stood with my back against the wall, took a deep breath, then checked my watch. Only half an hour to go.

Just as I was about to go in the kitchen to check on the food, the doorbell rang. Cassie must have forgotten something.

'Hey!' I pressed the buzzer.

'Hey, it's me.'

Already?

He'd arrived early.

My stomach flipped.

Mike was at my door. I didn't know exactly what would happen in the next few hours, but it was possible that our friendship—in fact, our lives—were about to change forever…

CHAPTER TWENTY-ONE

I t was funny. For as long as I could remember, friends and colleagues always came to me for advice. Somehow they saw me as the logical one. The woman who was calm in a crisis and knew what to say or do. And often they were right. But not today. Right now I wasn't feeling calm at all. My heart was beating at about five hundred miles an hour and my stomach was churning with a mixture of nerves and excitement.

These nerves were clearly caused by all of the expectations I'd put on things *happening* today. I couldn't help it, though. It was like so much was building up to this moment. After yesterday, I didn't want to have another missed opportunity.

Putting that kind of pressure on myself wasn't good, though. Somehow I needed to get out of my own head and try to relax. Follow the advice that I'd give to other people and allow things to happen naturally.

There was a knock at my flat door. I took a deep breath before opening it.

'Hey, Bells!' Mike stepped in all smiles and of course looking drop-dead gorgeous. I felt my knees buckle and reminded myself to keep calm. He was wearing grey track-suit bottoms and a vest top, which showcased his beautiful biceps again. He opened his arms wide, inviting me in for a hug. *Heaven help me.*

'Hey, you.' I wrapped my arms around his broad back and rested my head on his shoulder. He smelt all fresh and woody. I didn't know what shower gel and aftershave he used, but I loved it. I wondered how long was reasonable to hold onto him before I let go. I held on for another minute or so before pulling away. Any longer and I would've melted into a puddle. 'That's a big bag. What you got in there?'

'Well…' He followed me into the kitchen. 'I thought I'd get a selection of drinks, so there's two different bottles of Chardonnay to choose from, gin, a bottle of tequila and some Bacardi Breezers: for old times' sake…'

'Amazing, thanks! Are you trying to get me drunk?' I rested my finger on my chin.

'Let's face it, Bells, if I wanted to do that, it wouldn't take much. You only have to take one sip of something alcoholic and you're tipsy.'

'Oi!' I poked his solid abs. Didn't take me long to give in to the temptation to want to touch him. 'I'm not quite that bad. Not sure I'll be drinking the tequila, though…'

'Fair enough. But it's here if you change your mind. I also got cheese balls and a cheesecake for dessert. The selection was a bit limited.'

'No bread and butter pudding, then?'

'Nope. And to be honest, you ruined me with your

bread and butter pudding. I don't know how you made yours, but nothing I've ever tasted since has been as good.'

That used to be Mike's favourite dessert. Thanks to Melody's bread obsession, there was always plenty in the kitchen when we all lived together, as well as butter and milk, and although I usually had to buy the cream, it didn't take long for me to whip up. I hadn't made one in ages.

'High praise, thanks! Food's almost ready, so I'm just going to set the table.'

'Oooh, look at us being all grown up and eating at a table. Makes a change from juggling plates on our laps on the sofa or our beds. Let me help you.'

As we laid out the cutlery, Mike and I chatted easily. Earlier he'd played basketball with some friends and was in good spirits. I was so glad it wasn't awkward. In fact, it was almost as if yesterday had never happened. I just hoped that didn't mean his feelings had changed...

After pouring the wine, I dished out the food, putting a portion in a Tupperware container to freeze for Cassie to taste the next time she visited, then brought the plates to the table. We both got stuck in. It turned out pretty well, so it wasn't long before we'd devoured every mouthful.

'So, now that we've lined our stomachs, I'm going to have something a bit stronger. Seeing as I'm working tomorrow and need a clear head, the earlier I drink, the more time I'll have to get it out of my system. Fancy one?'

'What are you having?'

'Do you even need to ask?'

'Tequila?'

'Yep!' He smiled. He reached in the shopping bag for the lemon he'd bought and opened the cupboards, looking for the salt.

'Okay, go on, then. I'll have one shot and that's it.' A feeling of déjà vu washed over me as I recalled the last time I'd drunk tequila. I quickly pushed the thought away and helped Mike carry everything into the living room. After putting it all on the coffee table, we both sat on the sofa.

Mike sliced up the lemon and I sprinkled the salt onto the back of my hand in anticipation.

'Ready?' he poured the tequila into the glasses.

'As I'll ever be…'

He counted to three and we both downed it in one.

'Nope.' I winced. 'Still not a fan.'

'Some things never change,' said Mike. 'And actually, I think that's a good thing.'

'Yeah?'

'Yeah. I mean, not for everything, obviously, but for the important things.' Mike looked me deeply in the eyes. 'Like this. *Us*. It's like no time has passed. It doesn't feel like we haven't seen each other for so long. These past couple of weeks have been great. I've really missed this. Being with you.'

My heart flipped. It was like he'd reached into my brain, read my thoughts and said exactly what I was thinking.

'I feel the same. I've really enjoyed spending time with you.' I held Mike's gaze and the corner of his mouth turned up.

'Can I ask you a question, Bells?'

'Course.'

'What happened… with us? Why didn't you keep in touch? Was it because of what happened at your parents'?

On the night of our graduation? Because I've regretted that ever since it happened. I wish I hadn't—'

'It's okay,' I jumped in. My stomach sank. It wasn't okay. It had ruined me. But I didn't want him to dredge it up again. 'You said it was a mistake, so let's forget about it.' Talking about what had happened would just reopen the wounds. I didn't know what had changed and why Mike hadn't liked me before but seemed to like me now, and it was probably better that it stayed that way.

'No!' Mike grabbed my hands. 'You've got it all wrong. When I said it was a mistake, I didn't mean kissing you. I meant the *way* it happened. You were tipsy and I didn't want you to regret it. I didn't want to feel like I was taking advantage of you. You were too precious for that. If we were going to move from being best friends to something more, I wanted it to be special.'

What?

My head spun as I attempted to make sense of what he'd just said.

'I'm confused. So, you *wanted* to kiss me?'

'Kiss you? I wanted to do a *lot* more than kiss you, Bells! I wanted to make love to you. Run my tongue over every inch of you…' Hearing those words sent shock-waves in between my legs. 'But you weren't Rebecca or one of my silly one-night stands. I couldn't risk fucking things up. If I was going to cross that line with you, that would need to be it. I'd need to take myself off the market. *For good*. And I'll be honest, I was also worried about whether I was ready. Mainly because of what had happened with my parents.'

'Do you mean their divorce?'

'Yeah. They got together too young. They met at seventeen, were married and had me by the time they were nineteen. Dad was Mum's first. I think that not being with anyone else was one of the reasons she cheated and eventually left. She felt like she'd settled down too early and missed out on life. So I was worried that we were too young to get serious as well. I also thought about my friends, the accident and my promise to get out there, travel and live life... I just had too much going on in my head. So I had to leave. Before I did something that would hurt you and ruin what we had.'

'But you *did* hurt me.' I couldn't hold it in any longer. I had to tell the truth. 'When you walked out, I felt like you'd rejected me. That you left because you didn't want me. Because you thought I wasn't good enough. Like you were comparing me to Rebecca and all the others and I fell short.'

'Oh God, no, Bella! No!' He shook his head and squeezed my hands tighter. 'That wasn't it at all. Nobody else could even come close to you. But I didn't know how to deal with everything. How to be with you and still do all the things I felt I needed to do to honour my friends' memory without screwing things up. And then when Rebecca came round, it was as if I'd been given a way out.'

'But if you thought I was so special, why did you sleep with Rebecca just hours after we kissed?'

'That's what you thought? *Fuck*. I'm so sorry. It wasn't like that at all. We talked and by the time we'd finished, it was after four in the morning. I fell asleep—fully clothed —then woke up late. I didn't do anything with her. When I said I saw it as a way out, I meant I thought it'd be easier to just go away with her. Then I wouldn't have to deal with my feelings. I could just tick a place I'd always wanted to go to off my list and try and figure out what to do later. But it didn't work. I spent the whole time thinking about you. We argued constantly, mainly because she was frustrated that I wasn't sleeping with her. I ended up moving out of the hotel into a cheap hostel. I should never have gone in the first place. It was the worst holiday I've ever had. Me leaving that night was never about our kiss being a mistake because of *you*. It was about *me* and *my* issues.'

All. This. Time.

All this time I'd thought that it was because there was something wrong with me. And now I found out that he'd actually wanted us to be together just as much as I had.

Shit.

I'd wasted ten years. Ten years of friendship, or maybe more, had been thrown down the drain. Never to be regained. A decade of questioning my worth. Always thinking twice about taking chances because I was afraid of being rejected.

'Why didn't you tell me?' I said.

'I tried! When I came round the next morning, I *wanted* to talk about it, but you pushed me away. I tried when I came back—I wanted to tell you that Rebecca and I had broken up, for good, but you never wanted to meet. Why?'

My stomach plummeted. He was right. He had tried. Several times and I'd pushed him away.

'I couldn't face hearing the reasons why you didn't want to be with me.' I hung my head. It all sounded so stupid now. Never had I wished I'd spoken up about my feelings more so than at this moment. If I had, we could have solved this. I had to take my share of the blame.

'You really don't get it, do you? I was *crazy* about you. To me, you were perfect and that was the problem. Bells, you were always the gold standard. Every woman I ever dated during uni never lasted long because they weren't *you*. Even in the past ten years, travelling to different countries and meeting so many different people, I thought that I could find someone to help get you out of my head, but I never did.'

Oh my goodness. He felt the same.

'I thought it was just me. I tried. I really tried to stop thinking about you, but you were just always there.' I exhaled. I'd wanted to say that for so long but had been too afraid to admit it.

'I had no idea. I just thought you'd moved on and forgotten about me. I was so surprised when Melody told me you were single. I thought there was no way you'd still be available. It's *you*, Bella.' He leant forward. 'It's always been you. I've liked you since the first time we met at freshers' week. But back then you were with Lance and I'd just got together with Rebecca, and then we became friends. And so many times, so many times I wanted to kiss you. To hold your hand, to make love to you. But you were just so perfect. So special. I couldn't fuck it up.'

For as long as I could remember I'd been afraid to make the first move with Mike, but not anymore. We'd wasted enough time and I wasn't going to waste another second.

'It's not too late,' I said as we both edged closer, our faces now just inches away. I could feel his sweet breath on my lips. My heart thundered against my chest, desire pulsing through my veins. After years of waiting, things were finally about to happen. *Properly.*

Mike's mouth crushed onto mine. *Those lips*. They were just as soft and delicious as I'd remembered. He slid his tongue into my mouth gently and every inch of my body sparked. I'd fantasised about kissing him properly so many times over the past decade, but my imagination didn't even come close to how good this felt. It was everything I'd dreamt of and more. How had I survived this long without feeling his lips?

Our kisses became more frenzied with every second. Heat and pent-up sexual frustration flooded our lips. We'd held back our feelings for so long. It was like they were locked in a cage and now they'd been set free, we couldn't pull them back.

I tugged at his vest, pulled it over his head, then ran my hands all over his firm, muscular chest. *Damn*. Mike pushed me back gently on the sofa and straddled me. I'd wanted him badly before, but now I felt him pressed against my body, a whole new level of desire and urgency hit me.

'I want you, Mike,' I panted.

Mike lifted my top over my head, tossed it on the floor, sat up and looked at me, lying there in just my bra and jeans. 'God, Bells. You have no idea how beautiful you are. Everything you're feeling, I feel the same. But I'm worried because… there's something…'

'Shh…' I pressed my finger firmly on his lips. 'We've wasted too much time overthinking and worrying. We've got a second chance to have something special. Let's not waste it. Simple question: do you want me or not?'

'Of course! So much. It's just I…' Mike paused.

We'd both agreed we wanted to take things further, so that was all that mattered right now. I was tired of overanalysing everything. Always being sensible. Always looking ahead. For once, I just didn't want to think. I wanted to live in the moment. Worry about tomorrow, tomorrow. I couldn't let anything get in the way again. I didn't want to spend another decade filled with regrets. We had to just go for it.

I pushed Mike back on the sofa, then stood up. I unfastened my bra and whipped it off before sliding my knickers and jeans slowly down my legs. I pulled them off my ankles and stood there. Naked. I was completely vulnerable and open to more rejection, but I didn't care.

'Jesus, Bells.' Mike's eyes burned with desire. 'I knew you had a gorgeous body, but…'

Before I could catch my breath, he jumped off the sofa and scooped me up into his arms.

'I really want to bend you over this sofa and make love to you or have you up against that wall, but if you're sure you want to do this, I'm going to do things properly.' He carried me towards the bedroom.

'I don't care where we do it. I just want you inside me.'

He kicked the door open, laid me down on the bed and climbed on top of me. Mike started kissing my neck before trailing his tongue across my shoulder, then down to my breasts. He began circling my nipples and I whimpered. I couldn't help it. I felt utterly helpless. Consumed by the heat from his mouth.

As his tongue started to flick my nipple, he reached down in between my legs.

'Fuck, Bells. You are so wet. I love it.' He began stroking me and I cried out. It was like I'd been electrocuted. How could one man's touch be so powerful?

Mike started kissing down my belly button, going lower and lower, until—

Ohhhh…

The second I felt his tongue between my legs, I felt like I was going to explode.

I lifted my hips off the bed, pushing myself into him. 'You taste so good, Bells,' Mike groaned and buried his head deeper. The sensations shooting through my body were almost too much for me to handle. Hearing the sound of his deep, sexy voice and feeling the heat from his warm breath was a powerful combination.

At first he started circling me, so slowly, with long, lingering strokes. I was in heaven right now. Every inch of me trembled with desire. Mike gradually picked up the pace. The flicks of his tongue became more urgent, with each one sending me closer and closer to the edge.

I dug my nails into his back. This was the definition of pure pleasure. I wanted it to go on forever, but I knew I was close. I felt the wave building and building; the room started spinning and the blood flooded through my veins at what felt like a thousand miles an hour.

I wasn't ready for it to end. If I could just hold on for… just…

Too late.

I raised my hips, screaming with pleasure. I'd never been noisy during sex, but then I'd never experienced an orgasm like this before either. It was like I'd been hit by a tornado.

I squeezed my eyes shut in an attempt to regain consciousness. When I was able to strain them open again, I saw Mike lift his head.

'I feel like I could have done that forever.' He licked his lips.

'Definitely no complaints from me,' I gasped.

'Good to know,' he smirked.

'Although…' My chest was still heaving, but I wasn't done with him yet. I'd waited too long for this to stop half-way. 'Thinking about it, I do have one: you're still wearing clothes. I can help you to resolve this issue if you like?'

'Oh really?' Mike moved from between my legs and straddled me.

'Yes, *really*…' I tugged at his tracksuit bottoms. Excitement pulsed between my legs as I peeled them down along with his dark grey boxer shorts. As his rod sprang free, my eyes almost flew from their sockets.

The rumours really were true. I'd known Mike was a big boy, but *wow*. Length *and* girth? This was the stuff of dreams.

I slid my hands hungrily up and down him.

'Fuck, Bells,' he groaned. 'You are literally killing me right now.'

'*I'm* killing *you*?' I continued stroking him. 'You have no idea what you're doing to me. I want you inside of me so badly. *No*—it's gone past the wanting stage. I *need* you inside of me.' Using my other hand, I reached into my bedroom drawer and pulled out a condom. 'But first, it's my turn to taste you…' I rolled him over onto his back.

'I'd love that, you have no idea how much, but I won't last. Just thinking about having your mouth wrapped around my cock is enough to make me come. If you really need me inside you, Bells, let me do it, right now.'

'I'm ready.' I tossed the cushions resting on the duvet

onto the floor. I wanted to make use of every inch of this bed. 'Do it.'

Mike rolled me off him, sending me onto my back again, quickly ripped open the condom packet and made fast work of sliding it on. He spread my legs, then thrust inside.

I gasped.

Oh my God.

This was finally happening. I'd fantasised about this for what felt like forever, and after waiting so long, Mike Jones was finally inside me.

We rocked back and forth and it was good, but something wasn't right. Although I felt every inch of him, something was off.

'You're holding back.' I looked up into his eyes. Mike paused. 'I can feel it. I know you've got it in your head that I'm all sweet and innocent, but I don't want to be anymore. I want you to fuck me.' I raised my voice cautiously.

It felt weird saying that out loud. It was like something in me had shifted. I'd suddenly transformed from good girl Bella into naughty Bella and I liked it. I was sick and tired of toeing the line all the time and being so rigid. I always held back, and look where that had got me. Nowhere. I wanted to let go. To be bad for a change.

'What did you just say?' Mike frowned.

'You heard me,' I said firmly. 'I said I want you to *fuck* me, Mike. *Hard*. I've wanted this to happen since our graduation night. Actually, well before then, so don't hold back. Give me everything you've got.'

'Well, well, well…' Mike raised an eyebrow. 'I can't

remember ever hearing you swear. I had no idea you had such a dirty mouth…' His eyes darkened.

'I swear just like everyone does.' I gripped his bum firmly. 'I just save my expletives for when they're really needed. Like right now. So stopping *fucking* talking, Mike, and *fuck* me.'

'You asked for it,' Mike growled before thrusting inside of me at full power.

He got my instructions loud and clear and really went for it with gusto. As he pounded into me, I wondered if I'd bitten off more than I could chew. But those thoughts didn't last long. Now this was finally happening, I was going to make the most of every second. I wrapped my legs around his back, pushing myself into him.

He went deeper and deeper, causing my body to spark with every electric thrust. Then he reached between my legs and began stroking my swollen clit. I was going to come again. I could feel it. I dug my nails into his back and lifted my hips, pushing harder and harder against him.

And then I felt it. The pleasure tidal wave. Zipping from my head, down my spine, through my legs right down to my toes and just *everywhere*.

'I can't… I…'

I felt like someone had put a bomb inside me and pressed the activate button.

As I exploded, Mike continued to pump in and out before growling loudly. He then collapsed on top of me.

Mike rolled off onto his back, and we lay there for a while, our chests heaving.

'So… we did it…' Mike turned to face me. As we looked into each other's eyes, he ran his hands slowly down my body.

'We did… thirteen years of foreplay must be some sort of record, but it was definitely worth the wait.' I grinned.

'You have no idea how many times I'd imagined doing this, Bells. Now that I think about it, that's probably a good thing,' he laughed. 'But I didn't ever dream it would be as amazing as *this*.'

'Me either.' Having sex with a friend should feel weird or strange somehow, but for me, everything just felt so right. I'd known we connected emotionally, but the physical connection was the final piece of the puzzle. Mike really was the whole package.

'I've never been addicted to anything before, but I already know I'm addicted to you, Bells. I just want to do that again and again. I should probably warn you now… I've got a *big* appetite and all I want is you. I want to devour every inch of you. Like I said earlier, I want to have you everywhere in this flat: on your sofa, against the wall, in the shower… fuck.'

I moved my hand between his legs and started stroking him. 'No complaints from me.' I could already feel him getting hard and loved that he was so turned on. I was too. Naughty Bella had returned and was dancing on my shoulder. I couldn't wait to feel Mike, over and over. 'I'm ready to go again when you are.'

CHAPTER TWENTY-TWO

I stretched out my arms. As a flashback of the night before popped into my head, I felt a big smile spread across my face. The tingles now racing through my body and the soreness between my legs confirmed it wasn't just a dream. It really *had* happened. Three times. I'd officially moved out of the friend zone with Mike. We'd crossed the line in the most magnificent way.

I rolled over to look at him for added confirmation, but the bed was empty. Perhaps he was in the bathroom or…

No. I wouldn't allow myself to think the worst. I trusted Mike. There was no way that he would have woken up this morning and decided that us getting together was a mistake. That was in the past. Everything I'd thought about him not wanting to be with me was wrong. He liked me as much as I liked him. I felt it. We had a connection. A deep bond. We always had.

I got out of bed and checked the bathroom, kitchen and living room. There was no sign of him, and his trainers were gone.

As I returned to the bedroom, I spotted a piece of paper on the floor. It must have fallen from the bedside table. I picked it up.

Morning, beautiful Bells!

Wish our amazing time together didn't have to end, but have to go home to get changed for work. You were sleeping so peacefully, I didn't want to wake you.

See you soon!

M x

My shoulders immediately relaxed. Of course he'd need to go home. He couldn't exactly rock up to the lesson in tracksuit bottoms and that delicious vest top that clung to every inch of his solid pecs and abs. Just at that moment, I had another mental image of me removing his clothes, and my whole body sparked again.

Yesterday, round one had been swiftly followed by a second. After that, we'd fallen asleep in each other's arms for a few hours, woken up and had dinner. We'd then attempted to watch some TV on the sofa, but it wasn't long before we were at it again. By the time we'd finished, it was fast approaching midnight. Neither of us had the energy to check what time the last train and tube were, and as we agreed that we'd needed to get some sleep, I'd suggested Mike stay over. It was no surprise that I'd slept through the whole night. I hadn't had a workout like that in years. I was already looking forward to the next one…

I jumped in the shower and couldn't stop smiling as more memories of last night flooded my thoughts. After eventually dragging myself out, I slipped into a long dress, which made a change for a Monday, and floated out the door.

I looked up and the sky was bright blue. There wasn't a cloud in sight. I wasn't sure if it was just me, but the birds seemed to be singing louder than usual. I felt like bursting into song myself and skipping down the street. I couldn't remember the last time I'd felt this happy.

The train pulled into the platform right on time and I got a seat straight away. This really was shaping up to be the best Monday. A teenager opposite me had music blaring from his headphones, and rather than getting irritated, I found myself humming along.

My phone pinged and I pulled it out of my bag.

Cassie

So… I didn't hear from you last night. How'd it go?

Me

Sorry. I was busy…

Cassie

Busy, or getting busy???

Me

Yep! It happened!!! And it was AMAZING!!!

Cassie

Yay! I knew it! Sooooooo happy for you! Fill me in later, yeah? I'm already at work and my boss is breathing down my neck.

Me

Thanks, Cass! Will do. Fancy meeting at the weekend? Maybe on Saturday for lunch? Still feel bad about you leaving early yesterday. I saved you some food and put it in the freezer.

Hope your boss isn't too demanding today.

Cassie

Saturday sounds good! And no worries about yesterday. So glad it was worth it! Thanks for saving the food too. Better go. Love ya! x

I sent Cassie a row of kisses and as I did, I started thinking about how great it was kissing Mike. Even though it had only been hours since we were together, it already felt like a lifetime ago. I couldn't wait to see him again and press my lips against his. *Mmmm.*

I knew Sophia and Melody would also be keen to hear what had happened last night, so I fired off a couple of texts to let them know. Melody was the first to reply.

Melody

FINALLY!!!!

Melody

I don't like saying I told you so, but I TOLD YOU SO!! Really happy for you, Bella-boo! xoxo

I wasn't expecting Sophia to reply until after work, but minutes later, my phone pinged.

Sophia

Holy shit!!! This is the best news!! Go you! Still on for dinner on Thurs if you're able to take the night off from studying? Can't wait to hear everything!! xxx

I replied to thank her and confirm that I was definitely up for meeting. If I was seeing both Cassie and Sophia this week, I'd have to pull all-nighters probably every night to get my assignments done, but I didn't care. What Mike always said was true: life was for living. Right now I was convinced that if I looked up *cloud nine* in the dictionary, there would be a giant photo of me. Mike and I had enjoyed a magical day and night together. And knowing that my closest friends were so happy for me too just accentuated the feelings of joy.

As I entered the building, a teeny flash of fear jumped into my mind, making me wonder how things might be between us during the lesson and whether it would be awkward, but I quickly brushed those thoughts aside. I trusted Mike. Everything was going to be absolutely fine.

I literally sailed into the classroom and from the moment Mike looked up from his desk and our eyes met, I knew I was right. A smile spread across his gorgeous face. God, he looked hot. He was freshly shaven and it took every inch of self-control to resist racing over to him, running my hands across his smooth, perfectly sculpted jaw, taking his face in my hands and kissing him.

'Good morning!' I beamed.

'Morning, Bella,' Mike replied. 'Did you have a good weekend?'

'It was *amazing*, thank you.' I grinned. 'How was yours?'

'Mine was pretty amazing too, thanks. Especially yesterday…' He winked. My stomach flipped. I quickly looked around the class to see if anyone else was watching us, but we were in the clear. Faye was chatting to Petra and Craig. I went over and joined in the conversation. I needed to take my mind off Mike and my naughty thoughts. Something told me that was going to be an impossible task.

I felt a huge sense of relief. Our teaching practice session had finished and now we were just waiting for feedback.

'Faye,' said Mike.

'Yes.' Her voice trembled.

'You did great, just try to take it slow. You want to make it easier for your learners to understand. And remember, it's best to keep the TTT—teacher talking time—to a minimum. It's something that can happen to all of us when we're nervous. If you ask a question and the room falls silent, don't just talk even more. It could be that your learners don't understand, so try rephrasing the question in a shorter way and use concept-checking questions, okay?'

'Okay, thanks.' She bowed her head and scribbled down notes into her notebook.

'Bella…' Hearing Mike say my name sent shivers down my spine. He'd done that so many times last night…

'Yes?' My voice shook. I sat up straight and attempted to focus and not act like I was imagining him kissing every inch of my body, which was *exactly* what I was thinking about right now.

'Overall, you did a great job. I know you want the lesson to be perfect, and I can tell you spent a lot of time prepping, but try to avoid overplanning. When you're teaching English as another language, you have to allow for more contingency time than if you were teaching to native speakers. For example, if your learners don't understand, like I was saying to Faye, you'll need to find a different way to explain, which will add minutes to your lesson plan. If you pack too much in, you'll struggle to rejig things.'

I nodded. He was right, of course. If overplanning and overthinking were an Olympic sport, I'd definitely win gold. I'd have to work on reining it in. I was glad that Mike had been honest and wasn't giving me special treatment just because we'd started sleeping together.

'If you plan for eighty percent and have something fun like vocab bingo to fill in a couple of minutes if you need it, you'll be better off.'

'That's a good idea, thanks.' Adding games to the end of a lesson obviously wasn't something that I was used to doing.

'Anything to add, Graham?' Mike asked.

'I think you pretty much covered it,' he said. 'Just remember to grade the language to suit your learners. There were just a couple of words that might be too advanced for elementary level.'

'Okay,' I replied.

Mike went round to everyone in the class, giving his feedback and sharing the thoughts of the learners that had come in to help us practice. Afterwards, we split into groups to discuss it further. I was put with Faye and Petra.

'I know we're supposed to be talking about the TP sessions'—Petra rolled her eyes—'but can we all just take a moment to appreciate the *glory* of our tutor?' She fanned herself and licked her lips. 'Not Graham—obviously I'm talking about magnificent Mike. I swear to God he is the finest man I have ever seen. I don't see a ring on his finger. Does anyone know if he has a girlfriend?'

My eyes widened and my cheeks burned. I caught myself, then tried and failed to act casual.

'Um…,' I stuttered.

'I think he has,' Faye jumped in. I didn't know what

had given her that impression, but I was glad it took the heat off me responding.

'Shame,' Petra sighed. 'Then again, even if he has, doesn't matter. He might still be up for some fun…' She winked.

I wanted to shout 'hands off, he's mine!', but I bit my tongue. I supposed this sort of thing came with being with a man who was so attractive. But I trusted Mike. Crossing the line with me was one thing. There was no way he'd get involved with someone like Petra. I didn't think anyone in the class liked her.

Home time came around quickly. I desperately wanted to see Mike tonight, but after taking off so much time at the weekend, I had a lot to catch up on.

'Bella, do you have a minute?' Mike called out as I walked towards his desk. I'd deliberately taken a long time to pack up my books again so everyone else could leave the room.

'Course!'

Mike headed to the door, stuck his head outside, looked both ways, then closed it.

He strolled back towards me, his eyes burning, pushed me against the wall gently, then planted his lips on mine.

My heart thundered against my rib cage. God, his mouth felt so good. But this was so risky. Our lesson had only just finished. Anyone could walk back in…

He slid his tongue into my mouth and my knees buckled. Thank goodness he was holding me tight. I dropped my bag on the floor and suddenly I didn't care about what could happen.

As we kissed, it was like the whole world around us melted away. All that existed were sensations. The feel of his soft lips, the gentle flicks of his tongue, the sweet scent of his minty breath and the velvety smoothness of his chin resting on mine. I had no idea how much time passed. Probably a few minutes, but even if it was hours, it still wouldn't have been long enough.

When we reluctantly came up for air, I opened my eyes to find Mike staring at me, almost in a daze. Like he was mesmerised.

'I've been wanting to do that all day,' he growled. There was fire in his eyes again. 'That and a whole lot more…'

'*Really?*' I raised an eyebrow. 'What does *a whole lot more* involve exactly?'

'Hmmm… me, you and that desk.'

'You mean, me standing there while you sit and mark my work?' I teased.

'Not exactly. Let me clarify: you *on* my desk and me removing your knickers. With my mouth…'

I closed my eyes and groaned as I pictured the scene. The thrill of how it would feel to have Mike's head buried between my legs, combined with the idea of doing something so forbidden, made my whole body spark.

'God, I would love that,' I gasped.

'Fuck, Bells. I really don't know what to do about all of this. I want you, but we better not do anything here.'

'I wish I didn't have to study tonight. I want you too. No, I *need* you.'

'Same.' He glanced between his legs. His hard-on strained against his trousers. 'But I've got to work late tonight.' He paused. 'Unless…' He stood back and I could literally hear the cogs in his brain turning.

'What are you thinking?'

'Of a way that we can get what we want and still be able to do our work tonight. On the fifth floor, they're redecorating some of the classrooms, so they're out of action. Meet me in the one right at the end of the corridor in ten minutes. Then we can pick up from where we left off…'

'Okay,' I said before more questions about whether we might get caught invaded my thoughts. 'See you there in ten.'

CHAPTER TWENTY-THREE

I tiptoed up the stairs, looking behind me every few seconds to check no one was there. With every step, my heart beat faster. I felt like a criminal trying to avoid capture.

When I reached the fifth floor, it was eerily quiet. Most of the classrooms up here had glass walls, so were more revealing than the room we used for our lessons downstairs. Thankfully, though, there were frosted panels across the middle, so you could only see in if you went right up and peered over.

I walked to the end of the corridor and saw that the door was cracked open. I stepped inside. There were white sheets covering the furniture and I could smell freshly painted walls. As I looked towards the back, I saw Mike perched on top of an uncovered desk in the corner, smirking.

'Well, hello there,' he said.

'Hello,' I replied. As I walked over, Mike stood up,

pulled me into him, wrapped his arms around my waist and closed his mouth over mine. My lips moved hungrily against his. He spun me around and pushed me gently onto the desk.

'You still up for doing this, here?' he panted.

'Yes.' The word spilled out before I even had time to think. 'You don't know how many times I've thought about you taking me on a desk.'

'I doubt it's as much as I have.'

'Are you sure it's okay, though? I don't want us to get caught and you get fired or something.'

'It is risky, but all the workmen have gone home and most of the lessons have finished apart from a couple of evening classes on the first floor, so there's no reason for anyone to come up here. We should be fine.'

As soon as those last four words fell from his mouth, I pulled him closer, tugging on his belt. His hands slid underneath my maxi dress and glided up my thighs, causing the fabric to rise higher and higher. My whole body vibrated with anticipation.

I unzipped his trousers and reached inside his boxers, curling my fingers around him. Mike groaned, then crushed his mouth against mine. The pace of the kiss quickened and his fingers climbed until they were between my legs, brushing against my underwear. He slipped his hand underneath the smooth fabric.

'Mmm,' he groaned, kissing my neck, 'You're soaked, Bells. I love it.'

'Can you blame me? I'm spread across a desk with a hot guy about to make love to me. This is the stuff I see in films.'

'Oh really?' He looked up at me, desire burning in his eyes. 'What kind of films do *you* watch?'

'You know. Just films…,' I panted. I was finding it hard to talk whilst he was touching me. Mike continued stroking my clit with one hand whilst reaching in his back pocket with the other and pulling out a condom. 'Here.' I took the condom. 'Let me do it.'

I released my hand from around him, opened the pack and slid it down him. I was glad at least he was prepared. I didn't have any protection with me. Lately I'd never had any need to carry anything around in my purse.

Before I'd had a chance to catch my breath, Mike had rolled my dress up around my waist, pushed my knickers to one side, pulled me to the edge of the desk and slammed inside me.

'Oh God,' I groaned, wrapping my legs around him. I rocked my hips in time with his as he thrust deeper and deeper.

Mike started kissing my neck again, pulled down the top of my dress, followed by my bra, then took my nipple in his mouth, sending shockwaves through me. I raked my hands through his hair and the scent of his delicious woody shampoo flooded my nostrils.

As he continued sliding in and out of me, I felt like I was about to explode. I couldn't believe this was really happening.

Here I was in a classroom with Mike, my teacher, screwing me on the desk. Even though it was after hours, there were still lessons going on in the building. Someone could walk in at any moment. A trainee from our class. A cleaner. Even another tutor. This was so dangerous. And yet somehow I didn't care. I didn't want him to stop. It felt too good.

'We shouldn't be doing this,' Mike whispered in my ear, as if reading my mind. If I was feeling more like myself—sweet, good, pure Bella—I would have pushed him away. Told him he was right. That this was totally wrong and illogical. And I almost did, until he picked up the pace and pumped in and out. Harder and faster.

'Oh God.' I tried to catch my breath. That felt unbelievable. There was no going back now. 'I know we shouldn't, but... please don't stop. I'm close.' I threw my head back, gripped his bottom and pushed him further inside.

Fire burned through me. I never normally reached the edge of climax this quickly, but the thrill of doing something bad, having Mike's mouth and hands on my body and feeling every inch of him inside of me, was an explosive cocktail. I honestly didn't know how much more pleasure I could handle.

'Close isn't enough.' Mike lifted his head from my breast. 'I want to take you all the way.' He released a hand from around my waist, reached down and circled my clit with firm strokes, causing it to pulse, then spark like a firework display.

I gasped sharply as my legs shook. Mike wanted to take me all the way, and as my whole body pulsed, I knew I'd reached my destination. My gasps became long, loud moans as I shuddered, then completely fell apart.

Mike continued thrusting until he came and collapsed on my shoulder.

'Wow,' I panted. 'That was...'

'Yeah...' Mike's chest heaved and he struggled to speak. 'It really was.'

My head was spinning. In the best way. Mike rested his face on my chest. I didn't want to move from here. I just wanted to sit and enjoy the feelings rushing around my body.

We stayed still for a few minutes, the sound of our heavy breathing vibrating through the room.

Just as we'd caught our breath, I heard a noise and froze.

'What's up?' Mike whispered.

'Did you hear something?'

He stepped back and zipped himself up quickly. We both glanced at the door, then over the frosted glass panel. There was no sign of anyone. *Thank God.*

The reality of what we'd just done hit me. I climbed down from the desk and my dress dropped back down to my ankles. My legs wobbled. It was hard to stand.

'We should go,' said Mike, echoing my thoughts. 'Just in case. You leave first, then I'll wait awhile before going down.'

'Okay.' I nodded. 'I'll go to the bathroom on the third floor to clean up and will text you once I've left the building.'

'Cool.' He leant forward and gave me a long, slow kiss. 'Speak later.'

'See you in class, tomorrow, *sir*,' I smirked.

I smiled, then walked towards the door, glancing both ways before slipping into the corridor and down the stairs.

Well, that was unexpected.

This time, I glided down the staircase. I was buzzing.

If someone had told me forty-eight hours ago that I

would be sneaking out of a classroom after just having sex on a desk with Mike, I wouldn't have believed them. I didn't do that kind of thing. It was so out of character. So unscripted. So risky. But what Mike had said in the lesson earlier was right—I always overplanned. Thought too much. If this was what happened when you just went with the flow, I was converted. I felt free. *Alive*. Naughty...

And I couldn't wait to be bad all over again.

CHAPTER TWENTY-FOUR

I collapsed on the bed. If we kept this up, I wouldn't need that gym membership I'd been considering.

It was now Tuesday evening, and when Mike had arrived earlier, we'd lasted all of twenty seconds before crashing into the bedroom. There was something about seeing him dressed in his smart trousers and crisp white shirt with the sleeves rolled up to his arms and the top buttons undone that drove me wild.

After showering and cleaning up the kitchen, I'd returned to the bedroom and looked through my drawers for a T-shirt to sleep in. I spotted an old one at the back and giggled. I wondered if Mike would remember it. I pulled it out, ready to show him. The shower switched off and soon afterwards, Mike came in with a towel wrapped around his toned waist.

My eyes bulged and my whole body tingled. That sight would never get old. I walked over and tugged at the towel.

'Oh, no, you don't,' Mike smirked, waving his finger. 'No more sex for you tonight, young lady.'

'What?' I cried. 'Why?'

'Why?' He climbed under the duvet, threw the towel onto a chair and casually put his hands behind his head. Didn't he realise that seeing his bare chest and muscular arms like that wasn't helping me fan the burning flames between my legs? 'One, because I've got to teach tomorrow, so I'd either have to leave now or at the crack of dawn to get changed, and two, because as much as I want you, I don't want this to just be all about sex. We don't know how much time we have together, so when you think about me, I don't want to be remembered only for the number of orgasms I gave you.'

'Sounds like a pretty good way to be remembered if you ask me. *Mike Jones: Giver Of Multiple Orgasms*. Has a nice ring to it, don't you think?'

Mike gave a half smile. His comment about us not knowing how much time we had together sounded a bit morbid, but because of what had happened to his friends, I knew he was all about creating memories and making the most of life, so I understood where he was coming from. From what he'd told me, I guessed that sometimes Mike's grief struck him at odd times, so what he'd said was probably down to him reflecting in the shower.

'Okay.' I sat at the edge of the bed. 'I promise to try not to objectify you and use you just as a sex object. Tell me what I can do to show you that I see you as more than just a piece of meat.'

'First I need to know how you're getting on with your assignments.'

'Not too bad. After I got back from our *extra lesson*

yesterday, I studied for about six hours, then during lunch today, and I crammed in two hours before you arrived this evening.' I was surprised I even had the energy to go two rounds tonight.

'Good. Don't want you falling behind because of me. In that case, if you think you can handle taking a few hours off, let's go on a proper date this week. We can dine somewhere al fresco and enjoy the weather. Have fun together outside of the bedroom.'

'I thought we did that yesterday… in the classroom…' I smirked.

'Yeah, about yesterday…' He paused. 'I don't normally do stuff like that. It was just… you do things to me, Bells. When I'm with you, sometimes I just lose my mind. All logic goes out the window.'

'I know it was a heat-of-the-moment thing. I felt the same. Sensible Bella wouldn't do anything like that either. Even kissing in public is a stretch for me.' I blushed, thinking I didn't even know who I was anymore. 'And of course I'll go on a date with you. I'm meeting Sophia for dinner tomorrow, but I'm free on Thursday if you are? Obviously it'll be an absolute nightmare having to spend time with a smart, gorgeous hunk like you, but I'm up for the challenge.' I grinned. Since coming out of the shower, Mike had become really serious, so I hoped my attempt at a joke would help lighten the mood.

The corner of his mouth twitched. It seemed like he was softening again, which was good. Hopefully showing him the T-shirt would make him break into a full smile.

'Look what I found.' I reached for the T-shirt and held it up.

'No way!' He beamed. 'I can't believe you've still got it!'

It was a *Friends* T-shirt that Mike had bought me for Christmas one year. He had the same one. I remembered the gift tag saying 'Friends Forever', which had made me happy and sad at the same time. Happy because I knew I did want to have Mike in my life forever, but sad because I knew I wanted him to be more than that.

Sounds cheesy now, but we used to wear the T-shirts every Friday night when we watched *Friends*. That half an hour was a little slice of precious Bella and Mike time. I used to hate when the credits rolled because I knew it meant that after we'd discussed our thoughts on what had happened in the episode, he'd get dressed and meet Rebecca or his mates and be gone all night. Sometimes Melody would drag me out or I'd meet Sophia, but usually I stayed at home, studied, read a book or tidied the house. Anything to try not to think about what Mike was doing or what I'd like him to do to me.

Finding this T-shirt today had a new significance, though, because Mike was back in my life and now we were more than friends, which was what I'd always wanted. It might have taken a long time for us to get to this point, but the fact that we had was all that mattered.

'Of course I've still got it!' I pulled it over my head. 'And it still fits! What happened to yours?'

'It's probably at my dad's. I saw it a few years ago when he summoned me to clear out my room because he was converting it into a gym. I attempted to try it on, and even though it didn't fit me, I couldn't bring myself to throw it away.'

That was no surprise. Mike had filled out a lot since

then in the best possible way. His arms and chest had always been well defined, but now his muscles were even bigger, so that large T-shirt would definitely be a tight squeeze.

'Hopefully your dad hasn't chucked it out.'

'He wouldn't dare! Anyway, time for bed.' He turned off the light. 'Night, Bells.'

Going straight to sleep was definitely a good idea. Especially if I planned to go out two evenings in a row. Easier said than done, though.

Mike sleeping naked in my bed and not being able to do anything? Something told me my willpower was about to be tested.

CHAPTER TWENTY-FIVE

I packed up my notepad and pens and left the library. I'd been here since the lesson had ended a couple of hours ago to help my guilt about going out with Sophia tonight. Luckily, I was meeting her at a restaurant in Soho, so it wouldn't take too long to get there.

I walked into the small, traditional-looking Italian restaurant. As the waiter showed me to the table towards the back, I was surprised to see that Sophia had already arrived.

'What the…?' I said as she stood up to give me a hug.

'I know! I'm here before you!'

'What happened?'

'I told myself I wasn't going to let *anything* get in the way of seeing you tonight. I couldn't wait to hear all about what happened with you and sexy Mike. I know this is a big deal!'

Sophia arriving early was a big deal too. She often worked fifteen-hour days and had been even busier since winning her recent big pitch, so I knew that every second counted. We were already doing pretty well, meeting up twice in the past few weeks. During her really busy periods, it wasn't unusual for us to go months without seeing each other.

'It really is, Soph. I don't even know where to start! Maybe we should order drinks and food first. I've got a *lot* to tell you!'

I filled her in on the full story of what had happened on our graduation night (now Mike and I were together and had cleared up what was really going through his mind when he left, it was less embarrassing).

After previously getting Mike's permission to mention it to my closest friends, I also shared basic details about the tragedy he'd experienced, and understandably, Sophia was horrified.

I then told her about the near-miss on Saturday, how things had finally come together on Sunday, and of course our classroom escapade on Monday evening.

'There is no way you are telling me that you let Mike fuck you on the desk at school. *No way*.'

'Sssh!' I looked around nervously, suddenly feeling self-conscious. 'It was a lot less crude than it sounds. But it was really exciting.'

'I bet! I'm just shocked. I mean, I'm a good girl when it comes to sex. I'm probably more vanilla than a tub of Häagen-Dazs, especially these days. But *you*, my dear bestie, you're even *more* innocent, so hearing this is difficult to get my head around.'

'Believe me: no one is more surprised than I am. It's like Mike brings out something in me.'

'Yeah! Your inner *freak*!' Sophia laughed. 'Sounds like you've been having some epic sex sessions. Must feel so good to be desired like that…' Her voice trailed off.

'Everything okay with you and Rich?'

'Yeah… fine. Just you know, working long hours doesn't leave much time for fun in or outside of the bedroom.'

Although Sophia said things were okay between her and her long-term boyfriend, Rich, lately I'd be sensing that all wasn't as well as she made out. He was a lovely guy and I know he'd always been super supportive of her business, but something just seemed like it was missing.

I was also worried that Sophia was so focused on work that she'd forgotten how to live. I should know. I'd been guilty of doing the same in the past to some extent. But now I realised the joys of being less rigid, I wanted my friend to experience the benefits too.

Still, I couldn't claim to understand the pressure she was under. Being a teacher was very different to running a company. I supposed shouldering the responsibility for the livelihoods of staff and big client budgets meant fun had to take a back seat.

'Want to talk about it?' I softened my voice.

'God, no!' Sophia shook her head. 'We're not here to chat about me. I want to hear more about *you* and what it's like to *get it on* with your ten-year crush! Or are we saying it's a thirteen-year crush, seeing as you liked him when you first started uni?'

'Oh God! Thirteen years sounds so sad. Let's stick with ten years. Slightly less tragic. Plus, that's when we were both single—I started to crush on him hard and I *really* hoped things would have happened.'

'Ten-year crush it is, then! Sooo…'

'So… to answer your question, it's kind of difficult to put into words what it's like for us to finally be together. It still seems so surreal. Mike makes me feel so… alive. It's as if during the ten years that we were apart, I just existed. Life was good, but now, everything just feels so much *better*.'

'Multiple orgasms will do that to you!' She grinned. 'I'm glad he lived up to his reputation. It could have gone completely the other way.'

'That's true.' In my mind I'd put him on a pedestal and built him up to be this sex god, so imagine if when it came down to it, we just hadn't clicked? Thankfully that wasn't a concern. 'He definitely delivered on his rep and then some! Now I understand why those women always screamed so loudly.' I pictured myself at uni trying to sleep with a pillow over my head, desperately trying to drown out the noises of Mike and whoever was in his bed. 'We have this insane connection. This is *it*, Soph. Mike's *the one*. I've never felt so happy!' My heart flipped.

There was no doubt about it. Mike had blown my belief about it being impossible to find a man who was the total package out of the water. He had it all. Brains, amazing personality, good looks, chemistry and so much more.

'Oh, darling!' Sophia squeezed my hand. 'I'm so happy for you. No one deserves this more. Especially after how long you've waited. It was fate, you two meeting again. And Mike? How does he feel about everything? Do you reckon he's on the same page? I know in the past he's had some commitment issues…'

'He feels the same,' I said quickly. 'I can sense it. He

said that's why things didn't happen before, because he wasn't ready and wanted to do things properly with me.'

'That sounds promising.'

'I know I've spoken a lot about the amazing sex we've been having, but Mike said he wants me to remember him for more than just that, so he's taking me on a real date tomorrow.'

'*Remember him*?' Sophia frowned.

'Yeah.' I waved my hands dismissively. 'Just a turn of phrase—because of what happened to his friends. That's why he often talks about creating memories and living life to the full, that kind of thing. That's all he meant.'

'Hmmm.' Sophia rested her finger on her chin. 'Interesting choice of words. Anyway, I suppose it's great that he wants to take things out of the bedroom and spend quality time with you.'

'It really is.' I grinned. We could very easily spend every night at my place eating in and rolling around my bed. I certainly wouldn't complain. But him wanting us to go out publicly, especially given the whole blurred tutor-trainee lines right now, showed he was taking it more seriously than the one-night-only approach he'd taken to dating whenever he and Rebecca were on one of their many breaks.

'I love the fact that you're throwing caution to the wind and living in the moment, but just be careful. I don't want you getting too carried away and ending up hurt.'

The mention of something bad happening instantly made my stomach sink. I knew Sophia didn't mean any harm, though. We were both acute overthinkers who planned and questioned almost everything, so she was only looking out for me.

'I hear what you're saying. I'm desperately trying to hold back and be pragmatic and sensible about it all, like I normally would, but it's really difficult. I just want to shout from the rooftops that we're finally together. It was so hard speaking to my mum this morning and not saying anything. She'd be over the moon. Dad, not so much, but hey.' I shrugged my shoulders as if it didn't bother me. Of course it did, but I didn't want to think about that right now.

'Oh yeah… I forgot how much they hated each other.'

'Yep,' I sighed. 'On the one hand, I know I should keep calm—I mean, it's only been a few days since we got together. But then on the other, I've always been so cautious about everything. So part of me says I shouldn't overthink. I should just live in the moment and feel all of the emotions.'

The thought of letting go and being completely free made my heart beat faster. It was like a mixture of fear and excitement.

'I'm no expert…' Sophia took a sip of her G&T. 'I've been out of the dating scene for what feels like forever. But everything you're saying and feeling seems perfectly normal to me. It could just be a case of finding a balance. You've spent so long holding back your feelings from Mike and playing it safe, and that caused you to be apart for ages. So I reckon you should continue that leap of faith, enjoy your time with him, but also keep tuning into your gut to be sure he definitely is as committed as you are…'

That was the second time Sophia had mentioned Mike's commitment. It was true. He had had commitment issues in the past. That was another reason why I'd thought that if, by some miracle, he did like me, he probably wouldn't be looking for anything long-term, so that had ruled him firmly out of the relationship equation. I knew that I wanted a family, so the person I was with needed to want that too.

But after he'd helped that little boy at the skate park, I remembered Mike had said he *did* want to settle down, and the feelings he had for me seemed genuine. So even though it was very early days, my gut felt good. I was sure he was in it for the long haul. Just like me.

Sophia went to the toilet and I pulled my phone out of my bag. There was a text from Mike with the details for tomorrow evening.

Mmm, tomorrow…

It was crazy. I'd only seen Mike a few hours ago and I already had withdrawal symptoms. I really missed him. I had it *bad*.

I couldn't wait to hold, kiss and make love to him again. Our date couldn't come quickly enough.

CHAPTER TWENTY-SIX

I t felt like there were dozens of butterflies in my stomach, dancing with excitement. I was standing outside a tube station in Kensington, waiting for Mike to meet me for our date.

I still didn't know where he was taking me. When he'd texted last night, he said it was at a 'secret location'. I couldn't wait to find out where we were going.

'Excuse me, miss, are you alone?'

I spun around to see Mike flashing his incredible smile. One thing he had told me was that the dress code for tonight was 'Beach Party', and he was definitely dressed for the occasion. He'd changed into a colourful Hawaiian shirt which looked surprisingly cool and a pair of dark jean shorts that showed off his solid calves.

'Not anymore.' I grinned before leaning over to kiss him firmly on the lips.

'Mmm, lucky me. You look incredible.' Mike kissed me again. I'd changed out of the jeans I wore to class and was wearing my favourite orange maxi dress and sandals. 'I missed you last night.'

'Me too.' Hearing him say that made my heart sing.

Mike took my hand and led me down one road and then another. It was a lovely warm summer evening, so it was the perfect weather for a stroll. A few minutes later, Mike stopped in front of a hotel.

'We're here.'

'A hotel?' I frowned. So much for not making things between us just about sex…

'Oh… no. We're not here for that. Actually…' Mike reached into a leather rucksack on his shoulder and pulled out his tie. 'Do you mind if I blindfold you?'

'So you take me to a hotel and then ask to blindfold me and yet I'm supposed to believe this has nothing to do with you wanting to have your wicked way with me?' I laughed.

'Yes! I promise. I want it to be a surprise.'

'Okay. I warn you, though, I'm wearing mascara and eyeliner, so I can't guarantee I won't get it all over your tie.'

'Don't worry. And I'll try not to smudge your make-up. I know how long it takes to do that pretty wing thing in the corners.' He smiled. He was right. Thankfully when I'd done my eye make-up in the toilets at school this evening, it hadn't taken too long, which was surprising as I didn't normally wear a lot of eyeliner, but there were still days when I just couldn't get it even.

Mike came up behind me and lifted the tie over my head. I could feel the heat from his body and his scent flooded my nostrils. Everything went dark as I felt him gently tie a knot at the back. He took my hand and a sense of calm rushed over me. Having his big palm wrapped over mine was just so reassuring somehow.

'Okay, walk forward. There's a small step coming up… just here,' Mike said. I lifted my feet and then followed him slowly. 'Not far to go now.' I could hear music. The volume increased the more we walked. It sounded tropical. The smell of a barbecue hit me, and I felt my mouth watering. 'Wait here, Bells.'

I heard Mike give his name to someone and say he had a reservation for two. A minute or so later I sensed him standing in front of me. 'I'm just putting something over your head, okay?'

'Okay,' I said, intrigued to know where we were and when we could get stuck into the food because it smelt divine. Mike then went behind me and untied his tie.

'You can look now.'

I opened my eyes, and *wow*. How was this even possible? It was like we'd been transported from the streets of London to some sort of tropical paradise. There were palm trees, real sand, a beach hut with a thatched roof and a guy dressed in a Hawaiian shirt serving a couple at the bar. At the back was a chef in front of a BBQ and it was all set against some sort of painted sea view backdrop which was really authentic.

I looked down to see that Mike had put a flower garland over my head. He was wearing one too, along with a pair of hilarious yellow-and-green sunglasses, which had palm trees on the top.

'Welcome!' said a waitress clutching a tray of coconut shells filled with bright red liquid. 'Would you like a cocktail?'

'I'd love one!' I took the shell, which had a straw and

umbrella inside. So cool. It smelt like it had a lot of rum in it. Reminded me of when Mum got together with Aunt Janet and they'd make cocktails and reminisce about their childhood in St Lucia. I'd love to go back there one day and learn more about where Mum had grown up.

After Mike took his cocktail, he led us over to a couple of deck chairs and we sat down. 'This place is amazing!'

'Yeah. When I saw it, I thought it'd be perfect for our date. Bells…' He took my hands in his. 'I'm really sorry that we didn't get to Bali together. I'd always wanted to go on holiday with you, so I know this doesn't exactly compare, but I thought for the evening we could just, you know, pretend that we are away together.'

'That's so lovely. I already feel like I'm on holiday. They've done a great job with the place. The surroundings, the music and these cocktails. It's perfect. And even though we haven't been on holiday yet, there will be plenty of time to do that in the future. We can still go there.'

'I hope so. What would you like to eat?' Mike quickly picked up the menu. 'They've got burgers, so that's definitely a given, and seafood. I hear the ice creams are pretty good too.'

'Yes, to everything!'

'Great!' Mike jumped up. 'I'm on it.'

Whilst Mike sorted out the food, I slipped off my sandals. It felt so nice to feel the sand beneath my toes. Being here made me long for a holiday, somewhere hot.

I wondered what Mike's plans were for the half-term holidays in October. Maybe we could go somewhere together.

'Juicy burger, fresh off the barbecue, along with

seafood skewers and a spicy hot dog for my beautiful Bells.'

'Why, thank you.' I took the plate from Mike as he sat down on the deck chair beside me.

'I see you've made yourself comfortable.' He glanced down at my feet.

'Couldn't resist. I feel like I'm on holiday. Thanks for arranging this. You were right. It's nice to get out and make the most of the weather.'

'You're welcome. Glad you like it.'

'So, I was just thinking about holidays. You were always one to have a million and one destinations on your to-visit list. What's on it these days?' I thought this was a safer question than asking directly whether he wanted us to go away in a couple of months. I didn't want to come on too strong.

'So many places.'

'Like where?'

'Um, Asia, you know… like Vietnam… places like that.'

'Haven't you been there already?'

'Yeah.' Mike glanced down at his cocktail, then took a large sip. 'What about you?'

'I haven't really thought about it that much. Normally I'd go and visit my parents at their other place in Cornwall, but obviously I've been busy. Maybe I could squeeze in a mini-break or long weekend somewhere once the course is over, before I have to go back to work.' I left the comment in the air, hoping he'd pick up on it or maybe suggest we do something together.

'Cool…' He shifted in his seat.

'How about you?' I filled the silence. He hadn't got the

hint, so I tried being more direct. 'What's your plan once the course finishes next Friday?'

'Um, I've got some stuff… kind of in the pipeline.' He took a bite of his burger, removed the straw from the cocktail, then downed the rest. 'Talking of work, did you speak to Sophia about getting some voluntary business English teaching experience? We could look at some websites now to see if any companies are looking for volunteers.'

'Now?' I frowned. 'But we're supposed to be on a date.'

'I don't mind. Why don't you do a search on your phone whilst I go and get us some more drinks?' Mike jumped up and headed to the bar. I looked down at the little table. The waitress had just bought over two extra coconut shells, which were resting in front of us. They were both full, so I didn't understand why he'd got up so abruptly.

And I knew it was kind of him to offer to help me look for opportunities, but why now? I didn't want it to dominate our night together.

Whilst Mike was waiting to be served, a woman with a clipboard approached him. Mike looked over at me, smiled and nodded. Then he left the queue and started walking back towards me.

'Change of plan. You're right. This is supposed to be a fun date. All career stuff is now banned. So no more talk of lessons, teaching, work or future plans. Let's just focus on tonight. Deal?' He held out his hand.

I paused for a moment, feeling confused about what he'd said earlier, but then pushed it out of my mind. I wasn't going to overthink. I liked the sound of enjoying ourselves much more.

'Deal.' I shook it firmly.

'Glad to hear it. Because I've just signed us up for a limbo competition.' He grinned.

'Limbo?'

'Yep.' Oh no. I winced, thinking about how embarrassing it would be. I'd never been good at beach games.

'The winner gets a bottle of champers. We can totally do it. Starts in ten minutes, so just enough time to finish our food.'

Mike made quick work of the rest of his burger, kebab and sausages and we both inhaled our cocktails. It was so sweet I almost forgot there was any alcohol in it, but I quickly remembered when I went to stand up. Wobbly, alcohol-fuelled legs probably weren't ideal for limboing, but I definitely felt a bit more relaxed. Mike took my hand and led me over to the back of the garden, where the limbo pole had been set up. It looked like the woman was signing up a few more guests.

'Ready to win?' He kissed me softly on the lips.

'I don't know about winning, but I'll give it my best shot!'

The lady explained the rules, and before we knew it, we were all lined up ready to see how low we could go. The calypso music blared from the speakers, and we all took it in turns to walk underneath the limbo stick.

The bar started really high, so I was instantly lured into a false sense of security. But as it got lower, I realised my weak knees weren't going to last much longer.

Everyone clapped as I approached the pole once again with my back facing towards the ground, then bent myself backwards. I narrowly missed it touching my chest. Mike whooped with pride at my efforts before gliding underneath like the stick was twenty feet high.

A few of the guests started dropping out. That meant my turn came round even faster. I looked at the bar and didn't rate my chances. I had to try, though. I edged closer and bent my knees and body as far back as I could. Just as I thought I'd made it, my chin caught the bar. I lost my balance and fell backwards into the sand. Dammit.

Mike rushed over and scooped me up. 'You okay?'

'Yeah.' I wrapped my hands around his neck. 'Just wounded pride. I was so close.'

'You did great.' He pushed his mouth on mine and gave me the sweetest kiss.

'Mmm, I might have to topple over more often if that's what I get as a reward,' I said when we came up for air.

'You know you don't have to do anything to get a kiss from me. I'm already yours.'

My heart melted and I pushed my lips firmer onto his. At that moment I didn't care that we were surrounded by people or in the middle of a competition. Mike was the only person that existed.

The cheers from the other guests brought us back to our senses.

'Look at us. Getting carried away again like a couple of horny teenagers!' I laughed. 'You're a bad influence. Let's continue this kiss later. You've got a bottle of champagne to win for us.'

'Okay.' He put me back down on the ground. 'If my Bells wants a bottle of champagne, that's exactly what she's going to get!'

He gave me another swift kiss, then ran back over to the pole and breezed underneath again. There were only two other people in the running, and my money was definitely on Mike. It would be difficult for anyone else to match the power of his strong, muscular legs.

Three quickly became two. Mike swung his hips to the music as he approached. He was confident and it showed. After he glided below the pole, I cheered. The other guy didn't even get halfway underneath before tumbling over, and Mike was declared the winner.

'Congratulations!' shouted the organiser.

Mike lifted me up, spun me around and kissed me. We then walked over to claim our bottle of champagne.

'You did it!'

'*We* did it!' Mike corrected. 'Your kiss gave me the power to win, so it was a team effort.'

'If you say so,' I laughed.

'Do you mind posing for a photo?' said the organiser, who was now clutching a camera.

'Only if you send us copies,' said Mike. 'You up for a photo together?'

'Yeah, okay.' I smiled.

Mike and I struck a few different poses, culminating in him wrapping his arms around me and giving me another lingering kiss, whilst the lady continued snapping away.

'You two make a beautiful couple,' she said. My heart fluttered with happiness. 'If you write down your email addresses, I'll send you the photos.'

'Thanks.' I scribbled down my address. Mike wrote down his and we returned to the bar.

'Up for one more cocktail before we head home?'

'Definitely.'

'And I hope you don't mind'—Mike turned to face me —'but I packed a few bits to leave at your place. You know, toothbrush, toiletries, change of boxers so I can stay tonight. Those early-morning treks back to get changed were killing me. I left my trousers, shoes and a shirt in my locker at school. Or you're welcome to come and stay at mine, but it's a bit basic and not as close to a station as your flat is.'

'Of course I don't mind.' I beamed. We'd had a wonderful date together and he wanted to leave some stuff at my place. That was a good sign. Not just for tonight. It showed he was thinking ahead. About staying over for multiple nights. 'It's a great idea!'

And just like that I knew. This really *was* the start of something special. He was on exactly the same page as me. Mike wanted us to have a proper relationship and a real future together just as much as I did. There was no need for Sophia to worry about Mike's commitment. Everything between us was going to be just fine.

CHAPTER TWENTY-SEVEN

I couldn't believe it was the last week of the course. The last three weeks had flown by. Mike hadn't been joking when he'd said on the first day that it was intense.

I hadn't seen him since he'd left my place on Friday night. We both agreed that with such a big week ahead of me, I had to dedicate the whole weekend to making sure I'd done everything I needed to.

After Mike had gone, I went into the bedroom and found a bright yellow gift box on the bed. Inside, it was filled with little pampering treats, including a scented candle, bubble bath, an eye mask, a mini bottle of Chardonnay and a pack of cheese balls. He'd also written a note.

Hey, Bells!

Just a few goodies that might come in handy after burning the midnight oil. Don't work too hard!

M x

. . .

So sweet. I'd put that to good use on Saturday night after a long day of studying.

The only time I'd left the house was to buy a jewellery-making kit for Melody that I'd spotted in the window of a craft shop on the high street the day before. I'd posted it straight away, hoping it would arrive today and cheer her up. She was still struggling to find work. She'd also found damp and mould growing in the bedroom she shared with Andrea and the landlord was dragging his feet about fixing it. I really felt for her.

I'd got a lot done on Saturday and Sunday, but still had a pile of work to finish, which meant I couldn't see Mike tonight. Not even for a little after-hours fun upstairs in the empty classroom. Mike had a meeting straight after the lesson, so that was ruled out too.

Sounded crazy, but I was climbing the walls. I wanted him so badly. Before Mike and I had been reunited, I'd easily gone several months without sex, but strangely now, I was yearning for it after just a few days. I was addicted to him. And I think knowing I couldn't have him made me want him even more.

Everyone filed out of the classroom for lunch and I hung back. I stood several feet away from his desk, in case somebody walked past the open door.

'I miss you,' I whispered. 'I *want* you.' Mike's eyes met mine and instantly darkened.

'I miss you too.' He lowered his voice. 'Do you know how many times I've had to stop my dick from hitting the desk every time I've looked over at you today? Feels like I haven't felt you for weeks, not days.'

'I wish we could be together.' I took a step closer. 'Even for a few minutes.'

'Well… there's only one decorator working on the classroom upstairs now, and I heard in the staff room earlier that he'd called in sick, so…'

'Sounds like it's fate.' I felt a tingle race down my spine as I thought of the thrills we'd had upstairs before.

'Meet you there in ten?' Mike grinned mischievously.

'Make it five.' I turned on my heel, headed for the door, then hurried along the corridor.

There were students milling around after their lessons. Probably deciding whether to go out for lunch or head to the library, the canteen or coffee shop on the ground floor. I slipped through the door to the staircase. There were a few guys a couple of flights above, but they exited on the third floor to go to the library.

I opened the door to the fifth floor and it was deserted, just like before. *Excellent*.

Mike wasn't there when I arrived, so I made myself comfortable, propping myself on the desk in the corner. Memories of last time rushed through my mind. I was looking forward to a repeat performance.

Whilst I waited, I took a textbook out of my bag and started reading it.

'Hey,' Mike whispered as he walked towards me. I put the book on the desk beside me and almost melted into a puddle when Mike's mouth crashed against mine.

Good Lord.

He kissed with so much passion. Mike trailed kisses from my lips, along my cheek, down my neck and across my chest.

'Ohhhhh…,' I groaned.

'Let's try the chair today.' Mike leant over and pulled it out. 'Please take a seat,' he smirked before crawling under the desk directly in front of it. I watched as he grabbed fistfuls of my maxi dress and pushed it up to my waist. Next, he bit the top of my knickers and started dragging them down with his teeth.

Oh. My. God.

I raised my hips partly to make it easier for him, but mostly because I was overcome with pleasure. He hadn't even touched me yet and I already felt like I was going to explode.

Just as he buried his head between my legs and put his mouth on me, sucking oh-so-slowly, I heard a noise. I bolted up in the chair.

'I think there's someone coming!' I whispered. Mike stopped. The sound of footsteps grew louder.

'Shit!' Mike poked his head out from the desk to look, then dived back underneath. I quickly pulled the dust sheet over it so he was obscured, pushed the chair right up against it so that only the top half of my body was immediately visible, grabbed the textbook I'd been reading before and held it up in front of my face.

A second later, Petra's head peered around the door. She was about to leave when she spotted me and came in.

'*Ahhh…* hello, Bella,' she smirked. 'What are you doing here?'

'I'm, erm… studying. I came up here because it's quiet.'

'Oh, really?' She frowned. 'Why don't you just use the library?'

'It was… noisy… strange for a library to be noisy, I know,' I rescued myself. It was a ridiculous thing to say. 'I just find it easier to think up here.'

Petra's eyes darted around the room. I wondered if she

could see Mike's feet under the desk. Hopefully it was covered like the bottom half of my body. Just as I was wondering that, I felt Mike's fingers gently stroking my clit. Either he thought she'd left or he was a thrill seeker, getting off on the fact that we'd almost got caught.

I should have been mad because I found it hard enough to concentrate on lying without him touching me, but the sensations were doing all sorts of wonderful things to my body. It felt so good, I wanted him to continue.

Oh God...

My toes curled against the base of my sandals and I gripped the book tighter. My whole body vibrated.

And never mind Petra seeing Mike's feet. My dress was literally around my waist, so if she came any closer and saw me from the side, she might get a glimpse of my naked bum.

'Have you seen Mike?'

'Mike?' My voice went up several octaves as Mike slid his fingers inside of me. I tried and failed to stifle a gasp. That felt unbelievable. 'I... I...' I struggled to speak. 'Our tutor? Why would... I... why would I have seen him?'

'I just thought I saw him come up here, that's all...'

Oh no...

Mike stopped.

Things just got real.

Jesus. What the hell was I doing?

Suddenly I came to my senses. I was up in a classroom in the middle of the day, with hundreds of students in the building, with my knickers on the floor and my teacher's hands in between my legs. One of the other trainees in my class had just come into the room and almost caught us in the act.

Mike could get in big trouble for this. Irrespective of our history. And who knew what they could do to me? Throw me off the course? Would his assessments of me be invalidated or be seen as biased because we were sleeping together?

This was crazy. Stupid. Nuts.

'Oh…I…' I had to compose myself. Our future depended on it. 'Well, if I see him, I'll let him know you were looking for him.'

'So you *haven't* seen him, then?' Petra narrowed her eyes.

'I told you, I've been up here, studying.'

'Hmm…' She turned to leave. 'If you say so. But if you do see him before our lesson starts again in half an hour, tell him I'll speak to him then. Looks like we've got a *lot* to discuss… by the way, Bella, your textbook is upside down.' Petra walked out the door.

Dammit.

I wasn't sure how, but something told me that Petra knew *exactly* where Mike was and what we'd be doing in this classroom.

But what worried me the most was that she didn't seem like the kind of person to keep something like this to herself…

CHAPTER TWENTY-EIGHT

I t had been three days since Petra found me in the classroom and yet she hadn't said a word.

Whenever she saw me, she'd smirk or wink, and she'd been flirting with Mike, but that was nothing new. I didn't trust her. I felt like she had something planned. And not something good either.

When Mike and I had chatted about it on the phone that night, he'd told me to just focus on finishing the course and that he'd handle it. We'd both agreed we needed to keep our distance at school. No more sneaking off to classrooms or even meeting outside nearby. We had to play it safe. There was only one day of the course left, so it wasn't long to wait.

I hadn't seen Mike after lessons all week to give myself time to finish my assignments. Our teaching practice was all done, we'd been assessed, and tomorrow we'd find out our provisional results. Knowing I'd done everything I could, I'd invited Mike round for dinner.

'That smells *so* good!' Mike said as the sweet aroma of

cream, sugar, nutmeg and sultanas filled the air. I went to the kitchen and opened the oven. Not only had I become a lot more relaxed by not sticking to my rigid food menu every day like I used to, I'd also decided to make dessert, something I hadn't done for ages. I'd whipped up a bread and butter pudding especially for him. It had always been his favourite.

'It's almost ready.' I returned to the living room and sat beside him on the sofa. 'I hope it's okay. It's been a while since I've made it.'

'I'm sure it's going to be delicious. It always was.' He kissed me on the cheek. 'What's up?' My mind had wandered.

'Just thinking about Petra. Has she said anything to you yet?'

'Bells…' Mike wrapped his arm around me. 'Don't worry.'

'I'm trying, but I've worked so hard for this and I don't want her messing things up for me or ruining your career.'

'That's not going to happen.'

'Thank God we only have one more day left. Then we can be together. *Properly*.'

The idea of having unfettered access to Mike was so appealing. Being able to walk around everywhere hand in hand and kiss publicly wherever we wanted to, without worrying about being seen by other students or teachers. Although, given our history, people should understand that our relationship wasn't the same as Mike having a fling with a trainee he'd just started teaching, we still had to be careful. Holding back for twenty-four hours was nothing compared to spending a lifetime together.

'Fancying watching something?' Mike said quickly. I

thought he'd be more enthusiastic about being able to be more open about our relationship, but even if he didn't say it, I was sure he felt the same.

'Okay. I'll get dessert.'

When I returned to the living room, Mike wasn't there, but the TV screen was on and something was paused on the DVD player.

I put the plates down on the coffee table. Seconds later, Mike came strutting into the room and I burst out laughing.

'Oh my God!'

'What do you think of my new vest?' Mike smirked.

He was wearing his old *Friends* T-shirt, except he'd cut off the sleeves. Whilst that helped his arms fit, the rest of it was straining against his chest.

'I think if you keep breathing, it's going to split in two!'

'That'll give me a chance to show you my Incredible Hulk impression.' He grinned. 'You didn't believe that I still had the T-shirt when you showed me yours, so when I went to my dad's earlier this week, I found it.'

'I'm glad you did! Seeing as you're wearing yours, it's only right that I put on mine too.' I quickly went and pulled my *Friends* T-shirt out of my bedroom drawer and changed into it before rejoining Mike on the sofa.

'Mmm-mmm,' Mike licked his lips. 'Looking even better on you now than it did back then. In honour of our outfits, I thought we could watch a couple of episodes like old times. What do you think?'

'I'd love to!' I thought back to that awful date where that stuck-up guy was horrified to hear that *Friends* was one of my favourite TV shows. Each to their own and all that, but this was one of the many reasons I knew Mike was the man for me. We had so many things in common.

'I found the box set at my dad's, so thought I'd bring it round. Let's go all the way back to season one. Pick a number between one and twenty-four.'

'Um…ten!'

Mike scrolled through the episodes.

'Good choice. It's *The One with the Monkey*.'

After pressing play, we tucked into the bread and butter pudding. And Mike gushed about how delicious it was. This was lovely. Curling up on the sofa with the man of my dreams, watching TV. So simple, but so enjoyable.

'Ah. New Year's Eve… that episode pretty much sums up how awkward it can be if you're not dating or are with the wrong person. There's always so much pressure for it to be the perfect night. So sad that things didn't work out with Phoebe and the scientist guy, David,' I said as the credits rolled. Being all loved up made me watch this episode differently. 'They seemed to have a real connection, so it's a shame that he had to leave to go to Minsk for three years.'

'Yeah,' Mike sighed.

'Well, technically he didn't have to leave. He turned the grant opportunity down and she encouraged him to go and put his career first.'

'Do you think she did the right thing?'

'Ultimately, yeah.' This really was like old times. Mike and I often dissected the storylines after the show and discussed what had happened and whether we agreed with the decisions the characters had made. 'As deep as their connection was, if he'd stayed, he might have resented her, and it was a big opportunity for him, so he couldn't just turn it down,' I said.

'Well, maybe they could have tried to make it work long-distance rather than just ending things completely. Then she wouldn't have been so heartbroken.'

'No, I disagree.' I shook my head. 'Phoebe made the right decision. Long-distance relationships rarely work. Look at me and Lance. And we were both in the same country. Phoebe and the scientist guy were looking at travelling between America and Russia or Belarus or wherever Minsk is. It would have been difficult for that to go the distance. What she did was perfectly logical. Better that she be heartbroken at that moment rather than stringing out the inevitable.'

'But don't you think that—' The phone rang, cutting Mike off mid-sentence. I'd learnt my lesson from last time, so I let it ring. 'Aren't you going to answer?'

'It's okay. It's my mum. I'll text her in a minute to see if everything's okay.'

'It might be important. You should get it.'

'You sure you don't mind?'

'No, go for it. I'll load up the dishwasher.'

As predicted, it was my mum. She was calling to tell me that they'd just got home from Cornwall. They'd stayed a lot longer than planned. I didn't know how she got onto the subject, but it wasn't long before she asked how things were going with my love life.

For once, when she asked, my heart didn't sink. I actually *had* a love life and was deliriously happy. I was with an amazing guy and one that I knew she'd approve of.

I remembered when we'd spoken last week and how much I'd wanted to tell her about Mike but had held back.

Then I thought about my conversation with Sophia about continuing to throw caution to the wind. Things were going well with Mike and after tomorrow, he'd no longer be my tutor and we wouldn't have to hide our relationship. Maybe it was time to stop being so cautious, feel my emotions and start shouting about it from the rooftops like I'd wanted to.

My mum loved Mike and Mike loved her, so why hold back? Then I remembered Dad. He hated Mike. Once I told Mum, he'd find out too…

Sod it. I was tired of worrying about what he thought. I'd almost finished the course and Mike and I were together, so he'd just have to accept it.

'Actually, I *do* have some news on the romantic front…' Saying that out loud sounded so good.

'How exciting! Please tell me that news includes a certain man called Michael?' She'd already guessed.

'Yes, it does.' My stomach flipped. 'Mike and I are *finally* together!' Just at that moment, Mike came back into the room and froze. Mum's screams of delight, which almost burst my eardrums, must have startled him. His eyes widened.

'Oh, darling! That's amazing news. Is it serious or is it just a fling thing? Should I get excited?'

'No, Mum, it's not just a fling!' I rolled my eyes. As uncomfortable as it was discussing my sex life with my mum, I felt okay with saying that, especially since we'd both agreed that we wanted this to mean more than just something physical. 'It's serious. We're in a relationship.'

'Excellent! Is he there with you now?'

'He is indeed!' I beamed.

'Wonderful! Let me speak to him!'

I held the receiver to my chest.

'Mum would like to have a word.' I smiled, then put the phone on loudspeaker. Mike was still rooted to the spot.

'Um, I-I need to go to the toilet. I've got a bit of a stomach ache,' he said quietly as he backed out of the room. 'Apologise for me, please, and tell your mum I said hello.' He darted into the bathroom.

That was odd. Mike used to love chatting to my mum.

'Er… sorry, Mum. Mike's in the toilet. He's got a bit of a stomach ache, but he sends his regards.'

'Poor love. You haven't poisoned him with your cooking, I hope,' she chuckled.

'Thanks for the vote of confidence!' I hoped I hadn't. I'd made sure the chicken was cooked through, and I felt absolutely fine. Mike had too, up until five minutes ago. It didn't make sense.

'What was all that screaming about?' I heard Dad come towards the phone.

'Bella was just telling me some great news. Her and Michael are finally together!'

'What?' Dad's voice boomed. 'Not that useless, rude, waste-of-space lout from your university? He's not good enough for my daughter!' I quickly hit the button on the phone to take it off speaker. Even though Mike was in the bathroom and knew Dad wasn't a fan of his, I didn't want him to hear.

'That's not true, Dad. He's an excellent teacher now and—'

'Teacher? *Him?* That cretin couldn't teach his way out of a paper bag. *Good God.* Standards have really slipped. Whatever school hires him must be desperate. He's probably slept with half of the students too. I know his type. He's flighty. I bet he doesn't stay in his jobs long. Probably leaves before he gets the boot after they discover how hopeless he is.'

'You're wrong!' I raised my voice. 'I'm sorry, Dad, but you're just going to have to get used to the idea that we're together.'

'I refuse to. He'll hurt you, Bella. I'm just trying to protect you.'

'I don't need protecting, Dad. I'm thirty-one years old, for God's sake!'

'Everyone, just calm down,' Mum said softly. 'Maybe we should arrange a dinner or something, invite Michael over so that we can get to know him, properly?'

'Yes,' I exhaled. 'That's a good idea.' I heard a noise in the hallway. 'Look, I better go. I'll speak to you over the weekend, Mum,' I added, deliberately not including Dad. My cheeks burned thinking about what he'd just said about Mike.

I'd considered mentioning the course and Mike being the tutor, but one bombshell was enough for one night. Plus, if I told Dad, I wouldn't put it past him to call the school and report our relationship just to cause trouble for Mike. I already had Petra to worry about. I didn't need any more stress. Made more sense to tell them about everything after tomorrow evening.

'Okay, darling,' Mum said.

I hung up the phone. The flat seemed so quiet. I walked down to the bathroom to check on Mike, but the door was open and he wasn't there. I peeked into the bedroom. No sign of him there either. When I came back into the hallway, I realised his shoes were gone.

I returned to the bedroom and there on the duvet was Mike's *Friends* T-shirt neatly folded beside a note.

Sorry, Bells. Something came up and I had to go. Need to be fresh for the last lesson, so let's both get some rest tonight and talk tomorrow after class. Just know that no matter what, I care about you deeply.

Mike x

What?

I plonked myself down on the bed. I didn't understand. Fifteen minutes ago, everything had been fine. We were having a lovely evening. Then Mum called and he'd gone all weird. I was the one who'd said I wouldn't answer the call because I didn't want to interrupt our evening, but he'd insisted.

Was it because I'd told her about us and he still wanted our relationship to be kept secret? Or maybe he was mad because he'd overheard what Dad had said about him?

And what was with that *no matter what* sentence? He cared about me *deeply*? I was all in, madly in love with Mike, and he just *cared deeply*?

As for leaving without saying goodbye, that made no sense.

You didn't need to be a detective to see that something wasn't right. Something was going on with Mike, and I needed to find out what.

CHAPTER TWENTY-NINE

The woman sitting beside me on the train jumped. Even though I'd covered my mouth, my yawn was so loud I must have scared her. I'd hardly slept a wink last night.

After reading Mike's note, I'd paced up and down, wracking my brain, trying to work out why he'd left so abruptly.

I'd chewed it over on the phone with Sophia for almost an hour. Her conclusion? She didn't think Dad was the reason Mike had left—he'd already shown he wasn't afraid to stand up to my father at uni. Instead she reckoned hearing me mention our relationship to Mum had freaked him out.

Sadly, the gnawing feeling in my gut told me Sophia might be right. Just like she'd questioned when we'd gone to dinner and I'd also feared early on, despite saying he had changed, Mike was afraid of commitment. Hearing the word 'relationship' out loud must have made it real and he couldn't handle it. If that was the case, he could have at least waited until I was off the phone to talk it through. Him leaving like that just made me feel like I was being rejected all over again. But this time, rather than burying my head in the sand, I wanted to know the truth. Immediately.

Even though he'd said we'd speak today, I didn't think it was fair to leave me stewing overnight, so I'd tried calling later that evening. *Twice*. But both times it had gone straight to voicemail. Eventually, I'd told myself to try and get some rest and I'd drifted in and out of sleep. Waking up today was a struggle, but I'd forced myself out of bed, then onto the train.

It was time to face the music. I was now outside the classroom and my heart thumped against my chest. I'd arrived early hoping I'd catch Mike alone, but as I walked through the open door, I saw I was wrong. Faye and a couple of the other students were already there and deep in conversation with him. How could he be laughing and smiling with them when I had so many questions swimming around in my head?

I said my good mornings to everyone. Rather than greeting me with his usual sunny smile, Mike was more subdued. The corner of his mouth turned up slightly. He said good morning back but avoided my gaze. This was so weird. How had we gone from being so close and connected to feeling like strangers in a matter of hours?

Just as I was about to ask if we could speak privately, the door opened and the other trainees spilled into the room.

'Looks like we're all here.' Mike stood in front of the whiteboard. 'And twenty minutes early too. I'm impressed. Sadly it's our last day together… today I'd like to go through continuing professional development and give you some career advice. And of course, later you'll find out your provisional grades. Let's get started, shall we?'

Mike and I didn't get to speak at lunchtime. He was busy with Graham. When we returned to the classroom, it was the moment of truth: where we found out our results.

My progress reports during the course had been good, so I was confident that I'd at least pass. But until I saw my grade in black and white, I couldn't be sure.

Graham handed out our candidate report forms individually. There were a mixture of squeals and quiet groans.

'I passed!' Faye screamed. I glanced down at my form, my heart beating fast.

No way.

I'd achieved a Pass A.

My eyes widened and I read the form again, just to be sure. It was right. I'd got the highest grade.

'Yes!' The words escaped my mouth before I'd realised. I wanted to jump up and down on the table, then sprint around the room and hug everyone. Even Petra, who'd been giving me weird looks all morning. I couldn't believe it.

No matter how hard I'd tried at school, I'd never got straight A's. I often just missed out. Take uni: whilst Mike and Sophia had both achieved first-class degrees, I'd got a 2:1. Still a perfectly acceptable result—the second-highest grade—but I'd still wished I'd done better. I supposed I was just too hard on myself. I felt like, being the daughter of a teacher, I should excel at everything, but unfortunately I didn't always quite hit the mark. But I had today.

Even though the grade was provisional and still had to

be sent off to the official body for confirmation, it was still looking super positive. I was so happy.

'What did you get, Faye?' asked Petra.

'I got a Pass C!'

'Sounds like you just scraped through by the skin of your teeth,' Petra sniped. That was uncalled for. Faye had worked really hard.

'I thought I was going to fail, so I'm chuffed!' She grinned. 'How about you?'

'Pass B.' Petra sat up straighter. 'And you, Bella?'

'Pass A…'

'Well, we all know how you got *that* mark, don't we…?' She narrowed her eyes. Mike passed our desks and must have caught the end of the conversation.

'Petra, can I speak to you a second, please?' Mike said. She got up and walked to Mike at the front of the class. I could see their mouths moving, but with all the noise and excitement from everyone discussing their results, I couldn't hear what they were saying.

Oh God.

I *knew* she wouldn't let this go. She'd found out about us and now was implying that I'd only achieved that grade because I was sleeping with my tutor.

No, no, no. This was *not* how this was supposed to happen. I wanted to achieve this qualification on my own merits.

I had done this course to be free from the 'special treatment' label that had plagued me during school and throughout my teaching career. I wanted to escape from the feeling of getting a job because my dad was my boss. But instead I'd just swapped it for securing top marks because of sexual favours.

This was so wrong. I'd worked hard all month. My assignments were good. I had strong feedback from my teaching practice sessions.

Then again, as much as I didn't like her personality, Petra was a great teacher too. At least as good as me, so was she right? Did I get marked higher because of my relationship with Mike?

'Here.' Faye reached in her bag and pulled out some Haribo Star Mix. 'Have a sweet. I can see you're fretting. The sugar will make you feel better.'

'Thanks.' I tipped a handful into my palm.

'Don't you worry about a thing.' She rested her hand on my shoulder. 'You earned that grade fair and square. You're the best teacher in our class by a clear mile. She's just jealous. Of your talent and, you know…' She glanced over at Mike.

'You know?' My eyes bulged.

'Just an inkling… I don't think anyone else does, though. And it doesn't matter. Like I said, I reckon you were marked fairly.'

'I appreciate you saying that.' My shoulders relaxed a little. 'It means a lot.'

'No worries, honey. Thanks for all your help during the course. Can't believe it's over already!' said Faye. 'You coming for drinks at the pub afterwards?'

'Yeah,' I said.

Truth be told, I'd rather just go home and feel sorry for myself, but I needed to speak to Mike about last night. Plus, now this Petra thing had just unravelled, I wanted to make sure that I *had* been marked fairly.

My stomach plummeted. This should be a happy moment for me. I'd finally achieved my dream grade and now it was being overshadowed because Petra knew Mike and I had been up to no good in that classroom. Maybe I was better off being sensible and toeing the line after all. Right now, this whole *living life on the edge* thing seemed way too stressful.

It was official. The course was over. Four weeks of blood, sweat and tears had resulted in me finally achieving the PEFLITC qualification I'd wanted for years. Despite what Petra said before, I felt a sense of achievement. Whereas earlier I'd just wanted to go home, now I'd changed my mind. I *should* celebrate.

Faye and I walked to the pub and discussed our future plans. Whilst I explained that I wouldn't use my qualification for at least another year, Faye was itching to travel and put it to use immediately.

'I've already seen some jobs in Spain that I want to apply for. I feel much more confident than I did when I started. Thanks to Graham, but mainly to Mike. He's a brilliant teacher.'

Yeah, I said to myself. I'd thought he was a great boyfriend too, until he'd gone all weird on me.

We stepped through the pub door. It was different to the more modern one Mike and I had gone to at the start of the course. It had the traditional decor—dark wooden bar and furniture with burgundy carpets. It looked like it had a pretty large beer garden, which was ideal for a hot day like this.

I spotted Mike coming out of the gents' and knew I had to seize the opportunity.

'Sorry, Faye, I just have to talk to Mike quickly. I'll be back in a sec.'

'Good luck…,' she whispered.

I rushed over to him.

'Sorry about last night,' he said before I'd even had a chance to say anything. His gaze fell to the ground.

'Pretty shitty you just walking out like that. What happened?'

'I can't talk about it here.' Mike waved at one of the teachers who'd just come through the door. 'Later. I promise.'

He headed outside to the beer garden, where everyone had gathered. I stood next to Faye and watched Mike from the corner of my eye. It wasn't long before a swarm of female students had surrounded him. It was like being at the reunion all over again. I needed a drink.

After asking Faye what she'd like, I went to the bar and ordered a Malibu and orange for her and a Chardonnay for myself.

Within minutes of returning, I'd almost drained the glass. My head spun a little. Partly from the rush of alcohol, but also because of the many unanswered questions that had been swirling around my brain for too long.

I knew Mike had said we'd speak later, but I couldn't wait. I edged closer to him.

'Thank you sooo much again for all your help, Mike.' Keri, one of the other trainees in our class, rested her hand on his shoulder.

My eyes narrowed. I'd seen her gazing longingly at him before, but she hadn't been as forthright with her flirtations as Petra had. She'd clearly decided to wait until the course was over before making her move.

'You're welcome, but I was just doing my job.' He shrugged.

'True, but you're really not like other teachers,' she gushed, twirling her hair around her fingers. She was totally flirting. 'I really feel like you're always willing to go above and beyond the call of duty... I had a few questions, but I left them on my notepad at home. Would it be okay to take your number and call you about them over the weekend?'

Mike squirmed a little, then caught my eye. I knew I was scowling.

'Of course I'd be happy to answer your questions if you email them to me. My address is in the welcome pack everyone received at the start of the course, but I can give it to you again now, if you want to write it down?'

'Might be best to cc in the general department email too just in case, seeing as Mike will be leaving us soon. That's also on the pack,' added Esther, the director of training, who'd just walked over with a few of the other tutors and caught the end of the conversation.

'Oh... okay,' Keri sighed. Her little plan to get Mike's number had failed. I couldn't blame her for trying.

'I know I'm speaking on behalf of all of the trainees and your colleagues when I say we'll be sorry to see you go, Mike.' The other tutors nodded. 'Sure we can't persuade you to stay?'

Mike fidgeted. As confident as he was, sometimes he got uncomfortable with public praise or attention about his work, which explained why he'd started sweating. Although I was annoyed with him, I couldn't deny that Esther was right. He was an amazing tutor. I'd learnt a lot from him this past month. Not just in terms of the course content, but his teaching style. Mike was always so calm, cool and relaxed. He made everything look so effortless.

Despite having asked him a few times, Mike hadn't told me about his new position, but whatever school he went to next would be lucky to have him.

'Um, well, I've really loved it here, so you know— maybe in the future, I'd love to come back, if you'll have me.'

'In a heartbeat!' She beamed. 'So, are you looking forward to your new role in Vietnam? Sounds like a brilliant opportunity. It's next week that you leave, isn't it? You must be so excited!'

I froze.

What did she just say?

My throat tightened and my stomach felt like it had just plummeted down a hundred-foot lift shaft.

Either my hearing needed testing or Esther had just asked Mike if he was looking forward to going to Vietnam. And not for a holiday. She used the word *opportunity* like it was for work.

He had a job in another country. Not across the channel in France or somewhere in Europe, but in Vietnam. *Asia.* Practically on the other side of the world.

She said he was leaving *next week.*

And he hadn't told me. This—*us*—wasn't serious for him after all. It was just a fling. He hadn't changed. He wasn't ready for commitment. He was rejecting me. Again.

My thoughts swirled around my head so quickly, I felt faint.

I looked at Mike, who was now sweating profusely. He held my gaze this time and swallowed hard.

'Er, yeah, it's a great opportunity...' His voice trailed

off. 'Would you excuse me, please, Esther? I just need to grab a glass of water. I think all the heat is getting to me.'

'Better get used to it, Mike. Vietnam is a lot hotter than London!'

Mike got up and dashed inside the pub, signalling with his eyes for me to follow. I wanted to give him a piece of my mind, but I needed a moment. It was like my whole body was paralysed.

All night I'd worried about the fact that he'd left my flat without saying goodbye and left a cryptic note. Little did I know that would pale in significance to the bombshell that had just been dropped. How could he do this to me? Especially after what had happened before.

'You okay?' Faye tapped my arm. 'Bella?'

'Huh?' I slowly regained consciousness. 'Yeah… I… I'm just going to the toilet. Think I've drunk too much and it's gone straight through me.'

I pushed my body forward, willing my legs to support me, praying that I'd have the strength to put one foot in front of the other. Luckily, I made it inside. I saw Mike pacing up and down by the toilets.

My shock turned to anger. I stormed towards him. Mike spotted me and he dragged his hands over his face.

'Bells, look, I'm so sorry… I wanted to tell you. I tried… before things happened, but…'

'You should have tried harder!' I snapped. 'How could you do this to me? After everything that happened before?' My chest tightened.

'I didn't mean to hurt you, and this isn't like before.'

'It is! You're leaving! Just like you did before. No, actually, you're right. This *isn't* like last time. It's worse.'

'Let's go somewhere more private and talk properly. I was going to tell you. This evening.'

'But that doesn't change the fact that you're going! What more is there to talk about? I told you, this was it for me. I told you I was all in. And you just used me. Took advantage of poor, sweet little gullible Bella. I'm such a fool! Well, that's the last time you reject me. Now it's my time to walk. Have a nice time in Vietnam. And don't bother looking for me at the twenty-year reunion, because I won't be there. Find some other sucker to fall for your charms. I'm sure you'll have lots of takers.'

I stormed out of the pub, desperately trying to hold back the tears, but it was no use. I heard Mike's footsteps behind me and I ran and ran. I just needed to get away. Away from the pain and humiliation. Away from him.

I'd thought this was it. That I had a second chance at love. But I'd just made the same mistake twice. I should have trusted my gut and stayed away from that reunion.

What an idiot.

But I wouldn't make the same mistake a third time.

Mike and I were over. I never wanted to see or hear from him ever again. And this time, I really meant it.

CHAPTER THIRTY

I *t's official.*
Eating your body weight in ice cream, pizza and chocolates did *not* have a positive long-lasting effect on heartbreak.

Taking inspiration from the romcoms I'd seen where the main character used food to nurse a broken heart, on the way home last night I'd gone to the supermarket and filled my basket with a load of junk.

Over the past twenty-four hours, I'd consumed two tubs of Häagen-Dazs (strawberry cheesecake and cookies and cream), one large meat feast pizza, a slab of dark chocolate and a family-size packet of crisps. And my heart *still* felt like it had been trampled on by a herd of bulls, then fed through an industrial shredder before being incinerated.

Feeling guilty about all the rubbish I'd put through my body, I'd also just eaten two oranges in the hope that the vitamin C might help boost my mood, but nope. I still felt like crap.

I should've known better than to give my heart to Mike. I knew him so well, but yet I had chosen to ignore the foundation of his existence: to have fun, travel and enjoy life. Commitment and settling down to have a relationship in one country was not part of his plan. I'd always known that, but foolishly believed that *I* was special. That *I'd* be the one to miraculously tame him and that I'd be enough to make him stay. *So stupid.*

Lesson learned this time, though. I'd known something was off when he'd avoided talking about his plans after the course. And when he'd acted weird last night too. But I hadn't heeded the warnings from my gut, and now I was feeling the consequences.

My buzzer went. If that was Mike, I'd be so angry. He'd been messaging and calling almost non-stop since last night.

The first few times I'd replied and answered, because I didn't want to be rude and ignore him. Just because he'd acted like an arsehole didn't mean I was going to forget my manners. He'd apologised multiple times and asked if we could meet to talk properly. But I told him there was nothing more to say. He had a new job—a great opportunity by the sounds of it—so he should take it. I then told him I'd be hanging up the phone and not to call again, and that if he did, I wouldn't answer.

He ignored me, of course, and continued to call and text, but I forced myself not to answer. I'd already warned him that I wouldn't be responding, so if he chose to continue trying to communicate, that was on him.

But in his last text, he suggested he could come round to talk. As soon as I read that, my chest tightened and my face burned. There was no way I could allow that to happen. So I broke my ban and replied to say:

NO. I don't want to see you again.

If that wasn't firm and clear, I didn't know what would be.

The buzzer went again.

I stormed over to the intercom and picked up the receiver.

'*What?*' I snapped.

'It's me. Buzz me up, please.'

'Cass?' We'd had plans to meet for brunch earlier, but I'd cancelled. Now it was almost eight in the evening. I buzzed her in and opened my flat door.

She was lugging a big bag up the stairs.

'I come bearing healthy food!' she stepped inside, slid off her sandals and gave me a kiss on the cheek. 'I won't ask if you've put that nightdress on because you're going to bed early or if you've had it on all day because you're too sad to get changed. Oh…,' she added as she walked into the kitchen. 'I think I've got my answer…'

It looked like a bomb had exploded. The pizza box was open on the counter, with multiple half-eaten crusts, plus bits of meat and peppers that had fallen off. There was an empty bottle of wine beside it, the two containers of ice cream, dirty plates and cutlery, plus all the packets of the other junk I'd devoured but hadn't put in the bin. In all honesty, considering how I felt, the fact that I'd even bothered to bring everything into the kitchen rather than just leave it on the sofa or on the bed where I'd eaten most of it was an achievement in itself.

'I was just about to tidy up…'

'Tidying up isn't important right now. I can do that. I know you said you didn't feel up to seeing anyone today, but I also know what heartbreak feels like, so I thought I'd check on you and bring you some proper food. A wise cousin of mine once told me that eating crap after a break-up always seems like a good idea at the time, but it also makes you feel, well, like crap afterwards, so eating healthily is important for keeping your strength up.'

I vaguely remembered saying something like that when Cassie had broken up with a boyfriend a year or so ago. It was weird having it quoted back to me. If only I'd taken my own advice and remembered that *before* I'd gone to the shop last night.

'You didn't have to.'

'I know, but I *wanted* to.' She unzipped the bag and started taking out containers. The spicy scent flooded my nostrils. 'So tell me: how are you feeling now? One percent better? Ten percent worse?'

'I'm fine. Much better than last night when I called you. *It is what it is.*' I felt so embarrassed now I thought about how I'd phoned Cassie on the way home from the station, tears and probably snot running down my face as I'd told her what had happened. She'd offered to meet me then, but I'd said I'd go straight to bed when I got home.

Just as I'd walked through the door, Sophia had called me back. Her mobile had been switched off when I'd tried earlier, just before Cassie, so I'd relayed everything to her too. I hadn't told Melody. She had too much on her own plate to be loaded with my problems.

In a way, I was glad I'd only told two people. Now in the cold light of day, I realised that reliving the whole nightmare by going over and over it again wasn't going to help or change anything. I just had to move on and try and get on with my life. I'd done it before, so I'd have to do it again.

'Really?'

'Yeah. Of course, the situation isn't ideal, but there's no point crying over spilt milk. What's done is done. We had a nice time together, so I just have to put it down to experience and move on. It's better to have loved and lost than never to have loved at all.'

'Got any more clichés you'd like to add?' Cassie rolled her eyes.

'What?'

'You're acting like a robot. Spouting all that nonsense you'd find in some sort of self-help break-up recovery book. You've just found out that the love of your life is moving to another country and didn't tell you. Anyone would find that news devastating. You don't have to act sensible all of the time. You are allowed to feel emotions, you know: hurt, anger, frustration and whatever. You didn't do anything wrong.'

'I did. I should have known better. I should have trusted my gut and not got involved in the first place.'

'Yeah? So what was your gut feeling when you and Mike went for a walk on the South Bank just after the course started? Or when you spent your evenings here together on the sofa or when you were enjoying the limbo dancing at that pop-up beach bar? Was your gut telling you your feelings were wrong then too?'

Dammit. Cassie spoke a lot of sense, which was

annoying. Overall, everything *had* felt so right. Like we were meant to be. But clearly that was because I had been thinking with my heart and my hormones. Not my head.

'That's irrelevant. What's important now is that Mike is leaving. It doesn't matter how I felt when we were together. We can't be anymore. He lied to me. He made me fall in love with him all over again when he knew he was leaving. And he's moving to another country. Those are the facts. It's over.'

Saying those words out loud cut like a knife. Mike really was leaving. I tried my best to put on a brave face, but inside I was crumbling. Cassie was my younger cousin. She looked up to me. I couldn't let her see me like some blubbering mess. I had to be strong.

The truth was, my brain felt like it was on a high-powered spin cycle with so many thoughts racing around and around at once. No matter how much I went over it all, I still couldn't understand how he could do that to me. He must have known how hurt I would be, and still he didn't care.

'I'm not saying that Mike isn't a dick for not telling you, but there must be a reason why. Don't you think you should at least hear him out?'

'I've thought about it, but no. Either way, it changes nothing. Even if he had the most rational and logical reason, which I doubt, it doesn't change the fact that he's accepted a job abroad. I'm not going to be the one to hold him back. He's a free spirit. Always has been, always will be.'

The more I thought about it, the more I realised the significance of things he'd said to me. For example, about how important it was for us to enjoy the moment. And then there was that time where he'd said he didn't know how long we'd be together and to make the most of it. He hadn't just been thinking about his friends. He'd known it was because he'd be leaving. The signs had been there, but I'd completely missed them.

'The fact is,' I continued, 'unlike Mike, I'm looking to settle down. We're just not compatible. It wouldn't work. In a way, he did me a favour. At least things ended before we got even deeper. It's for the best. Anyway, I'm done talking about this.' I opened up the container and saw that it was Cassie's home-made chicken stir-fry, which was always delicious. 'This looks amazing, thank you. Let's eat.'

CHAPTER THIRTY-ONE

Like most people, Monday mornings weren't my favourite, but this morning stung more than usual. I was desperately trying to be positive and force myself out of bed to *seize the day* and get on with my life. I really wanted to do all the things that I'd advise my friends to do if they asked for advice on getting over a break-up, but it just wasn't working. I knew I'd feel better after having a shower, so why did climbing off my mattress feel harder than lifting fifty-tonne weights? It was as if my mind and body were being controlled by two different people.

I stared at the ceiling and thought about how much had changed. This time last week I'd been so happy. I'd been filled with joy and hope. The world had been my oyster. Today, though, I felt pure sadness. Despite finishing my course, which was a goal I'd had for so long, I wasn't feeling the euphoria that I'd hoped for. Just sorrow, which quickly turned into frustration. How could I allow my feelings for a man to bring my mood down so much? I knew I should be stronger, but right now, I didn't know how to be.

I'd thought that with every day that passed it would get easier. That the pain would become more bearable. But if anything, it became worse.

After I'd sent Mike that message on Saturday saying I never wanted to see him again, he'd stopped texting. Which was what I'd asked him to do. Repeatedly. But now he had, I missed him. My chest ached, constantly. My stomach was in knots and I just felt... empty. It was similar to the vacant feeling I'd had for all those years, but more intense. I felt off balance. It was like Mike had become part of my life, and now he was gone, there was a giant hole.

My cheeks suddenly felt damp. I rubbed the back of my hand over them. I'd been crying and I hadn't even realised it. The reality finally hit me. This was it. No more Mike. Ever again. No more seeing his smile. No more hearing his laugh. No more eating burgers together, bingeing on episodes of *Friends*. No more walks by the river. No more feeling his soft lips or being wrapped in his arms. Just emptiness. Day after day. Forever.

My phone rang. I instantly jumped up and grabbed it from my bedside table, praying that it was Mike. That he'd ignored my stupid requests to leave me alone and was calling to declare his love for me. I glanced at the screen, my heart beating faster, but it wasn't him. I quickly wiped my tears and took a deep breath.

'Hey,' I said, hoping that I didn't sound like I'd just woken up or like a blubbering mess. It was Sophia.

'How you doing?' Her using those words instantly reminded me of Joey's famous saying in *Friends*, and thinking about *Friends* of course reminded me of Mike. Was this how it was always going to be? Constantly thinking of him every minute of every day, wherever I went and whoever I spoke to? This was unbearable.

'Um, to be totally honest, not great.'

'I can only imagine how shitty you must be feeling right now. I wish I could just come round and give you a big hug.'

'Thanks, hon. How's it going over there?' Sophia was away on a press trip in Paris.

'Full-on, but it's going well. Anyway, I'm calling with some good news, which I hope will help cheer you up a little. Remember you said you wanted to get some business English teaching experience to add to your CV?'

'Yeah…' Mike reminder number three million and one popped in my head as I remembered it was him who'd recommended I ask Sophia.

'Well, before I left, I had a nail emergency and I popped into a local salon to fix it. Normally I only ever go to my clients to get a manicure, but I couldn't go away on a trip with a bunch of top beauty journalists with chipped nails. Anyway, I was speaking to the owner, and she said her staff found it difficult to chat with the customers because their English wasn't great, so I asked if she'd be interested in someone coming in to help them and she thought it was a great idea. I told her all about how amazing you are and she just texted to say she'd love it if you could come and see her on Thursday morning to discuss it. What do you think?'

'Oh my God, Soph! That would be amazing! Thank you!'

'Awww! So good to hear a bit of happiness in your voice.'

I started to feel a bit tearful again. Thankfully this time, they were tears of gratitude. How was I so lucky? To have such good friends to look out for me and help me like this. I was so used to being the one to step in and help others. I enjoyed it, but I wasn't used to asking for help myself. Somehow I just always felt like I should have everything figured out and do it on my own. But Sophia's kindness, first with signing me up for the course and now with this, had taught me that amazing things *can* happen when you open yourself up and let others support you.

'I'm so grateful. I really appreciate you thinking of me.'

'Of course! What are besties for? So… have you had any more thoughts about talking to Mike?'

'It's difficult.' I paused. 'I want to, but… I don't know. He really hurt me.'

'I get that. He must have a reason for not telling you. I reckon he's a good guy. Think about hearing him out…'

The knots in my stomach tightened. Had I made a mistake by pushing him away without giving him a chance to explain?

'Maybe…'

'I'm really sorry, but I have to get back to these journalists. I'll message later to check on you and to send the details for Thursday, okay?'

'Okay, thanks again, and have fun!'

'Press trips aren't as glamorous or as exciting as they sound, but I'll try!'

We both hung up.

I felt my shoulders loosen a little. I was just saying earlier how quickly life could change, and look: fifteen minutes ago I was lying on the bed, feeling sorry for myself. Now a great opportunity had been offered to me.

Suddenly there was hope. When it came to my career, anyway. I had a lot to be thankful for. It was bittersweet, though.

Under normal circumstances, I would have called Mike to share my excitement. I was one step closer to achieving my dream career one day and he was the first person I wanted to tell. But yet I couldn't, because we weren't speaking.

I hated this.

It was like something was missing. Like pizza with no cheese or a burger with no ketchup. Thinking of food made my stomach rumble and reminded me of the last burger I'd eaten, which of course was with Mike, when we'd gone for a walk by the river…

I really, really needed to stop thinking about him.

Some food and a shower would help. I was about to go in the kitchen when my phone chimed again. As much as I tried not to, I felt myself holding my breath as I glanced at the screen. It wasn't Mike, but I instantly knew the message was about him when I saw who it was from.

Melody

Mike told me what happened…

Melody

Such a shame that he's pissing off to Vietnam. I swear I didn't know, B. He should've told you.

Melody

He said you don't want to speak to or see him again. I know you must be cheesed off, but I still think you should hear him out and try and find a way to make it work.

Melody

You and Mike were apart for ten bloody years. And I know you didn't find anyone in that time that even remotely compared to him. Trust me, as you get older it's even harder to find a decent bloke.

Melody

I know he screwed up, but Mike is your soul mate. You've been given a second chance to be together. DON'T WASTE IT!!!

Melody

Considering you're both English teachers, you two are bloody awful at communicating!

Melody

If I set something up, would you meet him?

I picked up my phone, walked to the living room, sat down on the sofa and tried to process everything Melody had said in her string of texts. One day I should ask her why she always sent so many instead of putting everything into just one. Maybe it was because she wanted to use up as much of her free text messages allowance as possible.

In the grand scheme of things, I knew it didn't matter. I was just stalling. Thinking of something trivial to avoid focusing on what she'd said and the question she'd just asked me. I read her last text again:

If I set something up, would you meet him?

Would I?

As if sensing that I was mulling over her question, she sent another text. As I read it, I felt like I'd been punched in the stomach.

Melody

Remember, Mike is leaving in JUST FOUR DAYS... and HE'LL BE GONE FOR A YEAR. A WHOLE TWELVE MONTHS. MINIMUM!! Are you really okay with him moving to the other side of the world without at least hearing why he didn't tell you or without saying goodbye?

A year?

Made sense he'd be gone for that long. Lots of over-seas teaching posts were for that length. I just... I just hadn't known for sure. Because he hadn't told me. And I hadn't stopped to listen so he could explain.

Four days.

Mike would have left by the end of the week. We'd just found each other after a decade apart and now I was about to lose him all over again.

My chest tightened and I could have sworn there were a thousand leeches inside my body, sucking every drop of blood and draining away my energy. My head spun. I picked up my phone and started typing.

Me

No. The truth is, I wouldn't be happy to leave things like this. I'll give him a chance to explain. I'll meet him. Tomorrow evening.

I knew hearing why he'd deliberately done something that he'd known would hurt me would be difficult. Seeing him again and knowing it was for the last time would feel like being stabbed in the heart. But I also knew the alternative was much worse.

I'd already spent a decade not knowing why he'd walked out that night, and it had eaten away at me for years. I couldn't repeat my mistake. That night when he'd left that mysterious note, I'd said I wanted to find out the full story, and I wasn't going to bury my head in the sand. So if this was really going to be it and he wasn't going to be in my life ever again, I needed to know why.

Tomorrow was going to be a big day. Meeting Mike could destroy me emotionally. It was going to be tough, but someway, somehow, I had to find a way to be ready for it.

CHAPTER THIRTY-TWO

It was fast approaching five o'clock and I was on my way to see Mike.

Melody had arranged for us to meet in front of the London Eye at five-thirty. I was pleased that it was somewhere neutral.

Once again, my stomach was in knots. I couldn't remember a time over the past five days that it hadn't been.

I'd imagined a million different scenarios of how things could go, ranging from me running off in tears, to managing to hold it together and agreeing we could remain friends and meet up when he returned to the UK. But deep down, I knew that wouldn't be an option. Seeing him again would only dredge up all the emotions that I would have inevitably spent months trying to suppress.

I knew today would be goodbye. It was the only way I could truly move on with my life. But at least hearing him out meant I'd be able to do it at peace. Without wondering every day why he'd done what he had.

I quickly replied to the texts Sophia and Cassie had sent wishing me luck and an aggressive one written entirely in CAPS from Melody checking I was on my way.

I stepped out of the station and the warm summer air hit my skin. It was a hot day in London. I was glad I'd allowed extra time to walk to our meeting point so I wouldn't arrive dripping in sweat.

I'd thought I was nervous before, but when I saw Mike striding towards me, my stomach went into overdrive. The knots unravelled and transformed into a million butterflies fluttering around at high speed, and my heart thudded so strongly it threatened to burst from my chest.

He was a vision.

Mike had the sleeves of his white shirt rolled up, exposing his gorgeous forearms, and his confident walk just oozed sex appeal. As he got closer, I saw the corner of his mouth twitch and I hoped he was going to burst into the full-blown smile I loved, but instead, his face tightened.

'Hi,' he said cautiously.

Oh. No big bear hug either. To be expected, but I'd do anything for one of his huge cuddles right now.

'Hey,' I said quietly.

'Thanks for meeting me. Would you like to find somewhere to sit, stand or just walk? It's up to you.'

'Don't mind.' I shrugged my shoulders.

'Let's sit over there for a bit.' He gestured towards the bench opposite the river. 'So, I've gone over and over what I wanted to say to try and find the perfect words to justify my actions, but I keep drawing a blank. I know you've probably come here hoping for some grand explanation, but I can't lie to you, Bells. The truth is, there really is no valid excuse. I'm a dick and I messed up. Big time.'

'What? That's it?' I frowned. I didn't really know what I was expecting him to say, but it was definitely a lot more than that.

'Pretty much. At the reunion, I was so happy to see you again and I genuinely wanted to meet up so we could chat, but after you didn't reply to my text, I just thought it wasn't mutual. But when you turned up in my class, I thought it must be fate and then... after we started spending more time together, all of my feelings for you came flooding back. Well, I don't think they ever really went away. And then when I realised you felt the same, I saw that we had a chance and I took it.'

Mike sighed and shuffled in his seat. Once he'd composed himself, he started talking again.

'I'd liked you for, what, thirteen years and then suddenly you were there in front of me, and I know it's lame, but I couldn't help myself. For once we were both single, we both wanted to be together. It felt right. So I went for it. Obviously I accepted the job long before we reconnected, and I did try to tell you about it before we slept together, but you said we shouldn't overthink things or waste our second chance to share something special, so I kept quiet.'

'So you're blaming me?'

'No!' He shook his head. 'Not at all. I'm just telling you what happened. I tried, but I know I should've tried harder and not been so fucking selfish. I'd waited so long for that moment and I didn't want to ruin it. The more time passed and the better things became between us, the harder it got to tell the truth and the more reasons I found to convince myself that telling you wasn't a good idea. Like, if I told you, you might be upset and you wouldn't focus as well on the course, so it'd be better to wait until afterwards, which was true. I really wanted you to do brilliantly. I just… I'm sorry.'

Mike was staring me straight in the eyes and I knew he was genuine. I was surprised by his honesty. He could've made up a load of excuses or an elaborate story, but he hadn't. I could tell he was speaking from the heart.

I tried to process how I was feeling and what I thought about what he'd said. I took my mind back to that time at my flat when things had happened. I did remember him saying he needed to tell me something, and he was right: I had dismissed it. Just like him, I'd waited so long for that moment and I hadn't wanted anything to get in the way.

If Mike had told me he was leaving at that point, would it have changed anything? If I was being truthful, I didn't think so. I probably would've convinced myself that we'd just do the deed, I'd get over it and wouldn't catch feelings. That I'd be fine and we wouldn't do it again. But it was obvious that after one fix of Mike, he would be impossible to resist. So in a way, us sleeping together was inevitable.

Yes, I'd said we should focus on living in the moment, but that was that particular day. I knew there would've been no right time to break the news, but he could have tried.

By not telling me, Mike removed my opportunity to make an informed decision. If I'd known soon after we'd first got together, maybe it might have been less painful. I could've better protected my heart. Prepared myself mentally.

I wouldn't have started planning our future together or taken the emotional leap of convincing myself to believe in love again.

And I *definitely* wouldn't have told my mum that things were serious between us. She'd called practically every day since, asking when we'd both be coming round for dinner. I just hadn't had the energy to break the news to her that it was just a fling. For Mike anyway.

I could just hear Dad now saying 'I told you so'. I hated that he'd been right about things with Mike not ending well.

'I understand why it was difficult to talk about leaving. We were both swept away in the moment. But you really hurt me.'

'I know.' Mike hung his head. 'I should have acted better. Especially after what went on between us before. I wasn't sure what to do, so I put off telling you until I could work it out. I have to be honest with you again, though, Bella: I'm really sorry that I hurt you, but I'm *not* sorry that things happened between us. I've travelled all over the world a lot over the past decade. Seen amazing things, met many different people and had some incredible experiences, and yet the time we've spent together over the past month has hands down included the best moments of my life.'

Pow.

His words hit me straight in the gut. I wasn't expecting him to say that at all. The thing was, I felt exactly the same. Those precious four weeks with Mike were pure happiness. Everything had been so effortless, fun and just wonderful. Although we hadn't done anything crazy, like go sky-diving, the time we'd spent together doing simple things had given me the biggest rush of adrenaline and joy. Never had I felt so alive and whole.

'I enjoyed my time with you too, I'm sure you know that, but you deceived me, Mike. You made me feel like we had a future. Together. I told you this was it for me. And you made me think that we were both on the same page. That you were ready to commit to something long-term.'

'I am!' He took my hands in his. I didn't resist. My brain was too busy whirring, trying to process what he'd just said. It didn't make sense. 'This doesn't have to be the end. I've thought about it a lot—especially last Thursday night. That's why I left so abruptly. Watching that episode of *Friends* reminded me that I couldn't delay telling you any longer. I got scared. I didn't want to lose you like the scientist guy lost Phoebe. I know it was bad for me to go whilst you were talking to your mum, but if I stayed or if we spoke later on the phone, I knew you'd be able to tell there was something wrong. And if I was going to drop a bombshell, I needed to at least have some options to offer you. And now I do. We can still make it work.'

'How?' I pulled away and folded my arms.

'We have options. For example, we could have a long-distance relationship…'

'No.' I shook my head. 'Look at what happened with Lance and me.' If I couldn't make a long-distance relationship work when I was in the same country as a guy, how would it survive when my boyfriend was on the other side of the world?

'That's ridiculous. You can't compare what we have to your relationship with Lance. That's like me comparing you to Rebecca. There's no contest.'

He had a point, but I just didn't see that working. Although we'd known each other for a long time, our relationship or whatever this was was still too new. I couldn't see how it could survive something that challenging at such an early stage.

Knowing Mike like I did also felt like part of the problem. I knew he said that he'd changed, and I admit, when I was with him, it really seemed like he had. But I was still worried about whether he'd be able to commit or if he'd get bored after a few months and want to *seize the day* with someone else. It was too risky. And we'd both be miserable apart.

'Is that really how you want to spend the next twelve months? Being sad? Missing each other? Talking on the phone or through a computer screen on Skype? Wishing away our lives as we count down the days until we see each other again?'

Just thinking about it made me feel ill. I pictured a calendar on my wall, marked with rows of X's as I desperately crossed off the dates like an inmate waiting to be released from prison.

And after those twelve months, what then? What if it didn't work? We would've wasted another year of our lives. I wanted to settle down and start a family soon, with someone who was truly committed and preferably lived in the same country as me. I didn't have time to waste.

'If that's what it takes!' Mike nodded. 'But look, if long-distance doesn't suit you, then like I said, we have options. I could just stay here and find someone else to take my place.'

'Absolutely not!' I shouted. 'I already told you my thoughts on that sort of thing when we watched that episode of *Friends*.' On reflection, maybe I was overly harsh. Maybe, like Mike, the scientist guy was happy to pass up on the job for love and wouldn't feel resentful either, but it just didn't seem right. 'I don't know what this job is, but it must be something good, so I'm not having you give that up for me.'

'It's a director of studies role at a really great school in Vietnam, and even though, yes, it is a good opportunity, I'd turn it down if you wanted me to. There'll be other jobs.'

'Nope. Like I thought, it's not just an ordinary teaching job. That sounds like a big deal. A management role that will give you a lot of responsibility and new challenges. I'm guessing it's an opportunity you've probably wanted to be offered for a while.'

'Yeah, but like I said, something else will come up in the future. There is one other option…' He paused as if he was considering whether or not to say what was on his mind. 'How would you feel about coming with me?'

'What?' I shouted.

'Come with me: to Vietnam. That way we'll be together every day.'

'That's ridiculous!' I blinked quickly several times. He couldn't be serious. That was even crazier than the long-distance suggestion.

'Why? If you ask me, it's the most logical solution. Your goal is to teach English as a second language. Having your PEFLITC definitely helps, but without more long-term, specific experience, it'll be harder to find jobs in London. So what better place to get it than in Vietnam? I have a lot of contacts there, so I'm sure I can help you find a job teaching kids.'

There were so many things wrong with his suggestion that I didn't even know where to start.

'I can't just hop on a plane to Vietnam *hoping* that I'll find a job. I've got responsibilities here. A mortgage and a steady job with a steady income that I can't just give up on a whim.' I wiped my forehead. Just thinking about all this was making me sweat. 'That's why it's better for me to think about it next year, when I've had more time to plan. By then hopefully I'll know if I'm going to be promoted too.'

'I hate to break it to you, but a promotion, whether it's in a few months or a few years, won't help. Staying there, working under your dad, isn't right for you. You don't enjoy your job, and taking on more responsibility isn't the solution. Plus you know how it is in schools like that. Once people get promoted, they end up hogging that role for years. It could be ages before another opportunity comes up. Your dad is probably just dangling the carrot to make you stay. He doesn't think you'll ever leave. He thinks he can keep you there forever. Don't let him. Show him you're strong by following your dreams, on your terms.'

If I was being honest, I knew there was an element of truth in what Mike said. This past month, I'd felt so alive in the classroom. And I'd really enjoyed the challenge of teaching overseas students. It did feel like a better fit for me, so I'd definitely pursue it in the future. But not yet. It was too soon.

'And anyway'—I waved my hand—'when I do decide to pursue that path, I'd prefer to teach adults, so that's the kind of experience that I'd need. I've spent years teaching kids, and whilst most of them are lovely, it's very challenging. If I'm going to change jobs, I'd like to teach people who *want* to be there.'

'But that's the great thing about Vietnam, Bells! Teachers there are really well respected, and the students want to learn. It will be completely different to what you're used to. Trust me. Yes, you'd need to teach children first, but once you'd built up your experience, there'd be more opportunities to teach adults. And of course, if you don't feel comfortable just hopping on a plane, I can just let you know of any jobs when they come up, then you can apply or just come over. We can make it work.'

It was good to hear that teachers were held in higher esteem there, but no. It still wasn't feasible. I would have to give notice. If Mike suddenly found me a job during term time, I couldn't just up and leave. That would be too disruptive to my pupils.

And going to Vietnam wasn't part of the plan. All my research so far had focused on China. I didn't know the first thing about Vietnam. I'd have to start my groundwork all over again.

Then of course I'd need to sort out my flat. It would have to be rented. Which would involve giving it a fresh lick of paint or redecorating to maximise the rental value. I needed to cover as much of my mortgage as possible.

After that, I'd have to invite several estate agents round for valuations and choose which one to go with. They'd then need time to put it on the market, conduct viewings—who knew how long it would take to find a suitable tenant? That alone could take months. Which was exactly why teaching abroad in the next year or two was a more logical option. I could only go once I had all of my ducks in a row.

'I can't just up sticks and fly over whenever a job comes up. I'm not a student anymore, Mike. I need time to rent my flat, give a whole term's notice, build up my savings…' God, I'd forgotten about increasing my contingency fund. I needed to have enough in the bank not to worry if things didn't work out and I couldn't find a job straight away. My chest tightened. 'These things need to be planned sensibly.'

'Bells…' Mike stroked my cheek, making my whole body tingle. I swear, what with all the stress and my brain spinning at a hundred miles an hour, I didn't think I could take much more before I passed out. 'I can see you're freaking out, so I'm not going to push it. All I'm saying is to think about it. It's not as crazy as it seems. I know you're a lot more sensible and logical than I am. That's what makes you *you*. And I respect that. But sometimes, in order to grow, we have to step outside of our comfort zone. Sometimes we can't wait for everything to be perfect or plan everything so far in advance. We have to take chances. Tomorrow isn't promised to any of us.' He hung his head. 'I know that better than anyone. Why wait to leave your job? Why not hand in your notice now?'

I understood what Mike was saying. The circumstances surrounding what had happened to his friends had given him a different perspective on life, and because of that, for as long as I'd known him, he'd always been a risk taker. He'd never committed long-term to a job or home or anything. He didn't know any other way. But my idea of stepping out of my comfort zone was trying Peri-Peri chips at Nando's rather than the standard fries or choosing extra hot sauce for my chicken instead of hot. I didn't gamble with things like my career, my home or my future.

'Sophia's lined up a potential business English opportunity for me. I'm going to see the lady on Thursday.'

'That's fantastic!' Mike's eyes sparkled. He threw his arms around me and squeezed tight.

Oh, how I'd missed this. Breathing in his scent, the sensation of his heart vibrating against my chest, the firmness of his shoulder as my head rested on it. This felt like home.

After a couple of minutes I pulled away. I was enjoying it too much. I needed to start getting used to us being apart. Mike holding me was making that more difficult.

'Thank you.' I smiled faintly. I knew he'd be happy for me. Even if it meant me staying here, Mike was always supportive. 'Although I'm starting at the bottom of the ladder and it'll be harder, it's still possible to get some experience in London to add to my CV and still have the security of a full-time job. It makes sense to stay here, plan, then go when the time is right.'

'I'm happy for you. I really am. I just... I meant what I said before. This wasn't a fling for me. I *do* want things to work between us. I'm ready to go all in: with you. So all I ask is that you think about it. I'm leaving on Friday. I hope that I'll see you again and we can be together, but I just need you to know that I love you. I know I've never said it out loud to you before, but I really, really do. I always have, and whatever you decide, know that I always will.' He kissed me gently on the lips. 'Bye, Bells.'

As Mike released my hands and walked away, I melted.

He loves me.

Mike had finally said those three big words.

I felt the same. With all of my heart.

I brought my fingers to my mouth, reliving the feeling of his soft lips pressed against mine. I wished I could kiss Mike every day. Wake up beside him in the morning and go to bed with him next to me every single night.

But how?

It seemed impossible.

If I left, we'd be together, but I'd risk losing my flat, my stability and my income. So basically I'd be giving up my whole life on a whim. Crossing my fingers that things worked out.

But if I stayed, I'd have a job and the opportunity to pursue my dream career in the future, but no Mike. I'd feel empty all over again.

My whole life and future hung in the balance. And I had no idea what to do about it.

CHAPTER THIRTY-THREE

That wasn't right.

My key wasn't working. I tried it again, then noticed the colour of the door was different. I took a step back. It wasn't working because this was the wrong bloody building. I'd been in such a daze that I'd completely walked past my own block and wandered up the path next door.

I turned back and opened the right gate this time.

'Bella!' a voice called out. I turned around.

'Mum? What are you doing here?' She walked up and wrapped her arms around me. 'You haven't been answering my calls or messages. I needed to make sure you were okay.'

She squeezed me tighter and I started to sob.

'Mike's leaving.' I rested my head on her shoulder and breathed in her sweet perfume. It was the same one she'd worn since I was a little girl. I still found it so comforting.

'Oh, sweetheart, I'm sorry. Let's go upstairs and you can tell me all about it.'

Whilst I cleaned my face, Mum prepared the tea. We sat down and I told her everything. About the course, Mike, and him inviting me to Vietnam and not knowing how I could make it work.

I also told her how Dad made me feel stifled, and although I knew he didn't like Mike, I said I was convinced he'd find fault with any guy I brought home. He wasn't keen on the few boyfriends he'd met and in hindsight, with good reason. But Mike wasn't like the others.

'He's not just overprotective with me, he is with you too. Don't you miss not going to see your family in St Lucia or going *anywhere* abroad? Don't you get tired of going away to the same place every year?'

Before, I'd thought that having a routine was a good thing, but lately I'd been questioning it. Maybe variety *was* good.

'I've just got used to it. Most of my family have either moved to other places around the world or passed, so it's not so much of an issue now, but yes, in the past I did find it difficult.'

'Why did you put up with it?'

'I know you find it hard to believe, but your dad is a very emotional and sensitive man. He doesn't like us going abroad not because he's controlling. It's because he's afraid. He used to be a lot more adventurous. When he was twenty-one, he went travelling around South America with his friends. But then…' She paused, went to talk, then paused again, like she was debating whether to continue.

'Tell me. Please,' I pleaded.

'But then, his younger sister came over to visit one summer and they made plans to travel to a nearby island. She wanted to get a boat, but he insisted on flying, and the plane crashed. It was hours before anyone found them, and both his sister and the pilot died. It really hit him hard. She was only nineteen. He blamed himself for taking the plane when she hadn't wanted to and feels guilty that he couldn't save her. He's been afraid of flying ever since. And I don't mean just getting nervous or sweating a bit. I mean full-blown panic attacks. He didn't want you to see him like that. He was embarrassed by it. That's why he doesn't like flying and why he's afraid for us to take planes too—because he wants to keep us safe.'

I shivered. I knew about his phobia but hadn't realised the full story. His experience was so similar to what had happened to Mike.

That must have been horrific for Dad. No wonder he'd clammed up or left the room when I'd tried to raise the flying issue before. Wish I'd known sooner, though. It explained a lot.

One thing the similarity of Mike's and Dad's tragedies showed was how differently people handled grief and traumatic events. Whilst Mike used his pain to motivate him to go out and live life, Dad still lived in fear. Afraid to travel. Afraid to let his loved ones stray too far from him.

'I didn't realise. Now I understand why he's so over-protective about me travelling.'

'Yes. With his parents gone and the rest of his family scattered in different places, we're all he has and he worries that something will happen to us. Especially you. Even though you're all grown up, you're still his baby. You're his world. I know he's terrible at expressing his feelings, but he's afraid of losing you. I think that's why he wants you to stay at the school. So he can protect you. When you were away at university, he constantly worried.

He was paranoid about you having an accident or someone spiking your drinks or taking advantage of you. That's when he vowed to always keep you close.'

That explained why he hated Mike so much. After seeing him drunk and then cavorting on the sofa with that girl, he probably thought I was shacked up with a sexual predator and thought his fears had come true.

I knew Dad's actions were motivated by love, but by trying to protect me in the way that he was, he was actually harming me, both mentally and professionally.

I already suspected that although he hadn't meant to, he'd passed on a lot of his fears to me. Maybe that was why I was always afraid to do anything adventurous or try anything too different or scary.

'So he wants me to stay at the same school forever, so he can keep an eye on me?' I shook my head. 'He'll just end up pushing me away.'

'I know. I've told him that will happen if he doesn't change. Especially if he doesn't accept that you want to be with Mike.'

'Well, looks like he won't have to worry about that anymore.'

'So that's it, then? You're just going to let him go? You're not even going to try?'

'I want to, but I don't know how, Mum.'

'When me and your Dad got together, it wasn't easy. We came from different backgrounds. We had different skin colours. People were more close-minded back then. There was a lot of prejudice. Strangers would stare. Call us names and sometimes threaten violence. At times it seemed impossible. Different members of both of our families and even so-called friends thought our relationship was wrong and did all sorts of wicked things to keep us apart. But your dad fought for us. We loved each other. That was the important thing. It was the glue that held us together. We knew we were strong enough to get through anything. If you really believe Mike is the one, find a way around your obstacles. Fight for him.'

Mum wrapped her arm around me and I rested my head on her shoulder again. I knew that it had been challenging for them, but hearing her talk about it now made me see things in a whole new light.

My parents really did love each other, deeply. They'd both sacrificed a lot to be together. Made compromises, and despite their ups and downs and the forces that were against them, they'd found a way to make it work. Thirty-three years later, they were still married and happy. She'd given me a lot to think about.

My phone chimed, jolting me from my thoughts. I lifted my head and reached for it on the coffee table.

It was Melody asking how it had gone with Mike and letting me know she was on her way to the doctor's.

'Oh, no!' I gasped. Andrea had developed a cough and she was worried it had something to do with the mould in the bedroom. 'Poor thing!'

'What's happened?' Mum asked. I filled her in on Melody's situation.

'That's awful. Such a shame that she doesn't live closer. I'd gladly help her out. I miss having children around the house. Hopefully if you patch things up with Mike, that could change soon…' Mum smirked.

'Mum!' I rolled my eyes. 'Stop!'

I'd love nothing more than to give her a grandchild in the near future.

Having a child with Mike would be a dream. But we'd have to find a way to at least be in the same country first…

Even after talking it through with Mum and thinking about all of the valuable insights she'd given me, the reality was that sadly, I was no closer to working out how to make that possible.

CHAPTER THIRTY-FOUR

I was so glad to be going to the nail salon this morning. I desperately needed a distraction.

I'd overloaded on coffee to compensate for my lack of sleep both on Tuesday evening and last night. Since meeting Mike two days ago, I'd been tossing and turning, thinking about everything Mike had said, plus Mum's advice to fight for him, and wracking my brain about what to do.

By seven this morning, I'd abandoned all hope of getting any shut-eye and just got up to finish preparing for today's meeting.

The salon didn't have much of a website, so there wasn't a whole lot I could research online, but yesterday I'd tried anyway before planning my route and making some notes on how I thought I could help them. Even though this probably wouldn't be a paid opportunity as they were a small business and I was building up my experience, I still had to take it seriously.

Because I had been too upset over the weekend to even

contemplate ironing, I didn't have an outfit prepared like I normally would. And in a way, it felt kind of nice. *Freeing*.

If I'd planned a meeting outfit in advance, I would've chosen something formal and dark. But right now, I needed something bright to lift my mood. I might be feeling grey inside, but I wanted to project a happy, positive image. I quickly selected a silky yellow top and a pair of white trousers. After getting dressed, I applied some mascara, styled my hair, then was out the door.

I found the salon easily on the high street and walked in.

A small, dark-haired woman greeted me with a warm smile.

'Hello, I'm Bella. I've got an appointment to see Hanh.'

'Hello! That is me. Welcome!' Her English seemed good. 'Come!' She ushered me through the salon. It was small, with four nail stations and a couple of pedicure chairs. The technicians were diligently working on the hands and feet of the clients that filled every chair.

Hanh led me to the back and we sat in a small staff room. She reiterated what Sophia had mentioned on the phone. The salon was doing well, but she was concerned that her staff only understood basic English and weren't able to have a conversation with clients, and she was keen to enhance the customer service experience.

'I can definitely help you with that. I can teach them some common conversational phrases and we can do different role-plays —perhaps tackling different topics or scenarios once a week. So general interaction, dealing with challenging customers… is that the kind of thing you're looking for?'

'Yes! This would be perfect. How often could you come?' She took a container of food from the fridge and put it in the microwave.

'Would once a week be okay? I'll be back at school full-time from September, but maybe I could come after work in the evenings or for an hour on a Sunday morning? I'm guessing that weekends are busy for you.'

'I like this idea. Thank you. I do not have a lot of money to give you, but we can do your nails if you like?'

'That's very kind of you,' I said. I didn't really paint my nails. Occasionally I put a bit of polish on my toes during the summer so they'd look nice in sandals, but other than that, I kept them pretty bare.

'It is no problem.' The microwave pinged and she removed the container. It smelt divine. My stomach betrayed me and let out a loud rumble. So embarrassing. 'Someone is hungry! It is pho. I share with you.' She took two bowls from the cupboard and started dishing it out. It looked like soup with flat rice noodles and chicken.

'Oh, no. I couldn't ask you to do that. It's your lunch. I'm going home after this, so I'll make something.'

She shook her head. 'I always share. You try Vietnamese food before?'

'You're from Vietnam?' My eyes widened.

'Yes. Everyone here is from Vietnam. You know it?'

I swallowed hard. Of all the places she could have been from, how was it possible that she hailed from the very location that Mike was going to? This was too weird.

'No—I mean, I've heard of it obviously, but I've never been. My boyf…' I paused to correct myself. 'I have a friend who is moving there. For work. Tomorrow.' My heart sank. Saying those words was like chewing on barbed wire. It hurt like hell. *Tomorrow.* It was so soon.

'That is wonderful! Your friend is very lucky. You will go to visit, yes? I will give you the details of my family. My daughter is in Ho Chi Minh City with her family. If it is not too far from where your friend will stay, you can meet them. They will help you and your friend.'

I didn't know what to say. Hanh had only just met me and she was about to put me in contact with her family. So generous.

'I-I… thank you. I'm not sure if I'll be going, but… I'm hoping to go to China in a couple of years instead. To teach English. Have you been to China?' I wanted to keep the conversation upbeat, and talking about Vietnam only reminded me that Mike would be leaving, so I tried to steer Hanh in another direction.

'China is nice, very big and modern, but Vietnam is my home, so of course I think it is wonderful!' She grinned, acknowledging her bias. 'Friendly people, delicious food, very cheap to live. We have nice beaches and scenery. You must go!' She passed me a bowl and spoon before starting to eat the warm broth.

'Thank you.' I took a mouthful. Wow. This tasted amazing. I was tempted to shove the whole lot down my mouth. 'This is so good!' Hanh smiled, then went over to a computer in the corner of the room.

After turning it on, she moved her mouse around the screen, clicking on different folders. Suddenly her face lit up.

'Come look.' She summoned me over to sit with her. 'I show you photos.' She scrolled through a variety of pics on the screen.

There were pictures showing azure waters and white sandy beaches, others showing evergreen forests and waterfalls, lush countryside views showcasing what looked like every shade of green, and a colourful bustling city with lots of people on motorbikes or scooters. 'This is Vietnam.'

God. It looked beautiful. My heart instantly fluttered.

'It's stunning.'

'Yes. It is.'

'I'd really love to go, but I don't know how.'

'How? You buy ticket and take plane,' she laughed.

'Of course, but I have to give a lot of notice, and my flat... but I really want to be with him...' What was I doing? This was supposed to be a professional meeting. I shouldn't be offloading my personal problems onto a stranger.

'Aha!' Hanh's face beamed. 'You go for love! Lots of work for English teachers in Vietnam. Finding new job is easy. But finding new love? That I think is more difficult... wait here.' She got up again, went into a drawer and pulled out a plastic bag. 'Take this.' She handed me a book. It was a *Lonely Planet's Guide to Vietnam*. 'I find in charity shop and was going to give it to one of my client who wants to visit, but I think you need it more.'

'Thank you for this, but it's too generous. I can't take it.'

'You *must*. Read it and you will see. I have a customer now.' She scooped the last of the food in her mouth.

'Well, at least let me give you some money for it?'

'Not necessary. You come and give lesson this weekend, yes? That is fine. Call me tomorrow to arrange the time. Okay?'

'Sure. Okay. Thank you.' I put the book into my bag and followed her out into the main part of the salon. 'Speak to you tomorrow.'

'Yes.' Hanh nodded. 'Remember to read it. Then book ticket and take plane. Sometimes things do not have to be complicated.'

As I left the salon, I wondered if that could be true.

My phone chimed. It was Cassie, asking about the meeting and ranting about her flatmate. Couldn't be easy living with someone like that. Especially knowing you'd signed a contract, which meant you couldn't leave anytime soon. I felt for her. I did for Melody too. Her landlord was still dragging his feet about sorting out the damp in her place.

Hold on…

What if…?

Suddenly it hit me. Maybe Hanh was right. Maybe things *didn't* have to be so complicated.

I'd just had a brainwave and found a solution to one of my problems.

Maybe there *was* hope after all…

CHAPTER THIRTY-FIVE

I sat down on the bus and pulled the book Hanh gave me out of my bag. I tried flicking through it, but my mind was racing, turning over the possibilities that had flooded into my brain.

Before I explored my idea further, I needed to mull it over a little more, make sure I was a hundred percent certain of my decision.

Hanh was right. Vietnam looked amazing. I knew Mike had been a few times before, and there was no way he'd return if he didn't love it. I realised, especially over the past couple of weeks, that with a few exceptions, Mike and I liked the same things. So if he loved it there, I was confident I would too.

Yes. I was seriously considering going. Just thinking about it made my heart race. It was a scary decision. Probably the biggest I'd ever made in my life. Was I sure? Kind of...

A notification sounded on my phone. It was an email from an address I didn't recognise. The subject line read:

Here's Your Gorgeous Photo!

I opened it up and saw it was from the event organiser at the hotel Mike and I visited a couple of weeks ago.

Hello, Bella and Mike,

Hope you're both well. Thank you once again for visiting our pop-up beach bar and taking part in our *How Low Can You Go? Limbo Competition.* Mike, you were a very worthy winner! I hope you enjoyed the champagne.

Please find attached a copy of the photograph as promised. You two make a gorgeous couple!

If ever you're looking for a venue for parties, events or even weddings… we hope that you will consider us.

Please let me know if there's anything further I can assist with.

Kind regards,

Persephone Rogers

I clicked on the photo.

OMG.

My heart almost burst with joy. Persephone was right. It was a beautiful photo. Mike wasn't looking at the camera. His head was turned and he was gazing straight at me. Looking at my face with such love and adoration. As if I was the most precious thing he'd ever seen.

No one had ever looked at me like that before or made me feel so loved. But that was Mike all over. I always felt special and supported whenever he was with me. It was like, with him by my side, absolutely anything was possible.

My happiest moments had always been when we were together. And the saddest were when we were apart.

Ever since I'd walked out of that pub on Friday, right up until seeing him a couple of days ago, I'd been miserable. Even knowing I'd passed the course and with the exciting opportunity at Hanh's salon. Just like over the past decade, I'd done everything I could to try and forget him, but I couldn't get Mike out of my head. I couldn't just turn off the feelings I'd had for so long like a tap. And thinking about it, why should I?

This was under *my* control. The difference between now and before was I knew how he felt. He actually *wanted* to be with me. Us being together finally *was* possible. If I wanted to, I *could* be happy. The only thing holding me back now was fear.

I'd been living in fear all of these years. Afraid of letting my dad down. Afraid of telling Mike how I really felt because I was scared of rejection. Afraid of asking what really happened that night. I'd wasted so many years of my life.

By letting Mike walk away, I'd be repeating the same cycle. I'd be letting fear rule my life again because I was afraid of taking a leap, leaving my job and joining him in Vietnam. But he was right. Life was for living. Not next year or the year after. *Now.*

Why wait to travel? I'd played it safe for far too long.

Melody's words also rang in my ears.

You and Mike have been apart for ten years. Did you find anyone in that time that even remotely compared to him? Trust me, as you get older, it gets harder to find someone. He's your soul mate. Don't waste this opportunity.

There was no doubt in my mind. Mike was *the one*. Melody knew it, Sophia knew it, Cassie knew it, my mum knew it—everyone close to me knew it. So what was I playing at? If one of my friends were in this situation, I'd tell them to go for it. It was time I took my own advice. It was time to step out of my comfort zone.

And it was at that moment that I knew that I not only wanted to go with Mike to Vietnam, I *had* to go.

Before, I'd thought that going would be completely illogical. But now I saw that *not* going would be illogical. Letting a man who loved me unconditionally slip through my fingers would be plain dumb. Giving up on the opportunity to travel and gain invaluable experience pursuing the career I'd dreamt about for years would be stupid.

Yeah, it didn't fit with my original plan, but so what? *When the plan doesn't work, it's time to change the plan.*

I quickly texted Melody.

Me

I'm doing it—I'm going to Vietnam with Mike!! Not sure how or exactly when yet, but I'm going!

I'll message him this afternoon to arrange to meet tonight or before his flight tomorrow so we can work out the logistics.

I'm scared, but excited!! xxx

I don't think a minute passed before her reply came through.

Melody

YES!!!!! That's my girl!! Glad you saw sense! Soooo happy for you both! Message me tonight once you guys have met up.

Melody

Even if it's at midnight! I won't be able to sleep until I know it's really happening!

Me

Will do! Wish me luck!

Melody

You don't need it! You two are going to be great together. Always have been. Always will. xoxo

Me

Thanks for always rooting for us! Speak later xxx

Right. Time to change that plan. First, starting with my brainwave. I dialled Cassie's number.

'Hey!' she answered quickly.

'You okay to talk a second?'

'Yep. Perfect timing, just about to go on my lunch break. Hold on whilst I go outside.' Without realising it, I crossed my fingers. If this worked, it would mean a huge weight would be lifted off my shoulders. I held my breath as I waited for Cassie to come back on the line. 'All good now, what's up?'

'So… I got your text earlier. Thanks for messaging about my meeting. It went well, but that's not the reason I'm calling. In your text, you went on a bit of a rant about your flatmate…'

'Don't even get me started on that. Seriously, Bella, she is driving me up the wall!'

'Yeah, I know, which got me thinking… I know you've still got some time left on your contract, but are you still looking for a place to move to after that?'

'Yes! It's a nightmare, though. Everywhere is either too

expensive or miles away from a train station. All the flat shares I've seen are with weirdos or the places are disgusting shitholes. I don't know what to do.'

'Well, what if I told you that a one-bedroom flat had just become available with very reasonable rent, in a great location?'

'I'd say you're lying. I check the property websites religiously every morning, lunchtime and night. I even looked half an hour ago and there was nothing.'

'That might be because this flat just became available literally two minutes ago and hasn't been advertised. It's in Streatham, with two train stations nearby and is being rented out by a very kind landlady…'

'Wait, what?' Cassie paused. I could literally hear the wheels in her brain turning. 'Are you talking about *your* flat?'

'I am…'

'But…? Are you…? Have you decided to go to Vietnam with Mike?'

'I have!'

Cassie screamed down the phone and my eardrums almost burst.

'Oh my God! That is the *best* news! I am so happy for you! And proud. I know this can't have been an easy decision, but I really believe you guys are meant for each other. You're going to have the best time!'

'Thanks! I really hope I do. So is that a yes to renting my flat, then? I'll be gone for a while and I'd feel so much better knowing you were there. I probably can't go straight away because of my notice period, but that could tie in nicely with when your contract ends. You'd be helping me out because then I wouldn't have to bother with estate agents, viewings and all that stuff.'

'Er, *yes*! Not just *yes*. A big fat *hell yes*!'

'You might need to share the flat, though, with someone. Don't worry, she's lovely and I already know you'll get on well. I need to ask her first, though, and I've still got some other things to sort out, but I'll let you know later, okay?'

'Yes! And I'm more than happy to share with someone. If you vouch for them, that's good enough for me. And she can't be any worse than my awful flatmate. Thank you! You've saved me more than you know. And congrats! Does Mike know yet?'

'Not yet. I need to arrange to see him. Better go.'

'Can't wait!'

I exhaled. That had gone even better than expected. Step 1a done. My flat would be in safe hands, which was a huge relief. I'd need to work out the rent, but I knew it would be fine for Cassie. As long as I had enough to cover the mortgage and she took care of the bills, that was all that mattered. I already felt lighter.

Now for Step 1b… I dialled her number.

'Hey, Bella-boo?' she said. 'You texted Mike?'

'Not yet, but I will. How's Andrea doing?'

'Not great, but we're going to try sleeping in the living room tonight, see if that helps.'

'Actually, your accommodation was the reason I was calling. How do you fancy coming to live at my place? I hate the idea of you being in that awful house. If you don't find somewhere by the time I go to Vietnam, why don't you move in? My mum could look after Andrea during the day to give you time to look for work or whilst you go to work part-time or something.' The line was silent. 'Mel?' Suddenly I heard sobbing down the phone.

'Th-thank you…,' she stuttered. 'You have no idea what that would mean for me. For us.'

'Don't worry. We'll get you back on your feet again, hon. You'd be sharing the place with Cassie, too, though— would that be okay? Maybe you and Andrea can have my bedroom and Cassie could have the sofa bed in the living room or something. Not perfect, I know, but you could share the bills, so you'd both be paying next to nothing. What do you think?'

If I'd had two bedrooms, it would have been so much better, but I still thought it could work. I could even get some sort of divider in the living room or something so there would still be a separate sleeping/living space for Cassie.

'I think you've just made my day, my week, my month and my year! It'll be amazing. I love Cassie, and I remember when she met Andrea she was really lovely with her.'

That was true. Cassie was great with kids.

'Maybe you can have girly nights in too.'

'OMG! It will be so nice to have someone to chat to in the evenings. I can't wait!'

'Brilliant. I'll let Cassie know the good news and talk to you later.'

Step one had gone well. Now it was time to address step two: tackling the current job situation. In other words, speaking to Dad.

Something told me this wasn't going to be easy.

CHAPTER THIRTY-SIX

I'd called Mum to check Dad was at home. He was.
Which meant it was time to face the music. I was
going to tell him everything. And hand in my notice. It
was the only way.

I knew he loved me and wanted to protect me in his
own way, but it was too much. I had to strike out on my
own, properly. Live my life away from his shadow.

Yes, handing in my notice without a job lined up and
going to Vietnam was a risk. It was *huge* for someone like
me. But I believed in myself. I was a good teacher. Dedicated, loyal and hardworking. There were other jobs and a
whole new world out there, and I wanted to enjoy it as
soon as possible.

If I handed in my notice now, there might be a chance
of leaving by half term in October, but if I waited too long,
he'd probably make me stay until Christmas or even
January. It was now or never.

Worst-case scenario, even if things didn't work out in
Vietnam and I had to come back to the UK, I could always

do supply teaching. I was confident that I'd be okay, though. By that time I'd have some overseas teaching experience under my belt, so my CV would be even stronger.

Speaking of which, I had to believe that I *would* find a job quickly in Vietnam too. Mike said he had contacts there and I was pretty resourceful myself. Even if something hadn't come up by the time I'd served my notice, I'd have time on my hands. Maybe I could just go anyway. Surely it would work in my favour being based over there because I'd be ready to start immediately.

And even if things didn't take off as quickly as I hoped, I had savings. Although it wasn't as much as I'd planned, it'd be enough to keep me going for a while. Like Mike said, I had options. I could find another job, but as Hanh reminded me, Mike wouldn't be so easy to replace.

I checked my watch. It was one-thirty. If Mike was teaching today, he'd be about to start another lesson soon, so it'd be better to text rather than call. I couldn't wait to tell him the news! But first, I needed to get this over and done with.

'Hello, Dad,' I said as he opened the door.

'Isabella,' he said flatly. He was still angry. I had to go through with it, though, regardless.

We walked into the living room and sat down at opposite ends of the sofa.

'I'll keep this short.' I took a deep breath. My heart thundered against my chest, but the quicker I said the words, hopefully the better I'd feel. 'I need to hand in my notice. I've been studying the PEFLITC course over the past month and I've passed. In fact, I got the highest mark: a Pass A.'

Which reminded me, I still needed to talk to Mike about my grade. Hopefully there'd be time for that later. First things first.

'I want to go and teach English as a second language. Mike has been doing this for years and he's leaving to go to Vietnam…' I paused, reading Dad's face. He was grinding his jaw. But I'd started, so I needed to finish. 'He's got an amazing job over there and he's asked me to go with him. And I'm going to say yes.'

'You'll do no such thing!'

'I *am* and I *will*,' I said firmly. 'I'm going.'

'Teaching abroad is for kids. That's something you do after university. You're an established teacher. You need to stay at the school, with me. It's not safe to fly all that way.'

'Dad,' I said calmly, resting my hand on his. I knew he was worried about me, but I couldn't let his fears ruin my chance for happiness. 'I know you want to keep me safe, but you're suffocating me. You can't keep wrapping me up in cotton wool. I'm a grown woman. You have to trust and believe that I'll be okay. If you really love me, you have to let me live my life. Even if it means I'll be away from you.'

'That boy's no good for you, Bella. He's not responsible. You've got a good job. I know you're upset about the promotion, but something will come up in the future. You just need to—'

'No! I've made up my mind. I hope you can accept my decision and be happy for me. But if you can't, it's too bad. I'm leaving anyway.'

I'd been upset about the promotion. For a long time. But now I thought about it, I was glad Dad hadn't given me the job. It wasn't really what I wanted. I wanted to do something I felt passionate about, but still have time to live and enjoy myself. To feel free. Not be given more responsibility.

'I just want what's best for you, Bella. I can't believe you're choosing that boy over me.'

'It's not about choosing you or Mike.' I shook my head. 'It's about choosing *me* for a change. Going after what *I* want. What I think will make me happy.'

I also owed it to my pupils to follow my dreams. I thought about Mandy, who'd come to me the week before the end of term. The girl who'd wanted to go to college but her parents didn't want her to. How much she seemed to struggle with deciding what route to pursue. But she was thirteen, so that was completely understandable. I was more than twice her age, so I should know better than to let my father dictate my future.

I'd started the course to prove to Dad that I was capable of doing more, but really it had shown me that, as well as being capable, I had to follow my own path. Even if it meant disappointing him.

In life, there would always be naysayers, doubters or people who wanted to hold me back. Whether it was through their desire to protect, like Dad, or for more malicious reasons. But I couldn't let anyone, not even my father, rule over me anymore. I needed to step out of the shadow of his expectations. Step out of my comfort zone and do what felt right, for me.

'Anyway, you can't just resign like this. I need it in writing.'

I picked my phone out of my bag. If he needed it in writing, I'd email him right now. I touched the screen and there were two missed calls and several messages from Melody.

I clicked on the text icon. Maybe she had some questions about the flat. The first message was marked URGENT and of course was in CAPS.

Melody

URGENT! URGENT! URGENT!

GET YOUR ARSE TO THE SCHOOL RIGHT NOW!

Melody

MIKE IS LEAVING TONIGHT. He changed his flight. I repeat: MIKE IS LEAVING TONIGHT.

What? My stomach sank. Why? I skimmed to the next text.

Melody

He said he hadn't heard from you, so there was no point in hanging around in London.

Melody

I THINK HE'S TEACHING UNTIL FOUR. THEN GOING STRAIGHT TO THE AIRPORT. GO! GO! GO!

Oh no! I hated knowing that Mike thought I didn't want to see him. That I wasn't serious. Nothing was further from the truth.

There was no time to lose. I had to go and tell him. Right now.

CHAPTER THIRTY-SEVEN

'I've got to go.' I kissed Dad on the cheek and rushed out of the living room.

Mum was in the hallway, eavesdropping on our conversation.

'Where are you going, sweetheart?'

'I'm going to fight, Mum. I'm going to try and catch Mike before he leaves.'

'Ooooh! Just like in the movies!' She squealed. 'That's my girl! Go get him, darling!'

I ran out the door and down the road whilst glancing at my watch. It was just gone five past two. I should be fine, as long as the train came quickly.

I rushed onto the high street and ran for a bus that was approaching. It would be quicker to jump on that to the station rather than walking. Even though it shouldn't take me more than an hour to get to the school, there was no time to lose. I had to tell Mike I wanted to come with him.

As I raced down to the platform, a train pulled away.

Dammit. If I'd been thirty seconds earlier, I could've caught it.

I glanced up at the departures board. The next one wasn't for another twenty minutes. It was at times like these that I wished Streatham had a tube station. Tubes came a lot more frequently than trains.

Whilst I waited, I messaged Melody to let her know I was on my way. I tried calling Mike too, just in case, but it went to voicemail. Stood to reason. He always had his phone switched off during lesson time. Still, it wouldn't hurt to send a text just in case.

Me

I'm coming to see you right now! Please don't leave until we've spoken!

Next, I quickly emailed Dad. If he said he needed my resignation in writing, I'd give it to him. I wrote a quick message, asking him to confirm the earliest possible leaving date, then clicked send. That was good enough for now. If he really was going to insist on doing things formally or needed a letter, I'd deal with that tomorrow. Right now, I had more pressing priorities.

After what felt like more than twenty hours rather than twenty minutes, the train finally pulled in. I sat down and started to think about what I would say to Mike. Maybe it was something I couldn't plan. I'd just have to see how the words came out. Even if I messed it up, it didn't matter. I was just so excited to tell him I was coming to Vietnam!

Once I got out of the station, I practically ran all the way to the school. Sprinting in the sunshine was not a good idea, because by the time I'd arrived at 3.20 p.m., I was dripping with sweat.

I entered the building. I'd just realised I'd forgotten my pass. Even though the course was over, they still gave us a few weeks' grace in case we needed access to the library. Without it, there was no way for me to get to the class-rooms. Bummer.

I went to reception and there was no one there. I could wait for Mike to come out at four or I could jump the barriers. But I'd already done enough risk-taking for one day. Could you imagine if security carted me off some-where and that was the reason I didn't get to say goodbye?

No. There was usually always someone here. Maybe they'd nipped to the loo. I just had to be patient.

Five minutes later, Kalpna returned to the desk. Thank God. It was someone I knew.

'Hey!'

'Hi, Bella, how are you?'

'I'm okay, but I could be better. A whole lot better. Could you do me a favour, please, and let me through? I've forgotten my pass.'

'Sure!' She buzzed me in.

'Thanks!' I raced up the stairs and along the corridor to the classroom. I peeked through the door, but it was empty.

Shit.

I ran along the corridor, checking every room. Mike always taught on this floor, but maybe he was somewhere else? I climbed up the stairs to the floor above and checked there, but there was no sign.

I was wasting time. It was already almost quarter to four. I had fifteen minutes to find him.

I returned to reception, my heart now racing.

'Kalpna, sorry, I need another favour. I need to find Mike, urgently, but he's not in his classroom.'

'Mike? He's gone. Today was his last day here. Think he's going to Argentina or Vietnam, somewhere like that. Can't remember where he said.'

'Yeah, I know. He's going to Vietnam. But he was supposed to be teaching until four and it's only 3.45.'

'Oh, right. Erm… oh yeah! He's teaching an extra class over at our other site.'

'Where's that?'

'It's near Leicester Square. I should have a map here somewhere…' She started rooting through her drawers.

I looked at my watch. It was almost ten to four. I could either run out now and try and find it by myself or stand here idly, waiting.

'Is it far?' I asked, praying that it wasn't.

'Um, maybe about five or ten minutes' walk. It's down a little side road. A lot of people say it's hard to find, but it really isn't once you know how.'

Exactly what I didn't need to hear.

'I'm sorry, I can't seem to find the map, but if you—'

'Don't worry.' I rushed through the doors. 'I'll figure it out.'

I ran back outside, heading towards Leicester Square. There was a black cab on the corner waiting at the traffic lights, so I asked him for directions. I contemplated jumping in the cab, but from the look of the traffic, rush hour had already started, so it'd be much faster on foot.

After getting directions from the cabbie and then three other people, I finally found the school, which, like Kalpna had said, was tucked away down a narrow road. I burst through the doors and found a security guard at the desk.

'Hi there.' I pulled a tissue from my bag to wipe my forehead. 'I'm a student at your Covent Garden site and I urgently need to get through to one of the classes, but I've left my pass at home. Please can you let me in?'

'Sorry, luv. No can do. If I had a pound for everyone who tried that line, I'd be a millionaire by now.'

'It's not a line! It's true!' I protested, wondering if it was really possible that a lot of people tried to get access to the school when they weren't really students here.

'Well, of course you'd say that, wouldn't you? We get all sorts trying to get in and steal books or computers. And there's the safety of our students to think about.'

'I get it. I understand. I'm also a teacher, so—'

'So a minute ago you were a student, and now you're a teacher…? Hmmm…' He rested his finger on his chin. 'Sounds like someone's telling porkies.'

'I am! Not the telling porkies bit. I mean, I am a teacher, but I also studied the PEFLITC course here.' He must be new. It wasn't unusual for teachers to also be students. 'Look. It's *really*, *really* important that I get to a classroom by four, before the lesson ends.'

'Well, you're out of luck, luv, because it's already ten past.'

I glanced at my watch and my eyes widened. Crap. He was right. Melody had said Mike was leaving straight after his lesson for the airport, so he was probably already on his way.

Even though I'd raced here and arrived as quickly as I could, it hadn't mattered.

Mike was gone.

I was too late.

CHAPTER THIRTY-EIGHT

I walked slowly towards the exit, my head low and my shoulders hunched. I must have just missed him. So close. I was so close.

No.

I wasn't just going to give up that easily. Like Mum said, I had to fight. I could still find him. Go to the airport or something. But first, I'd try calling again.

I hit the dial button on my phone. It went straight to voicemail. He must not have switched it back on yet, which meant he wouldn't have seen my text either.

I was about to take another step towards the door, then paused. Mike was always friendly and sociable. I couldn't really imagine him finishing bang on time and racing out the door to catch a cab seconds later. He'd hang around for a bit. Checking his trainees had everything they needed, saying goodbye to his colleagues and giving them big hugs. So maybe he'd been held up in the classroom. Maybe he was still in the building somewhere and that was why his phone was switched off. It was a long shot, but I'd come too far not to try.

I turned on my heels and strutted back to the security guard. I needed to get through those gates, and this time I wasn't going to take no for an answer.

'Please. I really need to get to one of the classrooms. I'm begging you. This is literally a matter of life or... or *no life*.'

'Don't you mean life or *death*?' he chuckled.

'Yes. *Yes!*' I added, realising that it was true. 'You absolutely could say that. If I don't get to see him, my heart will die and shrivel up. Do you want that on your conscience?' I folded my arms.

'You're not one of those crazy stalkers, are you, with a crush on your teacher?'

'Of course not!' Well, I *did* have a crush on my teacher, but I wasn't crazy. *Yet...* 'Please! If you're worried, you can come with me. Or better still, call Kalpna at the Covent Garden site. She's the one that sent me here. She can vouch for me. I'll even write down my full name and show you some ID so you can check your student database or something. I must be on the system somewhere.'

By the time I'd shown him my driver's licence, he'd searched the database and spoken to Kalpna and finally agreed to let me in, it was almost twenty-five past four. There only seemed to be one entry/exit point, and Mike hadn't come out, which meant I really must have missed him. As sociable as he was, I doubted he'd hang around for almost half an hour knowing he had a flight to catch. I still had to try, though.

Mr Jobsworth the security guard said there were only two lessons on at the moment. One in room four and the other in room seven. I went to check room four first. I heard laughter, but the pane of glass on the door was covered, so I couldn't peek through it to see if he was still there.

I knocked, but there was no answer. Time was ticking. I had to know if this was the right room or whether to go to the other one.

I opened the door and slowly peeked around it but couldn't see. There was no other option. I had to step inside.

At the front of the classroom there was a Big Bird. Not as in the flying variety. Big Bird as in the character from Sesame Street. The teacher was wearing the costume and talking to a room full of children in Spanish.

This had to be the wrong room because Mike's lesson had finished half an hour ago whereas this was still in full swing. Plus, he taught English, not Spanish, and to adults, not kids. I quickly turned around and tiptoed back towards the door.

'*Hola!*' shouted a little boy who looked about six years old. 'Who are you?'

'Um…' I paused before turning to face him. The whole class now had their eyes fixed firmly on me. 'My name is Bella.'

'Are you our new teacher?'

'No—I'm looking for… never mind. I've come to the wrong room.'

'Hey, Bells!' said a voice that I instantly recognised as Mike's. But where was he? Suddenly, Big Bird whipped off his head.

'Mike? What are you…? Oh thank goodness!' Relief flooded through my veins and before I could stop myself, I rushed over and threw my arms around him. 'I thought I'd missed you. Melody said you were only teaching until four. I thought you'd already left!'

The whole class wooed. I'd forgotten they were even there. I had so many questions about what he was doing here, but they could wait. I'd found him. I wasn't too late!

'No, my last lesson *started* at four. I'm finishing at five. So in half an hour.' Mike smiled. God, I'd missed that magnificent smile.

'Is this your girlfriend, Mike?' said another little boy, who looked much taller than the other one. I didn't think these sorts of personal questions started at such an early age, but I supposed it wasn't every day a woman burst into a classroom and threw her arms around the teacher. I hoped Mike wouldn't get in trouble…

'I don't know, Elliot.' Mike's mouth twitched. 'I hope so. *Are you, Bells?*'

'Er…can we talk… privately? Maybe *after* your lesson?' *Talk about being put on the spot.* When I'd raced over here to tell him how I felt, I didn't think I'd have an audience. 'I think it's better to chat to you when we're alone.'

'I've got a taxi booked after the class finishes, but…'

'Tell him!' shouted one of the girls in the classroom. 'Tell Mike if you want to be his girlfriend!'

Wow. I didn't know who these kids were, but they were a feisty little bunch. They were all sitting around in a semicircle, glaring at me with their little arms folded as if to say, *Come on, woman. Get on with it. We're waiting. Put Mike out of his misery.*

Sod it. Right now I still had adrenaline racing through me. I'd never done anything crazy like this before, and if I waited half an hour for his class to be over, I might lose my courage and chicken out.

'Well, I came to say…' I looked around at the kids, feeling self-conscious.

'Come on, Miss Bella!' shouted the same girl. 'You can do it!' I liked her energy. She was right. I could. And I would.

'I wanted to say yes. *Yes*, I'll be your girlfriend and *yes*, I'll come with you!' I looked at Mike. He was frozen to the spot, looking absolutely ridiculous in his bright yellow feathered outfit and big orange feet. Still totally adorable, though.

'You'll… did you just say you'll come? To Vietnam?'

'Yes! I love you. I don't want to be without you ever again. So if coming to Vietnam is what it takes, then count me in!'

'Oh my God, Bells!' Mike picked me up and spun me around. The whole class clapped and cheered.

'Yay!' said the supportive girl.

'But what about your job? Your dad?' Mike frowned and put me back down on the ground.

'I went and saw him this afternoon and handed in my notice.' I thought that saying that out loud might make me feel regret or disloyalty, but actually, I'd never felt more sure about anything before in my life. 'He's hurt right now, but he'll be fine. So will I. There's lots of jobs out there, but there's only one of you, Mike. I've lost you before. I can't do that again.'

As the words left my mouth, Mike's eyes sparkled. I could tell he was happy.

'God, I love you, Bells.' He picked me up, squeezed me tighter and gave me another sweet peck on the lips. I knew we both would have preferred a long lingering kiss, but we had an audience, so had to keep it PG.

'Are you going to get married and have babies now?' said Elliot.

'My mum said that women don't have to get married and have babies anymore if they don't want to!' the girl huffed, folding her arms.

'Um, yeah, that's right, India, everyone has the right to choose,' said Mike. 'But if Bella wants us to, then I'd be very happy for us to get married and have children together in the very near future.' He kissed me gently and my heart flipped. This was it. Mike and I were starting our life together. And he'd just declared in front of a room full of witnesses that he was all in. Ready for everything. The whole nine yards.

'Hooray!' a group of children whooped.

'Can we come to your marriage?' asked Elliot.

'Can you call the baby Poppy like me?' said another little girl.

Mike and I looked at each other and burst out laughing.

'I think maybe now's a good time for me to go…' I squeezed his feathery arm. 'I'll wait for you outside. Bye, everyone!' I waved. 'Nice to meet you.'

'Bye, Miss Bella!' they said in unison.

CHAPTER THIRTY-NINE

That was the last of the children gone. I finally had Mike all to myself.

'So…' I came into the classroom as he started packing up the various colourful language materials. 'Spanish lessons?'

'Yeah, I help out with them sometimes as a favour. I enjoy it. Well, not so much the dressing-up bit—it's like a sauna in this costume—but the lessons. Teaching kids can be fun sometimes.' Mike stepped out of his outfit and quickly changed into a fresh white T-shirt and the grey tracksuit bottoms that I liked. Those were the same ones he had worn that night we'd first got together at my place, so they'd always be my favourite.

'I didn't even know you spoke Spanish. A man of many talents…'

'You haven't seen anything yet, Bells.' He pulled me into him and gave me a long, slow kiss.

Eventually we came up for air.

'I could literally do that all day,' I gasped.

'Me too… so let's continue…' He pushed his mouth onto mine. 'I've spent the last week worrying that I'd never get to kiss you again, so we've got seven days of kissing to make up for, plus at least ten years. That's a *lot* of snogging.'

'No complaints from me. Although…' I glanced at my watch and sighed. 'You've got the cab booked. Won't you be late getting to the airport?'

Unsurprisingly, he wasn't as concerned. Mike just shrugged his shoulders. 'If I miss the plane, I'll just have to stay here longer, won't I? In fact, why don't I? It won't really make a difference if I go a few days later. I don't start properly until a week on Monday. I planned to go this weekend because I was going to catch up with some old friends and chill out a bit. But when I booked my ticket, I didn't know I was going to see you again…'

'But won't you lose your money?'

'I'll figure something out. I have a contact at the airline. He's the one who switched the flight to today, so he should be able to help me change my ticket again. If not, it doesn't matter. It's only money. You're worth so much more. Spending time with my Bells is priceless.' He gave me another long kiss.

My stomach flipped. Mike always made me feel so amazing. And I loved how he was able to be so spontaneous. Before, I'd seen his desire to travel and have fun as flighty, but now I really saw how good it was to let go a little and enjoy life more.

'Well, if you're sure…'

'I am.' He grabbed his phone and started typing out a text. 'Just cancelled the cab. So as I was saying, I am definitely sure. There's just one condition, though.'

'What's that?'

'I'll need to crash at yours. Someone's already moving into the flat I was renting tomorrow, and I don't fancy living with my dad and his new girlfriend.'

'Hmmm.' I put my finger on my chin. 'Let me think. Having you, one of my favourite people in the world stay with me, giving me big hugs whenever I need them and having amazing sex on tap… sounds like torture, but I suppose I can suffer, if it helps you out. Consider it my good deed of the day.'

'Oh, *thank you*. I promise to repay you with burgers filled with extra gherkins, lots of *Friends* binge-watching sessions, and of course multiple orgasms…'

'Mmmm.' I kissed him again. 'Sign me up!'

'And I can help you prepare for the move and start looking for jobs over there. It'll be fun. After all these years, we'll finally get to go away together.'

'Yep! And for maybe six months too—depending on when I'm able to come over.'

'More than just six months! For a whole lifetime. This is it, Bells.'

'It is for me too.'

'Good to know.' Mike exhaled. 'Especially seeing as I've just declared in front of a room full of witnesses that I plan to marry you and have kids.'

'Yes, you did!' I laughed. I'd thought the same thing. Something told me that India and Elliot would be more than happy to testify if ever I needed them to.

'I mean, I haven't even proposed yet and we've already got wedding venues offering their services too. Did you see that email from the hotel with our photo earlier?'

'Yep. Her hint was about as subtle as a sledgehammer!

She was right about one thing, though, we *do* make a great couple.'

Mum, Sophia, Cassie and Melody had all said the same. I couldn't wait to update them later. It was confirmed. Mike and I were finally together. *Properly*. They'd be so happy for us.

'Definitely, Bells. I'm really glad we got a second chance to spend our lives together. Not everyone gets this lucky, so for as long as I'm on this earth, I intend to enjoy every single moment with you. I'm all in.'

As he wrapped his arms around my waist and squeezed me tight, I knew he meant every word.

Mike was no longer just my ten-year crush. Now he was my best friend, my partner, my cheerleader and my lifetime love. Like Melody said, we were going to be great together. We always had been. And I knew with all my heart that we always would be. *Forever*.

EPILOGUE

March 2018

M um and I lay back on our sun loungers, watching the waves crash against the white sand. This was paradise.

As we glanced along the beach, we saw three familiar figures walking towards us.

'Look at them.' Mum grinned. 'Hard to believe those two used to hate each other.'

I clocked the big smiles spread across both Dad's and Mike's faces. 'Yeah. What a difference eight years can make.'

I thought back to when I'd first told Dad I wanted to leave the school and London to join Mike in Vietnam.

We hadn't spoken for over a week until Mum had intervened and told Dad he needed to stop sulking and come and have an adult conversation with me or he'd lose his daughter forever.

It had been awkward at first, but we'd got everything off our chests. Eventually, he'd apologised and said as difficult as it would be, he'd try to come to terms with my decision, because all he'd ever wanted was for me to be happy.

I'd worried at first that he was just saying that and would revert back to his old ways once the new term started, but he'd really gone all out to help me. Dad was able to fill my position quicker than anticipated, so I'd just worked until half term, then travelled to Vietnam to join Mike in late October.

It wasn't easy being apart from Mike during that time. Especially after we'd spent the week before he moved to Vietnam living together. But thankfully we were able to Skype a few times a week and chatted on the phone in between. The English lessons that I'd been giving at Hanh's salon every weekend were a good distraction, though. What also helped us through was focusing on the bigger picture: what was a couple of months apart compared to the rest of our lives together?

Luckily, I found a job teaching at a school over there before I left London and Mike had already found us a place to live, so I'd worried needlessly.

By that time, my official PEFLITC certification had also come through. I had legitimately achieved a Pass A. Mike explained that even before we'd got together and Petra had caught us in the classroom, he'd spoken to both Graham and the director of training about the fact that we knew each other and arranged for Graham to assess my assignments and teaching practice. He wanted to make sure that I achieved my qualification fair and square.

Petra had apparently come to see Mike the morning after she caught us and said she'd keep our secret, as long as he gave her the same 'special treatment' he was giving me. In other words she wanted him to sleep with her. But he'd turned her down point-blank. He wanted me to focus on finishing my assignments, so had planned to tell me once the course was over.

When Petra made that comment on the last day about me only getting my grade because of our relationship, Mike told her that the director of training would be happy to talk to her. Particularly about her decision to blackmail a tutor. She quickly saw sense.

Vietnam was just as wonderful as Mike had promised. I loved everything about it. The school, my learners, the people, the culture, and wow: the food was to die for.

True to her word, Hanh had put me in touch with her daughter, who was amazing. She took us to so many cool places.

We did lots of travelling during the holidays, including to Bali, the destination I'd always wanted to visit with Mike. Which was where he proposed.

In the end, we loved Vietnam so much, we stayed there for two years before moving back to the UK, getting married and finding a place together in North London.

I joined some language training agencies and was booked for jobs teaching business English to overseas professionals, which was what I'd focused on during my last year in Vietnam. I was finally doing my dream career.

A few years later, just after Mike became an English professor, I fell pregnant and we had a beautiful son called Paul, who was now almost two years old. He really was the light of our lives.

Paul was also the apple of Mum and Dad's eyes. I thought Mum would be the most attached, but Dad was completely head over heels in love with his grandson. Paul had softened him a lot.

Dad and Mike were now just a few metres away from us. Dad was throwing Paul up in the air and catching him, much to Paul's excitement. His loud squeals of delight could probably be heard at the end of the beach. I didn't think Dad would ever have done that with me. He would have been too afraid of dropping me.

The counselling definitely helped. During our heart-to-heart, I recommended that Dad speak to someone to address his trauma. He resisted at first until I persuaded him to do a Skype call with Mike, who spoke to him about his experience and how he learned to live with his grief. He didn't admit it at first, but I know that hearing Mike's story and how he pushed forward despite his adversity inspired him and led him to eventually seek support.

That wasn't the only way Dad changed. He also booked himself on a fear of flying course. A year later he felt comfortable taking a short flight to Paris with Mum for the weekend. Then a few months after that, they went a little further afield for a summer holiday in Morocco.

Finally, last year, he felt brave enough to take a trip with Mum to St Lucia. She was so happy when he suggested it. He said the flight was nerve-wracking, especially when they experienced some turbulence, but he got through it. He'd faced his fear and I was proud of him.

Now here we were. All five of us, in St Lucia on holiday together. I was finally happy in all aspects of my life. Professionally and romantically. As well as being married to the most amazing husband and having the family I always wanted, I still had fantastic friends.

Melody was back on her feet with a little flat in London, working in a school during the week and making jewellery in her spare time, which she sold on Etsy.

Cassie was also doing well. After renting my place for two years with Melody, she'd got her own flat too and was in a relationship.

Sophia's PR agency was still thriving, and now that she'd broken up with Rich I had a feeling that there would be a lot of exciting things for her to look forward to in her personal life.

The last time I spoke to Faye, she was still in Spain teaching and was loving it.

Yep. Things were looking up all round.

'Mummy!' Dad had put Paul down and he ran towards me. I jumped up, opened my arms and gave him a hug.

'You're just like your daddy,' I said as Mike came up behind me and wrapped his arms around my waist. 'You give great hugs.'

'So do you.' Mike squeezed me tighter, then stood beside me. 'Look at this, Bells.' He stared at the sunset. 'Could life get any better?'

I glanced at our son and my husband. My heart was so full it could burst.

'Nope. This is happiness right here. I have everything I've ever dreamt of and so much more.'

Want more? Fancy finding out how Mike proposed to Bella? Visit: https://BookHip.com/PWPGFBB to join my VIP Club and download the *My Ten-Year Crush* Bonus Chapters for **FREE**!

Order book two in the series: *My Lucky Night* from Amazon now to read about Cassie's romantic adventures.

You can read all about **Sophia's love story** too by ordering *The Middle-Aged Virgin* and the sequel *The Middle-Aged Virgin in Italy* from Amazon today. Enjoy! x

ENJOYED THIS BOOK? YOU CAN MAKE A BIG DIFFERENCE.

If you've enjoyed *My Ten-Year Crush*, **I'd be so very grateful if you could spare two minutes to leave a review on Amazon, Goodreads and BookBub**. It doesn't have to be long (unless you'd like it to be!). Every review – even if it's just a sentence – would make a *huge* difference.

By leaving an honest review, you'll be helping to bring my books to the attention of other readers and hearing your thoughts will make them more likely to give my novels a try. As a result, it will help me to build my career, which means I'll get to write more books!

Thank you SO much. As well as making a big difference, you've also just made my day!

Olivia x

ALL BOOKS BY OLIVIA SPRING

The Middle-Aged Virgin Series
The Middle-Aged Virgin
The Middle-Aged Virgin in Italy

Only When it's Love Series
Only When it's Love
When's the Wedding?

My Ten-Year Crush Series
My Ten-Year Crush
My Lucky Night
My Paris Romance

Other Books
Losing My Inhibitions
Love Offline

All books available on Amazon.

The Middle-Aged Virgin

Have you read my debut novel *The Middle-Aged Virgin*? It includes Sophia from *My Ten-Year Crush* too! Here's what it's about:

Newly Single And Seeking Spine-Tingles…

Sophia seems to have it all: a high-flying job running London's coolest beauty PR agency, a long-term boyfriend and a dressing room filled with designer shoes. But money can't buy everything…

When tragedy strikes, Sophia realises she's actually an unhappy workaholic in a relationship that's about as exciting as a bikini wax. And as for her sex life, it's been so long since Sophia's had any action, her bestie has started calling her a *Middle-Aged Virgin*.

Determined to get a life and *get lucky*, Sophia hatches a plan to work less and live more. She ends her relationship and jets off on a cooking holiday in Tuscany, where she meets mysterious chef Lorenzo. Tall, dark and very handsome, this Italian stallion might be just what Sophia needs to spice things up in the bedroom…

But the dating scene has changed since Sophia was last single, and although she'd score an A+ for her career, when it comes to men, she's completely out of her comfort zone. How will Sophia, a self-confessed control freak, handle the unpredictable world of dating? And how much will she sacrifice for love?

Join Sophia today on her laugh-out-loud adventures as she

searches for happiness, enjoys passion between the sheets and experiences OMG moments along the way!

Here's what readers are saying about it:

"I couldn't put the book down. It's **one of the best romantic comedies I've read**." Amazon reader

"Life-affirming and empowering." Chicklit Club

"Perfect holiday read." Saira Khan, TV presenter & newspaper columnist

"Olivia has an innate knack for the sex scenes, which are very hot. **This book was steamy**, but with such a huge element of humour in it that when you read it **you will certainly giggle throughout at the escapades**." Book Mad Jo

"Absolutely hilarious! A diverse, wise and poignant novel." The Writing Garnet

Buy *The Middle-Aged Virgin* on Amazon today!

AN EXTRACT FROM THE MIDDLE-AGED VIRGIN

Prologue

'It's over.'

I did it.

I said it.

Fuck.

I'd rehearsed those two words approximately ten million times in my head—whilst I was in the shower, in front of the mirror, on my way to and from work…probably even in my sleep. But saying them out loud was far more difficult than I'd imagined.

'What the fuck, Sophia?' snapped Rich, nostrils flaring. 'What do you mean, it's over?'

As I stared into his hazel eyes, I started to ask myself the same question.

How could I be ending the fifteen-year relationship with the guy I'd always considered to be the one?

I felt the beads of sweat forming on my powdered forehead and warm, salty tears trickling down my rouged cheeks, which now felt like they were on fire. This was serious. This was actually happening.

Shit. I said I'd be strong.

'Earth to Sophia!' screamed Rich, stomping his feet.

I snapped out of my thoughts. Now would probably be a good time to start explaining myself. Not least because the veins currently throbbing on Rich's forehead appeared to indicate that he was on the verge of spontaneous combustion. Easier said than done, though, as with every second that passed, I realised the enormity of what I was doing.

The man standing in front of me wasn't just a guy that came in pretty packaging. Rich was kind, intelligent, successful, financially secure, and faithful. He was a great listener and had been there for me through thick and thin. Qualities that, after numerous failed Tinder dates, my single friends had repeatedly vented, appeared to be rare in men these days.

Most women would have given their right and probably their left arm too for a man like him. So why the hell was I suddenly about to throw it all away?

Want to find out what happens next? Buy *The Middle-Aged Virgin* on Amazon today!

Only When It's Love: Holding Out For Mr Right

Have you read my second novel *Only When It's Love?* Here's what it's about:

Alex's love life is a disaster. Will accepting a crazy seven-step dating challenge lead to more heartbreak or help her find Mr Right?

Alex is tired of being single. After years of disastrous hook-ups and relationships that lead to the bedroom but nowhere else, Alex is convinced she'll never find her Mr Right. Then her newly married friend Stacey recommends what worked for her: a self-help book that guarantees Alex will find true love in just seven steps. Sounds simple, right?

Except Alex soon discovers that each step is more difficult than the last, and one of the rules involves dating, but not sleeping with a guy for six months. Absolutely no intimate contact whatsoever. *Zero. Nada. Rien.* A big challenge for Alex, who has never been one to hold back from jumping straight into the sack, hoping it will help a man fall for her.

Will any guys be willing to wait? Will Alex find her Mr Right? And if she does, will she be strong enough to resist temptation and hold out for true love?

Join Alex on her roller coaster romantic journey as she tries to cope with the emotional and physical ups and downs of dating whilst following a lengthy list of rigid rules.

Only When It's Love **is a standalone, fun, feel-good, romantic comedy about self-acceptance, determination, love and the challenge of finding** *the one*.

Praise For *Only When It's Love*

'**Totally unique and wonderful.** Olivia's book has a brilliant message about self-worth and brings to life an important modern take on the rom-com. Most definitely a five-star read.' - **Love Books Group**

'I guarantee **you will HOOT with laughter** at Alex's escapades whilst fully cheering her on. If you like romance, humour and a generally fun-filled read then look no further than this **gorgeous, well-written dating adventure**. Five stars.' - **Bookaholic Confessions**

'Such a uniquely told, **laugh-out-loud, dirty and flirty, addictive novel**.' - **The Writing Garnet**

'I've never read a story so quickly to find out who she would choose! Five stars.' - **Books Between Friends**

'Cool, contemporary, but still wildly romantic! Yet another smasher from Olivia Spring! There's something about the way she writes that really endeared me to the heroine of this story.' - **Amazon reader**

'WOW WOW WOW!!!! *Only When it's Love* is **a dynamite love fest**. I read the entire story with the biggest smile on my face. In case you might have missed the million hints I've dropped, download the book today and jump straight in.' **Stacy is Reading**

Buy *Only When It's Love* on Amazon today!

AN EXTRACT FROM ONLY WHEN IT'S LOVE

Chapter One

Never again.

Why, why, *why* did I keep on doing this?

I felt great for a few minutes, or if I was lucky, hours, but then, when it was all over, I ended up feeling like shit for days. Sometimes weeks.

I must stop torturing myself.

Repeat after me:

I, Alexandra Adams, will *not* answer Connor Matthew's WhatsApp messages, texts or phone calls for the rest of my life.

I firmly declare that even if Connor says his whole world is falling apart, that he's sorry, he's realised I'm *the one* and he's changed, I will positively, absolutely, unequivocally *not* reply.

Nor will I end up going to his flat because I caved in after he sent me five million messages saying he misses me and inviting me round just 'to talk'.

And I *definitely* do solemnly swear that I will *not* end up on my back with my legs wrapped around his neck within minutes of arriving, because I took one look at his body and couldn't resist.

No.

That's it.

No more.

I will be *strong*. I will be like iron. Titanium. Steel. All three welded into one.

I will block Connor once and for all and I will move on with my life.

Yes!

I exhaled.

Finally I'd found my inner strength.

This was the start of a new life for me. A new beginning. Where I wouldn't get screwed over by yet another fuckboy. Where I wouldn't get ghosted or dumped. Where I took control of my life and stuck my middle finger up at the men who treated me like shit. *Here's to the new me.*

My phone chimed.

It was Connor.

I bolted upright in bed and clicked on his message.

He couldn't stop thinking about me. He wanted to see me again.

Tonight.

To talk. About our future.

Together.

This could be it!

Things *had* felt kind of different last time. Like there was a deeper connection.

Maybe he was right. Maybe he *had* changed…

I excitedly typed out a reply.

My fingers hovered over the blue button, ready to send.

Hello?

What the hell was I doing?

It was like the entire contents of my pep talk two seconds ago had just evaporated from my brain.

Remember *being strong like iron, titanium and steel* and resisting the temptations of Connor?

Shit.

This was going to be much harder than I'd thought.

Want to find out what happens next? Buy *Only When It's Love* by Olivia Spring on Amazon now!

ALSO BY OLIVIA SPRING

Losing My Inhibitions

Have you read my third novel ***Losing My Inhibitions****?* Here's
what it's about:

Finally free and ready to have fun...

**He's hot, single and off limits. She's just got her life together
after a messy divorce. Should she risk it all for a forbidden
fling?**

A year after leaving her controlling ex, Roxy's divorce is finally
official. She's got her confidence and career back on track and is
ready to start enjoying some no-strings-attached fun.

But just when Roxy thinks she has her dating plan all mapped
out, a hot younger single man unexpectedly appears. On paper,
he sounds like exactly what Roxy's been looking for, until she's
warned that he's strictly off limits. Getting involved with him
will put her career, home and everything she's worked for in
extreme jeopardy. There's a million reasons why Roxy shouldn't
give into his charms. The trouble is, he's just too tempting...

Will Roxy take a chance and risk it all to pursue a forbidden
fling? And if she does, can she find a way to let him rock her
world, without turning it upside down?

Losing My Inhibitions **is a sexy, laugh-out-loud romantic
comedy with a modern twist. This story is about self-love,
new beginnings, forging your own path in life and being true
to yourself**. It can be read as a standalone novel or as a prequel
to *The Middle-Aged Virgin* and *Only When It's Love*.

Here's what readers are saying about it:

"All hail the new queen of funny, sexy romantic fiction, Olivia Spring. A brilliant read with cringe worthy moments captured perfectly and **genius comedy that had me laughing out loud.** I can't wait to see what Olivia Spring conjures up next but I will snap it up. **All we need now is a movie deal for all three books. Five stars." Love Books Group**

"Oh my word. Ladies **if you haven't already read this, you are missing out**. **It's steamy, it's sexy and it's very funny.** There is a part in it, of which I can't repeat, that had me doubled up laughing. Totally loved it. **Five stars." Books Between Friends**

"*Losing My Inhibitions* is **the perfect mix of sexy, romance, drama and comedy which will have you laughing out loud. I would definitely recommend this book! It's perfect for a summer read**, chilled out in the garden with a glass of something lovely. Five stars." **Nicole's Book Corner**

"Well Olivia Spring, you've done it again. This modern girl's rom-com is about self-love, self-discovery, and to always be true to who you are. **I devoured it!" Girl Well Read**

"I really enjoyed reading this - some of the situations Roxy finds herself in **had me laughing out loud!** There's also a few steamier moments in there! Five stars." **Home Full Of Books**

"I read it in two evenings and it was brilliant!! **I couldn't put it down, I just had to know what happened next.**" Head In A Book 18

Buy *Losing My Inhibitions* on Amazon today!

AN EXTRACT FROM LOSING MY INHIBITIONS

Chapter One

At last.

I thought it was never going to end.

He'd been pounding away for ten minutes, grunting like a pig, and I'd been listening to the radio playing in the background, trying to figure out what advert the song before last was from. Was it the one advertising car insurance or the one for those panty liners that are supposed to keep you *cotton fresh all day long*? *It'll come to me…*

We should have just called it a night when he'd first struggled to get his machinery working. Based on tonight, it seems like what I'd read about some older men finding it difficult to get it up was true.

It was only about half an hour after he'd popped a little blue pill that he'd been able to get his little soldier to stand to attention, if you catch my drift. Which, unfortunately for me, was around the same time I started to sober up and wonder what the hell I was doing.

But by then, he was really excited, and it had been so long since my last time that I'd got myself worked up and was just as keen as him to give it a go. I mean, when I start something, I like to see it through. *Yep, I'm dedicated like that.*

I'd also read that there are lots of benefits of sleeping with an older guy. Apparently, after years of experience in the sack, they know their way around a woman's body better than a gynaecologist, so I thought I may as well give it a try. *Purely in the name of research, of course.*

But now I was really wishing I hadn't bothered. It was about as exciting as watching a hundred-metre snail race. And this guy wouldn't know his way around my anatomy if I gave him a map.

Still, at least it was over now. I was back in the saddle. First time since I'd left my ex-husband. Frankly, I hoped it got better from here. *Please tell me it does?*

I opened my eyes slowly and glanced up at his crepey skin and flaky bald head, which had tufts of grey at the side. His droopy man boobs hung above my chest, whilst the weight of his large pot belly pressed down on my stomach.

Dear God.

I must have had a lot more to drink than I'd realised.

Don't get me wrong. If I was looking for a relationship and this was a man I'd fallen madly in love with, then I wouldn't be so shallow. It was just that right now, I was looking for fun. To make up for the years I'd wasted with my ex. When I was dreaming of the day that I'd be free from Steve and with another man, this wasn't exactly what I'd had in mind.

I'd pictured a young, hot, sexy guy with abs that would

give a Calvin Klein model a run for his money, with a full head of dark hair I could run my fingers through. A stud who would have me screaming for more, rather than wondering when it would all be over.

It was Colette, my boss, slash landlady, slash house-mate, slash friend, who'd set me up with him at my divorce party earlier this evening. Now that I was officially free, Colette said some male company might be good for me, so she'd invited Donald, her loaded sixty-two-year-old boyfriend, and he'd brought his fifty-five-year-old mate Terrence along.

I knew that I was ready to get back on the horse, and it was already under control. My cousin Alex had been helping me. She'd given me a crash course in online dating two weeks ago, and I wanted to set up my profile ASAP so I could get going on the whole swiping thing, but this big work exhibition kept getting in the way. I'd been burning the midnight oil every night and often over the weekends too, trying to get everything prepared, which didn't leave me with any time for extracurricular activities. And after another long, tiring and stressful day, a hook-up was the last thing I was thinking about. But I guess the booze I'd been drinking all night had made me relax a little too much, so when Terrence had started flirting, my libido had woken up, curiosity had got the better of me, and I'd hastily thought, *Why not just get it out the way now?*

Big Mistake.

Oh well. You live and you learn. We all do things in the heat of the moment that we regret. As long as I didn't do it again, then it was fine. Which meant I better start thinking about how I was going to get this big sweaty oaf of a man off me. *Now.* I'd heard the effects of those pills can last for hours, and I definitely couldn't endure another round.

No way.

Remind me never to drink alcohol again.

Want to find out what happens next? Buy *Losing My Inhibitions* by Olivia Spring on Amazon now!

ACKNOWLEDGEMENTS

Time for one of my favourite parts of the book-writing process!

The first shout-out goes to my amazing bestie, Cams. Thank you *sooo* much for sharing your English language teaching knowledge and for your continued encouragement. I'm very lucky to have such a fantastic friend.

As always, a HUGE thank-you goes to my wonderful mum for reading multiple drafts of my manuscripts and giving excellent suggestions. You'd make a great editor!

Thank you to my incredible education consultants, Jade and Sophie. Your insights into school life were invaluable and made writing this book much easier.

So thankful for the talented ladies who make my novels shine: my brilliant editor, Eliza, proofreader, Lily, cover designer, Rachel, and website designer, Dawn.

My darling: *muchas gracias* for the love, hugs and laughter that inspire me to write every day. Really appreciate your constant support and understanding—especially when I'm burning the midnight oil to finish my drafts. You're the best!

To Jas, Loz, Brad and Jo, thanks for reading early copies of my manuscript and providing great feedback.

Sending endless gratitude to the wonderful book bloggers who read, review and shout about my novels. I value you so much!

And last but by no means least, sending a giant thank-you with sprinkles and a juicy cherry on top to *you*, lovely reader. I am so grateful that you buy and read my novels. It's because of you that I have my dream career!

Looking forward to writing the next acknowledgements page already!

Take care.

Olivia x

ABOUT THE AUTHOR

Olivia Spring lives in London, England. When she's not making regular trips to Spain and Italy to indulge in paella, pasta, pizza and gelato, she can be found at her desk, writing new sexy romantic comedies.

If you'd like to say hi, email olivia@oliviaspring.com or connect on social media.

facebook.com/ospringauthor

twitter.com/ospringauthor

instagram.com/ospringauthor

Printed in Great Britain
by Amazon